# THE TEARS OF AUTUMN

# CHARLES MCCARRY

# THE TEARS OF AUTUMN

THE OVERLOOK PRESS
New York Woodstock London

First published in paperback in the United States in 2007 by
Overlook Duckworth, Peter Mayer Publishers, Inc.
New York, Woodstock, and London

NEW YORK:
141 Wooster Street
New York, NY 10012

WOODSTOCK:
One Overlook Drive
Woodstock, NY 12498
www.overlookpress.com
[for individual orders, bulk and special sales, contact our Woodstock office]

LONDON:
90-93 Cowcross Street
London EC1M 6BF
inquiries@duckworth-publishers.co.uk
www.ducknet.co.uk

Library of Congress Cataloging-in-Publication Data

McCarry, Charles
The tears of autumn / Charles McCarry.
p. cm.
I. Title.
PZ4.M12265Te [PS3563.A2577]    813'.5'4    74-7419

Manufactured in the United States of America
ISBN-13 978-1-58567-890-7
3 5 7 9 8 6 4 2

*For Mother*

---

"To the living, one owes consideration;
to the dead, only the truth."

—VOLTAIRE *(Lettres Sur Oedipe)*

"The Pentagon's secret study of the Vietnam war discloses that President Kennedy knew and approved of plans for the military coup d'état that overthrew President Ngo Dinh Diem in 1963. . . .

" 'Our complicity in his overthrow heightened our responsibilities and our commitments' in Vietnam, the study finds. . . ."

—THE PENTAGON PAPERS, as published by
*The New York Times*

# THE TEARS OF AUTUMN

# ONE

1

Paul Christopher had been loved by two women who could not understand why he had stopped writing poetry. Cathy, his wife, imagined that some earlier girl had poisoned his gift. She became hysterical in bed, believing that she could draw the secret out of his body and into her own, as venom is sucked from a snakebite. Christopher did not try to tell her the truth; she had no right to know it and could not have understood it. Cathy wanted nothing except a poem about herself. She wanted to watch their lovemaking in a sonnet. Christopher could not write it. She punished him with lovers and went back to America.

Now his new girl had found, in a flea market on the Ponte Sisto, the book of verses he had published fifteen years earlier, before he became a spy. Christopher read her letter in the

Bangkok airport; her headlong sentences, covering the crisp airmail sheet, were like a photograph of her face. She made him smile. His flight was called over the loudspeaker in Thai; he waited for the English announcement before he moved toward the door, so that no one who might be watching him should guess that he understood the local language. His girl was waiting in Rome, changed by her discovery that he had once been able to describe what he felt.

Christopher walked across the scorched tarmac into the cool American airplane. He didn't smile at the stewardess; his teeth were black with the charcoal he had chewed to cure his diarrhea. He had been traveling down the coast of Asia for three weeks, and he had spent the last night of his journey in Bangkok with a man he knew was going to die. The man was a Vietnamese named Luong. He thought Christopher's name was Crawford.

They had met in the evening, when it was cool enough to remain outside, and walked together along the river while Luong delivered his report. Later, at a restaurant, the two of them ate Thai food, drank champagne, and talked in French about the future. Just before dawn, Christopher gave his agent money to pay for the girl, quiet and smooth as a child, who sat down beside Luong and placed her small hand in his lap. Luong smiled, closed his eyes, and ran his fingertips over the flowered material of the girl's dress and onto the skin of her neck. "No difference, silk and silk," he said. "Can you loan me some *baht?*" Christopher handed Luong two dirty Thai bank notes. Luong, his face reddened by drink, started to leave with the girl, then came back to Christopher. "Is it true that these girls will dance on your spine before making love?" he asked. Christopher nodded and gave him another hundred-*baht* note.

Christopher paid the bartender and left. He walked through the city with its smell of waste: dead vegetation, open drains, untreated diseases of the skin. The people who slept in the streets were awakening as the sun, coming up on the flat horizon, flashed into the city like light through the lens of a camera. A leper, opening his eyes and seeing a white man, showed Christopher his sores. Christopher gave him a coin and walked on.

When he reached the river, he hired a boatman to take him to the floating market. He had three hours to kill before going to the airport. It was cooler on the river, and he was just another white man among dozens who had risen early to be paddled past the grinning naked boys standing in the roiled waters and the market boats filled with odorless flowers and lovely fruits that had no taste. He bought some limes and shared them with the boatman.

The night before, in the toilet of a bar, Luong had put his thumbprint on a receipt for the money Christopher brought to him, his monthly stipend. While Luong cleaned the ink off his thumb with whiskey from the glass he had carried with him into the toilet, Christopher showed him the envelope. It was filled with Swiss francs, new blue hundred-franc notes. "I'd better keep this till morning," Christopher said. Luong, who always ended the night with a girl, nodded. They agreed on a plan for a meeting in the morning, checking their watches to be sure that they showed the same time.

Now, as Luong slept, Christopher took the envelope out of his coat pocket. He put the stamp pad inside with the money, sealed it, and dropped it over the side of the boat. The white envelope twisted in the moving brown water of the Chao Phraya and disappeared.

Christopher smiled at his own gesture. It was not likely that Luong would understand the message. He trusted Christopher. Luong knew, of course, that agents were sometimes sacrificed, but he did not consider himself an agent. He did things for Christopher and Christopher did things for him: though Christopher was white and Luong was brown, they had the same beliefs. "This money," he asked once, "it's good money, from people like us?" Christopher replied, "Yes." Luong was a subtle man, but Christopher, throwing ten thousand francs in secret funds into a tropical river, did not really believe that the Vietnamese would understand that the loss of the money meant the loss of Christopher's protection. It was more likely that he'd think there had been a mistake, that Christopher would come back, as he had always done. Luong would go back to Saigon and die.

Christopher was in no danger. If the secret police in Saigon interrogated Luong before they killed him, he would speak about a blond American named Crawford who believed in social justice and spoke unaccented French. Christopher had what no American is supposed to have, an ear for languages. He registered everything he heard, sense and tone, so that he understood even Oriental languages he had never studied after hearing them spoken for a few days. This trick was the fossil of his talent for poetry.

"Luong can vomit all over the floor about you," said Wolkowicz, the man from the station in Saigon. "The Vietnamese are never going to believe that an American can speak French the way you do. They'll figure some Frenchman has been passing himself off to Luong as an American, and we'll be off the hook."

"At Luong's expense. There's no reason to let him be arrested. You know they don't have any evidence he's tied up with the VC. He's not."

Wolkowicz put bread in his mouth and softened it with a sip of wine so he could chew it. Wolkowicz was self-conscious about his false teeth, but not for any cosmetic reason: his own teeth had been pulled by a Japanese interrogator in Burma during the Second World War, and there was a belief in the profession that a man who had been tortured, and stood up under it, could not afterward be trusted. He would know too well what to expect.

"Since when do facts make any difference?" Wolkowicz asked. "There's nothing you can do about this, Christopher."

"Luong is in Bangkok, waiting to meet me. I can tell him to stay there."

"What good would that do? Nhu told us he was going to grab Luong because he wanted to see if we'd warn him. If we do, Nhu will know we've been running Luong. We don't need that. We have enough trouble with the bastard without giving

**6**

him proof that Luong and that noisy little political party of his have an American case officer."

"They'll kill him," Christopher said.

"They'll kill him in Bangkok if they have to. We can't salvage him without blowing you and the whole political operation. One agent isn't worth it."

"Do me a favor, will you? Call him by his name. He's not an abstraction. He's five feet six inches tall, twenty-nine years old, married, three children, a university graduate. For three years he's done everything he's been asked to do. We got him into this."

"All right, so he's flesh and blood," Wolkowicz said. "He proved that when he struck out in Vientiane last month."

"He's not supposed to be an FI operator. He's paid to act, not to steal information. Luong was not the only one who couldn't find out what Do Minh Kha was doing in Vientiane in September."

"Action is what I wanted from Luong. He's supposed to be a boyhood chum of Do's. He should have walked in on him, like I suggested."

"Barney, Do would have shot him. He's a chief of section of the North Vietnamese intelligence service. Do you think he doesn't know who Luong works for?"

"I don't know what Do knows," Wolkowicz said. "I know Luong struck out on me."

"Luong reported what he saw—Do and the girl, constantly together for three days. At least he brought you back photographs."

"With no identification of the girl. Very useful."

Wolkowicz called for the check. They were sitting at a table at the Cercle Sportif. "Do you notice anything unusual about that girl in the white bikini?" he asked.

Christopher looked at a French girl who had just pulled herself out of the pool. She was wringing the water out of her long bleached hair, and her body curved like a dancer's. "No," he said.

"She has no navel. Look again."

It was true. The girl's belly was smooth except for a thin

7

white surgical scar that ran through her tan into the waist of her bathing suit.

"She had an umbilical hernia," said Wolkowicz, "so she asked them to remove it when she had a cesarean. The clever Vietnamese just removed her belly button altogether."

The waiter went away with the signed chit.

"Christopher," said Wolkowicz, "you're a conscientious officer, everybody knows that. But Luong is not your child. He's an agent. Go to Bangkok. Meet him. Give him his pay. Wipe his eyes. But leave well enough alone."

"You mean let Nhu have him."

"Nhu may not live forever," said Wolkowicz.

On the airplane in Bangkok, a stewardess handed Christopher a hot towel. Stewardesses disliked him. He had no sexual thoughts about them; combed and odorless, in their uniforms, they seemed as artificial as airline food and drink. He had been in nine countries in twenty days, flying in and out of climates and time zones, changing languages and his name at each landing. His appetites and his emotions were suspended.

The jet turned over the city. Sunlight flashed on a pagoda that quivered on the brown plain like a column of crystal; Christopher knew that the pagoda was faced with broken blue china saucers, smashed in the hold of an English sailing ship by a storm a century before. He stood up when the seat-belt warning went out and removed his jacket. The jacket was wool because he was flying into a cold climate, and it was clammy with sweat. It was the last day of October, 1963, and it would be chilly in Paris, where he was going to make his report.

Christopher organized his mind, sorting out what he had learned and what he had done in the past twenty days. When he closed his eyes, he saw the girl who had no navel beside the pool in Saigon, the brown girl he had bought in Bangkok for Luong, and finally the girl in Rome who was waiting with his book of poems to make love to him.

*Desire is not a thing that stops with death,*
*but joins the corpse and fetus breath to breath. . . .*

Christopher remembered what he had written well enough, but not so well as he remembered what had made him write. His grandfather's death had given him his first poem, eight quatrains in Tennyson's voice. The old man, lying in a hospital with the tubes removed from his arms so that he might die in his own time, thought that he was in a railroad station; as he ran for his train he met his friends, and they were young again: "Mae Foster! Your cheeks are as red as the rose! . . . Caroline! You're wearing the white dress I always loved!" Christopher's last poem was written in his own voice after he slept with a girl whose brother, who trusted Christopher as Luong did, had died for nothing. She sobbed all through the act.

After the girl had gone to sleep, Christopher wrote a sonnet and left it beside her; rhyme and meter came as easily to him as the technique of sex, and had as little to do with love. This happened in Geneva, on a night when snow had fallen, so that the gray city under its winter clouds gave off a little light. Christopher, as he stepped off the curb, was nearly hit by a car. The incident did not frighten him. It interrupted his behavior, as a slight electric shock will cause a schizophrenic to cross over in the mind from one personality to another. He saw what his poems had become: another part of his cover, a way of beautifying what he did. He went back to the bedroom of the sleeping girl and burned what he had written. She found the ashes when she woke, and knowing what they were because Christopher had written her other poems, considered them more romantic than the sonnet.

"Do you wish to sleep?" the stewardess asked.
"No," said Christopher. "Give me a large whiskey."

2

Christopher walked out of the Aérogare des Invalides, under the bare elms along the Seine. Autumn chill, smelling of wet pavement and the river, went through his clothes and dried the sweat on his spine. He walked across the Pont Alexandre-III, where he had once kissed his wife and tasted the orange she had eaten. The winged horses on the roof of the Grand Palais were black against the electric glow above the city. "The French do have the courage of their vulgarity," Cathy had said when, as a bride, she had first seen these colossal bronze animals trying to fly away with the ugliest building in France.

There were two policemen on the bridge. Each carried a submachine gun under his cape. Christopher walked by them and waited until he was in the shadows at the other end of the bridge before checking again to see that he was not being followed. Christopher knew Paris better than any city in America. He had learned to speak French in Paris, had written his book of poems and discovered how to take girls to bed there, but he no longer loved it. More, even, than most places in the world, Paris was a city where his nationality was deplored and his profession was despised; he could not stay there long without being watched.

Near the Madeleine, Christopher went into a café, bought a *jeton*, and called his case officer. When Tom Webster answered, Christopher heard the click of the poor equipment the French used to tap Webster's telephone. The volume of their speech faded and increased as the recording machine in the vault under the Invalides pulled power out of the line.

"Tom? Calisher here."

They spoke in English because Webster did not understand French easily; he was slightly deaf, and he had learned Arabic as a young officer. The effort, Webster said, had been so great that it had destroyed his capacity to learn any other foreign tongue.

"I'm staying with Margaret tonight," Christopher said.

"Then you've got better things to do than come over for a drink," Webster said.

Christopher smiled. Webster's tone of voice told him that he was proud of this quick-witted reply; he thought it made the conversation sound natural. Webster paused, sorting out with an almost audible effort the simple code they used on the telephone.

"Let's have lunch," he said at last. "Tomorrow, one o'clock at the Taillevent. I know you like the lobster there."

"Fine," Christopher said, and hung up. By the time he had climbed the stairs and ordered a beer at the bar, he had overcome the smile Webster's voice had brought to his lips. Webster was not very good at telephone codes. After seven years, he knew that any name beginning with a *C* was Christopher's telephone name. He was able to remember that "Margaret" was the euphemism for the safe house in the rue Bonaparte to which Christopher carried a key. It was the time-and-place formula that confused him. Christopher had spent many hours waiting alone in expensive restaurants like a disconsolate social climber because Webster was never sure whether to add or subtract seven hours from the time stated over the telephone for a meeting. Lunch at the Taillevent at one o'clock meant dinner at Webster's apartment at eight o'clock.

In other ways, Webster was a skillful professional. When he was still in his twenties, he had saved a kingdom in the Near East by penetrating a revolutionary organization and turning it against itself, so that the terrorists murdered each other instead of their monarch. The king he saved was still his friend. Like all good intelligence officers, Webster knew how to form friendships and use the friends he made. No human action surprised him or touched his emotions.

Webster and Christopher needed to make no allowances for one another. They lived in a world where all personal secrets were known. They had been investigated before they were employed; everything that could be remembered and repeated about them was on file, the truth along with the gossip and the lies. Gossip and lies were valuable: much can be understood about a man by the untruths that are told about him. Once a year, on the anniversary of their employment, they submitted to a lie detector test. The machine measured their breathing, the sweat on their palms, their blood pressure and pulse, and it knew whether they had stolen money from the government, submitted to homosexual advances, been doubled by the opposition, committed adultery. The test was called the "flutter." They would ask of a new man, "Has he been fluttered?" If the answer was no, the man was told nothing, not even the true name of his case officer.

11

To Webster, the flutter was the ordeal of brotherhood. He believed that those who went through it were cold in their minds, trained to observe and report but never to judge. They looked for flaws in men and were never surprised to find them: the polygraph had taught them so much about themselves—taught them that guilt can be read on human skin with a meter—that they knew what all men were.

They had no politics. They had no morals, except among themselves. They lied to everyone except their government, even to their children and the women they entered, about their purposes and their work. Yet they cared about nothing but the truth. They would corrupt men, suborn women, steal, remove governments to obtain the truth, cleansed of rationalization and every other modifier. To one another, they spoke only the truth. Their friendships were deeper than marriage. They needed each other's trust as other men needed love.

Webster recited these things to Christopher when he was far gone in drink. They were true enough. Webster, a phlegmatic man, had tears in his eyes; he had lost a young American in Accra. The boy had been shot by members of the Ghanaian service, who thought murder was the way in which secret agents dealt with their enemies. "What that kid really liked about this life is what we all like," Christopher said. "It's like living in a book for boys." Webster was outraged; he leaped at Christopher. "But he died! How many have you seen die? I can name them for you." Christopher gave his old friend another drink. "No need; I remember," he said. "But, Tom, be honest. If it had been you those black amateurs shot, what would have been your last thought?" Webster shook his head to clear the whiskey from his voice: "I'd laugh. It would be such a goddamn joke of a death." Christopher lifted his glass. "Absent friends," he said.

Webster was short and muscular. He had once held the shot-put record at Yale. He wore the clothes he had had in college, fifteen years before, and shoes he had inherited from his father that were a half size too small for him. Though he was homely and had no luck with women, he was amused by Christopher's good looks and the way girls came to him. "I'm the portrait you keep in your attic," he told Christopher. "Each time you sin, I get another wart."

Christopher, finishing his beer, remembered this and laughed aloud as in his mind he saw Webster as clearly as in life. The bartender took away his glass and didn't ask if he wanted another drink.

In the safe house, an apartment on the sixth floor of an old building behind the Ecole des Beaux-Arts, Christopher ate the food that had been left in the refrigerator for him, took a shower, and sat down at a portable typewriter. He worked steadily on his report until he heard the morning traffic moving on the quais along the Seine. He wrote nothing about Luong, except to include the receipt for the money he had thrown into the river. He burned his notes and the typewriter ribbon and flushed the ashes down the toilet.

Then, placing the typed report inside the pillowcase, he went to bed and slept for twelve hours. He dreamed that his wife, standing with the light behind her in a room in Madrid where he had slept with another girl, told him that she had given birth; even asleep, his mind knew that he had no child, and he ended the dream.


3

Tom Webster's apartment in the avenue Hoche had once belonged to a member of the Bonapartean nobility. Its salon preserved the taste of the marquis and his descendants. Carya-tids with broken noses stood at the corners of the ceiling; rosy women picnicked on the grassy banks of a painted brook that flowed along the wainscoting.

"Tom makes fun of the decor," said Sybille, his wife. "But really, in his heart of hearts, he thinks it's *très luxe.*"

"There's no need for all that before the other guests come," Webster said. "Paul knows that the chief decoration in all our houses is my scrotum, which you nailed to the wall years and years ago, Sybille."

"Does Paul know that?" Sybille asked. "But then he's

trained to notice everything, isn't he? Paul, Tom is always so glad to see you. He tells me in bed that you're absolutely the best in the whole company. In *bed*—what is the significance of that, do you suppose?"

Sybille Webster was a quick woman who liked to pretend that she was married to a slow man. Her fine face was more beautiful in photographs than in life. There were pictures of her in every room, and these were an embarrassment to her; she cleared away the frames when she invited strangers into the house. Webster married her thinking that he would want sex with no one else for the rest of his life, and he still gazed through his glasses at his wife as if she were, at all times, whirling about the room in a ballet costume. It was he who had taken the photographs.

Christopher took the drink Sybille had made for him and kissed her on the cheek. He handed his report to Webster. "Read the first two contact reports, if you have a minute," he said. "You may want to send something tonight."

"Why are you so good at the work, Paul?" asked Sybille. "Do you know?"

"People trust him," Webster said.

"Do they? Wouldn't you think that word would get around?"

"Oh, I think it has, Sybille," Christopher said. "You notice that Tom never leaves us alone."

"He's been that way ever since he started to flag," Sybille said. "That was, oh, the fourth day of our honeymoon. He took me to New York—the Astor Hotel. I was just a simple virgin from Tidewater Virginia. So many memories. Tom used to go to the Astor when he was a soldier and meet interesting people in the bar."

Sybille, sitting on the arm of Christopher's chair with her legs crossed, pointed a finger at Webster, who never gave any sign that he heard the things she said about him.

Webster tapped the report. "This is hotter than a firecracker," he said. "Do you think Diem and Nhu are really in touch with the North?"

14

"Why not? They sure as hell don't trust Washington anymore."

"What was Nhu like at the party?"

"Polite. I didn't ask him to his face what he was planning. Wolkowicz didn't like that."

"Screw Wolkowicz. All he wants to do is clean out wastebaskets."

"Well, he's expected to know everything that happens in Vietnam," Christopher said. "He doesn't see any sense in the things I do, running people like Luong. It upsets the police liaison. In a way, he's being logical. What good is building democratic institutions to Wolkowicz? Diem and Nhu don't like it, and they know who's doing it."

"What about Luong?" Webster asked. He drained his glass and held it out to Sybille to be refilled.

"Nhu is going to pick him up and kill him. They'll torture him a little first for appearances' sake."

Webster stared at Christopher for a second, then took off his glasses and rubbed his eyes. "Did you warn him off?"

"I was instructed not to," Christopher said.

Webster put his glasses back on his nose and resumed reading.

Sybille brought them another drink. "It surely is difficult for me not to overhear some of the things you two say to each other," she said. "Paul, do you want to play tennis with me tomorrow?"

"I'm going to Rome tonight."

Sybille raised her hands in protest. "But dinner!" she cried.

Christopher told her that his plane didn't leave until two in the morning, and Sybille went on with what she wanted to say as if he had not spoken to her. He wondered how Webster had found a way to propose to her; Sybille sometimes answered questions a day or a week after they had been asked.

"You don't know what a coup you're going to witness," she said. "Tom has invited Dennis Foley, the President's *right-hand man*. And I remembered that Harry McKinney is out of town, so I asked his lovely wife, Peggy, who thinks *she's* the counselor to the embassy instead of her husband. Peggy thought that about herself even when we were at Sweet Briar together. It's going to be a treat, Paul."

Webster put Christopher's report into his briefcase and locked it. "Foley's brother and I used to put the shot together," he said. "The brother's all right. I don't know this one."

"You've been to lots of meetings with him all week," Sybille said. "The entire embassy has been meeting with him. Foley came to Paris to tell de Gaulle who's really running the world. President Kennedy thought he ought to know—only de Gaulle won't give Foley an appointment. Wonderful JFK! Oh, that man is so sexy. He squeezed this little hand when he was here with the First Lady and I said, 'I, too, think you're absolutely irresistible, Mr. President.' "

"What did he say to you, Sybille?"

"He said, 'How nice to see you,' and sort of flung me down the reception line toward Jackie. Then she said the same thing and flung me again. They shake hands like a couple of black belts."

Webster grasped Sybille's chin. "Sybille," he said, "let's not have any of this Southern-belle chatter when Foley gets here. He doesn't know you."

"Oh, we're all going to be very respectful, Tom. I do think this administration has raised the whole tone of American life. Why, Peggy McKinney has been reading Proust in the original French and learning the names of all those new African countries. She says the people of Zimbabwe want rice and respect. I always thought they wanted money."

"Sybille, how about making this your last martini?" Webster said.

"I have to do something while you and Paul talk about betrayal and torture."

"We don't enjoy it," Webster said.

"Oh," said Sybille, "I think it makes you happy enough."

Dennis Foley, arriving with Peggy McKinney, did not have the air of a man who expected to have a good time. He nodded to Sybille and to Christopher when he was introduced, but did not offer to shake hands. Foley was a bony man who had played basketball in college, and he had still the manner, self-aware and faintly contemptuous, of the athlete. He had a habit of touching his own body as he talked, running a hand over the waves of stiff black hair on the back of his head, unstrapping his large gold watch and massaging his wrist. His eyes, pale blue with tiny irises, looked beyond the person with whom he was conversing. His face, which changed color rather than expression when he was pleased or annoyed by something that was said to him, was roughened by acne scars. Foley wore a two-button suit with a tin PT-109 clasp on a Sulka tie. Like President Kennedy, he drank daiquiris without sugar and smoked long, thin cigars. He had been talking to Peggy McKinney when he arrived, and he moved her across the vast room, away from the others, to continue the conversation. As Sybille and Christopher watched, Peggy lit Foley's cigar for him with a table lighter.

"Observe his gestures, listen to his voice," Sybille said. "He's turning into a JFK. All these New Frontier people are like that, have you noticed? It must be some royal virus. The closer you are to the throne, the worse the infection. Poor Peggy McKinney—see how she's trying to get everything just right? Way over here in Paris, all she can do is read Proust and take up touch football. She plays left end in the Bois de Boulogne every Sunday."

Across the room, Foley nodded brusquely, as if Peggy had told him everything he was interested in hearing. He brought his empty glass to Sybille.

"This is quite a place," Foley said. "How did you find it?"

"Oh, the French have this idea that Americans will rent *anything*," Sybille replied.

Foley's glance ran like an adder's tongue over Sybille's face and body, and a corner of his mouth lifted, as if he were rejecting a sexual invitation. "I'll bet you're the wittiest woman in

Paris," he said. "I'd like some soda water. Just plain, with an ice cube."

Sybille took his glass and went to the bar. Foley turned to Christopher. "Webster tells me you're just back from Saigon," he said.

"Yes."

"I understand you talked to Diem and his brother."

"I saw them at a reception Nhu gave. It was more a matter of overhearing what they said to others."

Foley took the glass Sybille handed to him and turned his back on her. "I've read some of your stuff in the magazine," he said. "I had a feeling you were holding back. Don't you write everything you know?"

"Usually. I don't write what I don't know."

"Look, let's cut the crap. I've got eyes—you work with Webster."

"Do I?"

"I can confirm it in thirty seconds if I have to. You're fresh from Saigon. You seem to circulate at pretty high levels out there. I'd like to hear your reactions. If they're worth it, I'll pass them on to the boss when I see him tomorrow."

The others overheard. Webster fell silent and put a cold pipe between his teeth. Peggy McKinney's face, as smooth as an ingenue's, was suddenly alight with curiosity; though she saw his name listed in the front of a great magazine and read his articles, she had never believed Christopher's cover story.

"The Americans are talking to themselves," Christopher said. "The Vietnamese say that the U.S. is working up to a coup to remove the Ngos."

"We know that the ruling family, and Nhu and his wife especially, are rabidly anti-American. What about that?"

Christopher shrugged.

"You think the U.S. government can work with a man like Diem?" Foley asked.

"Maybe not. He wants to stop the war and get us out of there. His brother is talking to the North. They have relatives in Hanoi, and Ho and Diem know each other from the old days."

18

"That's beautiful. Do you think we can countenance their talking to Ho Chi Minh behind our backs?"

Webster had begun to move across the room toward Foley and Christopher. Foley moved a step closer to Christopher, as if to prevent anyone stepping between them.

"They asked for our help," he said. "We've committed our power. You suggest that we stand by, tolerate corruption and wink at what amounts to Fascism, and let the whole project go down the drain?"

"I don't know that it would make much difference, except in terms of American domestic politics."

Foley's face had gone red. He tapped Christopher's chest with a blunt forefinger.

"The freedom of a people is involved," he said, "and that's all that's involved. If you think we're holding on in Vietnam because we're afraid of losing the next election, you don't know a hell of a lot about John F. Kennedy or the men around him."

"I've got no answer to that, Mr. Foley."

Webster put a hand on Foley's arm. "Sybille says dinner is ready," he said.

Foley continued to stare into Christopher's face. "What do you suggest we do out there?" he asked. "Nothing?"

"Sometimes," Christopher answered, "that's the best thing to do."

"Well, buddy, that's not the style any longer."

Foley put his glass into Webster's hand and strode into the dining room with Sybille and Peggy McKinney trailing after him.

5

At dinner, Foley's mood improved. He entertained Sybille on his right and Peggy McKinney on his left with stories about the President.

"There are dogs and kids, great books and great paintings and good music all over the White House," he said. "It's human again, the way it must have been under Franklin Roosevelt. If I want to see the boss, I just go in. You know you'll come out

19

of there with a decision. The door is wide open on the world. He's likely to pick up the phone and call some little twirt way down the ladder in the Labor Department. Imagine, you're forty and gray-faced, wearing a suit from Robert Hall, and for fifteen years you haven't even been able to get an office with a window. Then—*ring* and 'Mr. Snodgrass, this is the President. What the hell are you doing about migrant workers today?' It stirs up the tired blood." Foley looked around the table at the smiles of his listeners.

"The bureaucracy can use a little of that, believe me," said Peggy McKinney. "God, how we've needed to bring brains and style back into the government. The embassy just *crackles* with ideas and energy. *De l'audace, et encore de l'audace*—that's what the foreign policy of a great nation should be."

"Christopher was just telling me the opposite," Foley said.

"Oh? Well, so many of Tom's friends have to be cautious."

"What do you mean by that?" Sybille asked, with her elbow on the table and her wineglass held against her cheek.

"Oh, Sybille, come along now. We all know about Tom's friends," Peggy McKinney said. "Is it true," she asked Foley, "that the President putts when he thinks? I mean, does he really get out his putter and knock golf balls around the Oval Office? I think that's so lovely, do say it's true. I just devour all this gossipy stuff. You really don't have to humor me."

"I don't mind. I've just spent a week listening to Couve de Murville. Believe me, you're a welcome change," Foley said. "Yes, the boss putts occasionally. He'll do it at the damnedest times. The other day a couple of us came in with a recommendation. It was serious stuff. A decision had to be made—the kind of decision that would drive me, for instance, into agony. But his mind is like crystal. He's right on top of everything. He knew the situation—*felt* it, if you will, better than any of us. We gave him some new information. He absorbed it. We gave him the options. He didn't say a word at first. He got up, grabbed his putter, lined up a shot, and tapped it across the rug. We all watched the ball roll. Somehow—this will sound corny, but it's true—we all suddenly saw that golf ball as the symbol of the fate of a nation. Not a very big nation, not our nation, but a nation.

The ball ran straight into the cup. 'Okay,' said the boss. 'Go.' There's never been another like him."

Sybille turned to Christopher. "Paul has just seen a president out in Vietnam," she said. "A *little* president. Do tell, Paul."

"Oh," said Peggy. "Diem or Ziem, or whatever his name is. Horrid man."

"I'm interested," Foley said.

"There's not much to tell," Christopher said. "I stood by while he talked to somebody else. Or, rather, listened. The other man was an American."

"Who's that?" Foley asked.

"Carson Wendell. He's a Republican from California."

"I know about him," Foley said. "What poison is he spreading?"

"I don't think you want to hear it, Mr. Foley."

"Now I do," Foley said.

"You may not like this," Christopher said. "Wendell hates you people. He said Kennedy ran a dishonest, dishonorable campaign in 1960—lying about a missile gap that didn't exist and inventing a USIA report that was supposed to show American prestige abroad was at an all-time low."

"Losers have to have some excuse," Foley said. "What else?"

"Wendell told Nhu that Kennedy wasn't elected President —Nixon was. He claimed there's evidence that votes were stolen in Illinois and a couple of other states where there was a very small difference in the popular vote. The Democrats are in the White House by fraud, according to Wendell. He was very circumstantial, citing numbers and precincts to Nhu."

Peggy McKinney beat her fist on Sybille's tablecloth. "I've never heard such slander," she cried. "That man's passport ought to be taken away from him! I mean, *Christ.* . . ."

Foley unwrapped a cigar. "What did Nhu say to all that?" he asked.

"Nothing. I had a feeling he'd heard it all before."

Peggy McKinney opened her mouth to speak. Foley laid a hand on her arm. "People like Wendell and Nhu don't count," he said. "Power counts—and the right people are in power. I think we'll stay in power for quite a while." He grinned for the first time all evening, and sipped his wine. "In fact, if I can use one of the Republicans' more famous phrases, I think Mr. Nixon can look forward to at least twenty years of treason."

"Wit is back in the White House," said Peggy McKinney with tears of laughter in her eyes. "Let's drink to that."

## 6

Sybille led her guests into the salon for coffee. Peggy McKinney stood with Foley, her feet placed at right angles like a model's. She wore a pink Chanel suit, pearls, and a half-dozen golden bracelets on her right wrist. With her thin, nervous body and her bold features, she might have been taken for a Frenchwoman who had affairs. That, she told Foley, was the impression she had cultivated until the last election; the Kennedys had made her want to be an American again.

Tom Webster had said nothing during dinner. The evening had been spoiled for him by outsiders. Christopher operated all the time on hostile ground; in every country but his own he was a criminal. Outsiders, who did not know how fast betrayal traveled, could do him harm, perhaps even kill him, by knowing his name and speaking it at a cocktail party. Tonight Webster had entrusted Christopher's identity to two people who had no right to know it. He put his hand on Christopher's shoulder and began to speak.

He never got the words out. The doorbell rang and Webster went to answer it, closing the door behind him so that no other stranger could catch a glimpse of Christopher. The others went on talking; Christopher heard Webster speaking English in the hall.

When he came back, he held a perforated embassy envelope in his hand. He opened it and read the cable it contained.

"Wonderful," Webster said in a flat tone. "There's been a coup d'etat in Saigon. Some generals have seized power. The Saigon station says the coup has succeeded."

"What about Diem and Nhu?" Foley asked. He took the long white cable out of Webster's hand and read it. Peggy McKinney, not cleared to read secret traffic, stepped back discreetly; she gazed at Foley and her eyes danced.

"No one knows," Webster said. "The ambassador talked to Diem and offered him asylum, but he didn't accept."

"He's a dead man," Christopher said.

Foley handed the cable back to Webster. His face was expressionless.

Christopher watched Sybille put her coffee cup down, very gently, on the table. She sat in a corner of the sofa and looked out the window. Christopher, remembering the anecdote about the golf ball that symbolized a nation, stared at Foley, but the presidential assistant did not glance his way.

Tom Webster went to answer the ringing telephone. When he returned his hair was disheveled. "Diem is dead," he said. "So is Nhu. They were shot by a young officer in the back of an M–113 armored personnel carrier."

"American aid," said Peggy McKinney.

Foley let out a long breath through his nose and made a chopping gesture, as if to drive home a point.

Peggy McKinney, flushed and smiling, took five small running steps toward the middle of the room. Planting her sharp heels in the carpet, legs apart, she said, "All together, folks—three cheers!"

Lifting her thin arm, bracelets jangling, she cried, "Hip, hip, hooray!" She repeated the cheer three times. No one joined in.

Sybille put a fist to her mouth; Tom Webster fumbled for a pocket comb and ran it through his hair.

*"Paul,"* Peggy cried, pointing a long finger. "Did you do this? I'll bet you did, you sly spy—you were just out there in your false mustache."

"No," Christopher said. "I didn't do it and I don't know who did. I hope it really was the Vietnamese."

"Oh, come *on,*" Peggy said.

"Peggy, I'm going to tell you once more. I didn't know

23

anything about this, and I want that to be clear to you. Don't give me credit for murder, if you don't mind."

"Murder?" said Peggy. *"Surgery."*

"Jesus Christ," Sybille said. "Excuse me." She left the room.

"Did I say something?" Peggy asked, touching Foley's sleeve. "You'd think Sybille would be a little tougher, considering Tom's line of work."

"I guess Sybille's got the idea that assassination is foul work," Christopher said.

"Well, she can shed tears for both of us," Peggy said. "What happened tonight—what's the date? November 1, 1963—may show the world that the United States is going to take the initiative for a change. God knows they need to wake up to the reality of power in this world."

"You think assassination is the way to wake them up?"

"Oh, Paul, come on—a petty Asiatic dictator and a secret-police chief."

Christopher said, "Well, I have a plane to catch."

Peggy shook hands with him. Foley stayed where he was, across the room, looking Christopher up and down as if he wanted to remember every detail of his appearance.

In the hall, Webster helped Christopher into his raincoat. "There's one thing about this," he said. "Luong should be all right."

"Maybe," Christopher said. "I don't think they'd have had time to take him with them."

Sybille came into the hall on tiptoe. She put her arms around Christopher. "Sorry I fled, love," she said. "I've reached the age where everything reminds me of something that happened in the past. Wherever we go, it's corpse after corpse. God, how I hate death and politics."

Christopher walked up the shallow hill to the Etoile and found a taxi. The streets shone with rain. No one else was out walking. His mouth was dry with the metallic aftertaste of wine. He closed his eyes and tried not to hear the whine of the taxi's tires: he did not want to use any of his senses. In his mind, as if it were a clear photograph projected on a screen, he saw Molly's face, framed in russet hair and filled with belief. He had a sexual thought, his first in three weeks: it was a memory of the sun on her skin.

# TWO

1

They were in Molly's bed when she asked him about his poems. She lay on an elbow, her lips a little swollen, a strip of yellow sunlight running through her hair and across her cheek.

"Why didn't you ever tell me about your poetry?" Molly asked. " 'How odd,' I thought, when I saw the traditional slim volume, all covered with coffee stains, lying in a barrow on the Ponte Sisto. 'Here's a chap with my lover's name who writes poetry.' Then I read them, and it was your voice, you infamous wretch."

"I think I'd like dinner at Dal Bolognese tonight," Christopher said.

"Ah, things of the flesh and things of the spirit. Such an odd combination in an American. I want to know what you were like when you wrote those verses."

"Young."

"What was she like, the girl in the sonnets?"

"Oh, Molly—that was fifteen years ago. I invented her."

"Were you the man of her dreams?"

"She didn't like me at all, and when the book was published she liked me even less. She said people would think she wasn't a virgin."

"But you loved her."

"I was crazy about her."

"What was her name? Tell."

"Shirley."

"Shirley? Jesus—didn't *that* discourage you?"

"All right, what was the name of your first love?"

"Paul Christopher," Molly said. "That much is true. But now I find he has deceived me with a bird named Shirley. Paul, those poems are so good. I'm bloody jealous. Why don't you write like that now, instead of doing journalism?"

"I've lost the touch."

"Why didn't you tell me?"

"Because it didn't matter."

"It matters. What else haven't you told me?"

"Quite a lot, Molly."

"I've often thought so. Paul, I wish you'd *talk.*"

"I talk all the time. We agree that Red China should be in the United Nations. I ask you about Australia and your girlhood in the outback. I explore your reasons for hating kangaroos. I praise your body."

Molly kissed him and raised his hand to her breast. "Yes, all that, but you never go deep. I dream about you, I see you in your past, I see you in Kuala Lumpur and in the Congo when you're away. But you never *speak*—you're making me invent you, as you invented that girl."

"What do you want to know?"

"What is the worst wound you have ever suffered?"

"Ah, Molly—I'm bulletproof."

"You're covered with scars. Please tell me, Paul. I'll not ask you another question, ever."

Christopher sat up in bed, moving his body away from

Molly's, and pulled the sheet over both of them. "All right," he said. "Cathy could not bear to be alone. Her life, our marriage, took place in bed. She was a hungry lover, not graceful as you are. She needed sex, she'd scream and wail. Once we were thrown out of a hotel in Spain—they thought we were using whips. I knew she slept with men when I was away. I had no rule about it—it was her body, she could use it as she wished. She thought that showed a lack of love. She'd never believe I couldn't feel sexual jealousy."

"I believe it," Molly said.

Cathy had not been content to let their marriage die. She set out to kill it. Christopher realized soon after he met her that he had never been so aroused by a female; his desire for her showed him a part of his nature he had not known to exist; he was seized by a biological force that had nothing to do with the mind, and he was driven to have her as, he supposed, a father would be seized by the instinct to kill the man who attacked his child. Cathy was a lovely girl with elongated gray eyes like a cat's, perfect teeth, a straight nose, a lithe, frank body. She had been sent to college, and then to Europe to study languages and art, but she did nothing. She had superstitions, but no ideas; she had learned to play the piano and talk and wear clothes. She was beautiful and wanted to be nothing else. "What do you want?" Christopher asked her as they walked along a beach in Spain. "Not what other girls want—I'm not domestic. No children, no career. I want, Paul, a perfect union with a man."

Cathy believed that she was different from all other human beings. Christopher was the first man in whom she had confided; she thought he was more like her in mind and soul than anyone else could be. When at last they went to bed, she was rapturous. But her passion was all she had. She had no skill as a lover and could not learn.

After a time she sensed that this was the trouble. Cathy wanted to satisfy Christopher. He wanted to reassure her. They made love constantly, in bed, in the car. She would meet him at the airport naked under a raincoat, and remove the coat as they drove home, pulling the wheel so that he would turn into the ruins at Ostia Antica, where they would lie behind the broken stones of an old wall, shuddering on the cold earth in a rainfall. Because she was an American and his wife, he told her about his work—the nature of his profession, not its details. She thought that he kept more from her than official secrets—that he could not forget some other woman whose name he wouldn't reveal. She begged him to write about her. "You won't give me what you *are*," she said. "That's all I want."

Christopher loved to look at her. He bought her jewels and clothes and read to her. After a time, they lived in public as much as possible. They went to bullfights in Madrid, to the theater in London, they had restaurants they always went to and favorite drinks. Cathy loved to eat wild boar at Da Mario in the Via della Vite, she liked to sit up late on the sidewalk at Doney's, drinking Negronis.

When Christopher was away, she would ride through Rome on summer nights in his convertible with the top down. Finally, while he was in Africa, she met an Italian actor. After Christopher came back, she kept up the affair. She found other lovers. She went back to the actor. She would come home to Christopher, still wet, and want to make love. Christopher knew the Italian—he took Dexedrine and it made him violent. He was a Maoist who hated America; Cathy, who looked like a girl in an American film, was something he wanted to spoil.

Finally Cathy decided to break off with the actor. She had left some things at his apartment, dresses, jewelry, books. When she arrived, in the afternoon, she found him waiting with a dozen of his friends, all Italian except for a couple of Scandinavian girls. They were drinking *spumante*. The actor pulled Cathy into the apartment and threw her into the center of the living room. He had arranged the furniture so that the chairs were all around the walls, like a theater in the round. While his friends watched, the actor beat her with his fists. He punched her breasts, smashed her face. It went on for a long time—her nose and the bones in her cheeks were broken, some of her teeth were knocked out.

Cathy went downstairs to a coffee bar and called Christopher. When he got to her, her face was a mass of blood. Her hair was soaked with blood. She had vomited on her clothes. She wore only one shoe. Christopher took her to the hospital. The car was open. "Put up the top," she kept saying, "put up the top."

"I see," Molly said.

"Do you? Outside the hospital, I kissed her mouth. She was blinded by blood. I was enough like her by then that I would have pulled off her clothes right there, but they came out with a stretcher."

2

That evening, seated at Doney's while the crowd drifted by on the Via Veneto, they read the papers. Christopher saw, for the first time, photographs of the dead bodies of the Ngo brothers. Diem's corpse was closer to the camera, and a broad streak of blood ran from the wound in his temple over his cheek.

"What happens to your piece on Diem now?" Molly asked.

"I don't know. I cabled the magazine. They may want a fix, or they may not run it. They wanted something unflattering, but that may not seem appropriate to them now."

"You saw him?"

"Only for a few minutes. It's odd, you know, but no one knows anything about him, really. He was sealed up in his family, never talked to strangers. All the stuff about him in the papers was science fiction."

Piero Cremona, wearing a perfectly pressed tan suit and a silk scarf around his neck, came out of the crowd, lifting his hand in greeting.

"The famous American correspondent is back from—where was it this time, Paul?"

Christopher shook hands. "How's the world's best-dressed Communist?" he said.

Cremona ran the fingernails of both hands down the breast of his jacket, making the silk whistle. "The true revolutionary blends into his environment," Cremona said. "In the jungles of

Vietnam, I would wear the branches of trees. Here, this is my camouflage."

Cremona wrote political articles for *L'Unità*, the Communist newspaper. He signed his pieces with the *nom de guerre* he had used as a partisan; everyone but the police had forgotten the name Cremona was born with. Christopher avoided American reporters, and Americans generally, in Rome, but he had got to know a lot of Italians when he was learning the language. He never reported on them or carried out any intelligence activities in Italy; it was his rule never to operate in the country where he lived.

Cremona sat down with Christopher and Molly. He tapped the newspaper photograph of the dead Vietnamese. "The imperialist eagle devours its young, eh?" he said.

"Is that the line this week, Piero?"

"It's the obvious truth, Paul. Read my piece tomorrow. Brilliant. I've just come from the typewriter."

"Why is it so obvious? *Corriere della Sera* says the trigger was pulled by a South Vietnamese lieutenant."

"Yes, and the junta in Saigon says Diem and Nhu committed suicide," Cremona said. "Everyone knew it was going to happen—you have a man of action in the White House now. I predicted it weeks ago. A handful of dollars, a head full of bullets. Madame Nhu, when she was here last month, predicted it."

"Well, if you're right, it ought to be a very good thing for the revolution."

"The best, dear Paul, the best. Ah, you capitalist-imperialists are so adept at fulfilling the predictions of Lenin. You are eager for your own doom. Up to now, you've been growling in Indochina like a caged tiger. Now you must bleed, Paul. There will be chaos—generals cannot run a government in a civil war. Their army has always been a joke, now their country will be a joke. The U.S. Marines will land—they must. You're committed now to playing a bad hand."

"Last time I saw you, you were telling me that Diem and Nhu were a couple of Nazis."

31

"They were—but they were no joke," Cremona said. "Well, I must leave you. Molly, why does a beautiful girl like you consort with this running dog of Wall Street?"

"Our relationship is not political," Molly said.

They had made love all afternoon. While Christopher took a shower, Molly wrote five hundred words on Italian fashions for the Australian weekly she represented in Rome. Christopher found her at the typewriter, naked, with her glasses slipping down her nose and a yellow pencil clenched in her teeth, when he came out of the bathroom.

"Tripe," she mumbled. Molly wanted to live the life she thought he led, interviewing foreign ministers and film directors for a great American magazine. She kept all his articles, and would have typed them if he let her. Christopher did not want a secretary or a wife. He had hired Molly as an assistant two years before, to have someone in his office while he was away. It was important to his cover that someone answer the telephone and collect the mail. He kept nothing in the office, or anywhere else, that would connect him to his work as an agent. Molly could discover nothing.

Molly, who talked so beautifully, wrote badly, and she had never had an editor who knew enough about English to punish her for it. She asked too many questions when she interviewed; she had not learned to let her sources talk and betray themselves. Mostly she did stories about Italians, who liked the flat accent she used to speak their language, and tried to seduce her. She had beautiful legs and a soft way of smiling that made men want her.

Christopher had realized that he wanted her to stay with him after they had gone to bed for the first time. They had eaten lunch together on the first warm day of the year in the Piazza Navona. Molly had tied a scarf under her chin, and her bright hair was hidden. When Christopher spoke to her she searched his face, as though for some hint that he was mocking her. She spoke English with a public school accent, but when she talked Italian to the waiter her Australian intonations were audible.

She wore a gray sweater and a pleated skirt like a school-girl, and Christopher thought she was ashamed of her clothes, as she was ashamed of her Australian accent. He wanted to ask why she flinched when he talked to her; he thought she must be having a bad love affair. Her eyes were flecked with copper, and when she peeled a mandarine he saw that she had lovely, skillful hands.

Out of mischief, because she was so shy, he said, "Would you like to make love?" Molly replied, touching the corner of her mouth with a napkin, "Yes, I think I would."

Webster knew that Christopher slept with Molly. He sent her name in for a background investigation without mentioning that she was Christopher's mistress. "Do you want to read the file?" Webster asked when it came back from Canberra. "No," Christopher said. "She seems to be okay," Webster said. "If you have to live with a foreigner, an Australian is as clean as you can do." They did not live together; Molly kept her own small apartment. She didn't like the bed at his place, where Cathy had slept.

They walked to the restaurant through the Borghese Gardens. Molly did not hold his arm; she never touched him in public. Streetlights glowed in the branches of the trees. They paused on the Pincio and looked out over the dark city.

"We're too late for the sunset," Molly said.

After dinner, they drank coffee in the Piazza del Popolo. "Rome does smell of coffee in the winter," Molly said. "Have you ever mentioned that to me?"

She grinned at him. Christopher loved the scent of Rome, a mixture of dust and cooking and bitter coffee. When he had drunk enough wine, he described the aroma of the city to Molly, and they tried to separate the odors.

Molly had caught him in the middle of a thought. He didn't want to leave her, but she mistook what she saw in his face.

"You don't much like being loved, do you?" Molly said.

Christopher stopped himself from touching her. "I'm going to the States next week," he said.

"For how long?"

"A week, ten days."

"Will you be coming back to Rome, or going on?"

"To Rome. Maybe we can go someplace together."

Molly read his face again. "We're already here," she said.

## 3

David Patchen came to the safe house in Q Street at three o'clock in the morning. He was white with fatigue, and the glass of scotch Christopher gave him trembled in his hand. He drank it and poured another before he spoke.

"Dennis Foley wants your balls for breakfast," he said.

As a seventeen-year-old Marine on Okinawa, Patchen had been wounded by grenade fragments. The left side of his face was paralyzed. He walked with a limp. One of his eyes had been frozen open and he had learned not to blink the other; he wore a black eye patch when he slept. Patchen had no gestures. He was so still, like a hunting animal lying on the branch of a tree, that people would cough in nervous relief when finally he moved, and they saw that he limped.

Christopher was Patchen's only friend. They met in a naval hospital in the last days of the war and played chess together. While Patchen was still in a wheelchair, they were mustered with a handful o other wounded men to be decorated by a visiting admiral. Afterward, as Christopher pushed Patchen along a path planted with oleanders, Patchen unpinned the Silver Star from his bathrobe and threw it into the bushes. Both men were younger sons who had grown up in families in which an older brother was the preferred child. They were contemptuous of human beings who needed admiration.

Later, they had been roommates at Harvard. Another Harvard man, a few years older, took them to dinner at Locke-Ober's in the spring of their senior year. He ordered Pouilly-Fumé with the oysters and Médoc with the roast lamb, and afterward, in his room at the Parker House, recruited them for intelligence work. Neither man hesitated; they understood that what the recruiter was offering them was a lifetime of inviolable privacy.

34

Because people who had seen him remembered his wounds, Patchen remained in Washington. He was a natural administrator; he absorbed written material at a glance and never forgot anything. He knew the names and pseudonyms, the photographs and the operative weakness of every agent controlled by Americans everywhere in the world. Patchen never met any of them, and none of them knew he existed, but he designed their lives, forming them into a global sub-society that had become what it was, and remained so, at his pleasure. His hair turned gray when he was thirty, possibly from the pain of his wounds. At thirty-five he was outranked by only four men in the American intelligence community.

Christopher had gone into the field almost at once. It was thought that his book of poems gave him reality and an excuse to go anywhere. He began to write magazine articles after the brief notoriety of his poems dissipated.

They met once or twice a year in Washington. Patchen's wife was gone, like Cathy Christopher. Patchen and Christopher saw changes in one another, but the changes were physical. Their minds were as they had always been. They believed in intellect as a force in the world and understood that it could be used only in secret. They knew, because they had spent their lives doing it, that it was possible to break open the human experience and find the dry truth hidden at its center. Their work had taught them that the truth, once discovered, was usually of little use: men denied what they had done, forgot what they had believed, and made the same mistakes over and over again. Patchen and Christopher were valuable because they had learned how to predict and use the mistakes of others.

"Foley ordered me to destroy any report you'd filed on that theory of Carson Wendell's about the 1960 election," Patchen said. "I told him there was no report."

"Did he believe that?"

"Of course not. He's got the idea we run a gossip mill. You may have to write something, so he can burn it in his ashtray."

Christopher smiled.

"He wanted you fired," Patchen said. "The Director put a handwritten note in your file explaining that you were responding to a direct request for information and had no political motive."

"Does Foley believe that?"

"How could he? He lives on loyalty to one man, the President. He's had no experience with coldhearted bastards like you. No one but us can see that information is just information. Foley thinks you're an enemy if you don't agree with everything the President does, one hundred percent."

"So now everyone agrees with assassination?"

Patchen lifted his bad leg, using both hands, and crossed it over the other one. "Foley thought you were being emotional," he said. "I could kick Tom Webster's ass for bringing you two together."

"That doesn't answer the question."

Patchen hesitated. It was not like Christopher to ask for information he didn't need to have.

"The outfit had nothing to do with what happened to Diem and Nhu," he said.

"Foley didn't seem very surprised at the news."

"I can't explain Foley, or what he does," Patchen said.

Patchen opened his briefcase with a snap; he had had enough of this subject. He handed Christopher a newspaper clipping, the obituary of an Asian political figure who had died the week before of a heart attack.

"Did you see this? It isn't often that an agent dies of natural causes."

Christopher read the obituary. It said that the Asian would be remembered by history for three things: his autobiography, which made the world aware of the struggle of a whole people through the description of the author's own life; the Manifesto of 1955, which had influenced political thought and action throughout the Third World; and the statesman's success in driving Communists out of the political life of his country.

"Not even a chuckle?" Patchen asked.

Christopher shook his head. It was a convention that agents, even after they were dead, were called by their code names, never by their own. The Asian's pseudonym had been "Ripsaw."

"How much of Ripsaw's autobiography actually happened in his life?" Patchen asked.

"Most of the anecdotes were true as he told them to me. I just put in the parts where he had deep, deep thoughts. The Manifesto of 1955 I wrote on a plane, going down from Japan. It was the universal text—I'd done things like it before for some of the Africans. There just happened to be a guy from the *Times* in-country when Ripsaw issued it, so it got publicity."

"Don't you think it's funny, the way the *Times* is always reporting on you, and it doesn't know you exist?"

"That's what newspapers are for."

"Yes, to explain the real world."

"There is no real world, David."

Patchen smiled at the irony. He took back the clipping and closed his briefcase. He sat for a long moment with his good eye closed and a hand over the other one, sipping from his glass of whiskey. He took his hand away from his face and stared at Christopher.

"I've been thinking about you," he said. "I got out your file and read it; you've been through a lot in twelve years. You're losing your humor, Paul. I've seen it happen to others who stay in the field too long, do too much."

"Seen what happen?"

"Professional fatigue. I believe, in the case of Christians, it's called religious melancholy. Do you play with the thought of getting out? I know you like to be with this girl Molly."

"Sometimes I play with the thought. I'm tired of the travel, and once or twice a year I meet someone I'd rather not lie to."

"Molly wouldn't be enough for you, you know, any more than poetry was, or your wife. You say there's no real world, but if there is one, it consists of you and maybe a dozen other operators like you on both sides. You ought to be intoxicated."

"Maybe I am."

"No. Your agents are intoxicated. Foley is intoxicated. That's why you don't like him—you know how easily you could use him if he was a foreigner."

"Well, I'm going back out. I have to meet Spendthrift in

Léopoldville later this week, and after that I want to see what's left of the network in Vietnam."

"Who knows?" Patchen said. "You may find the atmosphere improved in Saigon. The embassy's traffic is full of bounce and optimism."

"I'll bet. Do you think the Foleys have any idea of what's going to happen to them out there?"

Patchen stood up. When he spoke, he turned the dead side of his face toward Christopher. "They're a funny bunch," he said. "They're bright. They believe in action, and at first that seemed refreshing. But they're almost totally innocent. They have about as much experience as you and I had when we were recruited, and there's no way to season them. They got into the White House and opened the safe, and the power they discovered took their breath away. *'Christ, let's use it!'* Power really does corrupt. They think they can do anything they like, to anyone in the world, and there'll be no consequences."

"But there always are."

*"You* know that," Patchen said. "For those who never smell the corpse, there's no way of knowing."

## 4

On his way out of America, Christopher stopped in New York to have lunch with the managing editor of his magazine. The man was fascinated with the internal politics of the magazine. In his eyes, Christopher was a good writer who delivered six articles a year according to his contract.

Christopher had been offered the contract after he wrote profiles of a dozen foreign statesmen whom no other journalist had been able to interview. It was good cover, but it created a security problem; Christopher could not be revealed to the editors.

The Director called the chairman of the board of the magazine; the two old men had been at Princeton together. The Director explained that Christopher was an intelligence operative in addition to being a writer. It was arranged that Christopher's salary, twenty thousand dollars a year, would be donated in a discreet way to the favorite charity of the chairman of the board. He either saw no reason to inform the editor of the magazine of Christopher's connection with the government, or forgot about it. In any case, no one at the magazine had ever mentioned a suspicion of Christopher.

The managing editor drank three martinis before lunch. He told Christopher he had thrown away his profile of Ngo Dinh Diem.

"My eyes glazed over," he said. "Diem was boring enough when he was alive. Who's going to read about a dead dinosaur? There's no American angle."

He asked Christopher to write fi e thousand words on the new Pope.

## 5

Christopher, alone, sat in a sidewalk café in Léopoldville. It had grown too dark to read, and the book he had brought with him lay closed on the table. Its pages, like Christopher's shirt and the tablecloth, were swollen with moisture.

Three gaunt adolescent boys ran among the tables of the café. Two of them carried armloads of wood, and the third clutched a piece of meat. It appeared to be the ribs of a large animal and it had begun to spoil; Christopher smelled its rancid odor. The boys crouched by a mimosa tree a few yards from the café and started a fire. The flames burst upward, licking the bole of the tree, silhouetting the thin boys, who threw the meat into the fire and danced away from its heat.

The child who had been carrying the meat darted away from his friends and came to Christopher's table, giggling as he ran. He was a leper. He snatched Christopher's unfinished bottle of beer from the table and ran away, hugging it against his chest with a fingerless hand. Back at the fire, he and his companions passed the bottle from mouth to mouth.

Christopher paid the impassive waiter and walked away. The unlighted streets were deserted except for an occasional Congolese, asleep in the dirt. By day, the concrete buildings, painted white or rose or pale blue like the Belgian sky, showed tropical sores and lesions. Now they were dark shapes, too geometrical to be natural, but emitting no more light than the forest that lay a few hundred yards away. Christopher walked in the middle of the street, to avoid the doorways. When he looked back, he saw the faint reflection of the fire in the high branches of the tree by the café.

It was too dark to see the river, but he could hear it. A power launch passed, showing no lights, and Christopher heard the canoes rattling at their moorings in its wake. He walked along the bank until he saw the outlines of a river steamer; it had once been white and its blunt stern was clearly visible against the sky. Christopher, leaning against a piling, waited until he saw a tall man go aboard the steamer. Then Christopher climbed the gangplank, crossed the deck, and went down a ladder into the interior of the boat. A candle burned in a stateroom at the end of a narrow gangway, and Christopher walked toward its nervous light. He heard Nsango behind him, and stopped.

"My friend," Nsango said.

Christopher turned around. The black, wearing the khaki shorts and torn singlet of a workman, embraced him. He took Christopher's hand in his own dry fingers and led him to the stateroom.

"I'm sorry to make you wait," Nsango said. "Did you come every night?"

"Yes," Christopher said. "Four times, but I never saw the light."

Nsango laughed. "I was in the bush. I was waiting, too. But I knew you would come back tonight. I saw you in the café, reading your book."

"Yes, I saw you across the boulevard."

"Ah, what eyes!" Nsango spoke rapid French at the back of his throat, with many extra *m* sounds as if his own language struggled to reveal itself. "Well, what news?"

"The Congolese think you're in Angola. Someone told the Portuguese you were camping along the frontier, and they told the police."

"Are they looking for me there?"

"They're watching the crossing points."

"Good. I'll go the other way." He laughed again.

"How did you explain this journey?"

"I told them in the camp that political organization was needed in some villages I know about. They probably think I have a woman somewhere."

"What's going on in Katanga?" Christopher asked.

"It's very quiet, my friend. I lose five or six men a week—they go back to their villages."

"Do you tell them to go?"

"Yes, they'll wait for me there. They don't like the new foreigners."

"There are new foreigners?"

"Yes, the Chinese have all gone away. They took their aspirin that made men bulletproof with them. But now we have others—some of them are black men."

"Stop talking like a native, Nsango. Who are they?"

Nsango guffawed. "They fell from the sky on great white leaves, master. Oh, we were frightened!"

Christopher had seen this man, who had the best political brain in black Africa, trembling in fear because he believed a spirit had entered his body as he slept; he felt it devouring his liver like a maggot. Christopher had brought a juju man from the Ivory Coast and he removed the spirit, sending it into the body of the man who had cursed Nsango. Christopher had given the juju man fifty ounces of gold for his work. He and Nsango had used the sorcerer again to carry out an operation they hoped would result in Nsango's becoming, in time, the prime minister of his country. They failed, and Nsango had gone back into the forest. Christopher knew he would never come out again, and Nsango, despite his diploma from the Sorbonne and his name that was known throughout the world, still feared enchantment and blamed it for his bad luck. Nsango was not, however, afraid of foreigners.

"They're Cubans," he told Christopher. "Three blacks, four whites." He removed a stained envelope from the pocket of his

41

shorts and handed it over. Inside was a roll of film and a sheet of paper on which the names the Cubans used were written in Nsango's neat missionary-school hand.

"When did they come?" Christopher asked.

"Maybe a month ago. First there was this one." Nsango pointed at the sheet of paper. "Manuel. He speaks good French. Then the others a few days afterward."

"How did they find you?"

"I suppose the Chinese told them."

"What do they want?"

"A revolution. They talk even more than the Chinese—we have meetings all the time. The men like it, there's a lot of beer, and they brought some very good guns."

"How many?"

"Ah, my friend, not so many. Some mortars. Not enough ammunition."

"Are they issuing the weapons to your men?"

"No, they're like the Chinese were at first. We must make our own weapons to make our own revolution. Spears and stones—Mao's teachings. We killed a South African for them— the capitalists have that mercenary camp still outside Elisabethville. We ambushed a jeep, the whites were drunk. One got away—he had a machine pistol, so we didn't chase him."

"Are you going back?"

"Yes, I'm the leader. We need the guns. The Cubans won't stay forever."

"Nsango, I think you're taking a chance."

"It's better than prison. What do they say about me in the papers?"

"In Léopoldville, nothing. But I see your name written on walls all over town: everyone believes you're alive. In Brussels, that your movement still is dangerous, and that you are more so."

"What would you do about these Cubans?"

"Let them stay," Christopher said. "It's better to have someone you know than to wait for someone you don't know to show up."

Nsango picked up the candle and held it next to Christopher's face so that he could watch his expression as he answered the question Nsango always asked.

"You still think I have no chance?"

"I don't say that. I can't help you—you have the wrong allies."

"But if, after all, I win, you'll be my friend, and your friends will expect me to remember past favors?"

"That's what they'll expect," Christopher said. "They're not always realistic."

"We'll see. When will you come back?"

"I don't know. If you want to see me, send a postcard. The one with the elephants if it's urgent. I'll use a postcard with a picture of Pope John. I'll come to Elisabethville on the sixth day after the postmark, ten o'clock at night. I don't think you should come to Léopoldville again—at least, not to meet me."

Christopher took a key out of his pocket and gave it to Nsango. "Deposit box 217, Banque de Haute Katanga, Elisabethville," he said. "In case you need it, there's a ticket to Algiers, a thousand dollars, and a passport with a visa for Algeria. It's a Camerounian passport, so don't go there."

"What good would I be to the movement, or to you, in Algiers?" Nsango said. "The old soldiers' home for revolutionaries."

"What good would you be dead?" Christopher asked.

6

Trevor Hitchcock knocked on the door of Christopher's hotel room at six in the morning. He was the son of missionaries, and he had spent his childhood in the Congo; he worked in the morning, slept in the afternoon, and drank through the night. His Presbyterian father had taught him to make no concessions to the climate and Hitchcock never went out in the sun without a coat and a tie and a Panama hat.

"Father made more converts than anyone in Kasai province," Hitchcock once told Christopher. "He thanked God for smiling on the Presbyterians. Then he learned, after about five years, that it was because he sweated like a hog butcher in his

43

black suits and his celluloid collars. The Congolese thought he smelled like a human being—the other missionaries, who wore shorts and took baths, smelled dead to them. That's what whites are called in the Lingala language—the dead."

Hitchcock read the cable Christopher had drafted in longhand after his meeting with Nsango. "What's the film?" he asked.

"As I said in the cable, pictures of the Cubans. Also photographs of some of their documents."

"Spendthrift took those?"

"Yes," Christopher said. "I gave him a camera in the old days."

"Spendthrift" was Nsango's pseudonym; Hitchcock was a careful professional who believed even the Congolese might have microphones planted in hotel rooms.

"I'll get this off this morning," Hitchcock said. "The Cubans are news to me. Do you believe it?"

"Well, there are the photographs. And Spendthrift has never lied to us, despite our lack of reciprocity in that department."

"You really thought we should have backed him all the way, didn't you?"

"Yes. He was better than any of the alternatives."

"Wrong tribe. Wrong time."

"He didn't take it personally," Christopher said. "He believes he's going to be running this country someday, and so do a lot of other people. His relationship with me is political money in the bank."

"Funny, isn't it?" Hitchcock said. "You recoil in horror from giving any of these people guns—that's the main reason Spendthrift struck out in '61. But if the world gets blown up, the bomb will be made with uranium and cobalt dug out of the Shinkolobwe by some black living in the Bronze Age."

"It won't be Spendthrift who drops the bomb."

"Or gets blown up by it. How were things in Washington?"

"Ecstatic," Christopher said. "The crisis managers are flying out to Saigon by the hundreds."

"Terrific. I hope they take along a few of the ones we've got here. What time does your plane go?"

"Ten o'clock tonight."

"Do you want to come out to the house for dinner?" Hitchcock asked. "I'll send your scoop, manage a crisis or two, and pick you up at six."

Hitchcock lived on the outskirts of Léopoldville in a large stucco house that still belonged to a Belgian trader. The Belgian fled to Brussels after Lumumba's troops raped his wife during the mutiny in 1960. Hitchcock's houseboys, three stocky men who laughed hysterically when he berated them in Lingala, were the same ones who had worked for the Belgian and opened the door to the drunken troops. One of the boys came into the darkened living room with a bottle of gin on a silver tray. He put it down and trotted across the tile floor, leaving the sweaty prints of his bare feet behind him. "Ice, glasses, tonic water, limes!" Hitchcock screamed. "We don't drink the stuff out of the bottle, Antoine!"

Hitchcock's wife flinched at the boy's wild laugh. She was a frail woman with thinning gray hair; as Christopher watched her, she pulled the cloth of her dress away from her body and placed a wadded Kleenex between her breasts. "It's the constant perspiration, it drives you mad," she said. Her damp skin had a reddish shine, as though discontent had burned away its outer layers.

Hitchcock drank six glasses of gin and tonic before dinner. The boys served cold soup and a large grilled river fish whose muddy flesh was slightly bloody along the spine. "Do you enjoy uncooked food, Paul?" Theresa Hitchcock asked. "The boys are defeated by the electric stove. We're all defeated." She smiled brightly and pushed her limp hair away from her forehead. "You'll excuse me? I have a headache." She went up the stairs.

"I'm sending her home," Hitchcock said. "She can't cope here—I don't know who can. My mother went mad as a hatter, you know. The old man told her to pray, but she thought the natives were going to gang her at any moment. Actually, they think white women are repulsive—like fish bellies."

Hitchcock had escaped from God and the Congo when he was eighteen, on the last freighter to cross the southern Atlantic before the Germans began to torpedo Belgian ships. His parents were buried in Kasai, in the red dirt of their churchyard. Hitchcock had studied German and Russian. "My idea," he told Christopher, "was to spend my life in cold climates. Whoever would have thought the Congo would become one of the hinges of American foreign policy? I grew up thinking uranium was good for curing cancer."

In his mind, Hitchcock still lived in cold climates. He sat at the table with the remains of the fish congealing on his plate, and sweat blackening the armpits of his seersucker suit, and talked about Berlin. He had been a famous operative there in the postwar years. Hitchcock liked to deal with Germans—they were always on time and they liked to be trained.

"You get to Zurich, don't you?" he asked Christopher. "There's a guy there you ought to know—you can't forget his name. Dieter Dimpel. I bought him a watch store in 1950—told 'em it was owed to old Dieter. So he's out of it. But go see him."

"I will," Christopher said. "I use up a lot of watches."

"Listen, Paul. Dieter is a midget—I mean he's a real midget. He's one meter, twenty-five centimeters high. Comes from Munich. Walks like Göring—he's got a big imaginary body he carries around with him. He used to sweep up in the beer halls. Knew Hitler in the old days, when the Führer would come in in his trench coat and mumble about taking over the world. They wouldn't let Dieter into the party because he was a freak, right? So Dieter goes to a forger and has a party card made. He gets himself an armband with a swastika on it and goes to all the Nazi rallies. Around 1943, some storm trooper grabs him. The forger had asked Dieter what number he wanted on his card. Dieter said, 'Oh, make it 555—that's easy to remember.' Unfortunately, 555 is the number of Adolf Hitler's party card. The storm trooper was nothing compared to the Gestapo when they got hold of Dieter. Forged credentials! A freak saying he's a Nazi! Using the Führer's party number!

46

"Off old Dieter goes to Dachau. He's resourceful as hell, he becomes a trusty. He escapes five days before the Americans come. He heads *east.* The Russians grab him. Dieter is a bit light-headed after two years on the Dachau diet, so he tells the Russians he's a Nazi. *They* put him in a camp. Well, of course he walks right through the wire and heads west again.

"I picked him up in Berlin in late '46—he's sweeping up in a beer hall again, wearing tiny *lederhosen.* Dieter is a bitter little guy. He knows he's smarter than Hitler, but he's only four feet tall. He wants revenge against the world. Good agent material.

"At that time we were trying to figure some way to get into the headquarters of a certain occupying power. No way to do it—troops on every door, bars on every window, bells and sirens wired up all over the place. Miller was running the Berlin base then, and he was full of stories of the good old prewar days in the FBI, when they used to sneak into the German ambassador's bedroom in Washington and come back with samples of his wife's pubic hair.

"Miller thought he was the world's champion burglar, but he couldn't think of a way to crack the GRU. However, *I* had Dieter. I recruited him by giving a whore a few marks to pretend she couldn't live without him. I gave him a cyanide pill to carry in a hollow ring—Krauts don't think you're serious unless you give 'em a cyanide pill.

"I had Dieter trained in rope climbing, in judo, I turned him into an acrobat. Dieter was a very strong midget. I put him through a course in clandestine entrance. Safecracking, photography with infrared, the works. After six months, he was the best burglar in Germany. Then, one dark and moonless night, I sent him down the chimney with a camera. Dieter came out a fireplace on the second floor, cracked every safe in the place, photographed everything, put it all back, and came out the chimney again. For three years Dieter went down the chimney once a month and did his work. Never left even a finger print. We sent him all over the place, doing the same. He got more stuff than any agent in the history of Berlin.

"One night, Dieter was shooting some agents' reports and

47

one of their colonels came in, working late. He turned on the lights, and here was this sooty midget with a camera and an infrared light set up in his office and the safe spilling all over the floor. Dieter whipped out his gun and shot the Russian right between the eyes. He dropped everything but the camera and went up the chimney like a rocket.

"I'm waiting in the next street. Lights go on, sirens go off, soldiers start coming out the windows. Dieter spent twenty-four hours hanging on to his rope inside the chimney—they couldn't find him, he couldn't come down. Next night, he sneaked over the roof and got away. Still had the camera, but he forgot his rope and they found it, so that ended that. He wouldn't have forgotten the rope, but all he could think about was taking a leak. The human element."

"How's he like the watch business?" Christopher asked.

"Okay, I guess. It pays for the girls. He takes pictures of them—he's a white-socks fetishist. Tell him you're a friend of Major Johnson. Old Dieter Dimpel. If you want to use a recognition code, give him the number of his party card, and Hitler's —555. He'll reply with the date of his arrest, June 4, 1943."

Hitchcock listened happily to Christopher's laughter. "I mean it," he said, "look Dieter up. He's useful." Telling the story had made him feel better; despite all he had had to drink, he was alert and smiling.

He drove Christopher to the airport. They shook hands in the dark interior of the car. "I'd go in with you for a farewell drink, but Theresa worries at night," Hitchcock said. "Christ how they change—had you noticed that, Paul?"

7

November is a rainy month on the Congolese coast, and Christopher was soaked when he entered the airport building after struggling through the crowd of porters between the curb and the entrance. In the ticket line an Englishman was having a violent argument with the airlines clerk, a laughing Congolese who told him that he had no record of his reservation.

"You'll bloody well hear about this!" the Englishman said.

48

"I'm a first-class passenger to London, and the booking was made a month ago."

The Congolese waved his hand in the Englishman's face. "Go away, go away—you have no reservation."

Christopher slid his bag onto the scale and handed the clerk his ticket. The clerk removed the five-hundred-franc note from the ticket, put it in his breast pocket with the rest of his bribes, stamped Christopher's boarding pass, and tagged his baggage.

"How much delay in the flight?" Christopher asked.

"That airplane will never be late!" said the clerk with another laugh.

Christopher took his passport out of his pocket, marked the page on which his visa was stamped with his boarding pass, and walked toward the passport control. A young Belgian priest carrying a transistor radio stepped in front of him. He tapped Christopher's green passport with his finger.

"You're an American?"

"Yes, Father."

"Your President has been shot."

"What?"

"President Kennedy—he's dead. Listen."

He turned up his radio. A Frenchman's voice on Radio Léopoldville was reading the news from Dallas. It was nine o'clock in the Congo, two o'clock in Dallas. The news was still a simple bulletin.

Christopher went back to the ticket counter and lifted the clerk's telephone. He dialed the American embassy. The duty officer did not say hello. He picked up the phone and said, "Yes, it's true. President Kennedy has been assassinated. The vice-president is safe. The President is dead. We have no details. Please hang up now." Christopher hung up the phone, nodded to the startled clerk, and walked toward the passport control.

Christopher never forgot anything. The tone of his mother's voice, the smell of a leper in Addis Ababa, the telephone number of the embassy in Kabul, the looks of a man killed by a car in Berlin as he crossed the street to meet him moved constantly through his mind. Now he thought of nothing. He went to the windows and looked out through the rain at the glistening jets drawn up on the tarmac. He felt a hand on his arm; the priest was beside him again.

"There's nothing more on the radio," the priest said. "They're playing music. Do you go to Brussels?"

"No, Rome."

"You're crying. Would you like to pray with me?"

"No, Father. I don't believe."

"It's a frightful thing."

Christopher thought the priest was talking about his rejection of faith. "For some," he said.

"For all. President Kennedy was a great man. That death should come like that to him—he was like a young prince."

"Yes, it's a great shock."

"You must have loved your President."

"I love my country," Christopher said.

"It's the same thing, perhaps."

"Ten minutes ago I wouldn't have said so, Father. Now I think you're right."

It was dawn when Christopher arrived in Rome. He bought the newspapers and read them in the deserted waiting room at Fiumicino while he waited for his call to Paris to go through. Sybille answered the Websters' phone.

"Tom's at the embassy," she said. "They've been up all night. We all have."

"Tell him I'm home if he wants me."

"I will. God, Paul, how I'm feeling this!"

"Yes," Christopher said. "The next time you see your friend Peggy, ask her what she thinks of assassination now."

# THREE

1

Christopher saw the truth at dawn on the tenth day after the death of Kennedy. He woke shivering with cold and covered Molly with the blankets that had slipped to the floor during the night. A rooster crowed on the hillside above Siena, and as he watched from the open window of their hotel room, the town changed color in the growing light from burnt umber to rose.

In the first sunlight, two figures in black hurried across a field and into the edge of a woods. These Italian farmers going innocently to work triggered Christopher's memory. Once again he saw men in black moving at a trot along the fringe of a forest, and an American in a flowered shirt lying in the weak morning light with the back of his head blown away.

The explanation struck like a bell in Christopher's mind. He knew who had arranged the death of the President.

All his life, Christopher's unconscious had released images, and he had learned to trust this trick of his mind. He often knew what men had done before they confessed their acts to him. (Cathy had thought him a fortune-teller. He had sometimes been able to see her lovers in her gestures—she would untie a scarf and pull the silk through her fist with a smile and Christopher would see her lifting her breast toward a stranger's lips. *"Did you see me, did you see me?"* she would gasp. It excited Cathy to know she could walk through the gates of Christopher's mind. She believed in dark powers.)

Christopher knew that this gift, which grew stronger as he grew older, was only a kind of logic. His senses received everything, he forgot nothing. Experience and information joined in the brain to provide explanations. It was like writing the first draft of a poem: words formed on the page without passing through the conscious mind.

Now, as he stood by the open window, he heard the plans being made for Kennedy's murder. He saw the messages being passed, saw the look in the eyes of the conspirators, watched the tension flow out of their faces when news of success was brought to them. He felt their sense of triumph like an electrical charge between them. He himself had been a part of such scenes often enough. He wondered why it had taken him so long to realize the truth.

Christopher had seen many men die for politics, and he knew that politics was merely the excuse their murderers used. Men killed not for an idea but because they could not live with a personal injury. Now he made the simple connection between the injury and the President's violent death. He understood the motive perfectly. He wondered if the murderers had foreseen that the death of Kennedy would drive the very memory of their existence out of the consciousness of the world.

Because they were who they were, the killers might have escaped suspicion forever. Christopher felt no anger, he wanted no revenge. The life he had led had burned away such feelings. He did not blame the murderers for what they had done. They had repaid an insult. He was only surprised that they had been able to do it so quickly. He would have expected them to be more patient, to choose a moment, such as Inauguration Day, when the humiliation would have been more intense. He supposed it had something to do with the stars; they would have horoscoped such an operation very carefully.

His mind worked tidily, sorting out the evidence he would need to illustrate the truth. Christopher hadn't yet discovered the details—how the money was handled or whether money was necessary, how they found the assassin and perfected his will to kill. They could not have told him their reasons, or who they were. It must have been easy to convince him that nothing was left to luck, that they had the power to rescue him. Christopher understood what had happened and why it had been inevitable. Putting faces to his theory was a matter of professional routine. He knew where to go, which men to contact. He thought he might very well be killed.

Christopher and Molly had been together in Siena for three days. Molly had chosen the hotel: the Palazzo Ravizza, built by some nobleman in the seventeenth century and now restored for romantic tourists. Molly loved the cold floors, the whitewashed walls, the carved black furniture, the curtained bed. She would not let him use the electricity; she bought candles in the town and they went to sleep with tongues of light all around them.

There was a dead garden behind the hotel; they ate breakfast there, wearing heavy sweaters under their coats. At night Molly's breath was scented with the white truffles she'd had for supper. They dined at a restaurant where the waiter brought a shallow basket heaped with truffles to their table: he would hold them under Molly's nose one after the other until she selected the one she wanted. They ate pasta with truffles, truffled chicken, truffle soup. "The taste penetrates the brain," Molly said. "Even you are beginning to taste like a truffle, Paul."

The night before, as they walked across the brown dish of the Piazza del Campo, Molly began to sing in the dark. "Come le Rose": this had been her favorite song ever since she had heard a street musician sing it at the table of an American couple at a sidewalk restaurant in Rome; the wife, gray-haired

53

and wrinkled, wearing clothes that looked ridiculous in Italy, had wept with happiness, though she could not understand the words.

When Molly began to sing, Christopher let go of her hand and stopped where he stood. She walked onward a few steps, then turned and ceased singing in the middle of a phrase. She smiled and lifted a hand in apology. "Am I making too much racket?" she asked.

"No," Christopher said. "I just realized that I love you."

Molly stood absolutely still, the smile still on her lips, her hand still raised, the sleeve of her coat pulled away from the bare skin of her wrist.

"Paul," she said, whispering as though she thought a whisper might make him understand her better. "Paul, it's all right to be happy."

In the morning, at the open window, Christopher remembered the look and sound of her and he realized, with a thrill of surprise, that he wanted his own life to continue.

2

They had lost a week in Rome before going to Siena. When he reached his apartment on the day after Kennedy's assassination, after the long taxi ride from the airport, he found his telephone ringing. It was Tom Webster; he made no effort to deceive the recording devices that monitored international calls out of France.

"I don't know what you can do about this in Rome," Webster said. "But there's total priority on this problem. This Oswald was a defector to the Soviet Union. He was in Russia from 1959 until June, 1962. The Russians are going crazy. They expect SAC over Moscow any minute. They keep telling everyone they didn't do it."

"I believe them," Christopher said. "Why would they?"

"I know. But it's a possibility that has to be considered. Headquarters wants maximum information from every point in the world. Who do you know down there, or anywhere, who might know something about this rotten bastard?"

"You want me to tell you over the phone?"

"Yes. Fuck it."

"You know all the names. There's no one in this town, except a couple of people who'd just be guessing."

"What about that journalist?"

"He'd just repeat the line, whatever it is. I can't believe they'd do it, Tom. Not with a man like Oswald. If I were the Russians, I'd think it was an attempt to put the blame on them. It might be."

"Let them worry about that," Webster said. "Our job is to tap in wherever we can and find out what we can. Anything. Every detail. Try the journalist—you never know."


Christopher met Piero Cremona in the Galleria Colonna. The brass band was playing waltzes as usual, and the music made Cremona angry.

"Italians!" he said. "There should be no music today."

Christopher was exhausted. He had not changed the clothes he wore on the flight from Léopoldville, and his shirt smelled of the sweat he had shed in the Congo. There was a newspaper on every table in the café, and a photograph of the dead President on every front page.

"How do you feel, my friend?" Cremona asked.

"I don't know, Piero."

"You Americans kill whole countries and it doesn't bother you," Cremona said. "But for America to be wounded—*ah!*"

"You enjoy the spectacle?"

Cremona tapped his coffee cup with a spoon. "No, I detest it," he said. "Politics is politics. Life is life. I hate Washington since the war—they don't understand misery. They don't know how to look into the mind of most of mankind, they think suffering—real suffering, which is at the center of everyone's history but America's—does not matter. But Americans are different, individual Americans. I saw them come into Italy in 1943, into an enemy country. They were alive, those soldiers, and they wanted everyone else to be alive, too. They handed out food, they screwed the girls, they got drunk. I've never forgotten how they were. There is a goodness in your people,

55

Paul. I'm very sad for them today. Maybe even *I* think there should be one country in the world where suffering is not permitted to exist."

"I expected you to tell me that this assassination is a small thing, compared to Hiroshima."

"No," Cremona said. "This is no small thing. Nothing is so terrible as to kill a symbol. The Japanese were Japanese; when a hundred thousand of them were vaporized by the atomic bomb, very few considered that anything important had happened to the human race. They were yellow creatures. The death of a hundred thousand Englishmen, maybe even a hundred thousand Italians, would have been different."

"Only the death of white men matters?" Christopher said.

"To Christians, yes. Do you think the whole Northern Hemisphere would be in a spasm of mourning if some brown president had been shot through the brain? This murdered man is an *American*. If a madman can kill an American president, then what is certain? 'Ah,' the miserable of the world will say, 'it's not possible, after all, to bribe history.' Everyone thought America could do it."

"You think Oswald is a madman?"

"Of course."

"It seems he's a Communist," Christopher said.

"Oh, Paul—you? You know what a Communist is. This man is a sick romantic. They didn't want him in the Soviet Union, they didn't want him anywhere."

"Have you found anyone who knows anything about him?"

"Everyone knows all about him. He occurs everywhere, sometimes he acts."

"What do the Russians say?"

"They'd kill him if they could," Cremona said. "I had a drink with Klimenko, the Tass man, last night. They're very angry."

"And very scared."

"Yes—and who can blame them?" Cremona drew a mushroom cloud in the air with a quick movement of his hands.

Oswald was dead when Christopher met Nguyên Kim on the Spanish Steps. Descending the stairway, he saw Kim speaking to a Vietnamese girl by the fountain in the center of the Piazza di Spagna. They were nodding vigorously in the Vietnamese way, and the tones of their language, like minor chords played on a complicated instrument, drifted through the noisy Roman square.

Christopher kept walking, hoping to pass by without being noticed. But Kim saw him, said a hurried good-bye to the girl, and rushed to greet him. A camera jounced against Kim's chest as he trotted over the cobblestones, dodging among the green taxis that swarmed around the fountain.

"Paul," he cried, "Paul, baby!"

Kim had learned to speak show-business English at UCLA; he held a master's degree in communications. He and Christopher had met often in Saigon. Kim knew Christopher as a journalist. He had acted as an unofficial press agent for his cousins, the Ngos; it was he who had taken Christopher to Ngo Dinh Nhu's reception.

"I'm here with Lê Xuân," he said. "Madame Nhu to you. I'm handling the press for her. It's like handling a kissing contest for a leper."

"How did you land that job?"

"I came out with the Nhu children when they left the country. That was one of the daughters I was just talking to."

Kim pointed at the girl. She walked through the crowd with two Vietnamese men and got into a curtained limousine. "Don't try anything," Kim said. "Those guys have got guns."

He told Christopher he had been looking for him for days and asked if Christopher was free for lunch. Molly was waiting in a restaurant. Christopher hesitated, then asked Kim to join them. There was no reason why Kim and Molly should not meet —Christopher could explain how he knew the man.

"A lot has happened since you left Saigon," Kim said.

"Yes."

"What will happen to your article about Diem? Did you rewrite it?"

"Yes, but the magazine will never use it," Christopher said. "They've forgotten everything since the assassination."

"I suppose they have. You mean the Kennedy assassination."

Christopher frowned; he did not understand at once what Kim meant. Then he remembered the murders of Diem and Nhu. "Yes. The others seem a long time ago," he said. "I was sorry about your president, Kim."

"And I about yours," said Kim. "Death comes alike to the high and the low."

They found Molly waiting in the restaurant. She had reversed an emerald ring Christopher had given her, as she always did when she waited alone for him in Rome, so that it looked like a wedding band.

"What will I call you?" she asked Nguyên. "I can't say Nguyên properly."

"Call me Kim. I like it better. There are millions, and I do mean millions, of Nguyêns in my country. My family are *the* Nguyêns, of course—my ancestor was the original Nguyên Kim, king of southern Vietnam. Bao Dai, the last royal ruler in my country, was a cousin of mine. So was Ngo Dinh Diem, who supplanted Bao Dai. I have a complicated family history, sweetheart, but I'm a simple man. So call me Kim. Let's have a bourbon on the rocks to start with."

Molly saw Christopher smiling at Kim. "You didn't tell me we were going to lunch with mod royalty," she said.

Nguyên raised his hands in protest. "Not I," he said. "I'm only a poor exile, hiding in Rome. I hope Paul still has his expense account. Until I can get to Beirut, I'm dead broke."

"Beirut?" Christopher asked.

"I have certain resources there, in a bank. We have learned to look to the future in my family."

"You seem to have had a bad time of it lately," Molly said. "Is Madame Nhu still in Rome?"

"Until tomorrow. Then she and the children go to Paris. I don't know why, but the French are pleased to have them."

"Have you been with them here?" Christopher asked.

"Off and on. I've been arranging her press interviews. Would you like to have one? For you, Paul, only two thousand dollars."

"Two thousand. Do you get many takers?"

"A couple of Frenchmen, some obscure fellow from an American weekly paper in Geneva. They never print the quotes she wants them to print."

"What are those?" Christopher asked.

"The truth," Kim said. "Last week the truth frightened them. This week it's in bad taste."

"What exactly is this truth?"

"What everyone knows and nobody will print—that Diem and Nhu were killed by you Americans. It really is incredible the way your government controls the press."

Kim's dealings with the press corps in Saigon had left him contemptuous of American reporters. "Intellectual sluts," he said. "Clowns, whores, sycophants." Kim liked bourbon whiskey, and he had drunk a lot of it on Christopher's last night in Saigon. Kim had unburdened himself. They had gone to the Restaurant Paprika for dinner; at the next table a group of drunken correspondents predicted to each other the downfall of Diem. "Six months ago those jokers thought Diem was the savior of Asia because I told them so," Kim said. "This year they're wise to Diem because of what some kid in the American Embassy tells them. You can have them the same way you can have dumb girls in California—put your hand between their legs and tell 'em you love 'em. They don't have minds—they have a clitoris between their ears."

Now he poured wine into Christopher's glass. "Did you hear about the other Ngo brother?" Kim asked. "Ngo Dinh Can —a vicious tyrant and torturer, Molly sweetheart. He used to run central Vietnam."

"I heard he was in jail."

"Chi Hoa prison, where the French used to crush yellow testicles. You know how Can got there? He went to the American consulate in Hué and asked for asylum. The Americans handed him over to the generals. I'd say Can has about a month to live. No doubt CBS will film the firing squad, so the world can see what happens to people who don't cooperate with the Americans."

"You're talking to an American, you know," Molly said.

"I know. That's the wonderful thing about them. They don't mind being insulted." Kim reached across the table and punched Christopher on the biceps. "Well," he said, "I guess you've got a big story in the States now. Are you working on it?"

"No, I haven't even heard from the magazine. The people who were in Dallas are the only ones who are writing this week."

"It's a great tragedy when a leader dies like that," Kim said. "There's no sense in it. A people just falls to its knees. Even the Americans—even you, I'll bet, Paul. It's a blow that strikes every person in the country."

"In the world, I should have thought," Molly said.

"Yes, I saw in the paper that Khrushchev cried," Kim said. "No one hates a murdered man if he's an American. These Kennedys were the real royalty of the modern age—too bad their reign was so brief."

They began to eat their spaghetti. "This is pretty good," Kim said. "I taste eggs and smoked pork. There should be more pepper in it."

Christopher said, "I must say you seem pretty cheerful, Kim, for a man without a country."

"Oh, I'll get by," Kim said. "We lose the country every once in a while, but we always get it back. We know a secret, Paul —in the end, nobody really *wants* Vietnam but us. All the rest of you have to learn that the hard way."

"Do you really think either branch of your family will ever get back in power?"

"Who knows?" Kim said. "Kings never come back, that's for sure. But the Ngos—that's another matter. They're very hard people."

"Yes," Christopher said. "But they're dead."

"Diem and Nhu are dead. Would you say the Kennedys are finished because the one who happened to be President has been shot?"

"No," Christopher said.

"People like the Kennedys and the Ngos always recover. One martyr wipes out all the bad memories. The Ngos have two martyrs."

"Are the two families really comparable?" Molly asked. "After all, the Kennedys are in America."

"What difference does that make?" Kim asked.

"They'll be safe there."

"Molly, my dear!" said Kim. "John Kennedy's funeral is tomorrow."

"That was the work of a lunatic," Molly said.

"Agreed. Will you now tell me that the assassination of Diem and Nhu was the work of sane men?"

"I don't know anything about that," Molly said.

"You're offended to have the two assassinations compared," Kim said. "Why should grief belong only to the Kennedys and the Americans?"

"It shouldn't. But, forgive me, Kennedy's death was more important."

"Ah, *Realpolitik* in such a beautiful young girl. Really, we backward people have no chance against you—even your women think in terms of power relationships."

"And yours don't?" Christopher said. "Didn't you just mention someone called Madame Nhu?"

Kim had been drinking a great deal of wine. When the waiter brought the second course, he asked for another liter. His face was flushed and his voice vibrated. The conversation excited him.

"Lê Xuan is a remarkable woman," he said. "She is more Ngo than the Ngos. I'll tell you a little family history. She comes from a Buddhist family, a very important family called Tran. She always felt that she was the least favorite child—she fought against her mother and father, she hardly tolerates her sister. She married Nhu when she was sixteen. She became a Catholic and an activist, she was imprisoned by the Viet Minh, she found out that the only real power for any human being is in a family that will die for its principles. In the confusion of the Japanese withdrawal in '45, one of her husband's brothers was killed by

61

Ho Chi Minh; Ho apologized to Diem and offered him half of his power, but Diem refused. Ho had killed his brother. Even Diem's country was not so important as that. Diem and Nhu triumphed, they fell—Lê Xuan saw all that happen. She has not lost heart, she knows the family goes on. There are many, many members of that family. She is one of them as she was never one of her own family. It means everything to her. She believes the family will rise again. She knows its strength."

Christopher watched Kim as he spoke. The Vietnamese had ceased eating; he pushed back his plate and poured more wine. He was speaking in a low, hard voice, his eyes fixed on Molly's. He seemed to have forgotten Christopher was there, and Christopher was content to let him go on.

"Its strength?" Molly said. "It's a family in ruins, hated in its own country, despised in the world, with its leaders destroyed by their own soldiers."

"So it would seem," Kim said. "It's good for the Ngos if the world believes that—especially now. That is part of their power, the insults of their enemies."

"I don't see any power there—I'm sorry," Molly said. She was angry.

"Oh, the Ngos have power," Kim said. "They're a force of nature. You can't understand it, Molly, but they're a great family. They forget nothing, they forgive nothing. Do you understand French? *Ils cracheront de leurs tombes.*"

Kim's speech had begun to blur. He shook his head violently, his small face was deeply flushed. Christopher knew the signs; Kim's capacity for alcohol was small, and he would soon need to go to sleep.

"Your Kennedys are not powerful in themselves," Kim said. "They live in a powerful country, that's all. They were working with their hands, unable to read, when the Nguyêns were kings of the land, and the Ngos were already wise men."

The waiter brought the bill. Kim handed it to Christopher without looking at it. He wiped his face with his napkin, and folded it carefully before putting it down at the table. He patted Molly's hand and pushed his chair back across the floor; the chair fell with a clatter behind him, but Kim did not look around.

He lifted his camera to his eye. "Smile," he said. "I want a souvenir of this most wonderful lunch." He took four photographs, quickly. He nodded, and walked out of the restaurant, carefully avoiding the chairs around the empty tables.

Molly watched him go. She closed her eyes for a moment, then smiled at Christopher.

"That's a bitter little man," she said. "What was that bit in French?"

"*Ils cracheront de leurs tombes,*" Christopher translated. " 'They would spit out of their graves.' "

Finally they went to Siena. Christopher wanted to be in a quiet place. For a week he thought of nothing but Molly. They walked through the old town with its thin campanile and its buildings that were the color of dry earth. The afternoons turned cold and they lay in bed, reading a novel aloud to one another. They drank hot chocolate with sweet Italian brandy in it. They woke each other often in the night. Afterward, Molly pushed her heavy hair away from her face and looked down, smiling, into Christopher's face. She fed the cats that gathered around her in the cafés. Christopher loved her so intensely that he felt her move in his own body.

It was Molly who liked to sleep with the window open. When the cold wakened Christopher on the last day in Siena, he noticed again that Molly slept with her lips parted, so that she seemed to be smiling over the day she had just lived through. It was only a few seconds after he had covered her and touched her hair that he went to the window, looked out, and realized what it was that Nguyên Kim, who looked like a brown child, had said to him in the restaurant in Rome.

Christopher went downstairs and booked one seat on an afternoon flight from Rome to the United States.

# FOUR

1

Patchen listened to Christopher's theory without speaking. They sat close together, away from the walls, in a sitting room at the Statler Hotel in Washington. Christopher had refused to use a safe house: they were equipped with microphones and tape machines. Even in the hotel room, he had turned on the television and the radio at full volume. Patchen's face was very close to Christopher's. The blue flicker of the television screen reflected in Patchen's glasses.

Patchen said, "Of course. Why didn't anyone else see it?"

"There's no evidence yet. It's just a feeling."

"It's obvious. No one else had a motive. All the other theories leave that out. No one had a strong enough motive—except these people."

"It looks like a perfect operation," Christopher said. "It

may be impossible to string everything together. They'll have had airtight security. Maybe only two or three people know—and there's no way of being sure who they are."

"Do you think they killed Oswald?"

"No," Christopher said. "If I'm right about how they handled him, it would have been wasteful. He didn't know who they were. They must have told him they'd get him out after the shooting, set him up as a hero under a fake identity. He would have believed that."

Patchen said, "They had to find somebody Oswald would trust. Someone he already knew."

"Who did he know? Nobody. All they needed was someone under discipline; the contact had to have bona fides. Probably a Communist of some kind."

"But how did *they* know about Oswald?"

"They went looking. He must have been in a lot of card files," Christopher said. "They had to have an American gunman. Only a nut would do it—no professional killer is going to shoot the President of the United States. Gangsters are too patriotic."

"How much have you put together?"

"Only the probabilities—but it's clear enough why they had to run the operation," Christopher said. "The psychology can't be questioned. They believed Kennedy had done this thing to them—whether he did or not doesn't matter. The way they think, they couldn't do anything but kill Kennedy in return. It's an imperative with them—insult for insult, blood for blood."

"Let's come back to that. How did they run the operation?"

"They had everything they needed," Christopher said. "First, total security. They had all the money they needed, and secure contacts all over the world. All they lacked was the assassin."

"How could they know Oswald would do it?"

"Oswald was easy enough to understand."

"They had no time to assess him. What if he turned them down?"

"They would have killed him," Christopher said. "He was

65

unstable. But I think they were confident he'd try it, and that he'd succeed."

"They needed confidence, if they thought they could get away with it," Patchen said.

"David, they've *gotten* away with it. No one even suspects them."

"Yes. Killing Kennedy made everyone forget they even existed."

"I'll bet that surprised them. They're going to be tough— they'll never believe we didn't think of them right away. They must imagine we've got a thousand men working on them right now."

"They don't know how dumb we can be," Patchen said.

Patchen massaged his bad leg, aware of the pain in it again. "No one is going to thank you for this, you know."

Christopher shrugged.

"Do you want to be assigned to this—do it yourself?"

"Yes."

"I don't know if it'll be possible. We'll have to tell the White House, and the liaison hasn't changed. It's still Foley. Johnson kept him on, with all the others."

"Who else can go? Who can you tell, even inside the outfit?"

Patchen rose and limped to the window; he bent the slats of the venetian blind and looked down at the traffic on K Street. The back of his suit was a mass of wrinkles, and he looked as if he had not slept for a long time. He expelled his breath; it was almost a laugh that he uttered.

" 'The dog it was that died,' " he said.

He touched Christopher's shoulder and pointed at the telephone. After Patchen had closed the door behind him, Christopher turned off the television and the radio. Molly's face, asleep and faintly smiling, flickered in his mind like the bleached electronic pictures in the mirrors of Patchen's eyeglasses. He sat down and waited for the phone to ring.

They met again after dark in Patchen's living room. The narrow row house still bore traces of Patchen's wife: a dying plant, chintz furniture. There were no photographs, no letters lying around, no odor of food and soap. The signs that anyone had ever made love in Patchen's house were disappearing.

Dennis Foley sat on the sofa with his long legs stretched before him. Grief had made him listless. The mannerisms Christopher had noticed in Paris were gone. Foley dressed as carefully as before, and he still wore the PT-109 clasp on his black knitted tie, but he had the look of a man who has been told that he has lost his health or his wife. What he had thought himself to be was in the past.

"You've met, I think," Patchen said.

Foley looked at Christopher without interest. "I haven't been briefed," he said. "Your people called to say you had something for the White House and we ought to take you seriously. Go ahead."

Christopher glanced at Patchen. "Who's been told?" he asked.

"The Director. He decided that the White House had to be brought in at once. No one else will be told without presidential authority."

"I can give you twenty minutes," Foley said.

Christopher remained standing. "I'll have to give it to you cold, Mr. Foley," he said. "It has to do with the assassination of President Kennedy."

Foley gritted his teeth and started to get up. "Take him to Earl Warren's people," he said. "That's the proper channel."

"It's too sensitive for that," Patchen said. "I know this is painful, but I think you should listen. You can reject what Christopher has to say after you've heard it, and you won't hear from him again."

Foley relaxed his grip on the arms of the chair. "All right," he said.

He stared at the floor as Christopher began to speak. After hearing the first sentence, his eyes snapped upward and fastened on Christopher's face. Christopher actually saw the pupils dilate, so that Foley's pale eyes changed color and darkened, as if his brain had commanded them to stop admitting light. Foley wore such an expression of pain that Christopher wanted to look away. It took Christopher, trained to report in clean sentences, very little time to summarize what he believed.

Foley went on staring into Christopher's eyes, but when he spoke, he spoke to Patchen. "It's insane," he said.

"No," Patchen replied. "It's logical."

"It's grotesque," Foley said; his voice had lost timbre, and he put a hand to his neck and cleared his throat. He began to cough, and in the midst of the spasm lit a cigar.

"It's grotesque," he repeated. "John Fitzgerald Kennedy and these people do not belong in the same order of nature."

"Nevertheless," Christopher said, "the possibility is there."

"How is it there—even the possibility?" Foley asked hotly. "How did they do it, how did they organize it? Give me the scenario."

"These things are less difficult than you think," Christopher said. "Tradecraft is a simple art."

"*What* is a simple art?" Foley asked.

"Tradecraft," Patchen explained. "It's jargon for the technique and practice of espionage. Go on, Paul."

"This is all speculation, Foley, and I like speculation even less than you seem to," Christopher said. "Bear with me for a minute."

"All right," Foley said.

"They needed an opportunity, and they knew it would come. American Presidents show themselves in public under security arrangements that are the laughingstock of the world. In addition to opportunity, they needed an assassin."

"So they reached into Dallas and picked out a psychotic like Oswald?" Foley said, his voice rising. "Come off it, Christopher."

"If I'm right, yes—they reached into Dallas and picked out Oswald," Christopher said. "His psychosis was the handle they had on him."

"Psychotics can't be trusted to function," Foley said, and Christopher, without surprise, again felt the man's stubborn resistance to what he was being told.

"I'd say he functioned very well," Christopher said. "You don't have to be sane to pull a trigger. You tell an agent who is obsessed with something, as Oswald was obsessed with his own impotence and the power of others, something that will inspire him to act out of the logic of his insanity."

"And what did they tell Oswald?"

"I don't know yet. I would have told him that I was a Soviet intelligence officer, and that we'd been watching him benevolently for years, here and when he was in Russia, knowing that he was capable of a great act that would change history. That would have fitted in with his fantasy."

Foley looked at his watch. "Half my time is gone," he said wearily. "Why does it have to be a conspiracy? Why can't Oswald have just *done* it for his own insane reasons?"

"One thing, and again it's speculation, but it fits in with the theory because it fits in with standard clandestine practice," Christopher said. "Oswald killed the President with a rifle. That's the tool of an agent, not the weapon of a lunatic. Every other President who has been killed or wounded by an assassin has been killed or wounded by a pistol—Lincoln, Garfield, McKinley. Both Roosevelts were attacked with pistols. Gandhi was killed with a pistol. Nuts like to smell their victims. Oswald used a rifle, and he left it behind like a professional and walked away. If he'd been a real professional, instead of something designed for one-time use, he would have got away."

Christopher was still standing. He had taken care to speak in a calm voice. He looked down at Foley, who had closed his eyes again; he was massaging the bridge of his nose to advertise his fatigue.

"I'd like to talk to you, Patchen," Foley said.

He said nothing more to Christopher and did not look at him again.

Patchen walked Christopher to the door. Foley was still sprawled in the chair with his hand to his face when Patchen returned.

"Get me a glass of water," he said.

When Patchen handed him the glass, Foley put it on the table beside him and opened his eyes; his pupils were still dark, as if bruised.

"How well do you know this Christopher?" Foley asked.

"We've known each other for twenty years," Patchen said. "We came into the outfit on the same day. I've backstopped his operations for more than ten years."

"Then you can't be very objective."

"You can check my assessment of Christopher with anyone else who knows his work," Patchen said. "Three things: first, he's intelligent and entirely unsentimental. Second, he will go to any lengths to get at the truth, he never gives up. Third, he is not subject to fear."

"Everyone is subject to fear."

"No. He'll walk into anything."

"Then he's crazy," Foley said.

"In that respect, maybe. But it makes him very valuable."

"This theory of his is as full of holes as a Swiss cheese—you know that, don't you?"

"I thought enough of it to bring you over here to listen to it," Patchen said. "The theory, as a theory with no hard facts to support it, is sound enough."

"Is it? In what way, exactly?"

"He's right about two things. They had a motive, and they had the skill and the experience to bring off an operation of this kind."

Foley leaped to his feet. Standing over Patchen, he pointed a finger at his face. "Let's get this straight once and for all," he said. "They had no goddamn motive. None."

Patchen's unblinking eyes did not change expression. "We both know they did, Dennis," he said.

Foley's face was closed and angry. Patchen knew why; he

understood that Foley, who had defended the living President with all the power of his mind, did not regard loyalty as something that stopped with death. Foley had stood next to the President of the United States, believing that everyone ought to love him as Foley did. He wanted to believe that only a madman would kill such a man as Kennedy had been; he wanted the world to believe it.

"I won't have any son of a bitch saying that what happened to Jack in Dallas was a *punishment,*" Foley said. He breathed deeply. "I want this matter dropped, right here and now," he said. "Send Christopher back to wherever he comes from. *Drop it, Patchen.*"

"You don't think this should be brought to the attention of the President?—two lines on a sheet of paper."

"No. It's not worth his time. If there is anything on paper, burn it. I don't think you grasp the implications of what this nut is trying to get us to believe."

"I see the implications," Patchen said. "All of them. So does Christopher."

"Who else is he going to go to with this?"

"No one."

"You're sure of that?"

"He lives in secret, Foley. He doesn't talk to anyone but us."

"You just told me he never gives up," Foley said. "What if he decides not to give up on this, then what?"

"Then he'll solve it, one way or another. He knows everybody in the world, and he's a very senior officer. He requires no support. He's what we call a singleton—he operates alone, goes where he pleases."

"Then you'd better bring him back here and put him behind some nice, safe desk," Foley said.

Patchen shook his head. "No. He'd resign. He doesn't need us—he's as well known as a journalist in the outside world as he is as an agent in ours."

"What you're telling me is that you have no control over him at all."

"No, I'm not telling you that. Control is not necessary. He

feels about the outfit the way you felt about John Kennedy. He'd do nothing to harm us, or the country. Of course, his idea of what's harmful to the United States might not be the same as yours."

Foley stared at Patchen, and then Patchen saw an idea being born behind Foley's eyes.

"Has Christopher ever been like this before—hooked on something?" Foley asked.

"Lots of times. He's usually been right."

"He's usually been right, or he's usually come up with data that supported his theory?"

"It's the same thing," Patchen said.

"It's not. When was the last time he saw a psychiatrist? Don't you have regular psychiatric controls on guys like him?"

"Psychiatric controls? When a man breaks down, we take care of him, that's all."

Foley said, "I've seen this guy twice. Both times he's been compulsive about something. It could be a pattern."

Again Patchen said nothing. A pulse was beating in Foley's temple; Patchen watched that.

"Christopher may have done great things in the past," Foley said. "I don't doubt it for a minute. But how long has he been out there—ten years, twelve? He's showing it. He needs a rest, David. You must have a quiet place where he can recuperate."

Patchen showed no surprise because he felt none. Foley, a much larger man, stood over him, giving off an odor of cologne and whiskey. Patchen understood how a woman about to be fondled by a man she does not want must feel. Foley, crude and emotional, seemed to him a ridiculous figure. Patchen's lips parted in a smile.

"Why don't you put that suggestion in writing," he said, "and channel it to me through the Director?"

Foley departed, leaving his glass of water untasted. Ordering Patchen to fetch it for him had been a way of emphasizing the difference in their ranks. In Foley's place, Patchen would have made the gesture at the end of the conversation, not at the beginning.

# 4

When Christopher came back into the house, Patchen played the tape recording of his conversation with Foley. Neither man said anything; the listening devices in Patchen's living room were voice-activated transmitters that could not be switched off. They put on their coats and went outside.

"The bars must still be open," Patchen said. "Let's walk. I'd like a beer."

They were alone on the sidewalk, and when they reached Connecticut Avenue the broad street was empty of cars, though the automatic traffic signals went on working: the lights changed to red along its whole steep length, like cards falling out of a shuffler's hand.

"What now?" Christopher said.

"It's over. The problem is, Foley believes you. He doesn't want your theory proved."

"You're willing to drop it?"

"Of course. If the White House doesn't want it, we won't do it."

"Well, it would have been nice if we'd got some Texan instead of Foley to talk to," Christopher said.

"The answer might have been the same. If the truth is known, the truth will come out. Nobody wants that—not even you."

"We know lots of truths that never come out, David."

"Not on this scale. This couldn't be hidden. It would blacken the name of the dead President. It would stand foreign policy on its head."

They were in front of a bar, and Patchen started toward its door. "Let's stop outside a minute," Christopher said. "You know what's involved here, David. If these politicians never know what happened, they'll do it again."

"Yes. They will."

"You don't think that's worth preventing?"

"I don't think it's possible to prevent it, Paul. You have a flaw—you think the truth will make men free. But it only makes them angry. They believe what suits them, they do what they

73

want to do, just like the slobs we're going to find lined up at the bar in there. Human beings are a defective species, my friend. Accept it."

"But don't you want to *know?*"

"Sure I do—I even say we should know, that we're doing damage to the outfit, not to say the country, if we don't pursue this to the end. But we don't run operations against the United States government."

"Foley is not the United States government."

"Foley would say you're talking treason."

"I'd say that's pretty melodramatic," Christopher said. "We were told from the beginning that our job is to keep the water clean. We feed the politicians information, they do what they want with it. But we don't doctor the information to suit political purposes, much less the emotional purposes of a short-timer like Dennis Foley. What Foley wants from us is a kind of treason —his illusions are more important than the truth."

"That's what I just got through telling you."

"We don't seem to be understanding each other very well, David. Would it help, do you think, if we spoke German?"

"Paul, you really are an arrogant bastard," Patchen said. "Your whole career has been a series of moral lessons for the rest of us. *You* won't use a gun. *You* won't betray an agent. *You* won't give support to a regime that tortures political prisoners. *You* won't countenance a coup against the Ngos, even though you've done more than anyone else to create a political opposition to them. Only *your* means justify the end. People have been telling me for years that you're more trouble than you're worth, and I'm beginning to see the point."

Patchen's voice did not change its tone; he might have been reading aloud from a newspaper.

"I guess I'm lucky to have had you as a protector," Christopher said.

"I can't protect you from these people. You're out in the open now, and they sure don't like the look of you."

"Foley's an amateur."

"We would have said the same thing about Lee Harvey Oswald."

74

"Yes, but he was operating against other amateurs."

"And he had professional advice."

"Yes, I think so."

A man and a young girl came out of the bar, holding hands. They stood in the doorway for a moment, looking up and down the street for a taxi.

"Have you tried the Cantina d'Italia, up the street?" Patchen asked Christopher, in a louder voice. "I think it's the best Italian restaurant in the world, outside of Italy."

The couple walked by Christopher and Patchen and crossed the street to the taxi stand in front of the Mayflower.

"You realize you're not going to be able to go out under our auspices," Patchen said. "Foley will have been on the phone to the Director. It won't be permitted."

"Then I'll do it on my own."

"You may die."

"That's always a possibility."

Patchen let a moment pass before he answered. "You really don't care, do you?" he said.

"Yes, I care. Less than some, I guess. I've never liked the death of others."

"How are you going to handle it?"

"Do you really want to know?"

"Yes. I want to understand what happens to you."

"I'll either find out very quickly or not at all," Christopher said. "I'll have to walk in on them and tell them what I think, and watch the reaction. I think they may want it to be known."

"*Want* it to be known?"

"Yes. Think about it. If no one knows, what was the point in doing it?"

Patchen absorbed this idea, then nodded his head.

"I'll fire you in the morning," he said. "If you live, and if you want to come back inside, it can be arranged. Foley won't last forever with Lyndon Johnson."

"The bar's going to close. Let's go in."

Patchen had one more thing to say. Christopher was surprised: it was unlike Patchen to be the one who prolonged a conversation.

"It takes about a month to inform everyone in the field of a resignation," he said. "I won't hurry it. You may want to talk to the people in the stations."

"Yes, there may be a question or two I'd want to ask."

"If you need support in any kind of an emergency, you know they'll give it to you. We'll justify it later."

Christopher smiled at him. "You shouldn't be saying these things. What if I'm tortured?"

Patchen waved away the pleasantry. "Speaking of that, I wouldn't rely too much on Wolkowicz. He and Foley are friends. The White House took an interest in Wolkowicz's career after the Bay of Pigs."

"Took an interest in his career?"

Patchen exhaled his dry laugh. "Wolkowicz was their idea of what a master spy should be. They all read those paperback books about secret agents. Wolkowicz carries guns and talks like a gangster. They were talking about Castro in one of the planning sessions—what to do with him after Cuba was liberated. Wolkowicz took out his revolver, removed a cartridge from the cylinder, and rolled the bullet across the table. In the Cabinet Room. That was when his star began to rise."

Patchen opened the door for Christopher. "Now let me buy you one last beer," he said.


5


Foley had not intended to return the phone call. When he saw the message on his desk he didn't recognize the name of the man who had called him.

"He's a Green Beret captain," Foley's secretary explained. "He's on his way to Vietnam. He said his sister is a friend of yours. Her name is Peggy McKinney."

Foley frowned and crumpled the slip on which the message was written.

"He said you and his sister met in Paris."

Foley remembered. He handed his secretary the ball of paper. "Set up an appointment for him today," he said. "Here."

He put a plain sheet of paper in his own typewriter and

began to write the letter he wanted Peggy McKinney's brother to deliver for him. Then he phoned a man at the Pentagon and arranged to have the captain assigned to an army intelligence unit stationed on Saigon.

When the captain appeared in Foley's office, he stood at attention in front of the desk. Foley, in shirtsleeves, grinned at him.

"Sit down, Captain," he said. "What can I do for you?"

"I didn't want to intrude on you—Peggy just asked me to call up and say hello."

"I'm glad you did. Peggy's terrific."

The captain was about twenty-five, dark and fine-strung like his sister.

"You know," Foley said, "it was right in this office that an officer like you was ordered to take the message to García."

"I guess those days are over, sir."

"No, they're not," Foley said. "I have a job for you. You are not to discuss what I'm asking you to do with anyone, not even your supervisor. I've informed the right person in the office of the Army Chief of Staff. You and he and I, and we alone, are to know about this. Is that clear?"

Foley gave him a sealed letter for Wolkowicz and told him what else he wanted him to do when he reached Vietnam. He gave him a photograph of Christopher; he had had to call the Passport Office himself in order to obtain it.

"His real name is Paul Christopher, but he'll probably be using an alias. Look at the picture and give it back to me."

"What channel shall I use to report?"

"You don't report. If you do the job, I'll know it. And, Captain, I won't forget you."

"I don't want anything for this," the captain said. "Sir, I loved President Kennedy."

"I know you did, son," Foley said.

# FIVE

### 1

Christopher stood on the steps of the Galleria Borghese and watched Molly walk across the park with the pine trees behind her. She had spent the morning at the zoo while he wrote his profile of the Pope, and she carried a bag of peanuts in her hand.

She wanted to look at Canova's nude Pauline Bonaparte and the Caravaggios before lunch. "Just those two things, Paul," she said as she made their plans. "You needn't look so suspicious." Molly could spend hours looking at painting and sculpture. "There are museum guards all over Europe who think you're in love with them, the way you hang about," Christopher told her. "Then you *know*?" Molly said. "Chaps with sore feet in dusty uniforms make me go all funny."

"Do you love me, now that you admit it, for my mind or for my body?" Molly had asked when he returned from Washington. Christopher could not separate the two. When he entered her, he felt himself grasped not so much by her flesh as by her idea of herself. Naked, she was as comic as a child; that was what had surprised him the first time he had her. He had imagined that she would be a solemn lover, but she laughed when she opened her legs, as if pleasure were a joke she played on life. They looked into each other's face when they made love, smiling and chuckling.

Now, as she came toward him, holding her hair in the December wind, he felt a smile pulling at his face, and when they kissed, he laughed. Christopher had a strange loud laugh that he could not control; strangers turned their heads when it exploded.

"Ah," Molly said, "I've just come from feeding a poor caged thing like you."

When the museum closed at two o'clock, they walked to a restaurant, and because it was Thursday, ate *gnocchi* and *bollito misto*.

Molly ordered a spiced pear and said, "Why does food seem so romantic when one's having a love affair? If I ate this much in a state of innocence, I'd weigh two hundred pounds."

When she had come back from Siena, she had moved into his apartment; she bought vases and filled them with roses and carnations. She put his books in alphabetical order, novels on one set of shelves, poetry on another, general works on a third.

Molly said she had driven Cathy's ghost out of Christopher's bed. "Did you really not mind the way she put horns on you?" she asked.

"Yes, I minded, until I saw her reason," Christopher said. "She knew more about my life than you do, Molly. Cathy was a gloomy woman. Maybe she wanted an existence that was as corrupt as she thought mine to be. It wasn't love, but it was the best she could do, to go down the way she thought I was going."

They were in bed, with Molly's candles burning on all the tables in the room. "I know nothing about your life—are you all that bad when you're away?" she asked.

"I never was, but when I was younger I had a tendency to melancholy," Christopher said. "I'd return from Lagos, still seeing the lepers catching coins in their mouths like dogs because their fingers had fallen off, and I'd betray a certain sadness. Cathy thought she knew another reason for my mood."

Molly lay still in the moving light. "Black girls?" she asked.

"That was the least of it," Christopher replied.

"It must have been your bloody silence," Molly said. "Have you any love for me when you're away, or does it start when you see me and end when your plane takes off?"

Christopher took a candle off the bedside table and held it up so that both their faces were in the light. "If I love you, Molly, it's because you've never been with me in all those places," he said. "I won't tell you, I won't take you. That part of it isn't life."

A tear ran down her cheek. He had never seen her cry before.

"I never thought there was any love in you at all," she said, "and now that you say there is, I want it all."

He blew out the candle. Molly drew his arm around her body, put her wet face in the hollow of his neck, and went to sleep.


2


The following morning, Molly came back from the post office with Patchen's letter. Christopher looked at the sterile envelope with his name and address typed on it and knew the sender: the characters that fell on the left side of the typewriter keyboard were fainter than the others. Once, as a joke, he had advised Patchen to get an electric machine to conceal these traces that his letters were typed by a man with one arm weaker than the other. He sent Molly out of the room and opened the envelope. On a sheet of cheap paper were typed two lines from one of Christopher's old poems.

*Death fell breathless behind us in our war-struck youth,*
*and winning that race, we lost our chance at truth.*

Below this, Patchen had typed: *"PSRunner/22X163/UBS (G)."*

The note was unsigned. Christopher put it in his pocket, lifted the phone, and made a reservation on the noon plane to Geneva.

Christopher was not known at the Union de Banques Suisses in Geneva, but they were used to strangers there. He told a clerk that he wished to discuss a numbered account, and he was taken into an office where a bald Swiss sat behind a bare desk. Swiss banks have a churchly atmosphere; Christopher judged from the furnishings in the bald man's office that he was the equivalent of a bishop. The man rose from a chair with a high carved back and shook hands, but did not smile.

"There is a numbered account here for me, recently opened, I believe," Christopher said.

"Will you state the number and the name, please?"

"It is 22X163," Christopher said, "and the name is P. S. Runner."

"One moment." The bald man unlocked a file and extracted a large card; he centered it on the polished surface of the desk before him and looked expectantly at Christopher.

"Do you require a signature?" Christopher asked.

"No, monsieur. Our instructions are to pay on demand, but you must furnish the second of two lines of verse."

Christopher quoted the line from Patchen's letter.

"It's in order," the bald banker said. "Do you wish to make a withdrawal?"

"What is the current balance?"

"A deposit of $100,000 has been made—that is, Swiss francs 432,512.65. You may have any amount, in either currency."

"Please give me twenty-five thousand dollars in hundred-dollar bills, and five thousand Swiss francs in hundred-franc notes."

The banker wrote on a form and pressed a bell. In a moment, a messenger returned with two long buff envelopes. The banker counted the money rapidly, sealed the envelopes, and handed them to Christopher. "Your balance is now

$73,865.74," he said. "When you call for more funds, you may come directly to this office without asking the *huissier*. It's more discreet."

Christopher nodded and put the envelopes in his breast pocket. Outside in the rue du Rhône he saw a man in a tweed Brooks Brothers overcoat limping through the crowd and thought for an instant that it might be Patchen. His letter bore a Swiss postmark, so he might have carried the cash to Geneva himself. Christopher followed the limping man for a block or two before he got a clear glimpse of his face, which was whole and handsome.

At a garage near the railroad station, Christopher rented a car with French license plates. There were no identity controls at the French frontier for motor traffic. The weather in northern Europe was already turning bad, and he drove over the Jura through fog and sleet. He did not want to leave any traces of himself on paper in France, so he did not stop at a hotel. He drove all night and arrived in Paris before the morning traffic had begun to move. He parked the car behind the horse barns at Longchamps and slept for three hours in the back seat. When he awoke, he touched the envelopes with Patchen's money in them.

### 3

It took Christopher half the day to learn the telephone number of Nguyên Kim.

"Are you still bumming meals?" Christopher asked, when Kim came on the noisy line.

They arranged to meet at Fouquet's. Christopher filled the gas tank and spent three hours circling the block until he found a parking place on the Champs-Elysées in front of the café.

Kim drank two large bourbons at Fouquet's and two more at La Coupole after they had driven through Montmartre and doubled back across the Seine bridges. Kim did not know the city, and the long ride with many detours down side streets did not surprise him. When they reached the restaurant, they were alone; as they pulled away from Fouquet's, Christopher had seen, in the rear-view mirror, the two men who were following Kim. One hurried around the corner to get a taxi while the other watched Christopher's rented Peugeot vanishing into a school of others just like it toward the place de la Concorde.

Kim ordered oysters. For an Asian, he was an adventurous eater, but he looked uncomfortable when he saw before him the thick green meat of a dozen *Spéciales* in their gnarled shells. He squeezed lemon over the oysters, and putting one into his mouth, opened his eyes wide and chewed. "They have no taste," he said, and sprinkled pepper over the ones remaining.

"Kim," Christopher said, "Let me see if I have this straight. The part of the Vietnamese family called the *toc* consists of all persons, male or female, who claim a common ancestry back five generations into the past, and forward three generations into the future. Is that right?"

Kim, still chewing, frowned. "Say it in French," he said. Christopher translated.

"Yes," Kim said, "That's it. Then there are the *chi* and the *phai*—different parts of the system."

"The *chi* is the important unit, is it? Those are people related in direct line of descent from eldest son to eldest son."

"People who belong to a *chi* think so. How do you know this stuff?"

"I'm not sure I do, that's why I'm checking. What's a *phai*?"

"There can be lots of *phai* in a family. That's people who are descended from younger sons."

"Can you belong to a *chi* on one side and a *phai* on the other?"

"Sure, everyone does. I'm a *chi* on the Nguyên side and a *phai* on the Ngo side."

"What about, say, Diem and Nhu—where did they fit in?"

"They were both younger sons," Nguyên said. "The eldest son was Khoi—the one I told you was killed in '45 by Ho's people."

"Do these categories mean anything in the modern world?"

"You bet your ass they do," Kim said. "What counts is

where you rank in the family. If the Nguyên kings had held on for another four hundred years, I'd be a prince of the blood royal. Nobody forgets that."

"Where do you rank in the Ngo family?"

"Way down—lower than Diem and Nhu did, even."

"They couldn't have ranked so low."

"Well, no, they didn't. They were listened to, and they contributed a lot to the family wealth in one way or another. But as far as the Truong toc was concerned, they were just a couple of kids who spoke French."

"The Truong toc?" Christopher said. "Who's that?"

"The head of the family. He's the oldest man of the main line of eldest sons. I guess maybe he was their great-uncle."

"What's his name?"

Kim chewed another oyster and gave Christopher a bright drunken look, filled with wariness. "Ngo," he said.

"Ngo what?"

"That's for me to Ngo and you to find out," Kim said, and coughed violently on the oyster that laughter had driven into his nose.

When he recovered, he wiped tears from his eyes and asked, "What do you want to know all this stuff for, anyway?"

"After we had lunch in Rome, I thought I might go back out to Saigon and do a piece on the Ngo family. You made them sound interesting."

"Well, they're not. They mostly sit around in dark little houses, eating smelly stuff and talking about the past."

"I find it hard to believe that this guy—the Truong toc?—could run the lives of men like Diem and Nhu," Christopher said.

"In politics, no. In the family, yes. He's the one closest to everyone's ancestors—very important stuff with us."

"He's in touch with everybody in the family?"

"Sure—that's all he has to do in life. Whenever there's a problem in the family, he settles it. Consults the ancestors, you know, and comes up with the answer. His house is the headquarters of the *toc.*"

"What if you're a militant Catholic, like Diem or Nhu—do you still worry about ancestor worship?"

Kim held a glass of wine to his lips with his right hand. With his left he made a gesture, palm upward, then downward, and lifted his eyebrows. He swallowed his wine and said, "It isn't a question of ancestor worship *versus* Jesus Christ Our Lord. I tried to tell you in Rome how strong the family is with us. You've got to picture a group of people to whom all the dead ones, going back forever, and all the living ones, including the ones who are going to be born from now to forever, are all *with you*, all the time. That's the Vietnamese family."

"I'd like to write something about this."

"Would you? You'd better do it on some other family. The Ngos are just a little anti-American right now."

"It would be a good chance for them to make a point or two," Christopher said. "I've got twenty million readers."

"Your readers wouldn't know a Truong toc from a third baseman, even after you told them. Paul, you're shitting me. I think you've got something up your sleeve. You think about that while I get rid of some of this wine."

Christopher watched Kim's progress through the loud restaurant. Sybille Webster, sitting at a table against the wall, put a finger along her nose and winked at him. Tom Webster watched the Vietnamese go into the toilet, then walked over to Christopher's table with his napkin clutched in his hand.

"Hi," he said. "How's every little thing?"

"Okay, Tom."

"A college friend of yours passed through a couple of days ago. He left a message for you."

"Did he, now? What was it?"

"It's a bit complicated. Why don't you come over for a drink when you ditch the little fellow?"

"All right. It may be late."

Webster nodded and went back to his table. When Kim returned, he changed to red wine.

"Have you been to Beirut yet?" Christopher asked.

"No," Kim replied, "I've decided to live oy my wits for a

while. I keep busy selling interviews with Madame Nhu. You're still not interested?"

"Not really, Kim. I know what she's going to say—and it's not publishable."

"You want to do a story about the Ngo family without talking to her? No way you could do it—you're too white, with all that blond hair and your big feet in wing tips. They wouldn't say a word to you."

Christopher shrugged. "I thought you might help out."

"I don't work there anymore."

"But you work, Kim. I'm not thinking of your doing anything for free."

Kim put down his wineglass and drew a short finger delicately around its rim. Christopher was reminded of the bald banker in Geneva, counting money. "Well," Kim said, "anything for the homeland. What seems reasonable to you?"

"A fair exchange. You give me ten good names—the Truong toc and whoever else you think might talk to me. I'd go to two hundred a name."

Kim shook his head. "You'd have to use my name to get in the door," he said. "I wouldn't want you to do that."

"Then give me some other name—there must be someone I can pretend to know. By the time they check, I'll be out of the country."

"Give me a piece of paper," Kim said. He pushed his plate aside and wrote rapidly with Christopher's pen, holding it between his second and third fingers. "I've given you addresses, too—the one with the asterisk is the Truong toc."

Christopher glanced at the list. "Who are the others?"

"Men to be careful of, Paul. I mean it. I think I know what you're after."

Kim laughed suddenly, staring into Christopher's eyes. "Oh, this ought to be funny, Paul. You want a name to use as a reference, eh?" He leaned forward and beckoned Christopher closer. "Tell them you know Lê Thu," he said.

"Lê Thu? That's a girl's name, isn't it?"

"Oh, yes, sometimes," Kim said. "Not always, though. Lê

Thu—can you remember that? Believe me, that name will open doors in Vietnam."

Christopher paid the bill. Outside, the café awnings were whipped by a hard winter rain. Kim fastened the button at the neck of his camel's-hair overcoat. "Jesus," he said, "I don't wonder white people are all screwed up, coming from a climate like this."

They walked together to the taxi rank at the corner of the boulevard Raspail. A tart standing against the wall of a building with her umbrella held over her head gave Christopher a miserable smile and cried, *"Au secours!"*

Kim stopped to inspect the girl. "How much?" he asked her in French.

*"Un napoléon,"* she replied, *"service non compris."*

Kim turned away with a look of contempt. "A hundred francs—for *that?"*

The girl called after him, "Seventy-five, it's raining."

*"C'est dégoûtant,"* Kim said.

Christopher stepped under the awning of a darkened shop. He handed Kim an envelope.

"Two thousand francs," he said. "You're doing better than the *poule,* and you don't have to stand out in the weather."

Kim weighed the envelope in his hand, then stuffed it into the pocket of his coat. His hair had been parted by the rain and his small round face was wet.

"I'm selling a bigger thrill," Kim said. "Remember the name—Lê Thu."


4

Christopher let Kim walk alone to the taxi. When the cab was out of sight, he went into the Dôme and ordered a hot rum. The zinc bar was gone, and the harp-backed straw chairs, but the manners of the customers had not changed. A boy in a ragged sweater stared contemptuously at Christopher's suit and tie; the boy held his girl's hand and pressed down hard with his thumbnail on each of her knuckles in turn, watching with a small smile as pain crossed her face.

Christopher watched the street. When he saw Tom and Sybille Webster get into a taxi, he paid his bill and walked around the corner to the Métro.

Webster opened the door before Christopher rang the bell. "How's Kim, the P.R. genius?" he asked.

"About the same," Christopher said. "Are we going to talk here, or do you want to go someplace else?"

"Wherever we go on a night like this, we'll be surrounded by four walls. Sybille wants to say good-night to you—or good-bye, or whatever."

Sybille had taken off her stockings when she came in from the rain, and she stood in front of the fireplace with her skirt lifted high on her freckled legs.

"Hello, cookie," she said. "Why are you in this terrible town when you could be in the sun?"

Christopher kissed her. "To see you for the last time—we can't go on meeting this way, Sybille."

"That's what David Patchen told me the other night. Oh, I realized I hated him when he sat right there with his eyes propped open like a bad statue's and said, 'By the way, Christopher's resigned,'" Sybille said. "As a conversationalist he's a *blowgun*—Paul, I know he's your best friend, but every time he comes here he has some bit of news, tipped with curare, that he fires into my poor flesh. Why does he come? Why doesn't he stay in Washington and stroke his computers?"

Webster handed his wife a glass of brandy. "We'll still see Paul," he said. "Blame him—he's the one who resigned, after all."

"I'd rather blame David Patchen," Sybille said. "Besides, it will never be the same. We can't assume Paul knows the same secrets as we do anymore. I've *seen* people go outside—they have the same faces as before, but they change. Little by little, what made them nice leaks out of them."

Sybille drank her cognac. "Oh, well," she said. "I'm going to bed like a good professional wife, so you two can have your last exchange of dark confidences. Are you sleeping here to-night. Paul?"

"I might, if that's all right."

"You know where—I'll put some towels out for you. We'll meet again in the morning." Sybille put a hand to his cheek and kissed his lips. "It's raining all over the world," she said.

Webster filled their glasses again. They stood together by the fire, smiling at Sybille's noises in the back of the apartment. Finally her bedroom door closed and Webster brought a sealed envelope out of his pocket and handed it to Christopher. There was no salutation on the note and no signature:

You wanted something on Oswald's movements before Dallas.

He was in New Orleans from 24 April to 25 September, working at insignificant jobs. He passed out leaflets for something called the "Fair Play for Cuba Committee."

On 25 September, for no apparent reason, he went to Mexico City by bus, arriving there on the morning of 27 September. He stayed at the Hotel Commercio ($1.28 a day).

On the twenty-seventh, he went twice to the Cuban embassy and once to the Soviet embassy to apply for visas; said he wanted to return to Russia, transiting through Havana. He was turned down at both places, and had a loud argument with the Cuban consul. At the Soviet embassy he spoke with Yatskov and Kostikov, both KGB types under consular cover.

Between 27 September and 1 October, he remained in Mexico City, but there is no information about his movements on those three days. He returned to Dallas, arriving 3 October, and went to work at the Texas Book Depository on 16 October.

He'd had the rifle for some time—bought it under a false name, "A. Hidell," on 13 March, by mail order.

On 1 November, he rented P.O. Box 6225, Terminal Annex, Dallas.

After our little dance on the sidewalk, I began to think about what you'd said. Maybe we're the ones with illusions, but it doesn't matter. See what you can do; if you succeed, I'd like to hear about it. But that's up to you.

The money in Geneva represents less than the total of your magazine salary over the past five years. We never found a way to give it to charity (something about accounting regulations), so it's been lying in a safe all this time. I found a way to give it back to you as a "termination bonus." As long as we call it that, it seems to be okay. There's more if you need it.

I wish I could arrange a nobler gesture. It's not possible. I do advise you to stay out of this country for a while. Your highly placed friend won't be in "power" forever, but while he is, you might as well realize you have no one here who can help you. He's serious about the straitjacket.

I've told Tom about your "resignation," to prevent his sending me cables asking where you are. He'll keep it to himself, even if asked directly. He knows nothing else, and shouldn't.

Good-bye.

Christopher read the first part of the note again to memorize it, and dropped it in the fire. Webster said, "What's all this about, Paul?"

"A word of farewell from David."

Webster brushed aside Christopher's reply with a motion of his hand. "I mean, what brought this on so suddenly?"

"Tom, it's not so sudden. You get tired of the life. I've been hanging around alone in hotel rooms in central Africa and Afghanistan ever since I got out of college. I don't want to do it anymore."

"It's not too convenient for the rest of us, you know. There are twenty-six principal agents in eighteen different countries out there who won't talk to anyone but you."

"They'll get along. Ninety percent of what they do, they do out of their own resources. They aren't photographing documents, they're running political movements. I've held their hands for a long time—let them go on alone."

Webster sat down heavily. "I'm not used to operating against you, Paul, and I don't like to do it. I think this smells very, very funny. Patchen doesn't give a shit about your agents, either. He wouldn't discuss handing them over to somebody else. It's like he expects you back after a short vacation."

"I won't be back, Tom. David knows that."

"Then what's he waiting for? He doesn't want word of your leaving to get around, isn't that right?"

"You read Patchen's mind if you want to. I've never been able to do it. What do you mean by operating against me?"

"Trying to get you to open up," Webster said. "Sybille may think things have changed, but I don't. We've never lied to each other, Paul."

"Then let's not start now."

"All right, I'll tell you the truth. I don't think you're out. I think you and David have got something going. You went to Washington without even telling us. I didn't know you'd been there until Patchen showed up on the doorstep day before yesterday."

"When I went to Washington, it seemed the thing to do, Tom. I'm sorry I didn't tell you—but I go a lot of places without telling you, when I pay for my own ticket."

"So you fly home at your own expense, resign, make plans to shack up in Rome for the rest of your life with that Australian you've got, right?" Webster said. "And a week later I spot you in La Coupole, with Nguyên Kim, with no French surveillance closer than wherever you lost it. The French are on him like ten pots of glue, all the time. You're telling me they took a night off so you two could eat oysters and gossip about old times?"

"Tom, I'm not telling you that—you're making it up."

"Well, I'm not making this up. Kim has run just over two million dollars through the Banque Sadak in Beirut in the last ten days. He's got couriers going every which way."

"He didn't mention that to me," Christopher said.

"The French have got him bugged. We couldn't get mikes in there because there's always someone in the house, so we're piggybacking the French wires."

Christopher laughed. "I'll bet the French are going to like that."

"They won't find out. We're not going to find out a hell of a lot listening to tapes. We need someone next to Kim—like you. But you're an outsider. I'm not telling you any more."

"I can guess," Christopher said. "You think they're talking to Hanoi—put us back in, and we'll let you in after we get rid of the Yankee devils."

"Maybe. But it may just be business. Kim's in touch with a heroin factory in Marseilles."

91

"Why? They've got more opium in Vietnam than they know what to do with."

"I don't know—maybe he's buying technology. If Kim can process it himself instead of shipping it raw, he'll make fifty, a hundred times the profit."

"Do you really think they're serious about the heroin business?"

"Kim sure as hell is," Webster said. "He puts in all his time on it, night and day. He wants to buy a factory. I'm certain of it."

Christopher grinned. "Were you in touch with your wire man today?"

"Yeah. How'd you enjoy your beer at Fouquet's?"

"Okay. You had nobody behind me after I left."

"Didn't I? I stuck a bleeper under the left rear fender of your fucking Peugeot, buddy."

Webster was filled with sly pride. He showed Christopher a rigid middle finger and poured himself another cognac.

"That'll teach me to believe in coincidence," Christopher said.

"You just aren't used to operating against a professional service," Webster said. "You're not going to explain a goddamn thing, are you?"

"Tom, there's nothing to explain. If you think I'm not out, you're wrong. I'm through. I don't work for you people any longer."

Webster took off his glasses. He was a young man, but there were heavy pouches beneath his eyes and broken veins under the skin of his face. "Okay, Paul," he said, "I'll say this—next to Sybille, you're the most sensitive human being I know. You don't think for a minute that I believe any of this. Patchen sat right here and told me to help you any way I could and to keep my mouth shut about it. That seemed a little unusual to me."

"If I need any help, I'll let you know," Christopher said. "One thing—have you picked up anything on the audio you have on Kim about somebody called Lê Thu?"

Webster thought, and shook his head. "I don't recall, but I've got some logs in my briefcase. Hold on." He looked through a sheaf of typed sheets. "No, nothing in these, Who's he supposed to be?"

"I think it's a she—Lê is a female indicator in Vietnamese names, like Lê Xuan, for Mrs. Nhu. It was a name Kim mentioned, as if he were playing a practical joke on me. Maybe he is."

"I can run it through for a name check, if you want."

"No," Christopher said. "Don't do that. I'm not entitled to such services. You've got to start remembering I'm a private citizen."

"I'll bear that in mind," Webster said. "Go to bed."

## 5

Christopher rose while it was still dark. He left a note for Sybille on the kitchen table and went down the carpeted stairs. In the cobbled courtyard of the apartment building he encountered the Webster's concierge. She was collecting the garbage, and she raised her wizened face, narrowing her eyes in the smoke of her morning cigarette. Her squint of suspicion changed to a smile.

"Husbands travel, don't they?" she said.

Christopher rapped softly on the lid of one of the concierge's garbage cans. "It's the age of the airplane—everybody can afford to fly," he said.

The old woman grinned. "But some have to take off early, eh?"

Christopher gave her a ten-franc note, and she trotted ahead of him through the rain to open the heavy door to the street.

He found a café filled with workmen and a few pallid whores; the girls sat at the tables by the window, talking about shops and movies with the kindness and generosity they have for one another. He was reminded of Webster; like him, the girls were aging too quickly, and they placed the same value on people who knew the things that they had learned. They understood one another's fatigue.

Christopher had two cups of coffee and went out into the rain again. By the time he had walked to Montparnasse, the rain had stopped and Paris was filled with its winter light, a dull atmosphere of mother-of-pearl. There was no one in the street behind the Select where he had parked his car. He felt inside the left rear fender until he found the transmitter Webster had put there. It was attached with a strong adhesive, and Christopher broke a fingernail prying it loose. He stuck it under the tailgate of a truck with Nice license plates.

Christopher headed north, toward Brussels. He reached the airport there by noon. In the tax-free shop he bought Molly a ring shaped like a cobra with rubies for eyes. That afternoon in the sunlight in Piazza del Popolo, he watched her slip it on her finger.

"A stealthy gift," she said. "What lovely surprise have you in store for me next?"

"I'm going to the Far East tomorrow," Christopher said.

"Christ. You just got back from there."

"I promise to love you the whole time I'm gone," Christopher said.

Molly removed the ring and put it on the table between them.

"Don't mock me in daylight with the things I say in the dark," she said. "One day I'm going to leave you alone in bed, Paul, and tell you nothing when I return except that I love you. You'll find the reassurance means quite a lot."

# SIX

———

1

The girl led him down one final dark street. This quarter of Saigon was all but silent, but Christopher knew it by day, and its clamor persisted in the heavy air, like rifle shots in the hours after a skirmish. He met the girl in a bar on Tu Do Street. He thought she might be seventeen. She spoke no French; her languages were Cochinese dialect and soldier English.

"My name is Honey," she told Christopher. "It rhymes with money."

She led him up an outside staircase, tapping his arm so that he would see the boy sleeping on the landing outside her door and step over the curled body.

When Christopher told her what he wanted, she did not ask his reasons. "You're not a bad man?" she said. Christopher said that he was not, and she believed him at once, as if no one had ever lied to her.

Christopher gave her money and she turned around modestly and tucked it away somewhere under her dress. As frail as a child's wrist, she sat on the bed and wove her hair into a long black braid.

"Maybe I can go visit my mother while you stay here," she said, speaking as quickly as the thought crossed her face.

"No," Christopher said, "I want you to be here, so that you can say I'm with you and deal with the people—I speak no Vietnamese."

Honey finished her braid and pulled her dress over her head. She wore narrow pants printed with bright northern flowers, daisies or black-eyed susans; her skin was almost the color of the dyed blossoms.

Christopher smiled at her, and she drew in her breath to make her breasts larger. "You change your mind?" she asked.

"No," Christopher said, "I just want you to be my sister for a few days, and not bring anyone else to this room."

She pulled a mat from under the bed and unrolled it on the floor. "Then I better sleep down here, brother," she said. She lay down on her back, drew her braid over her shoulder, and grasping it in both small hands, went to sleep.

Christopher covered her with a sheet and lay down on the bed. Honey had lighted a joss stick; its scent mingled with the stench that poured through the window like dust with sunlight. She made no noise as she slept. Christopher turned on his side and closed his eyes.

The girl had no papers, she had told him; therefore she had no existence, and if he came and went in the dark, they should both be safe enough. Heat, as palpable as the odors in the room, closed around his body.

2

Before it was light, Christopher started walking through the city again. He lost himself twice in cluttered dead-end streets, but he found Luong's house before the sun had wakened anyone.

Luong's wife, wearing a Western bathrobe that was too big for her, answered his knock. She did not know him, and fright showed in her eyes.

"Tell Luong that Crawford is here," Christopher said in French.

"Craww-ford?" she said.

Christopher repeated the name. "We're friends," he said.

She left the door ajar and Christopher stepped inside the house. A very young child sat up on a mat in the next room and stared silently at him. Christopher winked at the child; he could not tell its sex. Luong's wife, fully clothed, came and gathered it up; Christopher heard her speaking softly in another room, and in a moment saw her go by the window, with all three of her children following behind her. Her hair was loose, and as she walked she reached behind her with both hands and fastened it with a clip.

"How did you find my house?" Luong asked.

Christopher handed him an envelope. "I'm sorry I didn't see you in Bangkok. You'll need this."

"I waited three days," Luong said. "When I thought it was useless, I came back." He did not ask for an explanation; he was trained.

As they drank tea, sunlight filled the room. Luong had been much abroad. His parlor was furnished with Western sofas and chairs, and alpine scenes hung on the walls. The shrine of his ancestors, visible in a corner of an adjoining room, was crowded with cheap colored glasses filled with wax in which small flames burned on bits of cotton wick.

"Do you know anything of a person called Lê Thu?" Christopher asked.

Luong searched his mind. "Is Lê the family name or a given name?"

"I don't know. I hadn't thought it might be a family name. I assumed it was a woman's name."

"The Lê were kings of this part of Vietnam before the

97

Nguyên," Luong said. "It's a common family name, both in the North and the South."

"This Lê Thu has some connection, I don't know what, with the Ngo family."

"The Ngos are not very accessible these days. They're in mourning, you understand. And they're learning to be careful again, like everyone else."

"Can you find out the connection? But ask with care, Luong—it may be that opium is involved."

"I'll try. It may not be the sort of thing you can pay for."

"I need to know who this person is, and where, and what is the connection to the Ngo family."

"Where are you staying?"

"I'll come here tomorrow, just before dawn. If you want me before then, write the time and the English word *airborne* above the urinal at the Pussycat Night Club on Tu Do Street. Do you know it?"

Luong smiled. "I know it. Be careful what you sleep with from that place—they're all country girls and they don't know about precautions."

"We speak a great deal about precautions to each other, Luong."

"Well, it's a time to be careful. Why are you still asking about the Ngos? The important ones are dead, or gone away."

"This is a different matter. They still exist, as a family."

"Oh, yes," Luong said. "Everywhere. They buried a lot of money—and a lot of democratic elements too."

Luong's remark was not meant as a joke. On his home ground, when he was working, he was a serious man. That was what had earned him the Thai girl Christopher had bought for him in Bangkok, and his house in Saigon, on a street where flowers grew beside the dirt walks.

"What are people saying about the Ngos since Diem and Nhu died?"

"That their luck ran out. In Vietnam, that's always the explanation. We have no political analysts, only superstitions and fortune-tellers."

"And killers."

"Yes, we've always had a good cheap supply of those."

"Do you think you have some sort of personal luck that keeps you alive, Luong?"

"Of course. Everyone believes that. Even some foreigners believe it, but not you yourself. I saw that in you from the first —you believe in nothing except the force of human intelligence. Isn't that so?"

"I doubt even that."

"I thought so. But there are other forces. One waits, and a force moves; it's like water, soft and yielding, but also possessing great power." Luong smiled.

"Lao-tzu," Christopher said. "What's your lucky number, Luong?"

Luong hesitated. "Eleven."

"Has it come up lately?"

"Yes. Nhu wanted to kill me, you know. There were men waiting here for me while I was with you in Bangkok. But Diem and Nhu died while I was away, on November 1—the first day of the eleventh month, an eleven and a one, three elevens if you read from front and back."

"What was Diem's number?"

"That's well known. Seven, double seven. He came to power on July 7, as you may know, too."

"Does the number go on working after death?"

"I suppose so," Luong said. "Any combination of sevens would be good for Diem's spirit."

"Would it make sense to honor his memory on a day seven days after his death, or fourteen days, or twenty-one?"

"Oh yes," Luong said. "Triple seven, twenty-one, would be thought very auspicious. . . . But you're toying with our superstitions."

"No, I try to understand these things. It isn't necessary to believe in them to know they exist, even that they exert what you call force."

"Well, perhaps one wouldn't call such passive things a force."

"What, then?"

Luong searched his mind for the French word. "An elegance," he said.

## 3

No one in the tropics expects to see a white man at sunrise. Christopher did not live by the clock but by the rhythm of the place in which he found himself. In hot countries he moved on his targets in the cool of the morning. They were always surprised to see him. As he walked down Luong's street under the stunted flowering trees, he received startled glances even from the children.

A few blocks away he found a taxi with its driver asleep in a patch of shade. He woke him and gave him the Truong toc's address.

The Truong toc's house was sealed. Shutters were fastened, doors locked. The house stood in a small park, and as Christopher walked among the flower beds and the palms it seemed to him that the noise of life parted at the gate and flowed around the walls of the garden. The babble of voices and the whine of scooter engines that filled the streets on all four sides of the narrow house were deadened. Christopher knew the noise was absorbed by the trees and the high wall cloaked with vines, but he thought, all the same, of the passive forces Luong had spoken about.

No one answered his knock. He stepped back and looked upward at the blank windows, then walked around the corner of the house to a terrace where bougainvillea grew over a trellis. Heavy iron lawn furniture, curlicued and painted white, was arranged in the shade; green mold crept up the legs of the chairs, designed to stand on a lawn beside the Loire. French doors opened on the terrace. Christopher saw someone in white robes move quickly across the room within. An entire wall was taken up by an ancestor's shrine. Photographs of the dead and candle flames reflected in the panes of the terrace doors. The person inside was lighting a thicket of joss sticks on the shrine.

Christopher knocked again, and his fist rattled the glass.

The white figure turned around; he saw it was a young woman who stood at the back of the room and stared at him. He knocked again, and drawing out his voice in the elongated tones of a Frenchman who has lived long in Asia, called, *"Mademoiselle, s'il vous plaît!"* The girl came to the glass door, held up both palms, and shook her head violently.

Christopher rattled the door handle and spoke in a loud voice: "A word with you, mademoiselle."

She opened the door and, using the *tu* form, said, "Shut up. This house is closed."

"I know, and I understand," Christopher said. "But I've come all the way from Paris to see the Truong toc."

"He's not receiving visitors."

"I have an important message for him. It concerns his family."

The girl let breath burst from her nostrils. *"This* family?" she asked incredulously, looking at the color of Christopher's skin.

"Yes—truly it's very important to the Truong toc."

"Who are you? Have you a card?"

"No—no card. But give him this."

Christopher wrote on a page of his notebook, tore it out, and handed it to the girl. She folded the note without reading it, dropped her eyes, and closed the door again, turning the key in the lock. She pointed a finger toward the front of the house, and he went around to the main door. Fifteen minutes passed before it opened. The girl, striding in her *ao dai* like a Frenchwoman, led him through odors of fish sauce, furniture polish, candle smoke down a narrow hall to a room filled with books. She adjusted the blinds so that strips of light ran across the polished tile floor, and left him alone.

The Truong toc let Christopher wait for a long time. When he came in, he wore Vietnamese dress, white to signify his mourning. Without shaking hands, he sat down, holding the page from Christopher's notebook between his thumb and forefinger. "Why do you bring me this message?" he asked.

"I wished to meet you. I thought you would want to have this information."

"Well, then?"

"Your nephew, Ngo Tan Khoi, was garrotted after he entered his car in the parking lot of the casino at Divonne-les-Bains, on March 8, 1958," Christopher said. "He was buried that same night in the bottom of an open grave in the town of Gex, eight kilometers away. A woman named Marie-Thérèse Hecquet, for whom the grave had been prepared, was buried in it on March 9."

"By whom was he killed?"

"Not by your enemies. He was mistaken for a heroin dealer named Hoang Tan Khoi by the people who killed him. Your relative and the heroin dealer had the same given names and they were both Vietnamese."

"Who were these people?"

Christopher gave him the names of the French gangsters. "Machelon is dead," he said. "Gaboni is still in business; if one wishes to hire him, one leaves one half of a thousand-franc note in an envelope with the doorman of the Russian restaurant in the rue de Passy, in Paris. Gaboni will appear on the following Monday, at ten o'clock, in the public toilet on the Champs-Elysées, near the place Clemenceau."

"How do you have this information?"

"I had it from Machelon."

"Of what interest is it to me?"

"You now have it, in any case. I thank you for seeing me. Good-bye."

Christopher uncrossed his legs and gripped the arms of his chair, as if to rise.

The Truong toc handed Christopher the notebook page. It was a gesture to establish trust; he was returning the evidence. "And you are what—a policeman? You speak like a Frenchman, but you don't have the manners of the French."

"I'm not a policeman. This is a personal matter—I greatly admired the late Ngo Dinh Diem. I knew him slightly. When he was murdered, I wished to express my sympathies."

"You choose a bizarre method."

Christopher put the page of the notebook in his pocket. "If

I knew who killed Diem and his brother, I would tell you that," he said.

The Truong toc moved his hand and let it fall back in his lap. "How did you know of me?"

"I made inquiries. Your existence is not a secret. The dead boy in France—he was a member of the Ngo *chi*, was he not?"

The Truong toc opened his eyes. There was nothing involuntary about his expression of surprise; he wished Christopher to understand that he respected his knowledge.

"Yes," the Truong toc said. "We had hoped he wasn't dead, but of course there was no other ex̭ lanation."

Christopher looked into the flat face of the Truong toc; the old skin stretched over the bones of his head like the ruined glaze of a china plate recovered from the ashes of a burned house. The old man had the light behind him, so even the faint expressions he allowed himself could not always be seen.

"It did not matter to the parents," Christopher asked, "that Khoi was a Communist and an agent of Ho Chi Minh?"

"One accepts what a son becomes in politics. There is no choice."

"I would be glad," Christopher said, "if you could tell me something about President Diem. I met him only twice, but I thought him a great man."

The Truong toc folded his hands. "Many thought him a tyrant," he said. "He was not much loved outside Vietnam. Even in his own country, many never understood him. He hadn't the gift of the popular gesture. He once said that it was impossible for him to feel guilt."

"Yes," Christopher said. " 'He who loves the world as his body may be entrusted with the empire.' "

"Lao-tzu. You're a surprising man."

"One may read as one wishes. Do you believe President Diem loved his world, which was Vietnam, as he loved his own body?"

"They were the same," the Truong toc said. "And now the one is dead and the other is dismembered,"

"The family is partly in the North, partly in the South. Is it dismembered?"

"No, the family is one."

"And acts as one?"

"In matters that concern the oneness of the family, when it can. But it is weak, compared to the apparatus of the state and the weapons of the world."

"So are all families," Christopher said. "When the American President was killed, as Diem had been killed, I wondered if the members of *his* family had any thoughts about your family."

"Because we had similar sorrows? I would be surprised. We live far away, in a weak country."

"The assassinations came close together—only twenty-one days, three weeks, separated them."

"The Americans live in another world," the Truong toc said. "How can they compare their situation with ours? We cannot touch such beings. Perhaps time will touch them."

Christopher stood up. "When you communicate with Ngo Tan Khoi's parents," he said, "tell them I am sorry to have brought such news—and to have brought it so late."

The Truong toc, his hands folded in his white lap, called out a phrase in Vietnamese. The young woman reappeared and led Christopher to the door.

"What's your name?" Christopher asked.

She gave him a contemptuous glance and remained silent.

"If you want to be worthy of the Truong toc, you must learn to hide your feelings," Christopher said.

She opened the door and dropped her eyes, as if looking at the color of his skin offended her.

Christopher walked through the muffled atmosphere of the garden. Two Vietnamese in European clothes lounged by the gate. Christopher saw the outline of revolver butts under the thin white stuff of their identical shirts. The men watched him get into his waiting taxi, then one of them crossed the street to use the telephone in a shop.

Christopher told the driver to take him to the Continental Palace Hotel. He walked past the desk and up the stairs. It was still very early in the morning, and the maids were not yet active. He found an unlocked room from which the luggage had been removed. Closing the door behind him, he sat down on the soiled bed and used the telephone to call Wolkowicz.

## 4

Wolkowicz imagined that he was stalked by murderous enemies. He carried a heavy revolver in a shoulder holster and a smaller pistol strapped to the calf of his leg. A young Marine armed with a submachine gun drove Wolkowicz to work in the embassy and home again in a Mercedes with armored doors and bullet-proof windows. Wolkowicz's villa was surrounded by a concrete wall, and the house itself had been fitted with steel doors and shutters. There were submachine guns, steel helmets, and flak vests in every closet.

Christopher rang the bell and saw Wolkowicz's eye at the peephole. In the dark hall, Wolkowicz worked clumsily to refasten the bolts and locks with his left hand. He carried a pistol in his right hand and a newborn pig under his arm.

"I was just about to feed the snake," Wolkowicz said. "Have a drink if you want one."

Christopher made himself a gin and tonic with big clear ice cubes from Wolkowicz's American refrigerator.

"Nhu, where the hell are you?" Wolkowicz said. "Come on, baby, we haven't got all night. . . . He hides during the day, half the time I can't find him."

Wolkowicz shifted the pig to his left hand and replaced the revolver in his shoulder holster. He got down on his knees and looked under the furniture. "There you are, you son of a bitch," he said. "Come on out."

A young python glided from beneath the sofa and lifted its flat head. The pig squirmed sleepily in Wolkowicz's arms.

"I have to dope the pig, otherwise the house gets wrecked in the chase," Wolkowicz said. "I gave this one a Miltown in a can of beer. He's feeling no pain."

"Where'd you get the snake?" Christopher asked.

"Phnom Penh," Wolkowicz said. "I had to go over to see

Pete. The Cambodians run around with pythons draped around their necks. This is a nice one—I bought him from a taxi driver. He had him on the seat beside him. The problem is getting food for him. You don't have to feed him often, but he'll only eat live stuff. He likes chickens, but I can't stand the noise."

Wolkowicz put the pig on the floor and sat down heavily beside Christopher on the sofa. "You ever seen this done?" he asked. "It's kind of interesting."

The snake watched the pig fixedly. The drugged pig seemed surprised that it was unable to run; it gave a faint squeal and staggered toward the sofa. Wolkowicz gave it back to the python. With much slower movements than Christopher had expected, the snake attacked, wrapping itself around the pig's small body. The pig struggled briefly, then subsided, uttering a series of thin squeals like a baby drifting to sleep. Its head thumped on the floor.

"Look at the snake's eyes," Wolkowicz said. "This is the only time they change expression—he gets dreamy while he's squeezing."

It took the python a long time to swallow the pig's limp body. Toward the end, when only the pink rump still showed in the snake's widened jaws, the python reached around with its tail and pushed the pig into its throat.

"He'll sleep for days now," Wolkowicz said. "I never knew they used their tails like that—it's pretty interesting."

"You enjoy having him around the house?"

"I make sure I know where he is before I go to sleep—snakes are good pets. They've got dry, very smooth skin, like the local girls," Wolkowicz said, grinning. He grasped the snake's tail and pulled it across the floor and into a closet.

When he came back he said, "I heard you took a little heat in Washington."

"Oh, how did you hear that?"

"I got a personal letter from a guy. The way I read it, you're not supposed to be operating out here anymore."

"That's why I wanted to see you, to tell you I'm not operating. All appearances to the contrary, I'm now just an honest reporter, trying to make a living."

"That's why you showed up at the Truong toc's at five-thirty this morning, is it?"

"I'm doing a piece on the Ngos. I thought the Truong toc was a good person to talk to."

"Yeah. Well, what do you want from me?"

"I hear Don Wolfe is out here."

"That's right. He reported in last week."

"I'd like to talk to him."

"Call him up, he's around."

Christopher smiled. "I just wanted to go through channels. He works for you. I thought you might like to be present."

"I don't *have* to be present. He works for me, as you mentioned."

"Nevertheless," Christopher said. "If he's living next door, I'd be grateful if you'd call him over now. I don't plan to hang around Saigon very long."

Wolkowicz pursed his lips. "You're out, aren't you?" he said. "Patchen didn't bother to inform anybody, but news travels."

"I'm out, Barney."

"So what's in this for me?"

"If I run into anything, I'll let you have it."

"You'd better," Wolkowicz said, "or you'll never get into this country again. You believe that?"

"I believe it."

"Okay," Wolkowicz said. A short-range transceiver had been babbling on the coffee table while they spoke. Wolkowicz picked up the microphone and spoke into it.

"Why do you talk German on the radio?" Christopher asked.

Wolkowicz put his hand, covered with stiff black hair, over the microphone, as if it were a telephone receiver. "Wolfe can't speak Cherokee," he said.

Don Wolfe wore sagging Bermuda shorts, a T-shirt, and a buttoned seersucker jacket.

"You know the illustrious Christopher?" Wolkowicz said. "Tell him anything he wants to know."

Wolkowicz picked up a heavy attaché case and his radio and went out of the room. Wolfe removed his jacket, revealing a revolver in a shoulder holster. "Station regulations, we never go out without a gat," he said. "You don't believe in firearms, do you?"

"I always thought somebody might take it away from me and shove it down my throat," Christopher said.

"What can I do for you?"

"A lot, I hope. When did you leave Mexico City?"

"Let's see, this is December 15. I left on December 2—four days at headquarters to learn all about Vietnamese culture, then right out here."

"David Patchen says you worked on the Oswald thing down there."

"That's right."

"Are these dates right?" Christopher recited Oswald's movements in Mexico City.

"I think so. I haven't got your flawless memory."

"Who talked to the people at the Soviet embassy?"

"From our shop? I did."

"How were they?"

"The Russians? Scared shitless. There was a lot of pressure on them, you know. We had SAC in the air, and you have to admit it looked awfully funny—Oswald a onetime defector, chatting with the KGB in a foreign capital only a few weeks before he shot Kennedy. They were feeling the pressure."

"Well, that passed."

"I think we were a little hysterical ourselves—the Russians don't do things like that anymore. They're trying to be respectable, like us," Wolfe said. "When Ruby killed Oswald, everything settled down overnight. That was a real gift, from the Sovs' point of view."

"Did you have any surveillance on Oswald while he was in town?"

"No, why would we? You know what the manpower problems are. He was just a jerk who went to Russia once."

"Oswald was in Mexico City from September 27 to October 1."

"Well, to September 30, really. He left early in the morning of October 1, by bus."

"Who else was in town during those three days?"

Wolfe rolled back his eyes. "Jesus, half the human race. What do you mean?"

"Who passed through in that time who interested you? Third-country agents, I mean."

"Not Mexicans, not Americans. I don't know if I can remember them all, in the time frame. The Mexico City airport is the place where they all change for Moscow, Peking, and Havana, you know."

"What about Hanoi?"

"You mean Vietnamese? There weren't any. Does that narrow it down for you?"

"Not a Vietnamese. A third-country white man, who maybe had been to Vietnam very recently, or was on his way there."

Wolfe closed his eyes, reached under his T-shirt, scratched his narrow chest.

"There was only one fellow like that," he said. "Manuel Rogales is his passport name. He uses Manuel Ruiz, Manuel Linares—always Manuel, though. He's a protégé of Ché's."

"Where is he now?"

"I'm not in touch, Paul. If you find out, it'll be helpful. He's a great jungle fighter, he goes out and surveys revolutionary prospects for Guevara. He's been in Bolivia and Colombia, even Panama. He surfaced for about two months this year—mid-August to mid-October. Then he went to ground, as they say, and no one's seen him since. He's not in Cuba."

"He was in Vietnam in that period?"

"Yes," Wolfe said. "In Hanoi from early September to around the end of the month. I remember his coming through town on a Chilean passport. We got a photo of him from Mexican security at the airport."

"And after that?"

"We never saw him again. As I said, he pulled the chain on us." Wolfe sipped his drink. "Does one ask what all this is in aid of?" he asked.

Wolfe spoke like an Englishman and in colder climates wore suits that he ordered by mail from a tailor in London.

"Nothing, probably," Christopher said. "I'm just curious about the whole incident."

Wolfe nodded. "How's your bride?" he asked.

"Cathy? We've been divorced for three years."

"Have you? I guess I haven't seen you for quite a while. Your loss is somebody's gain—I always fancied that girl, Paul."

"Yes, she had a way about her," Christopher said. "Have you seen Wolkowicz's python do his act?"

Wolfe gave a high giggle. "Are you changing the subject or telling me the secrets of your bedroom?" he asked.

"Thanks for the dope," Christopher said.

"That's all right," Wolfe said. "Mexico can give you the exact dates and the Cuban's photograph the next time you get down there."

"I think I may already have a picture of him somewhere."

"*Do* you? Tell them that in Mexico. They love it when you chaps fly in and save the world over a long weekend."

Christopher smiled. "So does Wolkowicz. We're admired wherever we go."

## 5

Christopher left Wolkowicz's house the way he had come, through the walled gardens of the foreigners' compound. There was no moon, and only a few weak stars broke the black surface of the sky.

When he emerged into a quiet street, he was still alone. He didn't understand it; by now the Truong toc's men or the secret police should have picked him up. He walked for a mile or more on side streets, doubling back and wandering into cul-de-sacs as if he were lost, but there was no one behind him. Finally he turned and walked straight toward the glow and racket of Tu Do Street.

In the Pussycat Night Club, Honey sat on the lap of a Special Forces master sergeant. She wore his green beret on the back of her head and drank from a bottle of champagne. The

110

sergeant's bare forearm, covered with tattoos, encircled her. Christopher finished a bitter beer at the bar and walked across the room. Honey saw him and pointed a derisive thumb at the sergeant, whose face was buried in the hair at the back of her neck. Christopher winked at her. She wore the sergeant's badges and ribbons on her dress, and she inflated her chest as she had done the night before and giggled again.

Over the urinal, Luong had written *1230 Airborne*. Christopher spat on his thumb and wiped out the message; the blue ballpoint ink stained the ridges of his thumbprint, and he went back to the bar and scrubbed it off with beer and his handkerchief.

Honey put her hands on the bar beside him and said, "You coming home tonight?"

Christopher, watching the sergeant in the mirror, said, "Yes, but very late. Don't let the sergeant fall asleep."

Honey's face, like that of a bride in a photographer's shop window, was fixed in innocence.


Luong took Christopher's arm and led him through his darkened house to the bedroom. A picture of Christ, vermilion heart glowing through a white winding sheet, hung over the bed. Christopher had seen the original in Saint Peter's.

"It's not good to meet here," Luong said. "My wife wonders who you are."

"You can't go out at night."

"I can. But carefully. I have something about this name, Lê Thu."

Christopher was tired; he moved so that his back was against the head of the bed.

"I haven't put a person to the name yet," Luong said, "but there is something about it—it startled some of the people I asked."

"Startled them? Why?"

"I think perhaps there is no person, that this is a false name —but I suppose you expected that. *Lê*, as you know, comes from the old Chinese. It means, or suggests, 'tears.' *Thu* means 'autumn' in Vietnamese—therefore, 'the tears of autumn.' "

Christopher nodded. "As Lê Xuan—Madame Nhu's name —means the tears of spring."

"Exactly. I asked a man who takes messages into the countryside if he had ever heard the name. His reaction was interesting. He said nothing, as if he were thinking, and then something connected in his memory. He advised me to forget the name, and left me."

"Did you go on asking after that?"

"No. I had already asked others. There is a man I might see, but he's not in Saigon. He's in a village on the way to Bien Hoa. I had no reason to go today, but perhaps tomorrow I can drive there. We have a party cell in the village—he has not been unfriendly."

"Who is he?"

"He was a Catholic priest when the French were here. They thought he was running with the Viet Minh and they tortured him. They say he's a eunuch. He still lives in the church and wears priest's clothes."

"Does he still run with the Communists?"

Luong shrugged. "Who knows? He's a remote connection of the Ngos—his grandfather married one of their women while the Catholics were still in the North."

"Would he talk to me?"

"Not for money. Maybe for curiosity. There's talk about you —you went to see the Truong toc, I hear. They've been asking about a man who must be you. They think you're French, despite your looks."

"They haven't tried to contact me," Christopher said.

"They can't find you in any of the places you should be."

"And if I talk to this priest?"

"Then they'll find you."

"He reports to them?"

"He's their relative, my friend. You're a foreigner," Luong said. "There's a way to deal with him, Crawford. He's doing some business with opium—a lot more of the stuff has been moving in the last few weeks, I hear."

"Moving? How?"

"The VC are bringing it in from Cambodia, and from Laos, down the trail. I hear that the principal storage place is under the priest's church—there are VC tunnels running under the village. They control that part of the countryside."

"Then he is still running with the Communists?"

"Doing business with them. He's buying. He has a great deal of money, it's said, very suddenly. He never had any before."

"How would one deal with him? Offer to buy? Threaten to expose him?"

"I wouldn't make threats," Luong said.

"Show me where he can be found, exactly."

Luong drew a map on a page of Christopher's notebook, showing the roads to the village. He drew a row of *X*'s along the main line. "Ambushes at all these places recently," he said. On another page he sketched the village, showing the church and the room where the priest lived. Christopher studied the pages for a moment, then ripped them out of the notebook and handed them back to Luong. "What's his name?" he asked.

"With whites he uses the French style," Luong said. "Jean-Baptiste Ho."

Christopher stood up. Fatigue ran through his body like a painful injection. "Where can I get a car without papers?"

"Now? You're going out there at night?"

"Yes. I can get back before daylight."

Luong gave him the name of a garage. "There's one more person I can ask tonight about the name," he said. "I don't want to meet here again—have you a place in the city?"

Christopher, so as not to say it aloud, wrote the address of Honey's room and sketched the entrance. He looked at his watch. "I'll be back at five o'clock in the morning," he said. "Don't come after it's light."

"If I have anything by five o'clock, I'll come," Luong said.

Christopher shook hands with him. "One more thing—if Lê Thu means the tears of autumn as a name, how do you say it in the ordinary way?

"In Vietnamese? *Nuóc mắt mùa thu.*"

113

"It's more poetic in French."

Luong smiled. "You hear music in the language you know," he said.

## 6

The car was a Citroën with only thirty thousand kilometers on the odometer. Its soft fabric cushions and the air suspension took some of the ache out of Christopher's back and legs. There was a checkpoint at the Thi Nghe Canal bridge where the highway joined the avenue leading into Saigon; a young guard took the thousand-piaster note clipped to Christopher's press card and waved him through.

The Citroën made very little noise apart from the grip of its tires on the tar road. Christopher turned off the headlights, and by the time he was far enough away from Saigon to be in danger, he saw well enough in the starlight to drive as fast as the car would go. His eye followed the road through the trees and the low bushes, and the paddies shining in the darkness like coins. He saw no movement. He didn't think that anyone would expect to see a darkened car moving at 150 kilometers an hour, or be able to hit it with gunfire.

On the dirt track leading into the village, Christopher went more slowly, but still dust blew in the open windows and coated the interior of the car. The church was a small building standing by itself beyond the huts that lined the principal street. Light from the altar candles leaked through its thin walls. Inside, there were a few long benches with their ends lying in deep shadow. Like Patchen's house in Washington, the church was a place in which nothing involving human emotion had happened in a long time.

Christopher knocked, loudly, on the door behind the altar. The priest opened the door at once; behind him, the tiny room in which he lived was lit by a kerosine lantern. He wore a cassock, unbuttoned at the top so that his neck and his bony chest showed. Christopher heard a soft noise and saw a woman sitting upright on a plank bed; she turned her eyes aside and went to stand with her back against the wall at the far side of the room.

"I'm sorry to disturb you, Father," Christopher said. "I need your help."

The little priest threw back his head and looked Christopher in the eye. "It's very late," he said. "It's very dangerous, there are no army patrols at this time of night."

"So I understand, but it was important that I see you. You are Jean-Baptiste Ho?"

"And you are what—a Frenchman?"

The priest fumbled with the tiny buttons on his cassock. He had a facial twitch; his cheek moved, causing the right eye to open and close like a caged owl's. Christopher had never seen an Oriental with such an affliction. Remembering what Luong had told him about the priest's experiences with French interrogators, Christopher said, "Father, I'm an American."

"Ah? You don't look or sound it, if I may pay you that compliment."

"Well, I'm something of an outcast," Christopher said. "I have lived very little in America as an adult, so I haven't kept up with my countrymen's manners."

"You're an outcast—or a pariah?"

"Between the two, for the time being—like yourself, Father."

The priest still stood in the doorway of his room, with the motionless woman behind him. His twitch became more active, and he placed a hand, ropy with age, over his cheek. "Like *me?*"

"Like you," Christopher said. "Your relatives the Ngos were willing enough to tolerate an unfrocked priest who dealt with the enemy and used his church for cover. Perhaps you could be of service to them in small ways. But the new regime is less tolerant. How long do you think you'll last here?"

The priest called out a phrase in Vietnamese. His woman rummaged in a box and brought him an envelope filled with white powder. He turned his head away and snuffled heroin into his nostrils. In a moment his cheek quietened, and he

115

gestured Christopher to follow him. They sat down together on a bench near the altar.

"The regime makes a great deal of noise in the daylight," the priest said. "As you see, their soldiers are very quiet at night."

"That's fine for those who live only at night, like the Vietcong combatants. For those who wish to utilize the whole clock, it's inconvenient. When next you send a message to Kim in Paris, tell him to change banks. The Banque Sadak in Beirut is leaky."

The priest's twitch had stopped altogether. The heroin had had an effect and also, Christopher saw, it was not the present that drove the man's nerves out of the control, but a memory of the past. He put his hands in the sleeves of his soutane and gazed at Christopher.

"I've heard something about you, I think," he said. "You have a great deal of information."

"I have an appetite for it. Father, I have no curiosity about your traffic in opium or in politics. It's your affair. But it's the sort of thing, if it were to come to the wrong ears, that could send you to prison again. Where did the French put you?"

"Chi Hoa Prison."

"You have a relative there now—Ngo Dinh Can."

"Thanks to the Americans, yes. Thanks to them, I have no doubt Can's jailers have more modern equipment than mine did—the French are poor mechanics. They used field telephones, water, even their boots."

"Yes—and Can is guarded by Vietnamese, not Frenchmen," Christopher said. "That makes a difference."

"I suppose so. What is it you want?"

"I want to talk to you about a certain Lê Thu."

Like a man picking up a teacup to show that his hand does not tremble, the priest moved his eyes slowly from Christopher's face to the dusty altar and back again. "I know no one named Lê Thu," he said.

"My Vietnamese is very poor," Christopher said. "The name means 'the tears of autumn,' does it not?"

116

"You've come here to discuss Vietnamese names and their derivations from archaic Chinese? I'm not an expert."

"Father, I've given you some information, voluntarily. Perhaps I could give you more—I have an idea that your business with Kim is important. If you go on taking heroin, you'll soon be of no use to your family or your movement, and if the regime doesn't kill you, the drug certainly will. You will have had a personal experience of its effects when you go to your grave, and since you are a political man as well as a member of the Ngo family, I expect that you'll smile to think of the American soldiers you've doomed to be ruined like yourself. They'll be very young and very stupid."

"You have a morbid imagination."

"I've learned to understand revenge," Christopher said. "What I want to know I want to know for myself, not for any family or any government, or any other person. I understand that you won't believe that, but it's true."

"And what is it you want to know?"

"First let me tell you what you get in return. Silence. I'll tell no one—not in Saigon, not in Washington, not in Paris—what you are planning with heroin."

"Why not? Do you care nothing for your countrymen?"

"Yes. But I'll be truthful once again. They wouldn't believe it—they underestimate you. They think you haven't the intelligence or the resources, and they think they are too strong for you, as individuals and as a nation."

"Then they are weaker than I thought."

"No, they're not weak," Christopher said. "They just don't see that the weak can strike at them. The senses travel very slowly in such an enormous body as America's. Men like you can wound, but you cannot kill such a large organism. That's *your* weakness."

"So, what is it you want to know in return for your silence, and this lesson on philosophy?"

"Three things," Christopher said. "First, is Lê Thu the code name of the operation that was carried out on November 22 in Dallas? Second, how was the message transmitted from Saigon to the North, and then to the man who recruited the American assassin? Third, what is the name of your relative in the intelligence service of North Vietnam who recruited the man who, in turn, activated Oswald?"

The priest sniffed; the drug had fixed a smile on his face, and his body rocked slightly as if in rhythm with the movement of the heroin through his bloodstream.

"You're very direct," he said. "You must not be afraid of consequences."

"I'm careful of them. You've read detective stories, I suppose? The blackmailer always arranges that his information will pass into other hands if he is killed."

"You've told me it would not be believed."

"Not by any American you know about, or can conceive of. There are others who would believe it, and I advise you not to have contempt for them. As your recent success has taught you, contempt is a mistake."

"Ah—it's for these people that you want this information?"

"No, for myself. It's an intellectual challenge—I'm accused of believing that everything can be discovered and understood."

"If you already understand, or think you do, then why insist on discovery?"

"Before I realized what the heroin was for, I imagined that you had had revenge enough," Christopher said. "So one discovers something new every day."

The priest's tic was awakening again. His blinking eye seemed to register Christopher as an automatic camera freezes the motions of an athlete.

"Do you want me to give you the information, assuming that it exists and that I know it?" he asked. "Or do you merely want us—me—to know that you have this *idée fixe*?"

"Have you the information?"

"No."

Christopher stood up. "Then I'll be in plain view all day tomorrow in Saigon. If anyone wishes to talk to me, I'll be available."

Christopher walked rapidly out of the church. He checked

the doors of the Citroën for wires and looked at the motor and the undercarriage with a flashlight. There was no sign of explosives. Christopher had seen the woman go through a trapdoor in the priest's room after she had given him his heroin, but the village VC would be out on patrol, and unless some of them were lying along the dirt track that led to the highway, they would not have had time to get back. He turned the car around and drove out of the village.

Halfway to Saigon, Christopher saw shapes move in the darkness beside the road, a hundred yards ahead of the car. He turned on the headlights, bathing three armed men in their glare. One of them threw his arm in a floppy pajama sleeve across his eyes. Christopher turned off the lights and blew the horn. In the rear-view mirror he saw muzzle flashes, like the burners of a gas stove. There were no tracers; that gave him confidence. Rounds struck the road behind the car and ahead of it, but none hit the Citroën before it went around the next curve, rising with a sigh on its suspension, the steering wheel chattering in his hands.

## 7

As Christopher entered the city, the red sun touched a string of cirrus clouds on the eastern horizon. He looked at his watch and, remembering Luong, realized that he was late. He could see the shapes of buildings in the increasing light. The streets were still empty. There was the taste of dust in his mouth and his eyes burned from the strain of driving in the dark; he pulled the headlight switch and followed the yellow puddle of the low beams through the grid of Saigon's streets. He parked the car five blocks from Honey's room, locked it, and walked the rest of the way.

At the mouth of the alley, he met two Vietnamese. They had changed their white shirts for darker ones, but he recognized them. The men, walking rapidly, stopped when they saw him, then hurried by. Christopher turned around and watched them disappear into another alley; a motor scooter whined away, its rider shifting gears very rapidly.

Christopher climbed the stairs. The air smelled fresh, as if there had been rain in the night, and the sunrise washed across the roofs of the quarter. The boy was asleep again on the landing outside Honey's room, sprawled on his back with one trouser leg pulled upward on his hairless calf.

Stepping over the sleeping figure, Christopher looked down. It was Luong, his eyes staring, his black hair blown forward as if by the wind. Christopher kneeled and touched his skin. It was still warm; there was a black stain on his trousers where his bladder had emptied.

Christopher pushed back Luong's hair and saw the small blue hole on his smooth forehead. *"He's not your child,"* he heard Wolkowicz say. Christopher laid his palm on Luong's cheek and closed the eyes and the slack lips with his thumb and forefinger.

He opened the door. The Special Forces sergeant, wearing an identification bracelet with a delicate gold chain on his thick wrist, lay on his back with Honey in his arms. Her narrow body with its row of knobs along the spine rested easily on the sergeant's chest; she had left her hair unbraided. They were breathing together softly. Luong's killers must have used a silenced gun.

Christopher knelt beside Luong again and looked through his pockets. There was nothing for him there, or in the dead man's clenched hands. He was not surprised; no agent had ever spoken a last message to Christopher before he died.

8

Christopher started the Citroën without checking it for bombs and wondered if the tension on his wrist when he turned the key might be the last sensation his brain would ever register. But the warm engine started normally, and he drove to the post office, where there were coin telephones. He called Wolkowicz and told him what had happened.

"Tell someone to get there fast, before the people in the neighborhood wake up and dump the body," Christopher said.

"What difference does it make?" Wolkowicz said. "He was a *politique*—they won't investigate, they'll just close his file."

"As long as they get the body. He has a wife."

"All right, I'll put out a call, but don't expect any answers from the Vietnamese—if they went around solving murders in this town they'd never get anything else done."

Christopher thanked him. "That's okay," Wolkowicz said. "Funny how things turn out, isn't it? If he'd come back from Bangkok last month when he was supposed to, and they'd shot him then, his widow would've gotten a pension. But this sure doesn't sound like death in line of duty."

"It never does, after it happens," Christopher said.

In the lobby of the Continental Palace half a dozen foreigners, Americans and Frenchmen, waited in two docile groups for the early minibus to the airport. Christopher had not slept for twenty-four hours or changed his clothes for forty-eight. The Frenchmen stared curiously at his rumpled suit and unshaven cheeks; he could tell by their clothes and the way in which perpetual impatience had twisted their faces that they lived in Vietnam. They were not used to seeing dirt on a white man, and it annoyed them.

The *métis* behind the reception desk, who had his father's Norman nose and his mother's small bones and almond eyes, spoke English to Christopher as a matter of course. He said he had no room. When Christopher replied in French, the *métis* pushed a registration card across the desk and took a key from the rack. *"Pièce d'identité?"* Christopher handed him his American passport, and the clerk gave back a resentful look— he had lost his first bribe of the day through trickery.

Christopher sent the bellboy for the suitcase he had left at the Alitalia office. He shaved and took a bath; the tepid water coughed from the tap, rusty and smelling faintly of the river. He sat down and wrote a letter to Patchen. Using the English section of a Collins French-English pocket dictionary, he converted the words he had written into groups of numbers corresponding to the page, line, and column where they were found in the book. It was not a satisfactory dictionary for use in a book code; *heroin* did not appear, and he had to render the word as "next-stage morphine derivative." He might as well have been writing in German, he thought. Christopher burned the paper on which he had written his draft, and put the thin sheet covered with rows of numbers into an envelope with an American airmail stamp already affixed. He did not address the envelope.

Before he went to sleep, Christopher took no precautions apart from the useless one of locking the door. Precautions would serve no purpose. If Luong had been killed as a warning, Christopher himself would not be killed until whoever was running the assassins decided that Christopher had not taken the warning. The two men could have killed Christopher easily enough in the alley when they met him face to face. Or, if they wished to be artistic, they could have shot him after letting him discover Luong's body. The killers had no distinguishing features, they looked like any other young Vietnamese sharing a motor scooter and looking for a way to make a little money out of the war.

Each time Christopher began to dream, he reached into that part of his mind and stopped the pictures. Nevertheless, he saw the man run down in Berlin again, and a youth in Algiers with a bullet coming out his back in a plume of blood as if he had thrown a glass of wine over his shoulder, and Luong's photograph on a grave marker with a bright sacred heart glowing on his chest. While the Truong toc drank tea, Jean-Baptiste Ho showed Christopher pictures of all the Ngo dead, arranged among candles in the room in Siena where he had repeated to Molly that he loved her. Touching Christopher's arm as if he were an old friend, the priest said, "It would be beautiful to die of disgust, but you will not."

9

When Christopher awoke, he went to the American embassy and mailed his letter to Patchen, scribbling the false name and the post-office-box number in Washington across the envelope at the moment he dropped the envelope in the box.

He knew it would reassure Patchen to see that the message had passed through the U.S. mail only. It was undecipherable without the book that was the key to the code, but ciphers are incriminating in themselves.

The crowd of foreigners on the terrace of the Continental Palace Hotel reminded Christopher of travelers on the deck of a ship. Everything that interested them lay inside the rails; the Vietnamese, as alike as gulls, went by on the sidewalk, locked in a language that made no sense to white men. Christopher saw four Americans he knew, all of them journalists. He sat at the other end of the terrace with his back to their table and ordered a vermouth cassis. In the street, ordinary women in *ao dai* and trousers and bar girls in miniskirts that spoiled the grace of their slender bodies were out walking; a rawboned American girl carrying an armload of packages strode through the crowd, whistling a love song, her hair swinging.

Christopher waited. Dark had fallen, and most of the people on the terrace had gone inside to have dinner, when the girl came. She had changed out of her white gown into a linen suit, with a tangled necklace of pearls at her throat and her heavy hair coiled on her neck.

She paused in the doorway, saw Christopher, and walked straight to his table. She took the bamboo chair opposite Christopher, sitting on its edge with her spine straight. She wore a faint violet scent, and Christopher thought of Honey's bikini printed with foreign flowers she had never seen. Christopher did not speak again, except to summon the waiter; he let the girl order her own Coca-Cola.

"It's curious," she said, "this was the very first place I looked for you. I'm glad you're so easy to find."

"There aren't many places in Saigon to look for a foreigner," Christopher said. "I'm a little surprised that the Truong toc sent you—I had an idea he'd send a male relative."

The girl wrapped a paper napkin around the sweating glass the waiter had set before her. "I detest ice," she said. "It makes one feel no cooler to swallow these freezing drinks."

She smiled and lifted the glass; her gestures, like her face, were softer outside the Truong toc's house. She had the fine features of the Vietnamese young; her fresh skin was lighter than Honey's. She had had a better diet: the bones of her neck were covered with smooth flesh and her hair shone with health. Her small ears, pierced by the golden earrings of an engaged girl, were almost transparent.

"My uncle was impressed with you," she said. "He wasn't pleased that I had been rude to you."

"Neither was I. Perhaps we can come to the point. I'm a little tired, and very hungry."

"You repay me my rudeness, I see. You have the right. There's been death in our family, as you know, and it's difficult sometimes to remember one's manners. I'm exhausted with condolences—everyone comes to the Truong toc's house, and I'm tired of all the sadness."

"I understood. It's not important."

"My uncle would like to talk to you again."

"Would he? I have nothing more to tell him about your cousin."

"He knows that, but he would like to meet with you. What's your Christian name? We can't go on calling each other 'monsieur' and 'mademoiselle.' I am called Nicole, in French."

"Nicole? And in Vietnamese?"

She smiled. "Nicole is easier. And you?"

"Paul."

"Like the angry saint. I've always liked that name." She spoke French like a Parisian, with a studied musicality that paid compliments to the language. She was not speaking to him in the same way as before. Like an educated Frenchwoman, she had two voices: her natural speech for ordinary business, and a sweeter tone when she wished to be charming.

"I'd be glad to see the Truong toc again," Christopher said. "Has he a time and place in mind?"

"He asked me to bring you to him."

"That's kind, but I know the way."

"He's not at home tonight—we'd have to go to another place, and I'm not sure you could find it. It's in Cholon, and the streets are not easy there."

"All right. I have a car—but really I must eat before we go. I've had nothing since yesterday."

Nicole reached across the table and lifted Christopher's wrist to look at his watch. "It's only eight—we have time," she said.

During the meal Nicole talked about France. "I was educated to belong there, all of us were whose families had enough money," she said. "I think in French even now—it really is the language of logic. I separate people into French categories, intelligent or not intelligent. Everything is so simple in French, one knows the difference between things."

"And do you feel in French as well?" Christopher asked.

"Ah, no—a Vietnamese feels in Vietnamese. French is a language of the mind—Vietnamese, of the blood."

"You sound like Diem—what was he to you, an uncle?"

"A sort of cousin. Why should I sound like him? He hardly ever spoke."

"He spoke enough," Christopher said. "Is this mystical idea of Vietnamese nationhood something the mandarin class has invented? You're the only ones who speak of it."

"How would you know? You can only speak to people who understand French."

"That's true, and you all have this tendency to dramatize the Vietnamese side of your nature. You take such pleasure in tantalizing outsiders with your national mystery, as if it were something hidden, but in plain sight."

"And what, in your opinion, is that mystery?"

"A pride in your murders. It's not a quality that's confined to Vietnam. There's a tribe in Ghana that believes no one dies a natural death—when a man dies, they use magic to find who in the tribe has killed him, and by what spell. Then the dead man's son is given his father's sandals. When he grows big enough to wear them, he kills his father's murderer. Eventually, of course, he too is killed in revenge. It goes on, generation after generation."

"You think the Vietnamese question is as simple as that?"

"I think the human question is as simple as that, Nicole.

Intellectual systems are developed to justify the exchange of death; the system of the Ghanaian tribe is as sensible as Christianity or your own family's sense of aristocracy, or what the Americans call the dignity of the individual. In Germany, two thousand years of Christian teaching produced the SS. In Vietnam, two thousand years of colonialism produced this slaughter of peasants Ho Chi Minh calls a revolution and Diem never put a name to. It required only a hundred years of technology to produce the Hiroshima bomb. All achieved the same results—murder without guilt."

Nicole put down her knife and fork and leaned back in her chair, peering at Christopher as if his words had formed a frame around him. "You believe in nothing, then," she said.

"I believe in consequences," Christopher replied.

# SEVEN

## 1

Cholon was alive at night. The Chinese were everywhere, crouching in the street to eat rice, moving quickly through the din of voices and loudspeaker music on errands, exchanging goods for money. Christopher drove the Citroën through the boiling crowd; pedestrians banged on the thin metal hood to let him know that they were there.

"We'd do better to walk," Nicole said.

Christopher parked the car; the gray Simca that had followed them from the hotel stopped a block behind. Two Vietnamese, shorter than the Chinese who filled the street, got out of the Simca and vanished into the crowd.

Nicole led Christopher through a series of alleys; the mob thinned and finally disappeared altogether as they entered a narrow dirt street lined with the windowless walls of warehouses. Nicole opened a door that squealed across a concrete floor and grasped Christopher's wrist, guiding him along a walkway past piles of crates.

They went down a stairway and through a passage with dank earthen walls. Streams of rats whimpered around their feet in the darkness. At the end of the tunnel they climbed another stairway and Nicole rapped at a door. They were let into a dark hall that smelled of incense by a young Chinese. He opened another door, let them go through, and closed it behind them.

The Truong toc, dressed like a peasant in pajamas, sat on a divan; the priest, Jean-Baptiste, crouched on a mat on the floor, with his legs crossed under him and his feet clasped in his hands. Nicole knelt, poured three cups of tea, and handed them to the men. She and the Truong toc spoke to one another in Vietnamese. Christopher understood most of what they said; the Truong toc merely wanted to know if Christopher had come willingly. "He has no fear," the priest said, "there must be a reason why." Nicole left the room.

Christopher, leaving his tea untouched, faced the two old men. He supposed they might be sixty, but it was impossible to tell with Asians; one year they were fresh with youth, and the next their skulls came through their flesh as if their corpses were eager to escape into the grave.

"I'm glad to see you safe," the Truong toc said. "You take chances, going about at night as you do."

"He takes certain precautions, I'm sure," the priest said. "Your car is quite all right?"

The priest sniffed loudly and scratched his ribs. His eyes and his voice were clear, and his tic was quiet.

"Last night you asked my cousin, here, certain questions," the Truong toc said. "I am intrigued to know your purpose."

"It's simple. I hope for answers."

"He has none. Nor do I."

"Then there's no purpose in my being here," Christopher said.

"You didn't tell me that you knew my relative Nguyên Kim."

"It didn't seem important."

"After you left my house, I tried to puzzle out why you had come to tell me of the death of young Khoi. It made no sense. I concluded you wished to make yourself known to me in a way that would ensure that I'd remember you."

"My idea seems to have succeeded," Christopher said. He put his teacup on the table.

"You've certainly shown us that you are very direct. Are you working against time?"

"No."

"Then why," asked the priest, "do you behave like a man with an incurable disease? Really, it's very stupid to go about talking as you do and showing yourself as you do unless you care nothing for your life."

"I'll be direct again," Christopher said. "I hoped to shock you into speaking about the things I mentioned to you."

"You've shocked us," the Truong toc said. He paused, as if reluctant to say something rude. "If you are right in what you think, you must expect that we will kill you. Why, then, come here?"

"Let me ask you this: why waste a gesture, like Nicole in a Paris suit?"

"You know her."

"You must know I'd have come in answer to a telephone call or a note."

"And you must know that such things leave traces. An American dining at the Continental with a Vietnamese girl leaves no trace. It's the sport of the times."

"Were those your men who followed us across the river?" Christopher asked.

The Truong toc's eye sockets were filled with shadow; when he turned his face toward Christopher, he showed as little expression as an animal. "Now you waste a gesture," he said.

"Let me explain something to you," Christopher said. "What I said to you about Diem was honest—I thought him a great man in his way and I regret his death. I *would* tell you who killed him, if I knew."

The priest was scratching his skin now with great violence,

as if he was glad heroin had given him this evidence that his nerves were alive. "And in exchange for this worthy intention," he said, "all you want is for us to confess the murder of an American President and a plan to destroy the American army with heroin."

"Briefly, yes."

"Then you're a fool. What do you think this is—a film? We tell you everything, you escape with the truth, the world is saved. I believe you're insane."

"Then you should be frightened," Christopher said. "We're alone in this room. You are old. Even if I have no weapon, which is illogical, I could kill you both with my hands before anyone came. You don't seem to be afraid of that."

The Truong toc moved his face into the light. "Nothing is gained by this," he said. "Why exchange these threats?"

"It's useless," Christopher said. "I want to ask you a question. If I'm right, and your family arranged such a colossal revenge as the murder of Kennedy, what is the point of keeping it a secret?"

The priest threw his arms wide and began to speak; the tic was moving in his cheek again. He subsided when the Truong toc raised his palm. The Truong toc kept his eyes fastened on Christopher's face.

The Truong toc said, "Go on."

"You are the head of the family," Christopher said. "What do you want for it?"

"That it should continue," the Truong toc replied.

"No—that it should rule. You had power when Diem and Nhu were killed, and Can was put into prison. How long did it take you to achieve that? The whole length of the family's life. Are you content to wait another hundred generations for another Diem?"

The Truong toc made a brusque movement of his fingers, as if to summon the words from Christopher's mouth.

"If you kill a man for revenge, and he does not know why he died, and no one knows," Christopher said, "then what have you accomplished? Your own emotional release—and what use is that?"

130

The priest began to reply, but the Truong toc silenced him with another gesture.

"Say what you mean," the Truong toc said.

"I mean you have everything to gain and nothing important to lose by letting yourselves be identified as the assassins of Kennedy."

The priest had begun to sweat and tremble. He reached into his pocket with a fluttering hand and produced an envelope of heroin. With his eyes fixed on Christopher, he drew the white powder into his nose. After a moment he was quiet again.

The Truong toc returned his attention to Christopher. "That's certainly a novel idea," he said, his dry lips opening in a faint smile.

"It's logical," Christopher said. "To complete the act, you must be discovered. There may be a certain elegance in killing an American President with ignominy—using a man who appears to be a lunatic so that the assassination will be regarded as a bit of random madness. But it accomplishes nothing."

"Accomplishes nothing? The man is dead."

"But not his policies. When Diem was killed, he and Nhu were desperate to end American influence in Vietnam. They had no chance. But you do. Let it be known that Kennedy was shot in Dallas in revenge for the death of Diem and Nhu, and there will be such revulsion in the United States against Vietnam that you won't see an American face in your country, or an American ship in your harbors, for a generation to come."

The Truong toc flicked open his clenched hand as if releasing a bird into flight. "You'd give this country to the Communists?"

"Why not?" Christopher said. "Diem and Nhu were prepared to do so. At least the Communists are Vietnamese. Some of them are members of your family."

The Truong toc relaxed on his divan, steepled his fingers, tapped their ends together. The priest spoke to him in rapid Vietnamese. Christopher watched the Truong toc's impassive features and the priest's face, one side of it as unreadable as the Truong toc's and the other side in spasm. "Kill him tonight, in

131

the street, anywhere," the priest was saying. "No, he can do no harm," the Truong toc replied. Christopher realized the old man knew he understood Vietnamese.

"Mr. Christopher," said the Truong toc, speaking the name for the first time, "I'm curious—how did you come to hear the name Lê Thu?"

"Nguyên Kim mentioned it. He seemed to think it would be a great joke to use it as an introduction to you."

"And you thought it had great significance—that it symbolized this assassination you think we carried out?"

"I didn't know," Christopher said. "That was one of my questions."

"You've translated the name, I understand. It means 'the tears of autumn.'"

"Yes—if it's a code name it's poetic, but insecure."

"And you wish to know the name of our relative in the North Vietnamese intelligence service?"

"Yes."

"That is all you require to prove our guilt, and rid our country of the Americans, who, as you suggest, will destroy it for reasons of their own policy?"

"Yes."

As Christopher and the Truong toc spoke to each other, they smiled—more broadly with each question and answer. After hearing Christopher's final reply, the Truong toc laughed, a string of dry barks like the cough of a man who has swallowed smoke. His laughter was a compliment. Only a clandestine mind like Christopher's, free from values and concerned with nothing but the results of action, could have conceived the proposal Christopher had just made. The Truong toc had the same sort of mind. He was delighted to encounter another brain so like his own.

"We've heard a good deal about you since yesterday, Mr. Christopher," he said. "It all seems to be true. This really is a most clever provocation. I have no idea what purpose your masters think it will serve, but you may give them my answer. It is this: your hypothesis is absurd. How could we touch a Kennedy? They live in another dimension of power."

"Murder requires very little power."

"No, no, no. Mr. Christopher, Lê Thu is just a name. You will search in vain for any relative of ours who is a secret agent of Ho Chi Minh's. We accepted the death of Ngo Dinh Diem and Ngo Dinh Nhu—we are weak, Mr. Christopher. How could we do what you think we've done?"

Christopher rose. "Very well," he said. "I'll go on with my work."

"What bravado," the priest said. "You want what—admiration? You're mad—I'm more convinced of it than before."

The Truong toc stood and took Christopher's cold teacup from his hand and he drank from it with a smile. Christopher had not touched the tea. "You are not lacking in caution," the Truong toc said. "I have something to give you."

He reached into a pocket of his pajamas and brought out a gray envelope. Christopher opened the flap and looked at the photograph it contained.

It was a picture of Molly, smiling into the camera in surprise, a lock of her hair drawn tight between her thumb and forefinger. Half of Christopher's face showed in the photograph. It was the picture Nguyên Kim had taken in Rome after they had had lunch together.

The Truong toc looked steadily into Christopher's eyes. "You may have that print," he said. "I believe Kim has the negative."

Christopher felt a stab of panic. The Truong toc watched it flicker in Christopher's face. He bowed slightly. His brown scalp showed like shined leather through his thin hair.

2

No one interfered with Christopher as he left. The Truong toc showed no surprise when Christopher opened the door into the front of the house instead of going back through the darkened warehouse.

He moved through small rooms that smelled of burnt joss and cooking. There were no windows, only a streak of lamplight sifting through a series of doors leading to the front of the house.

133

Christopher moved quickly through the dim rooms; there was almost no furniture, nor any sign of Nicole or any other Vietnamese. In one of the rooms a withered Chinese woman sat in a large wing chair, staring at an oil lamp that burned on a low table in front of her; she paid no attention to Christopher.

He heard the noise of the street on the other side of a door, and opened it. Stepping into the crowd, he was borne along through the choked street until it opened into a larger thoroughfare. He searched the horizon for the glow of Saigon's lights. Finding his direction, he set off for the place where he had parked the car.

The crowd, mostly Chinese, was still very think but he stood head and shoulders above it, so that he could see into its depths. One side of the street was lighted by shop fronts; the other, running along the blank backs of godowns, lay in deep shadow.

He saw the first Vietnamese with his face in the full light of an open doorway; his expression had not changed since morning. Christopher looked for the other, and when he did not see him at once, knew that he must be behind him.

He turned around and saw that the crowd had parted. The second Vietnamese stood with his feet apart, poised like a diver on the balls of his feet. He was lifting a pistol with a steady sweep of his arm, wrist locked, both eyes open, mouth relaxed. Christopher recognized the technique. He leapt sideways toward the darkened half of the street. The gunman moved his arm instead of his whole body, and lost his aim. Two soft-nosed bullets hit the wall to Christopher's right. Two more rounds gouged shallow holes in the concrete. The gunman ducked behind the parked car, expecting return fire.

Across the street, the Vietnamese Christopher had seen first had a revolver in his hand; he was motioning people out of his way. The crowd made no special noise; people moved away from him in both directions to make room for the shooting. Christopher ran back the way he had come, past the parked car with the gunman hiding behind it. The crowd did not see him coming until he was well within it, running with his knees bent and his head bowed so that he was not much taller than the small people who surrounded him.

Christopher looked behind him. One of the Vietnamese was running after him at an easy trot, his long pistol held against his thigh, his head turning alertly from side to side. Christopher saw the other man move in the shadows by the warehouses. The two Vietnamese moved well as a team, like terriers used to hunting together. The crowd drifted toward the lighted half of the street.

Pushing bodies aside, Christopher plunged through the door of an apothecary's shop. A young Chinese looked up in surprise, then shouted in anger as Christopher went through a beaded curtain at the back of the store. A family of Chinese sat around a low table, playing cards. Christopher walked over the table, scattering the cards, and into another room. A window stood open in one wall. Christopher climbed through it, scraping his back on the sash. He fell into a space between two houses. The ground was littered with broken glass, and the passage was so narrow that there was no room for his shoulders. He moved through it sideways as quickly as he could toward a strip of light at its end.

One of the men who had killed Luong stuck his head out the window, braced his pistol against the sash, and took careful aim. Christopher turned his face toward the gunman, threw his arms into the air, gave a loud wordless roar that scraped the skin in his throat, and fell to his knees. The gun wavered as a spot of bluish flame blinked at the muzzle. Christopher did not hear the round go by, and he thought it might have struck him. He felt no pain.

He staggered into a bright street and saw a canal shining at the end of it. A young Chinese grasped his arm roughly and glared suspiciously into his face. Christopher smiled at him and struck him under the chin with the heel of his open hand; the boy's light body was lifted into the air by the blow, and he landed in the opposite gutter with his neck twisted. A knot of Chinese gathered around Christopher, shouting angrily, and followed him as he walked rapidly away.

The Citroen was parked in the shadows in the next block. Christopher headed for it, pushing the chattering Chinese roughly out of his way. There was no sign of the two gunmen. He was fifty yards from the car when two of the Chinese, young men with angry faces, realized that it belonged to Christopher. They broke out of the crowd and ran ahead. One of them opened a knife and knelt to slash the tires. The other darted around the Citroën, still screaming in a hoarse voice. He snatched at the door handle, and as the door began to swing open, Christopher remembered that he had locked it.

He fell to the ground with his arms around the two people closest to him. Afterward, he thought that he remembered the flash of the explosion lighting the flat face of the Chinese boy and the blast lifting the boy's thick black hair so that it stood on end. The noise was a long time coming. Before he heard the explosion, like the slap of a heavy howitzer, he saw the whole body of the car swell like a balloon full of water. The glass blew out and one door cut through the crowd like a great black knife.

Concussion sent blood gushing out of his nose. He could hear nothing except a high ringing in his ears. All around him, mouths opened in noiseless screams of terror. He lay where he was with his eyes open.

In a few moments a policeman wearing a lacquered American helmet liner leaned over him and spoke. Christopher pointed to his ears and said, "I'm deaf." He heard nothing of his own voice but felt its movement over his tongue. The policeman pulled him to his feet and led him toward the end of the street. He would have been killed by the fire truck that roared up behind them if the policeman had not pulled him out of the way.

3

"All I have to do is say the word and they'll slap a murder charge on you," Wolkowicz said. "Ten witnesses saw you break that Chinese kid's neck."

The Vietnamese police major had withdrawn when Wolkowicz arrived. Christopher's passport and a sheaf of Polaroid photographs of the bombed Citroën were spread over the top of the policeman's gray metal desk. Wolkowicz's face was bleached by the strong fluorescent light in the ceiling, his beard blacker than usual against his pallor. Christopher's hearing was returning, but his ears still rang, and Wolkowicz's voice sounded thin.

Wolkowicz tapped on the desk with the edge of Christopher's passport. "You'd better hear me," he said. "These guys can take two or three years just deciding if there's a case against you. You'll be eating rice and spoiled fish three times a day, and having a little chat with the *juge d'instruction* whenever he bothers to remember you're in jail. Believe me, it can go on for a long time."

"What do you want?"

"The story," Wolkowicz said. "What in hell was that all about? Your car blown up and five innocent bystanders killed, Luong dead in an alley, shots fired at you in the middle of a crowd. What do you think you're doing, for Christ's sake?"

Christopher looked around at the metal furniture, the chirping fluorescent lights, the air conditioner on the windowsill. "There seems to be a lot of American equipment in this room," he said.

"We're not going to talk here. I just want to know if you're going to bullshit me again if I take you out of here."

Christopher made a gesture. Wolkowicz pressed a button on the telephone. When the major returned, Wolkowicz walked with him back into the corridor. Christopher watched them through the half-open door, talking quietly and nodding.

The major came into the office. "There's one more formality," he said, gesturing for Christopher to follow him.

Christopher went with him down the hall and into another room. Honey, wearing her silk *ao dai*, sat on a scarred bench in the empty office. Her joints were locked in fright—fists clenched, neck rigid.

"Is this the American?" the major asked in Vietnamese. Honey nodded stiffly.

"Look at him," the major said.

Honey turned her head, a quick movement like that of a child forced to look at a corpse, and nodded again.

In the corridor, the major tapped Christopher's sleeve. "I believe you knew Vuong Van Luong," he said. "I believe you know he's dead."

"Yes."

"The girl saw you searching the body. You woke her when you came into the room—she believes you killed this Luong."

"She's not a very intelligent girl, major."

"No. But she has the power of speech, Mr. Christopher. We have her statement, and we'll keep her with us for the time being."

"I understand," Christopher said.

"I hope you do, Mr. Christopher. It can be very inconvenient for you if the police decide to take an interest in you. One violent death, and you can maintain that you're a victim of circumstances. But there have been six in less than twenty-four hours. Even in Saigon, that's too many."

The major was carrying a dossier. He held it up so that Christopher could see his name written on its cover. "You've formed a great many friendships here," he said. "Your passport will be returned to you at midnight today at the airport. You are already booked on the UTA flight to Paris. Don't miss the plane, Mr. Christopher."

The Continental Hotel was only a short distance from the police station in Tu Do Street. Wolkowicz sent his Marine driver to fetch Christopher's suitcase from his room and pay the bill. They waited in the car, the windows rolled up, until the driver returned.

At Wolkowicz's villa, Christopher threw away his blood-stained shirt and washed his face. The police doctor had painted the small cuts on his arms and chest and told him that his right eardrum had been ruptured by the explosion. He ripped the adhesive bandage from his cheek and looked at the cut on his face. His head ached. He took four of Wolkowicz's aspirin.

The villa was icy; Wolkowicz kept the air conditioning turned up so that his snake would sleep. In the living room, Wolkowicz gave Christopher a glass of bourbon and motioned him into a chair.

"Okay," he said. "It's gut-spilling time."

Christopher told him where he had been. He described the visit to Jean-Baptiste Ho's church, and his meeting with the Truong toc. He did not tell Wolkowicz what had been said, except to describe the movement of opium into Ho's church.

"Describe this guy who tried to shoot you," Wolkowicz said.

"He's been taught either by us or by someone who learned how to shoot a pistol from us," Christopher said. "When I turned around, he was in a crouch, bringing the pistol up, wrist and elbow locked, both eyes open, not using the sights. He fired two shots at a time in the prescribed manner. He's trained."

"Not very well trained," Wolkowicz said. "How many times did he miss you?"

"Four rounds that I know of, but I jumped off to the side. He didn't expect that. He didn't shift his feet, just swung his arm, so he lost his stance. And then, I was in a crowd and it was dark."

Christopher described his flight through the apothecary shop. "The kid in the street must have thought I was a burglar when I came out of that crack in the wall" he said. "I hit him to make him let go of my arm."

"I know these things mean something to you," Wolkowicz said. "I was bullshitting you about your killing him—all he's got is some busted teeth and maybe a slipped disc or two in his neck."

"I know. I saw him get up."

"And then the car blew up while you were still half a block away from it," Wolkowicz said. "I don't understand that."

"They wired the door on the driver's side. A Chinese kid ran ahead and yanked it open—he wanted to do me some damage. The priest saw me check under the hood when I was out there last night. You have to open the door to open the hood."

"The cops think there must have been a kilo of *plastique* in the car. I guess you're immortal, just like Patchen's always said."

"I was surprised that they were so public about it—why not wait until I was asleep in the hotel?"

"Maybe they thought you'd done enough talking. What did you say to them, anyway?"

Christopher's hearing continued to clear; when Wolkowicz shook his glass, he heard the ice cubes rattle.

"They're doing something with heroin," Christopher said. "Jean-Baptiste Ho is an addict, but for some reason his church is the depot. That country is VC-controlled. They bring in the raw opium from Laos, Cambodia—wherever it's grown. Luong told me there's a tunnel complex under the village. They keep it there. It's crazy, but that's the way they're doing it. They store it under the church."

"Did you confirm any of this?"

"The tunnels, yes. I saw the priest's woman disappear through the floor."

"Opium isn't heroin."

"Tom Webster thinks they're trying to buy the technology in Marseilles. Have you seen that traffic?"

"Yeah, I read the cables—two million bucks through Lebanon. But why take all the risk?"

"They figure they're going to have a big market in-country pretty soon," Christopher said. "The Yanks are coming."

"That's speculation—garbage," Wolkowicz said.

Christopher shrugged. "Okay, Barney."

"What's their objective? They've got enough money not to have to take chances like that."

"What chances? Jean-Baptiste is a member of the family— he's not going to talk," Christopher said. "If the police or the ARVN come smelling around, they'll see them coming ten miles away. They can blow those tunnels in thirty seconds."

"Thanks to you, they're probably moving the stuff out right now."

"Maybe. It doesn't matter. They'll do it some way—they're not in it to make a profit," Christopher said. "They want to send a few thousand junkies back to the States when all this is over. That's the purpose."

Wolkowicz tossed melting ice from his glass into his mouth and chewed it. "Why?" he asked.

"They think we killed Diem and Nhu," Christopher said. "They think we ought to pay for that."

Wolkowicz walked across the room and came back with a handful of ice cubes and a bottle of bourbon. He dropped ice into the glasses and filled them with whiskey. Handing Christopher one of the dark-brown drinks, Wolkowicz beckoned him to follow and walked out of the house. The garden was surfaced with gravel, so that Wolkowicz could hear footsteps approaching in the night. In the center of the garden was its only ornament, a bed of flowers surrounding an aviary. Wolkowicz paused by the cage and made kissing noises at the sleeping birds.

"You ought to come out in the daylight and have a look," he said. "Some of these birds are really pretty—they don't sing worth a shit, though."

Christopher sipped bourbon; his hands were steadier than they had been in the first hour or two after the explosion.

"Now that we're in the open air, how about coming clean?" Wolkowicz said.

"You're the only man I know who goes outside to get away from his own bugs," Christopher said.

"I think you told the Truong toc and the priest more than you've told me," Wolkowicz said. "I thought maybe you'd feel easier in your mind if we could talk in the open."

"I don't care where we talk. Even next to the birdcage. I've told you everything I can."

"Okay, it's your ass. But I know you're on to something besides a heroin racket—just remember that. I *know*. I'm going to be on you like a sheet of flypaper, Christopher."

"I'll be glad of your company, after tonight."

Wolkowicz took Christopher's arm and walked him over the crunching gravel to the back of the garden. "I'm going to tell you something I'm sure you know, Christopher," he said. "I don't like you and I never liked your operations. That's basic.

141

However, you've been around for a long time and I feel I've got an obligation to you—do you understand?"

"Perfectly, Barney. Spit it out."

"I've heard some things about you behind Mother's back. There's a certain guy in the White House you had some problems with—you follow me?"

Christopher nodded in the dark. Wolkowicz rattled the ice cubes in his glass after each sentence.

"Well, this guy sent me a letter. A Green Beret captain carried it out to me from Washington. In the letter he says you're around the bend with a crazy idea about something that could have dangerous consequences to national security. What he was asking was this: if you showed up out here, would I get in your way."

"And have you been getting in my way, Barney?"

"No. Who the fuck is he to tell me what to do in a letter delivered outside channels? However, remember the Green Beret."

"What about him?"

"Well, they're gung-ho sons of bitches. And they're amateurs. They're setting up all kinds of networks around here. You said the guy who shot at you looked like he'd had training. What kind of a handgun did he use—did you notice?"

Christopher thought for a moment. "It was a .22 automatic with a long barrel and a silencer—a Colt Woodsman or maybe the Hi-Standard that looks almost the same. The rounds didn't ricochet, they gouged big hunks out of the concrete like heavier ammunition when they hit, so I could have been wrong."

"Mercury in the bullets," Wolkowicz said. "Didn't you think it was funny the Truong toc would try to shoot you and blow you up, all on the same night?"

"I thought it was thorough of him."

Wolkowicz rattled his ice. "It's not a pretty thought," he said. "But I think you ought to consider the possibility that you've got people coming at you from two directions."

"You're telling me that Americans are trying to do me in?"

"If they are, maybe it's a case of too much zeal. Soldiers have a way of giving a hundred and ten percent—look at Diem and Nhu. The lieutenant who shot them thought he was a hero. Nothing was supposed to happen to them, the way I understood it."

"The way you understood it, Barney?"

"That's what the traffic said—stand back and watch. We had a guy carrying messages between the ambassador and one of the generals in the plot, but that was all. There was no mention of bloodshed. I guess they couldn't face it in Washington. I could have told the dumb bastards what would happen."

"Why didn't you?"

"You know why. I wasn't allowed to do anything, why should I say anything? The amateurs were running the show."

"I see," Christopher said.

"What happened to you tonight was more amateur stuff— shooting in a crowded street, chasing you through houses full of witnesses. I'll do what I can to shut these guys off—not that I think they're going to admit anything. That captain is just a kid. Whosis in Washington probably told him just what he told me —get in Christopher's way. The kid misunderstood—but that's not going to be much help to you if you end up like Luong, with pudding for brains."

"That was no amateur bomb."

"No," Wolkowicz said. "I'd say that part of it was real life."

Christopher put his hand in his pocket and touched the sharp edge of the photograph the Truong toc had given him. Molly's face, as perfect as Cathy's had once been, moved over the screen of his memory. He knew they would kill her if they thought he needed the lesson.

"What are you going to do?" Wolkowicz said. "The cops want you out of the country in twenty-four hours."

Christopher looked at the green dial of his watch. "It's two in the morning now," he said. "I'll make the deadline."

In the darkness, Wolkowicz was chewing ice. "We'll miss you, baby," he said.

Luong lay in his coffin with a bunch of bananas on his chest to confuse the appetite of the Celestial Dog, devourer of the entrails of the dead. A ring of candles burned around the edge of the coffin, and an oil lamp smoked beneath it. A child of ten, Luong's eldest son, stood at his father's feet, welcoming mourners. He wore a straw headpiece and a robe of white gauze, covered with patches to show his wretchedness. Christopher bowed to the corpse and gave the child an envelope filled with piasters, two bottles of Veuve Cliquot, and a satin banderole on which was written a compliment to the dead man.

"I was your father's friend," Christopher said.

"Tho spoke about you," the boy said. "I remember your visit."

In death, Luong had been given another name, Tho, and no member of his family would call him by his own name again. Probably they had never done so when he was alive. A Vietnamese's name is used only by officials and foreigners; those who know him call him by nicknames or a number that fixes his position in the family, so as not to provoke evil spirits.

Luong's son placed Christopher's gifts with the others on a low table beside the altar at the end of the coffin. No attempt had been made to conceal the bullet wound in Luong's forehead; his relatives had put rice in his mouth, and a white grain of it was visible between his lips. In his best clothes, Luong looked not much older than his son. Luong had been dead for a full day, and the weeping had ceased; his wife, wearing patched gauze like her children, sat in a group of women with a white veil covering her face.

Musicians played at the end of the room, and male relatives with white mourning bands tied around their foreheads were drinking and laughing at jokes. They stared at Christopher, who stood alone by Luong's coffin, and went on with their loud conversation. Luong's widow made no sign that she saw him. When he turned away from the corpse, an old woman approached and gave him a bowl of food. He thanked her in Vietnamese and she bowed.

Christopher ate the food. Guests continued to arrive, crowding into the small house and filling it with a babble of voices and laughter. Luong's picture of Christ with a burning heart had been brought out of the bedroom and hung beside a portrait of Buddha on the wall nearest the coffin.

A man detached himself from the group of male relatives and came toward Christopher with a cup of rice wine in either hand; he gave one of the cups to Christopher.

"You are my brother's friend Crawford," he said.

"Yes, I'm sorry for your family's sadness," Christopher replied.

"You speak Vietnamese."

"Very badly," Christopher said in French. "You are Tho's brother? You look a great deal alike."

"Yes, I am older by five years. My name is Phuoc."

"I don't want to intrude here. I only wished to pay my respects. I knew your brother well."

"We thank you for the gifts you brought," Phuoc said. "You knew he liked that sort of champagne. I told him often it would be his downfall." Phuoc looked into Christopher's face and gave an explosive high-pitched laugh. "The burial is tomorrow—will you come?"

"Alas, I'll be gone tomorrow. But my thoughts will be here."

Christopher finished his rice wine. Phuoc handed him his own cup. "Drink it," he said. "I have no use for it. Perhaps Tho told you I am a *cu si*—not quite a monk and, my brother always said, not quite a man. I observe the five interdictions of Buddha: no sex, no alcohol, no tobacco, no theft, no killing."

"Yes, he spoke about you. I believe he admired you very much."

"Did he? Tho lived without interdictions of any kind, except that he never betrayed a friend."

"That I have known for a long time," Christopher said.

"How much money did you bring?" Phuoc asked. It was a polite question among Vietnamese, who were always asking each other the details of their salaries and bank accounts.

"There are 175,000 piasters in the envelope."

"Very generous. In dollars or piasters?"

"In piasters—it's an odd sum, but it equals five thousand dollars."

"Piasters will be less embarrassing," Phuoc said. "It will be a great help to his widow. She must stay indoors for two years, as you know. She worries about the children—Tho insisted on expensive schools."

"He was right in that, of course."

"He was right in most things. He put money away, I believe more than a million piasters. My brother expected to die young, he often told me so. His was not the sort of life that lasts very long in a country as troubled as ours."

"He lived his life with courage, at any rate."

Phuoc laughed again, opening his eyes and his mouth wide and letting shrill notes escape from his throat; it was a mannerism of grief.

"For your friendship and your money, you should have something in return," Phuoc said. "Come with me for a moment."

He led Christopher down the hall and into his dead brother's bedroom. Closing the door behind them, he went to the window and looked out, then leaned his back against the wall. Incense burned on the dresser in front of a photograph of Luong.

"My brother was going to meet you when he died," Phuoc said. "Did you know that?"

"Yes. I found his body."

"Did he speak to you?"

"That doesn't happen," Christopher said. "He died instantaneously—you saw his wound."

"Can you tell me anything more about his death?"

"I saw the men who killed him. They walked past me as I entered the street where he lay. I did not, of course, know then what had happened."

"Would you know them again?"

"I saw them again. They shot at me." Christopher gave Luong's brother a description of the two men. "Both times they were in Cholon. I'd look for them, if I were looking, around

Dong Khanh Boulevard. They'll have money to spend, and that's where they'd go to spend it."

Phuoc absorbed the information. "Have you any idea what my brother wished to tell you?"

"No. I asked him to find a person named Lê Thu. Before he went out for the last time, he told me he had one more source to question—nothing more than that."

"Then he went to his death for you?"

"Yes," Christopher said.

Phuoc did not laugh again. "My brother always did as he wanted to do. It wasn't your fault. He thought highly of you. As it happens, I know where he went."

Christopher waited. When Phuoc did not speak again, he said, "Would your brother have wished you to tell me?"

"Oh, I think so," Phuoc said. "You paid, after all. He went to see a Chinese named Yu Lung. You know the name? Yu Lung is a respected astrologer and geomancer. He knows the stars and all the rest very well—it's a gift as well as a science. Very expensive. Yu Lung serves the famous in secret, he won't deal with ordinary men."

"Thank you. Where is Yu Lung's house?"

"In Cholon, near the Tat Canal, by the racetrack. Ask anyone. Yu's house is poor outside, rich inside—he's a Chinese."

Christopher rose, hesitated, held out his hand. Phuoc gripped it tightly and, holding it for a long moment, threw back his head and laughed again. "Luong—*Tho* should have asked Yu Lung about his own future, eh? Instead of asking questions for you, Craww-ford. Do you know what the Vietnamese name Tho means?"

"Longevity."

"Yes, my brother will be dead for a long time," Phuoc said. "Tho is also the word for a coffin that's purchased well in advance of death. We thank you again for the money."

## 5

Wolkowicz had given Christopher a car and a driver. "It'll save us both trouble," Wolkowicz said. "You don't seem to care who knows where you go, and I can't spare three men to surveille you until you get on the plane tonight."

"Who's the driver?"

"Pong's his name. He's a Thai, so he's disinterested. He'll take you where you want to go and wait outside—but don't go off and leave him. I'm responsible to the cops until you get out of the country."

The car was an air-conditioned Chevrolet with a two-way radio and local license tags. Pong was flicking dust from the waxed hood with a feather duster when Christopher emerged from Luong's house. Under the tail of his long silk shirt, Pong wore a heavy revolver. One of Wolkowicz's Swedish submachine guns was clipped under the dashboard, with three extra magazines stowed in polyethylene pouches tacked to the door. "Pong's got a reputation around town," Wolkowicz had said. "These people fear the Thais, and they couldn't be more careful of old Pong if we painted shark's teeth and a crazy eyeball on him, like a surplus B–26."

Pong put his feather whisk in the trunk of the car and sat quietly with his hands on the steering wheel until Christopher told him where to go. Then he moved off, turning the car into traffic as a good dancer would swing a woman onto a ballroom floor. He was a competent man.

All during the morning, while he was looking at Luong in his coffin and talking to Phuoc, Christopher had controlled the impulse to touch the photograph the Truong toc had given him. Now he reached into the breast pocket of his coat and brought out the picture of Molly. He looked at his watch; he could not be in Rome in less than thirty-six hours. It was useless to send a telegram. Molly wasn't trained, she wouldn't know how to hide, she would think the cable was a joke. Christopher was not used to feeling emotion; he was as surprised by his fear for Molly as he had been by his love for her.

Pong maneuvered the clumsy car through traffic on the quais along the Ben Nghe Canal. Sampans lay in the foul water, their decks swarming with boatmen whose joints bulged on their thin bodies like knurs on diseased trees.

"Driving this car is like being in America," Pong said, "so cool and quiet—I don't like to get out."

Christopher pressed the electric window control. The stench and noise of the canal and the heat of noon thrust through the open window like a beggar's hand. Pong made a disgusted sound in his throat and stared at Christopher in the rear-view mirror. He turned north, toward the center of Cholon.

Yu Lung's house was not far from the place where Christopher's Citroën had exploded. The wreck had been hauled away, but broken glass still glittered on the pavement and the flames had left a long smudge across the face of a building. A soup vendor stood with his car where the Citroën had been, tapping on a block of wood with two sticks to attract customers.

They drove through the neighborhood twice before they found the house. Once, emerging from a sea of tin-roofed hovels, they found themselves across the city boundary, trapped on a narrow road through fields of paddy. Pong stepped on the accelerator and, reaching through the steering wheel, worked the action of the submachine gun to put a round in the chamber. He found a place to turn around by a group of huts; Pong pulled the wheel all the way over and skidded the tires in an arc through the dust. Christopher watched a young boy, astride a buffalo in a water hole, disappear in the cloud of dirt thrown upward by the wheels of the Chevrolet, and then come out the other side, not having moved while the slow wind moved the dust over him and the buffalo.

"Stop in the shade," Christopher said, when they had passed Yu Lung's house for the second time. He wrote six dates, each followed by a time of day, on a page of his notebook. Then he tore five hundred-dollar bills in half, put five halves in an envelope with the notebook page, and placed the other torn halves in his wallet.

"Pong, walk back so they don't see the car," he said, "and give this to whoever answers the door. Make an appointment for me to see Yu Lung after dark tonight—but not after nine o'clock. Tell him I want horoscopes for the men born under the first four dates and times—he'll have to transpose the dates to the lunar calendar. I want to trace the connection between the birth dates and the last two dates, which are days and times when certain events took place. Have you got all that?"

Pong scowled and repeated Christopher's instructions. "Who do I tell him is coming?" he asked. "He may not want to see an American."

"Tell him I'm a friend of Lê Thu," Christopher said. Pong tapped the submachine gun to call Christopher's attention to it and stepped into the street. Pong rocked from side to side as he walked, as if the taut muscles of his squat body were disputing the signals from his brain.

When he came back, he nodded at Christopher. "Yu Lung will have the stuff for you at eight o'clock," he said.

"Let's have some lunch, then," Christopher said.

"Barney told me not to leave the car."

"Have you anything with you?"

"Sandwiches," Pong said, holding up a packet. "I made them at Barney's while you were telephoning the young lady."

"You're a good operator, Pong. Did you report that to Wolkowicz?"

"Yes, on the radio while I waited for you at the dead man's house. That's when he told me not to leave the car."


6

Nicole was waiting at the table on the roof of the Majestic, a Coca-Cola before her and the city spread out beyond her soft profile. She wore a different French frock; her hair was bound with a broad white ribbon that passed over the top of her head. Christopher sat down with his back to the view, so that he could watch the door and the room.

"I'm a little surprised you came," he said.

"You came last night when I invited you."

"Yes. I hope you have a quieter journey home than I had."

"You seem well. There's a cut on your cheek."

Christopher spoke to the waiter, who poured cassis in the bottom of a glass and filled it with white wine.

150

"You shouldn't drink wine at midday in this climate," Nicole said. "It's very bad for the liver." Her eyes looked beyond him as she watched ships move in the river.

"Well," Christopher said, "have you any compliments or messages for me from the Truong toc?"

Nicole smiled, a sudden sly glint of teeth and eyes. "He doesn't confide—I listen at doors. I listened last night, in Cholon. You took their breath away, you know."

"Did I? Then they have very good self-control."

"They don't know how to deal with you. At first they thought you were insane."

"And now?"

Nicole traced a pattern on the tablecloth with her fingernail, then looked up quickly into Christopher's eyes. "They think you're in a terrific hurry. That upsets them more than what you say you know, or suspect. They think you want to lay this theory out before the world as truth. They know you're a journalist."

"I've never concealed it."

"They know what else you are. You conceal that."

"Then I'm concealing it still. I'm only a journalist, Nicole. There's no one behind what I'm doing."

Nicole shuddered with impatience. "You suppose they don't know where you slept last night, or whose car you have today? Come, Paul—really."

"My embassy thought, for some reason, that I needed protection. I was glad to have it."

Nicole looked at him again and laughed shrilly, almost in the tones of Phuoc's laughter. The waiter brought them fish, poured more wine, and went away. Nicole ate deftly, saying nothing until she had cleared her plate. Her eyes moved busily over the landscape behind Christopher's shoulder; the sun filtering through the green awning changed the hue of her skin as she turned into the light or away from it.

"What you were saying to my uncles last night—were you serious?" she asked.

"About revealing what they had done? Absolutely."

151

"*If* they have done such a thing—let us have that plainly understood."

"All right. It isn't proved that they did."

"You think the proof would have the effect you described? Would the Americans leave?"

"Yes."

"It's logical," Nicole said. "The Americans would do what you say in the open, before the world. But what would they do secretly?"

Christopher shrugged. "I don't know. Not much. After all, it was a fair enough exchange."

Nicole drew in her breath. "You *are* cold-blooded. Would you speak in this way to an American?"

"I've done so. They don't like it any more than you do, Nicole."

Nicole touched the back of his hand with her fingertips. "Leave Vietnam," she said. "You don't understand us."

"Don't I? Tell me about yourself, Nicole. Where were you born? What were your schools? What is your future?"

She drew back her hand. "All that means nothing." She touched her temples. "You believe one lives in this part of the body, but I live in my three souls and my nine spirits, and there are a thousand vital points in my body. Each one of which touches a time or a date or a number in the lunar calendar, which you cannot even understand. I never speak my own name, nor does anyone who loves me. You haven't time, if you lived here for another fifty years, to begin to understand."

Christopher put a forefinger on her brow; she made no movement to avoid it. "If your brain stops," he said, "then all this wonderful system of mysteries stops, too, doesn't it?"

"In this body, yes. There are other forms, other forces that go on."

"You seem determined to convince me that Vietnamese culture is a secret code."

"And you seem determined not to believe me."

Christopher called for the bill. While he counted out the money, Nicole sat watching him, her upper lip caught between her thumb and forefinger. Christopher remembered how he had closed Luong's dead mouth, and again saw the grain of rice between his lips, magic against the Celestial Dog. It took him a moment to realize that Nicole's long fingernail was pressing into the back of his hand. When he looked up, she removed it, leaving a white half-moon on his sunburnt skin.

In Vietnamese she said, "My name is Dao. I was born in Hanoi. I am twenty-three. All that is worth loving will die around me before I have a child."

Christopher, giving no sign that he understood her language, folded his napkin into a neat triangle. "We seem to be back where we began," he said. "I thought we might to beyond gibberish today."

"You really don't believe in the importance of anything I've told you, do you?"

"Oh, yes, I believe in its importance, and you've taught me quite a lot," Christopher said. "But if there is one certain thing about codes, it's this—they can be broken. Tell the Truong toc I thank him again for the photograph he gave me last night. Tell him, too, that I have some pictures of my own."

"I don't understand that message."

"The Truong toc will understand. Like me—and like Diem and Nhu—he believes in consequences."

153

# EIGHT

1

"Barney ordered me not to leave you," Pong said. His eyes darted over the crowd in the narrow street outside Yu Lung's house. There was enough light to see movement, but not enough to distinguish faces. Bicycles drifted by, and an occasional motor scooter sounded its horn, scattering pedestrians and cyclists as it plunged past the parked car.

"If you stay here with the car you'll draw attention," Christopher said. "Go somewhere else, and come by again at exactly nine o'clock. I'll be here."

A cyclist peered angrily through the windshield and hammered on the hood of the car.

Pong said, "Okay, nine o'clock. If you're not here, I'll come inside."

He drove away through the crowd, touching the horn lightly in a series of Morse dots to clear the way ahead of him. Christopher was annoyed by Pong's unnecessary noise. Then he realized it made no difference—secrecy was of no further use to him in Saigon.

Yu Lung's house had a blind front except for a frame of carved wood, painted red, around the door. The lintel was low, and Christopher ducked his head to enter. A servant with a large flashlight showed him down a long hall to the back of the house. They walked past rooms filled with noise—plaintive Chinese music playing on a gramophone, loud voices, the beating of a spoon against a pot in the kitchen. But the hall itself was dead space. It was impossible to guess what sort of people lived behind the closed doors.

After the noise and the pungent smell of the house, Christopher did not expect to find Yu Lung looking as he did. The fortune-teller was a man of forty with a round prosperous belly under a checkered vest and a gold watch chain. He greeted Christopher not in a dim room hung with incense and calligraphy but in a brightly lighted office, sitting at a polished desk with gray-steel file cabinets behind him. There were two telephones and a photograph of his wife and her young children in a gold frame on the desk. Yu Lung rose from his chair with a smile and shook hands with Christopher. The pressure of his hand was firm and quick.

"Yu Lung," he said. "You're a friend of—who was it again?"

"Lê Thu." Christopher found himself smiling broadly—Yu Lung had made magic efficient.

Christopher took the torn halves of the five one-hundred-dollar bills out of his wallet and laid them on the desk. The Chinese produced his own portions of the torn bills from a desk drawer and spent a moment fitting them together on the glass top of his desk.

"Is the fee satisfactory?" Christopher asked.

"I've drawn the horoscopes for you," Yu Lung said. He spread six sheets of rice paper over the top of the desk. On each sheet he had drawn a circle; symbols connected by lines lay within the circle. A vertical row of Chinese characters ran down the edge of each page. Yu Lung looked expectantly at Christopher.

"I'm afraid I can't read these without assistance," Christopher said.

Yu Lung nodded. "As you no doubt suspected, there is a remarkable conjunction of forces between the four men and the two dates you gave me. The fates are acting quite strongly on one other. Do you wish a classical interpretation, or a Vietnamese reading?"

"Vietnamese, to begin with," Christopher said.

"I thought you might, so I've added the geomantic factors as well. Briefly, three of these men are either dead already or will be on"—he ran his finger down a lunar calendar— "the next conjunction of their forces, which will occur, in Western time, seven years from now on the dates you gave me for the events."

He pushed aside the charts that he had drawn for Kennedy, Diem, and Nhu on the basis of their birth dates and times.

"This fourth man," Yu Lung said, tapping the Truong toc's chart, "is active in the fates of the others. I see no danger for him. You understand, you've asked me to work from very limited information."

"I'm impressed with what you've done. How much faith have you in your results?"

"Well, you understand that the basis of horoscopy in our system is that the stars and all the other portents predispose rather than predetermine an individual's fate. A man's acts can alter his reading—in other words, he can avoid destruction through wisdom, or cheat himself of good fortune through stupidity. But the forces here are quite clear."

"And the factors other than horoscopy?"

"Yes, the geomantic factors. You understand the principle of geomancy, of course—one orients oneself to the natural world on the basis of harmony with the five natural elements, which are fire, water, metal, wood, and earth. None of these three men seems to have been in harmony with the world. In

156

Vietnamese terms, they were all under the influence of the Ma Than Vong."

"Which is?"

"A very colorful and malevolent force—the tightening-knot ghost. Ma Than Vong goads men to suicide, or into situations where their violent death is inevitable. One of the men, this one—a foreigner, I believe—am I correct?"

Christopher nodded. Yu Lung had shown him Kennedy's horoscope.

"The foreigner was a powerful man," Yu Lung said, "but his particular nemesis was Ma A Phien, whom the Vietnamese call the opium ghost. This man was predisposed to a death in the pleasures. Also, he was much involved with the *am*, the female spirit that stands for darkness and is associated with death. As for the others, who must be Vietnamese, there was a long period of the influence of *duong*, or the male spirit of light, or life. Then this force conjoins with the *am* spirit of the other man, and they are lost."

"By whose error?"

"Their own, of course. As I said, we are dealing with predisposition, not predetermination. The horoscope is incomplete, as you must realize."

"Incomplete? In what way?"

"There are other individuals involved. One in particular, who I could guess is a Vietnamese related in some way to the other two. Perhaps he lives elsewhere than in the place where his two relatives live, or lived. He exerts a force after their death. It's a key force. Without knowing his stars, you will not understand the others."

Yu Lung rocked back in his swivel chair with a faint squeal of metal springs and folded his hands on his stomach. "Would you care for some tea," he asked, "or a glass of scotch whiskey?" Yu Lung's face was circular like his charts—a small pursed mouth, a broad nose that moved when he smiled, arched eyebrows.

"It's the other man in whom I am interested," Christopher said.

Yu Lung laughed. "I thought it might be. You haven't the look of a man who pays five hundred dollars out of idle curiosity." He pulled Scotch tape from a dispenser and stuck the torn American bills together. "Have you chosen between tea and scotch?" he asked.

"Nothing, thank you. I may say you work swiftly from very limited information."

Yu Lung shrugged. "It's a settled science. One learns the principles, and if one has the gift, the situation opens itself very quickly."

"One would almost think that you had dealt with these particular horoscopes before."

"Ah, perhaps," Yu Lung said. "They are unique. All horoscopes are."

"Then you'd remember if you had done them before?"

"Yes, I'd remember. You say you are a friend of Lê Thu. How did you come by that name?"

"By chance," Christopher said, "though I suppose your philosophy would not accept that explanation."

Yu Lung waved a pudgy hand. "Chance is an accurate word in your language. A geomancer would call it the function of *feng shui*—the geomantic conditions. What you'd describe as being in the right place at the right time. These beliefs are ancient. Your people once held to them, like everyone else. They're preserved in your language, though you no longer hear the real meanings in what you say."

"You know something of Lê Thu, do you not?"

"I?" Yu Lung said. "It's a common Vietnamese name, quite a sad one—they might give it to a second child if the first had died, in order to discourage the bad spirits from taking this child as well."

"I was also a friend of Vuong Van Luong," Christopher said. "I believe you spoke to him a couple of nights ago."

"Luong. Yes, he came here."

"And asked about Lê Thu."

"I could tell him nothing of importance."

"He was shot dead after he left you," Christopher said.

"Not for that name, I think," Yu Lung said. He had a habit

of widening his eyes when he lied. He held Christopher's money in his hands, counting it over and over again.

"What are the ethics of your profession?" Christopher asked. "Your consultations are secret, I suppose."

"Oh, yes, absolutely. These are intimate matters."

"Do you keep records?"

"Of course. Clients come back. One keeps a complete profile of the case. Principles are fixed, but conditions change. One wants to see how forces have behaved in the past, so as to apply their logic to the future."

Christopher smiled at the man. "What is the maximum period of time over which a horoscope may be kept?"

"It's quite indefinite, but of course one can compute in terms of an adult lifetime. Thirty years. Say ten thousand days —that has a certain ring to it."

"I should think five thousand days would give one a complete picture."

"Fairly complete. Not all, but enough."

Christopher put a thick envelope on Yu Lung's desk. The fortune-teller kept his eye away from it. He drew one of the horoscope sheets toward him. With a red pencil he drew circles around groups of ideograms that ran down the edge of the paper. "The system I use is uniform," he said. "The top group is the date, place, time of birth. The next group is the name of the individual, if I have it. All the Chinese characters below are the description of the individual's fate. Do you see?"

"Yes."

Yu Lung straightened the pages, squaring their edges by tapping them on the glass top of his desk. He went to his file cabinet, unlocked it, and inserted the papers in a file so that a corner protruded from the top. Christopher's envelope still lay on the desk top.

"And now," Yu Lung said, "I must insist that you take a glass of scotch with me. It's quite an extraordinary bottle of Chivas Regal. I had it from a foreigner. I'll fetch it, if you'll be so kind as to wait."

Yu Lung left the room. Christopher took the file folder from the open drawer of the steel cabinet and opened it. There were seven sheets of drawing paper in addition to the ones Yu Lung had prepared for him. Christopher used Yu Lung's scissors to clip the ideograms from the edges of all the sheets. He put the long strips of rice paper, covered with Yu Lung's flowing calligraphy, in his inside pocket, with Molly's photograph. He closed the file and pushed in the lock.

Yu Lung, when he returned with the whiskey, did not glance at the file cabinet. He handed Christopher his glass before he poured whiskey into it, and smiled when Christopher held the empty tumbler up to the light.

"Will you spoil it with ice?" he asked.

Christopher shook his head. They touched glasses.

"You've spent a good deal of time in the East," Yu Lung said. "You've learned our manners—you don't make sudden noises or laugh in that peculiar way Europeans have. They guffaw and stare at one, expecting that one will put on an expression that exactly matches their own. One is not, after all, a mirror."

"Living in Saigon has not made you into a Vietnamese, Yu Lung."

"No," Yu Lung said, "though I was born here, like my father. We Chinese who live abroad call ourselves *hua-chiao*. The words mean 'sojourning Chinese.' A sojourn is by definition temporary. One of our poets said we are like migrating birds with our souls flying ahead of us to China; we take no interest in our landing places or even in our journey—we beat our wings violently, in pursuit of our souls. Vietnam is where I live, my dear fellow—but it is not my world."

Yu Lung widened his eyes in self-mockery. "I think one glass of scotch is quite enough for me," he said.

Christopher's envelope, containing fifty one-hundred-dollar bills, still lay untouched on the desk. Yu Lung had not acknowledged its existence. Christopher walked along the hallway behind Yu Lung. Outside Yu Lung's bright modern office, they were back in China. When Yu Lung drew close to shake hands, he gave off the bitter unused smell of an old man.

Pong was late. Christopher crossed the street and stood with his back against the wall of a tin shack. Cyclists and pedestrians moved over the beaten earth of the street. No one turned a face in Christopher's direction; he might have been as invisible as one of the spirits Yu Lung had spoken about. A new moon shone beyond the mist of Saigon's lights.

Pong came into the street driving too fast, blinking the lights to clear people away from the car. As he reached Christopher, he threw open the front door and slowed only enough to let him scramble into the seat beside him. Pong's eyes were fixed on the rear-view mirror.

"That gray Simca picked me up after I left you," Pong said. "I lost them for a while, but you can't hide this big car."

"Do you think they're still on you?"

"They were five minutes ago. They've got yellow headlights."

Christopher looked out the rear window. "Go out to the quais and head west," he said. "Let them find us."

"We should go back to the house."

"They'd be outside when we came out again. Let them follow."

Pong turned the car toward the canals. The two-way radio crackled. Christopher switched it off. "Turn off the dashlights," he said. "You may have to drive in the dark after a while."

As they made the long curve where the Doi Canal turned south, yellowish light flashed from the mirror onto Pong's face. "There they are," he said.

"Keep going," Christopher said. "When we get into the paddy, turn off the lights and drive fast. They can't keep up."

They were still within the city limits, but the car was racing through the swamps and paddy of the rural Seventh District, on the southwestern edge of Saigon.

"You know there are VC all over the Seventh District at night, don't you?" Pong asked. He pulled his revolver from its holster and laid it gently on the seat between them.

"I know. How far to the first big curve, so you can stop without their seeing your brake lights?"

"Maybe two kilometers," Pong said. "Just before the Cho Dem ferry."

Pong switched off the headlights and trod on the accelerator. The car pulled itself into the darkness, swaying on its soft springs over the uneven roadbed. Pong cursed as a wheel ran off the pavement and threw a burst of clods against the inside of the fender.

"Barney says driving this car is like screwing a fat woman —you don't know exactly where you are," Pong said.

Christopher pulled the submachine gun off the dashboard and worked the action. "This is what we're going to do," he said. "Listen, because I only have time to tell you once."

Pong listened. "Barney said no shooting," he said.

"Barney's not here," Christopher said.

Midway through a long curve, Pong pulled the automatic transmission into low gear and turned off the key. The car bucked and ran down to a stop, Pong touching the brakes lightly only twice.

Christopher got out while the car was still moving. He lay down on the slimy earth between the road and the paddy; the Simca had turned off its lights, but he could hear its motor far back and see flashes of red as the driver braked to keep it on the road.

The Chevrolet, its lights still out, stood broadside on the pavement. Christopher saw the rice move near the Chevrolet as Pong waded into the paddy, his revolver held above his head.

The Simca came around the curve with its tires shrieking, swaying from side to side. The driver saw the Chevrolet at the last moment and switched on his lights. For some reason he sounded the horn, and in the glow of the instrument lights Christopher saw him pulling the steering wheel to the right, hand over hand like a falling man clawing at the face of a cliff. The Vietnamese in the passenger seat braced his feet against the dashboard, his teeth bared in fear.

The Simca flew for an instant after it left the road. Christopher had no real idea of its speed until it struck the paddy, sending a great sheet of water into the air. There were three sounds one after the other: the hard slap of the flying car on the surface of the paddy, the splash of water hitting the road and the parked Chevrolet, and a brief shriek of pain from inside the wrecked car. The Simca turned end over end and settled into the paddy on its top. Its yellow headlights shone over the water, then sank below it to glow among the stalks of rice for a moment before they went out. It was very quiet; Christopher heard water filling the car and, when that stopped, the faint rustle of the rice, disturbed by the wind.

Pong, wet to the waist, came out of the paddy with his pistol in his hand and stood at the edge of the road. Christopher stood up.

"I thought they hit you," Pong said. He walked back and ran the toe of his sneaker, smeared with dark mud, along the skid marks.

Christopher waded through the paddy, still holding the submachine gun, and looked at the car. All four windows were under water. He beckoned Pong and together they rocked the car until it tipped over on its side. Pong opened the door; both men were crumpled together behind the wheel. He clambered onto the car, seized one of them by an arm, braced his feet against the door frame, and pulled the limp corpse out of the seat. He threw it into the paddy and pulled out the other body. Christopher helped him carry them through the water to the tar road, which was still soft from the afternoon sun.

Pong searched the bodies methodically, finding nothing but weapons and a little money. The man who had killed Luong had not attached the silencer to his .22; Pong found it in his trousers and held it up for Christopher to see. When he was done, Pong stood up and threw a handful of coins from the men's pockets into the water. He started to roll the bodies back into the paddy.

"Wait," Christopher said. "Do you have a camera in the car?"

Pong nodded and opened the trunk. He came back with a Polaroid camera, fitting a flashbulb into its reflector. He offered the camera to Christopher. "No," Christopher said, "you do it."

Pong knelt and took pictures of the dead men. The flashgun erased the shadows from their faces, so that they looked as Luong had looked, lying on his back with the morning sun shining into his extinguished eyes.

"Take two of each," Christopher said.

## 3

At Luong's house, the old woman who had given Christopher food that morning told him that Phuoc had gone away to pray. Christopher found him in the Xa Loi Pagoda, where the Ngos' enemies had waited for arrest only a few weeks before. He sent Pong, a Buddhist, into the pagoda. Phuoc came out alone and got into the car without hesitation.

Phuoc looked at the submachine gun and the two-way radio and turned his body in the seat, watching Christopher's profile. Christopher gave Phuoc the Polaroid photographs Pong had taken and turned on the interior light.

"These are the men," Christopher said. He opened the glove compartment and brought out the long-barreled .22 pistol. "This is the gun."

Phuoc examined the dead faces of his brother's murderers. Christopher turned off the dome light.

"How did they die so quickly?" Phuoc asked.

"They drowned. It was an accident. I wanted to talk to them, but they went off the road and overturned in a paddy."

"You wouldn't have killed them?"

"No. I would have given them to you."

Phuoc gave his sputtering laugh. "I see."

"Do you know them?" Christopher asked.

"How should I know them? They look like boys."

"So did Luong when I found him."

"Tho."

"All right, Tho," Christopher said. "Phuoc, have you ever seen them? If you have, tell me."

Phuoc slapped his palms together twice, sharply, in the dark. "Yes," he said, "they were outside Yu Lung's, drinking in the street when Tho and I came out the other night."

"You went with him to Yu Lung's?"

"Yes, I know Yu. His father taught me horoscopy."

"Did you sit with Yu and your brother while they talked?"

"Yes," Phuoc said, "but Yu said nothing of value. He wanted money, that's why my brother was coming to find you. He thought you would have it."

"What was Yu going to tell your brother in return for the money?"

"That wasn't clear to me. Yu can talk like a fool when he wants. When Tho spoke about Lê Thu, Yu became very alert. He talked about a voyage. 'Tears must be carried in a special vessel,' Yu said."

"What voyage? What vessel? He spoke to me in a very brisk way, like a French psychiatrist. Why should he talk to your brother in riddles?"

"I've known Yu since we were boys—he suits his approach to the client. He's Chinese."

"He said nothing more?"

"Oh, yes," Phuoc said. "He leaned across his desk and whispered, 'Five thousand dollars.' Then we went away, Tho to get the money from you. I came here—I sleep nearby."

Christopher touched the brake pedal twice, to signal Pong. Pong came out of the shadows, walking in a slight crouch, his head moving from side to side as if to catch a scent. Christopher was reminded of the drowned men, following him through the crowd in Cholon.

"I won't see you again," Christopher said.

Phuoc opened the door and seemed startled that his action bathed them in light. He still held the photographs in his hand; he glanced at them again before he closed the door, and gave them back to Christopher.

"One thing I know," Phuoc said. "This Lê Thu—it was the death name of one of the Ngo women. She was killed in '54, by the French or the Viet Minh, no one ever knew which, as she was coming down from the North. The Viet Minh brought her child, a small girl, to the Ngos. Their Truong toc raised her. It's said he loved her mother."

"The child was Dao, the one who calls herself Nicole?"

"Yes, Dao. It means 'peach blossom.' "

"Who was her father?"

Phuoc opened the door again. Sitting in the light with his face turned away, he said, "Do Minh Kha. Do went with the Viet Minh in the early days, and after they won, he gave up his wife to stay in Hanoi. She and all the other Ngos who were Catholics came south after Dienbienphu. The Truong toc had a great passion for this woman—Ho Chi Minh himself wrote a poem about it, how she had chosen a brave fighter over a rich man. Do chose the revolution over Lê Thu and the revolution killed her. So the Truong toc got the women he lost to Do after all—he keeps her altar, and he has her daughter."

### 4

Christopher called Wolkowicz on the car radio and, speaking German, asked him to bring two things to their last meeting. An hour later, he found Wolkowicz waiting in his Mercedes on the Yen Do Road, near the airport.

Wolkowicz walked from his car to the Chevrolet and got into the back seat. When Christopher told him what had happened, he showed his teeth.

"What did you do with the bodies?"

"Put them back in the paddy."

"The cops'll think it was the VC."

He handed Christopher an envelope. "Is this what you wanted?" he asked.

Christopher opened the envelope and looked at the photographs of Nicole and Do Minh Kha that Luong had taken in Vientiane.

"Yes. Thanks."

"You've identified the girl, right?"

"Yes. She's a relative of the Truong toc's."

"The chick you had lunch with?"

"Yes."

"What's the connection with Do?"

Christopher put the photograph back in its envelope. "She's a courier," he said.

Wolkowicz grunted. "All in the family. The generals would like to know that."

"Do this for me," Christopher said, handing Wolkowicz the envelope. He had addressed it to the Truong toc.

"I'll mail it in the morning," Wolkowicz said.

Christopher opened the car door. "Did you bring the Green Beret?" he asked.

"He's in the Mercedes."

Christopher walked to the other car and rapped sharply on the roof. Peggy McKinney's brother, wearing khakis, got out. Planes flew overhead, descending toward the airport with their landing lights on. Christopher had to shout above the noise of the jet engines.

"Come around in the headlights," Christopher said.

He handed the boy the Polaroid pictures of his dead agents. The young captain crouched so that the light fell on the pictures. He wore a heavy Rolex watch and a West Point class ring. He was very slender in a sinewy way and he had his sister's mannerisms: he held his body so as to display it to best advantage, but he had less control over his face.

Staring at Christopher, he stood up and held out the photographs. Christopher took them back. He handed him the pistols Pong had taken from Luong's killers.

"You've lost your amateur status," Christopher said.

# NINE

1

Christopher did not imagine that the Truong toc would be immobilized by a photograph of Nicole. He'd hide the girl, as Christopher intended to hide Molly, and try again to kill Christopher. But he would have to adjust his operations. All this would take time. Time was what Christopher wanted, and Molly's life.

It was raining in Rome and the Christmas decorations were up. The taxi driver let Christopher out by the door of his apartment on the Lungotevere. Christopher looked up and down the curving street and saw no one. One side of the street was open to the Tiber and the other was lined with old buildings whose heavy doors, built to accommodate horse-drawn coaches, were always locked. There was no place for surveillance to hide; that was why Christopher lived in this street.

Christopher's training told him it was better to see the opposition than not to. He did not know how quickly the Truong toc could move. He felt the beating of his own heart as he went inside and climbed the stairs. Molly should be asleep. He used his mind to make his body stop trembling.

Letting himself into the apartment, he walked across the marble floors, hearing his own footsteps. Molly had decorated a small Christmas tree and placed it on a table in front of one of the windows. The paintings that had been in the bedroom now hung in the living room. She thought that pictures should be moved from one wall to another so that the eye would be surprised to see them in a new place each day.

It was not yet six o'clock in the morning, and the rooms seemed cold in the wintry light that filtered through the windows. Christopher went into the bedroom. Molly was not in the bed. The clothes she had worn the day before were draped over the back of a chair, and a book she had been reading lay open on the bedside table.

Christopher pushed open the bathroom door. It was a windowless room; he turned on the light and, hesitating for a moment, pulled the shower curtain aside. The tub was empty and the tap dripped on a brown stain he knew was only rust. He was still wearing his raincoat and its hard material whistled softly on the door frame as he brushed against it.

Christopher looked at the bed again. There was a small lump in the center of the mattress. He threw back the covers and saw a bottle of champagne lying on the sheet; there were beads of moisture on the cold glass. He stared at the bottle.

Feeling something at his back, he turned around and saw Molly standing in the doorway, pushing her tangled hair away from her face. She wore one of his T-shirts and carried two wineglasses between the long fingers of her left hand.

"Double bloody damn," she said. "I wanted to be in bed with the wine poured when you came in. I forgot the glasses."

Molly pushed the hair away from her cheek and smiled. "I heard the taxi in the street," she said. "It woke me from a dream, and I looked out and saw you in the flesh, which was

169

what the dream was about. You must have come in like a cat burglar—I didn't hear you from the kitchen."

She shivered and placed one bare foot on top of the other. Her eyes were defenseless with sleep. Christopher took several deep breaths, but he could not regain control of himself: he had believed for thirty seconds that she was dead. Blood poured through his heart—he felt its temperature, as hot as tears on the cheek.

"Open the wine," Molly said. "Never too late."

Christopher picked up the bottle and began to peel the foil off its neck. He lost control of his hands; they leaped on his wrists and he dropped the bottle. It exploded on the marble floor. He put his quivering hands in his armpits and sat down on the bed.

"Paul," Molly said, "what's the matter?"

"Be careful of the broken glass," he said.

"What is it? Stop trembling, Paul."

She knelt beside him on the bed and put her hand on his forehead, as if he might have a fever.

"You're cold as ice," she said. "You've caught a chill."

When they made love, Christopher cried out as if he were in pain. Molly wanted to talk, but he put his fingers on her lips. After they had lain quietly for a few moments, he opened his eyes, thinking she would be asleep. But she lay on her side with her knees drawn up, gazing into his closed face. When he kissed her, she didn't open her lips or put her hand on him. He fell asleep.

He woke before she did. Molly found him sitting on the sofa with the long strips of Yu Lung's calligraphy spread on the coffee table before him.

Christopher rubbed her thick hair; it crackled with electricity in the damp winter air. Molly moved away from him.

"Don't stroke me," she said. "I'm not a cat."

"All right. What do you want?"

"To be told. What was the matter with you when you came home this morning? I thought you were going to scream when I walked into the room."

170

"I couldn't find you."

"Where would I be? Sleeping with an Italian?"

"I didn't consider that possibility."

"Then what?" Molly asked. ·I've never known anyone like you, Paul—each time you show your feelings you act like someone who's been caught in a lie. ·

"I'm trying to get over that."

"Well, I wish you'd hurry it up. I take you into my body. The least you can do is to tell me what it is that's made you so cold when you're not making love. When you get out of bed, you change, you know. I'd like to know whether you're yourself when you're lying down or when you're standing up. I used to think it was Cathy, but it's more than that, Paul."

"Yes, it's more than that."

Something had changed in Molly. Christopher looked at her for the first time without a memory of sex or a desire for it. Molly's personality had always been the force that lit her face or formed her gestures, something that made her physical beauty accessible to him. Now it leaped out of her flesh. There might have been two women facing him—one with Molly's body and the other, entirely separate, a spirit that had escaped from it.

"For Christ's sake, Paul, what is it?" Molly cried. "What am I to you? You confess that you love me at midnight, and go to America in the morning without a word. You go to Saigon for no reason and come back looking as if you've done murder. I thought your heart had dropped out of your body when I walked into the bedroom this morning with the wineglasses. Why were you so frightened?"

"I thought I'd killed you," Christopher said.

He told her about the photograph the Truong toc had given him.

"Was that the picture that odd little Vietnamese took in the restaurant?" Molly asked.

"Yes. I was stupid to let him see you."

"And you think they really would kill me in order to—what? Punish you for learning their secrets?"

"I know they would," Christopher said.

Looking steadily into her eyes, Christopher told her what his life had been. He gave her no details, just the fact that he had always lied to her. Molly gazed back at him while he spoke, showing no flicker of surprise.

She said, "Is this what drove Cathy to do the things she did —knowing you were a spy?"

"I think so, yes."

"Then she was a fool."

"You may not say so when you've lived with it for a while, Molly. Ninety percent of the time it's a foolish, joking sort of life. But once in a while something like this happens, and the joke stops."

"Do these people really go about murdering strangers?"

"Not usually. This time they're really threatened."

Molly moved for the first time since they had begun to talk; she crossed her legs, clasped her bare knee, and put her chin on it, as if listening to a story about creatures she didn't believe in.

"What do you have on them, for heaven's sake?"

"Molly, it's better that you don't know that."

"No," she said, "we're not going to have that again, Paul. If you don't tell me I'll go out into the streets and let them kill me. I won't go on with you."

"All right," Christopher said. "I believe they assassinated Kennedy. I have some proof, and before I'm done I'll have it all."

"I see. And when you have the proof, what good will it be?"

"I don't know, Molly. All my life I've believed that the truth is worth knowing, even if it leads to nothing. It usually leads to nothing. But what else is there?"

Molly touched herself, and with the same finger, touched Christopher.

"Yes," he said. "But I didn't know that always."

"It's funny," Molly said, after a moment of silence. "I won't say I'm not frightened. But it's too unreal."

"It's real enough," Christopher said. "I'm sorry you have to know."

"Know what? I've always known you were dying of shame.

Now I know why, and it's not so bad as it might have been. Whatever you've done, you've done for your country. Isn't that supposed to justify anything?"

"That's what we train ourselves to believe."

"Yes," Molly said. "I would like to know one more thing. Have you killed other men?"

Christopher closed his eyes. "Not with a gun or with my hands," he said. "People have died because I made mistakes, or by accident. Sometimes I knew it was going to happen and did nothing to prevent it. I don't know the difference between that and murder."

## 2

Molly made them a cooked breakfast. She put a new record on the phonograph and stood with her arm around Christopher's waist and a glass in her hand, waiting for him to laugh at the words of a new Italian love song.

After they ate, she gave him the mail and the telephone messages from the office. Christopher sorted out five of the telephone messages and pushed them across the table.

"Who's this?" he asked.

"Herman. I don't know whether that's supposed to be a first or a last name. He talks Italian with an accent."

"And this was the message?"

"Yes. It seems less mysterious now than it did then. He just kept saying he'd be standing by the *Pietà* in Saint Peter's at ten o'clock in the morning and again at four in the afternoon. Then he'd say, *'Molto urgente!'*—and ring off."

"Could you tell what sort of an accent he had?"

"Not really. A lot of tongue and lips in it."

Christopher looked at his watch. "It's three-thirty," he said. "I ought to be back in less than two hours."

Molly gave him a long look and then laughed. "Ah," she said, "the joys of love."

"Molly, you have to understand. This may be nothing—I may not even make the contact when I see who it is. But I have to know. It could be important."

"It could be a killer."

"In Saint Peter's? Shooting a man in front of the *Pietà* is the sort of thing a lover or a lunatic would do—not a professional."

"Kennedy was shot in Dallas, in the middle of a crowd of people with cameras."

"Yes," Christopher said, "but there's no way to kill the President of the United States discreetly."

"What you're saying is that if they kill you—or me, I suppose—they'll not simply kill us but destroy all trace of us. Isn't that it?"

"That's the idea, Molly."

They sat on opposite sides of a narrow table, and Christopher could see every detail of Molly's face. Her eyes were closed and she pressed her lips together, so that a web of lines appeared for an instant on her smooth skin. Tears ran through her lashes.

"My God, how cruel," she whispered. "They leave a person no meaning at all."

Christopher turned up the volume on the phonograph and told Molly what to do while he was gone. On his way out of the building, he used the stairs again, searching the hallways on each floor as he descended.

The day was as gray as slate. There was no one in the street except a shepherd, down from the Abruzzi for the Christmas season, who stood on the low wall above the river playing bagpipes. The shepherd's wild music followed Christopher across the Ponte Sant'Angelo, but no one was behind him, and he was still alone when he reached Saint Peter's Square. He walked through one of the colonnades of Saint Peter's, loitering among the pillars, but still saw no one following.

Inside the basilica, he walked along the left wall, pausing to look at paintings. In an alcove near the great altar he saw the original of Luong's picture of Christ: its meaning was being explained in German by a guide to a group of tourists. Christopher walked on, behind the main altar. Foreign priests were celebrating mass in the chapels along the sides of the basilica.

Gherman Klimenko, standing before the *Pietà* with a

**174**

guidebook in his hand, saw Christopher coming. He leaned on the chapel rail, as if to read Michelangelo's signature on the girdle of the Madonna, then snapped the guidebook shut and walked leisurely to the other side of the church. Christopher paused for a moment at the sculpture and watched Klimenko's gray-tweed overcoat disappear into the group of German tourists.

He followed Klimenko past Luong's Christ and saw the Russian get into the elevator that led to the roof of Saint Peter's. Christopher took the stairway, and Klimenko was already on the gallery, gazing down into the Vatican gardens, when Christopher got there. He went to the opposite side of the terrace and waited until a young couple finished taking photographs and descended the stairs. Klimenko turned and looked at him, and Christopher walked across the flagstones toward him.

"This has been very dangerous for me, coming to the same place at the same hours for three days," Klimenko said.

"I've been away. I only got your message today."

Klimenko had no hair and he was always cold. Even in Africa he wore a buttoned suit. He stared morosely at Christopher and pulled his fur hat tighter on his bald head; a sharp wind filled with rain blew the skirt of his coat and he leaned over and tucked it between his knees.

"I think you know what I want," Klimenko said.

Christopher remained silent. The great building and the trees in its courtyards absorbed the detonation of the Roman traffic, so that he and Klimenko stood in a pool of silence at the back of the roof.

"You won't answer me," Klimenko said.

"You haven't asked me a question, Gherman."

Klimenko turned his back to Christopher and rocked up and down on his toes.

"I'm worn out," he said, as if speaking to one of the Swiss guards pacing below them in the garden. He turned around again. "I want to make a contact," he said.

The wind nearly took Klimenko's hat and they both

reached for it; Christopher caught it and Klimenko screwed it down again on his forehead.

"Paul," he said. "We can only talk for ten minutes. Don't waste the time. You know what I want."

"I think so. But I can't help you, Gherman. Walk into the American embassy. You can be there in ten minutes in a taxi."

"Christopher—don't do this. They *know*. I've been running for a week. Where do you think they expect me to go? They're waiting outside the embassy in the Via Veneto. You know the system—a car is waiting around the corner. They'd have me before I could walk across the sidewalk."

Christopher shrugged. "Then go to Paris or Bern."

"You're my only hope. I've been waiting for three days. You don't know what it's like."

"No, I don't."

"Look," Klimenko said. "I have no more energy for charades." He seized Christopher's arm. "I told you, I'm worn out."

Klimenko's teeth chattered. He walked back and forth rapidly on the roof, swinging his arms around his body to warm it. He came back, close to Christopher, and spoke in a hoarse whisper.

"Paul—have I ever given a hint that I knew about you in all the years? Ever? How many times have I seen you, in how many places? We drank whiskey together in the bar of the New Stanley Hotel in Nairobi. We had lunch in the Fin Bec in Geneva, as if we were friends. We talked about opera, the ballet, the way BOAC is always late."

"I'm glad you have such tender memories," Christopher said, "but if you think you know anything about me, you're wrong."

Klimenko stood up to his full height. He was still a foot shorter than Christopher. Holding his clenched fists at his sides, he said, "All right. In 1959 you were in the Sudan; a Pole named Miernik was killed by the natives in the desert and you brought his body out. In 1960 you were meeting an agent named Horst Bülow in front of the S-bahn station at the zoo in Berlin; he was run down by a black Opel and killed before your eyes. In 1962 you penetrated the Chinese operation in Katanga with Alphonse Nsango and gave him gold to pay for the juju that broke one of their insurgent groups. In 1961 you were in Laos talking to a certain Hmong who is now a general. Your case officer is Thomas R. Webster, who lives at 23-bis, avenue Hoche, Paris. The chief of clandestine operations in Washington is David Patchen, and in practice you are answerable only to him. I can go on."

Christopher said, "If all that is true, why do you think I won't shoot you right now?"

Klimenko opened his eyes. "You people don't kill. We know that, too."

Christopher was not surprised at the quality of Klimenko's information, and he knew that Klimenko did not expect him to be startled.

Klimenko took Christopher's arm and walked him around the gallery. The mossy slope of Michelangelo's dome rose behind them. Christopher heard the wail of pipes, and saw a shepherd walking across the piazza below; the man wore a sheepskin tied around his waist with a rope and a red cap like the bagpiper he'd seen by the Tiber. Straining his eyes, Christopher saw that this man had a different face.

"They close this gallery at four-thirty," Christopher said. "We'd better go down."

"I didn't come out empty-handed, Paul. I can show you samples."

Klimenko's voice was growing thinner, as if he had suddenly caught cold. "Name a place," he said. "Just make sure it's secure."

"This is not my work."

Christopher put a hand on Klimenko's shoulder; the flesh was loose under his thick overcoat. Christopher had always liked the Russian, but he knew what mistakes he could make. "How long do you expect to stay operational if you go around in public like this?" he asked.

"Not long. You see what's happened to my nerves."

"Why did you come out? You've always been a loyal Russian, haven't you?"

The skin of Klimenko's sagging face was blotched, brown

177

and white like the meat of a bitten pear. "Loyal to Russia, yes —and I still am. I no longer agree with the line."

"It's no different than it ever was."

"No. But I am. One gets tired. Doubts become more important—Klimenko's Law: as life shortens, misgivings magnify."

"Then I'm sorry you've come to the wrong man."

"I can tell you how the arms come to the V. C. through Cambodia," Klimenko said in a rush of words. "I can tell you what we are going to do with the structure of the Cuban intelligence service. I can give you names you don't have. There's been a change in the funding system—I set it up, I know the banks and the account numbers. Paul, don't be foolish."

Christopher shook his head.

"I know what you think," Klimenko said. "You're worried about your cover. But you have no cover with us. We know about you—we've known for years. When you begin thinking about yourself you lose your profession. I know."

A Vatican guard appeared in the stairway door. "The gallery is closing," he said in Italian.

"Do you want to go down first?" Christopher asked.

Klimenko uttered a little laugh; he was in possession of himself again.

"It's comic how I fit the defector's pattern," he said. "I tell you how I love Russia, and offer you her secrets in exchange for safety. It's no wonder people like you and me exist, Paul—men are so predictable, so easy to use. I know what you'll do next. We'd better set up a meeting now. I don't want to use the telephone anymore."

"Gherman, I won't see you again. I can't help you. What I'm telling you is not technique, it's the truth."

"You don't believe in the quality of the merchandise."

"I care nothing about it one way or the other."

*"Signori,"* the guard said, "you must descend now. The gallery is closing."

Klimenko fluttered his gloved hand impatiently at the guard. He turned his back on the man and again put his face close to Christopher.

"There was an operation in the States last month," he said.

"The code word was Weedkiller. A million dollars went through a certain Swiss bank. An American got the money. A million dollars, Paul. Think about that."

"When?"

"The money went into the bank in Zurich on November 25. It was taken out the next day, just before the bank closed."

"By whom?"

Klimenko looked aside. "I don't tell you that now. When we meet again, when I have assurances—but not on this roof, in the rain."

"You'll have assurances when I have this information," Christopher said.

"Weedkiller?"

"Yes. All of it."

"Tomorrow," Klimenko said. "I can't wait longer than that."

Christopher nodded and smiled at the guard, who had come onto the gallery and was walking toward them with his arms thrown out and his shoulders shrugged to show that he was at the end of his patience.

"All right," Christopher said. "Five o'clock in the morning, in the Protestant cemetery behind the Porta San Paolo. I'll meet you on Shelley's grave."

"Romantic," Klimenko said.

He walked away, leaving Christopher to talk to the remonstrating guard, who might remember him.

### 3

In one of the souvenir shops near Saint Peter's, Christopher bought a postcard of John XXIII. He took a taxi to the main post office in the Piazza San Silvestro and, using the typewriter at the telegraph office, typed the name and address Nsango used in Elisabethville on it. In the message space he typed a Christmas greeting in French and signed the message with three initials. He could speak like a Frenchman, but his handwriting was plainly American.

He dropped the card in the airmail box outside and walked next door to the long-distance telephone office. When the call came through, the clerk put him in Cabin 10 as usual, and he could hear the tap sputtering on the line. Sybille answered.

"You're coming for Christmas!" she said.

"No, I want to invite you down here."

"My dear, we can't. We'd have to charter an extra plane to carry the presents my husband has bought me to make up for his guilty conscience."

"Is he there?"

"At five-thirty? Have you forgotten already what it is to be chained to a machine gun like a poor German private, rat-tatting away for the Fatherland?"

"Will you give him a message? Tell him I'd like to have lunch with him. Write down the date and time carefully—you know what his memory is."

Christopher gave her a formula that would bring Webster, if he understood it, to Rome the following afternoon.

The shops had just reopened and the streets were teeming. Christopher went into a jewelry store and bought an opal ring for Molly. He put it in his pocket and walked into the Rinascente next door; the department store was so crowded that he moved sideways through a pack of unmoving Italians. He went to the top of the store on the escalator and came back down the stairs, leaving by the front entrance. By the time he reached the taxi stand behind the Galleria Colonna across the street, he was certain that he was still alone.

He rang his own doorbell six times, four long and two short. Molly tapped on the inside of the door four times, and he rang again twice. He heard the locks turning and the chain rattling, and Molly opened the door. She held a bottle of champagne in her hand.

"Can you open this without fumbling?" she asked. "It's three thousand lire the bottle, you know."

Sitting on the sofa, Christopher told Molly to close her eyes. He put the opal ring on her finger.

180

"It's beautiful," Molly said. "But aren't opals supposed to bring bad luck?"

"A little superstition will do us good. Gaze into the stone, Molly, and live each day as if it were your last."

"What a wonderful sense of humor you have. Is all this business really a joke to you?"

"Isn't it a joke? Think of it—some little fellow with hate in his heart, deadly dramatic, stalking us in Christmas week. If he exists, he wouldn't even have been told who we are or why he's supposed to kill us. All he asks is a chance to be taken seriously."

"*I* take him seriously."

"Take his gun seriously, and his delusions," Christopher said. "But not him. He's just a man, and a weak and stupid one or he wouldn't let himself be used. We know about him. That cancels his value."

Molly kissed him. She wore no scent or makeup; he had always thought her as clean as a child. Molly did not like the image.

"After this morning," she said, "I go on the premise that anything is permissible. I've been reading your poems again. Explain what you meant by these lines:

> *"In the cave where my father grows,*
> *He sees my son undoubling from a rose."*

"Christ, Molly, I don't know. It rhymed."

"Open up," she said, pointing a finger.

"I loved my father," Christopher said. "He lived his whole life without doing anyone any harm. I think I hoped, if I ever had a child, that it would manage to stay innocent, the way the old man did."

"What was the cave?"

"Silence. He stopped speaking when he was about fifty."

"Stopped speaking? Altogether? Why? Was he mad?"

"My mother thought so," Christopher said. "So did I, for a while. Then I began to read a little more and I realized that he would have been treated as a holy man in most places in the world."

"On the other hand, he could have been mad."

"That's possible. He refused to give evidence."

"Not a word, not a gesture, to the end of his life?"

"Nothing."

"You behave as if you think what he did was rather beautiful."

"Oh, I do," Christopher said.

### 4

Christopher heated milk in the dark kitchen and drank a cup of cocoa before he woke Molly so that she could lock the door after him. She had slept naked and he embraced her long body, still warm from the blankets. He stood in the hall until he heard all the locks fall into place.

It took him ten minutes to inspect his car. It was still dark and he had no flashlight. He felt the motor with his hands and lay on his back on the cold cobblestones and ran his fingers over the frame. The car had been standing in the rain for a week and the engine started reluctantly.

Christopher drove up the Tiber, crossed it on the Ponte Milvio where Constantine had seen the sign of the Cross, and came down the opposite bank. The streets were empty. When he parked the car and walked into the cemetery, there was enough light to see the tips of the cypresses against a sky filled with sailing clouds.

He walked on the grass among the headstones to avoid the noise of his footsteps on the gravel pathways.

At precisely five o'clock, Klimenko, wrapped in his long overcoat, emerged from a row of cypresses. The Russian walked without hesitation to Shelley's grave, and Christopher thought again about Klimenko's tendency to make mistakes: he must have come to the cemetery the evening before and marked the spot.

"Good morning, Paul."

"Gherman. Did you case this place last night?"

"Why?"

"You knew right where to find Shelley."

"I came earlier this morning. No one has picked me up."

Klimenko lifted his feet, in pointed Italian shoes, one after the other out of the wet grass. "Nevertheless, I'd like to get under cover as soon as possible," he said. "All this standing about in the open isn't good."

"That grave over there is where Edward John Trelawny is buried," Christopher said. "He snatched Shelley's heart out of his funeral pyre on the beach at Viareggio. Later Trelawny was a secret agent in Greece with Byron. He thought Byron was a romantic amateur."

"Dung," Klimenko said. "Let's go over to the trees." In shadow, surrounded by the straight stems of the cypresses, Klimenko seemed more at ease. "What arrangements have you made?" he asked.

"If what you have is valuable, I can hand you over to someone this afternoon. They'll tell you what to expect."

"What will that be, roughly?"

"Safe transportation to the States, debriefing, a place to stay until you're ready to surface."

"I don't want money," Klimenko said. "That has to be made plain. No money."

"All right, I'll tell them. What do you have with you?"

"Your interest was aroused by Weedkiller. I've brought you something."

Klimenko removed his hat and turned out the sweatband. He handed Christopher three small photographs and a slip of paper with a series of numbers and letters written on it in red ink. The photographs showed two men in dark American suits and white shirts crossing a sidewalk. One of the men carried a large attaché case. The cameraman had been sitting in a car: the angle of the door showed in a corner of the picture. The faces were very clear.

"What bank in Zurich is the account number for?" Christopher asked.

"Dolder und Co., in the Bleicherweg. It's a small bank. This was a one-time usage."

"Who are these people?" Christopher held up the clearest photograph.

"The men who made the withdrawal. They spoke American English."

"Names, Gherman."

Klimenko shrugged. "They were couriers. The names they used on the hotel register were Anthony Rugged and Ronald Prince."

"Rugged and Prince? Come on, Gherman."

Klimenko reached into his hat and handed Christopher photocopies of two Swiss hotel registration cards. "The cards are genuine," he said. "What do names like that suggest to you?"

"Clumsy Americanization." Christopher looked again at the men in the photograph; they had dark, closed faces; one man's mouth was open, as if he had been chewing gum. "Probably Ruggieri and Principi originally."

"Something like that. I saw the passports they handed in at the hotel—genuine. Their names are Rugged and Prince."

"What was the million dollars for?"

"I don't know. I carried it from Stockholm. It was brought to me from Moscow by the head of my section. I made the deposit, and my instructions were to put the money in the account and leave Zurich at once. Center wanted no surveillance on the messengers."

"Why not? Is that your standard procedure?"

"No. Do you want me to explain the whole system now? Briefly, this is the only cash transaction in any amount I've ever handled where no receipt was required. I couldn't believe the irregularity of it."

"Why would they do it this way? A million dollars."

"Obviously security was more important than money. It was a very tight operation."

"You must have been given a deposit slip."

"No—they wanted no paper of any kind. Not even in the files at No. 2 Ulitza Dzerzhinskogo." Klimenko smiled bleakly when Christopher did not react to the address of KGB headquarters, spoken aloud.

"What was the withdrawal code?" Christopher asked.

"Also spoken, not written. To make a withdrawal, one cited the number of the account and gave the codeword *tortora*, which means 'dove' in Italian."

"Why Italian?"

"I'll come to that—it was an insecure code, there's a clue in it. But you know how incautious these administrators can be."

"Who accepted the money at the bank?"

"One of the directors, Herr Wegel."

"Where is his office?"

"Second floor, extreme northwest corner of the building. His name is on the door."

"Could you sketch the layout of the office from memory?"

"Yes," Klimenko said.

He produced a notebook and a pen and made a quick sketch, resting the pad on a gravestone as he drew.

"What's this?" Christopher asked, pointing to a scribbled feature on one side of the sketch.

"A fireplace," Klimenko said. "Herr Wegel had a coal fire going—he made a joke about being an unthrifty Swiss. I remember everything. I was worried about the lack of documentation."

"So you decided to take some pictures and ask some questions?"

"Yes. I'd already decided not to go back. I thought the information might be useful."

"Why didn't you just take the million and run?"

"Where to? Mars? Besides, Paul, to steal official money? Why should I do such a thing? What would they think?"

Klimenko still held his hat in his hand. Astonishment drew wrinkles on his bald head: he could betray his service and his country, but he could not bear that his colleagues should think him a thief.

"This is an intriguing little mystery," Christopher said, "but I don't see why it should interest us. It's incomplete. All you've given me is evidence of a big cash transfer and a couple of photographs. The rest is not even speculation."

"I can speculate, if you like."

Christopher waited.

"In the fifties, as you know, I was at the UN under deep cover as a Tass correspondent," Klimenko said. "Mostly I handled Latin Americans—they're easy, because they like women. Sometimes an African. My targets were all non-American, except one. I had a primary assignment targeted on a certain American group. The Latinos and the blacks were make-work. The American target was very, very difficult. I only made the recruitment three months before I was posted to Western Europe."

"And you handed over the American asset when you left New York in 1956?"

"No, there was no handing over. I made the recruitment and told the man to go fictitious until we made contact again. It wasn't really a recruitment. I didn't tell him anything about his employers. We didn't have him under discipline. He was an American patriot, he would have shot me if he had known I was a dirty Communist spy."

"What did you tell him?"

"That I represented a group in Belgium that might need work done in America. That my name was Blanchard. That the fee would be high. That he might not hear from us for years, but when he did, we'd expect action in whatever period of time we specified. I told him it might be as short a period as twenty-four hours."

"How did you bind the recruitment?"

"I gave him one hundred thousand dollars as a retainer. We wanted him to know we were serious."

"How did you set up the future contact?"

"Telegram and meeting. I rented a safe house in Chicago and put two unwitting people in it. The agent had the address. When he got a telegram from Naples saying, in Italian, that his uncle Giuseppe had died, he was to go to the safe house at 10:18 on the next night after the day of the week mentioned in the telegram as the day of his uncle's death."

"10:18—that sounds authentic," Christopher said. "Why do you people split the clock that way?"

186

Klimenko was annoyed by the digression. "It's just technique, it's supposed to discipline agents. In czarist days no one could tell time in Russia. After the revolution, people were shot for being late. It was part of the pattern of changing everything, making a new society."

"Who was the agent?"

"I told you it was a difficult target," Klimenko said. "It took me three years to make contact. I wasted time. I should have realized their security is almost the same as ours. All clandestine organizations are more or less alike. When I did, I went in with almost no trouble, after I'd established my cover with them."

"Who?"

"Franco Piccioni. He's called Frankie Pigeon."

"What is he?"

Klimenko laughed. "You have lived abroad for a long time, Paul. Think. What would someone called Frankie Pigeon be?"

"Mafia."

"Yes, Chicago. Frankie is an important American."

"But why? What would you need with him? You've got all the guns you need."

"You never have all the guns you might need. You know how it is. One of the *bolshoy chirey* has an idea—do you know what that phrase means? The big boils—that's what we call our senior officers, as if they will burst at any moment. It tells you something about the KGB. Anyway, someone had an idea in Moscow. I carried it out in the field. It was a contingency plan. Maybe someday they'd need a clean killing in the States. Then they'd have a man."

"But it was insecure."

"The Mafia is insecure? No one has ever convicted Frankie Pigeon of anything. It was compartmented very tightly. Frankie didn't know who we were. He likes money, a little on the side. It wasn't easy to find a man like Frankie—most of these gangsters won't deal with outsiders."

"How often did you use him?"

"Never, unless we used him last month. The idea all along was to employ him on a one-time basis against a target we couldn't reach. He'll never be used again."

Klimenko was shivering violently, and Christopher felt the cold seeping through his own raincoat.

"Really, we must get under cover," Klimenko said. "It's getting light."

"What was Pigeon used for?"

"That I don't know. But consider the sum involved. Consider the date."

"I have," Christopher said.

"I can give you a piece of hard information, Paul. Frankie Pigeon is a sentimental man. He always spends the twelve days of Christmas in the village of Calabria where he was born. He brings his wife and children with him on Christmas Eve and stays until January 7. I can show you on a map where he'll be."

"You can show me in the car," Christopher said.

Sitting in the front seat beside Christopher, Klimenko drew a sketch of the roads leading to Frankie Pigeon's house in the hills above Catanzaro, on the toe of the Italian boot. He handed it to Christopher.

"He takes two men with him," he said. "I don't know what their security arrangements are. He likes to hunt rabbits in the early morning and talk with the farmers in the evening. He goes for walks before dinner."

"I thought you said you didn't keep in touch."

"I kept myself informed."

"Is there anything else about this man Pigeon—as a person, I mean?"

"The weakness?" Klimenko said. "He's a snob—he's been bilked of thousands by genealogists attempting to prove that his mother's family, the Cerruti, are bourgeoisie from the north of Italy; but all the Cerruti are Sicilian from way back, shepherds and shoemakers. That's of no use to you."

"Then tell me something that is useful."

"Frankie Pigeon is a hypochondriac. He's morbid about germs—washes his hands all the time. He has a servant who spreads sterilized towels over the floor for him to walk on in hotels. He boils his coins before he touches them, won't handle paper money at all because of the danger of disease. You recognize the pathology—it's common enough in murderers."

The bleak shape of Monte Testaccio loomed above the car, with a cross mounted at its summit. "What's the name of that hill?" Klimenko asked.

Christopher told him. "It's made entirely of pottery—the jugs the ancient Romans used to transport wheat and honey from the eastern Mediterranean. It will appeal to your Leninist sense of irony that the Monte Testaccio, a dump, is the only remaining trace of the common people of the Roman Empire."

Klimenko laughed, coughed, and covered his mouth. "What are the arrangements?" he asked.

Christopher gave him an address and a key. "Be ready at five o'clock, precisely on the hour. The man who comes will say his name is Edward Trelawny. You'll reply, 'Do you still have Shelley's heart?' "

"Almost twelve hours. Can't it be sooner?"

"No. One last thing, Gherman—don't talk to anyone else about Frankie Pigeon for fourteen days. Then you can spill it."

Klimenko was swiveling his head, watching the approaches to the car.

"Do you understand?"

"Yes. I'll tell your friends on January 6. There'll be no trouble filling the time with other things, Paul."


## 5

Christopher began to talk while Molly was still in the room. Tom Webster gave her a cold stare and held up his palm.

Molly smiled and said, "Tell me the etiquette, Mr. Webster."

"Tom would feel more comfortable if you went into the bedroom and read a book," Christopher said.

When the door had closed behind Molly, Webster said, "What does she know?"

"That I'm a retired agent. She had to know what she was involved in, so I told her. She took the call from Klimenko, but she doesn't know his name or what he is."

"Klimenko?"

"That's what I have for you, Tom—Gherman Klimenko. He wants to defect."

"He's in Rome?"

"Yes, I met him twice, last night and this morning. You can pick him up at five o'clock."

"Why does he want to come across?"

Christopher shrugged. "He's pleading ideological disillusionment. I think he's just tired of the life, the way they usually are. Even Klimenko feels his motives are a little peculiar. He doesn't want to be offered money."

Webster stood up and looked at his watch. The phonograph was playing Molly's new love songs at full volume and Christopher had to strain to hear Webster's voice.

"Where is Klimenko?"

"In a minute, Tom. There are some things I need."

"You're bargaining with me?"

"No," Christopher said. "I'm going to ask a favor. You can have Klimenko whether you help me or not. What would I do with him?"

Webster sat down again and peeled the cellophane from a cigar. He watched Christopher through the flame of the match. "Wolkowicz sent a cable on your doings in Saigon," he said. "He sent somebody out to that church you visited—the cellar is full of opium."

"Is it? Well, that's a dividend for Wolkowicz."

"Like Klimenko is my dividend? For a retiree you're pretty active."

"I'm like a reformed tart," Christopher said. "People just won't believe I don't enjoy it anymore."

"You still won't tell me what you're up to? Wolkowicz is in a tizzy out there, and it's going to communicate."

"I'll be finished soon. Tom, I've gone as far as I can go alone on this. I need some support."

"Tell me what you're after, and you've got all the support you can use."

"No."

"Then no support."

"Okay, Tom," Christopher said, with no inflection in his voice. "Klimenko's at 6 piazza Oratorio, second floor. The name on the door is Busotti."

"What's that place?"

"It's a *pied à terre* Cathy had for herself. She gave me the keys when she left—there was a paid-up three-year lease."

"What does Klimenko expect?"

"All I gave him was a recognition code. Tell him your name is Edward Trelawny when you pick him up. He'll reply, 'Do you still have Shelley's heart?' He expects you at five." Christopher handed Webster a key. "You'd better knock before entering," he said. "He's nervous."

Webster stabbed the ashtray with his cigar, breaking it in half. "Let me ask you this—does this operation of yours have anything to do with the United States of America?"

"Yes."

"Will you tell me about it when it's all over? Have you told Patchen, or anybody, so that the file will be tidy if you get your brains blown out?"

"After it's over, I'll tell you if I can, Tom. Patchen knows. If I can't tell you, try him."

"Then you *are* working?"

"Not for the outfit, Tom. If you help me, you put your ass in hazard."

Webster breathed loudly through his nose, attempting to keep his patience. "What do you need?"

"I want you to take Molly back to Paris with you and keep her off the streets until New Year's Eve. She can stay with Sybille or you can put her in a safe house, but I want her covered twenty-four hours a day."

"Why is that necessary?"

"They've threatened her. I can't leave her alone—she has no idea how to protect herself."

"All right. Sybille and I are going to Zermatt for the holidays. We can take your girl along."

"Second," Christopher said, "I want you to fix it up with the Rome station so that I can use their villa on the via Flaminia for

191

a week, beginning day after tomorrow. It has to be the villa—I don't want any other safe house. Third, I need the stuff on this list by tomorrow night. It can be left in the villa."

Webster read the list and frowned. "*You* want weapons?" he said.

"Yes."

"All that stuff in Saigon must have shaken you up," Webster said.

"Parts of it did. Can you do all that?"

Webster ran his finger down the list. He said, "I think so. Rome will get credit for Klimenko—they won't be in a mood to deny you anything."

"You don't have to say the villa and the weapons are for me. Find out how to turn off the microphones."

Webster put on his coat. He opened his attaché case and held up a nine-millimeter Walther pistol. "Do you want this until I get back?"

"No. I'm going to stay inside."

Webster balanced the flat automatic on his palm, then put it in his pocket. "Look for me about ten," he said. "I may want to sleep here—Molly and I can get an early start in the morning."

Webster started to close the briefcase, then snapped his fingers and reached inside it for a copy of *France-Soir,* folded to the crime page. He handed Christopher the newspaper, tapping a small item with his forefinger. "I almost forgot to show you this," he said.

Christopher read the item:

### DEATH OF A CRIMINAL

About eleven o'clock last night, police were summoned to the public lavatories near the place Clemenceau to provide assistance to a man who had been found unconscious inside.

The attendant, Mlle. R. Calamier, told the guardians of the peace that the man entered a compartment about 10:15. Shortly thereafter, Mlle. Calamier, who was cleaning the women's portion of the public facility, heard sounds of a struggle through the partition.

It was a few moments later that Mlle. Calamier found the unconscious man, or the man she believed to be unconscious, in the compartment and summoned policemen on duty nearby.

The investigating officers found that the man was, in fact, dead. He had been struck a hard blow on the nape, judo-style. Police suspected at first that it was an affair of perverts.

However, medical examination revealed that the victim had died from a massive overdose of heroin. A portion of the hypodermic needle used to administer the fatal dosage was found in his arm, perhaps broken in the struggle that preceded his death. The police physician was not of the opinion that the deceased was a heroin addict: his body bore none of the usual signs of that habit, apart from the single fresh puncture in the forearm.

The victim was said to be Jean-Claude Gaboni, a Corsican born in Algeria. Gaboni was known to the police as a criminal type involved in the traffic in drugs. An investigation is in progress.

"You see?" Webster said. "Sometimes poetic justice triumphs."

Christopher handed back the newspaper. It had been six days since he had told the Truong toc about Gaboni, three days since the Truong toc had given him Molly's photograph. They were moving no more quickly than he'd thought they could.

"Do you still have Kim's place bugged?" Christopher asked.

"Yes."

"You may hear something about Gaboni on those tapes. If you hear anything about me, or about Molly, I hope you'll let me know."

"We're always a week behind on the logs because of the translation problem. They talk Vietnamese all the time."

"That's terrific," Christopher said.

"Wait a minute," Webster said. "How would Kim know about Gaboni?"

"I told them in Saigon about that mistake with young Khoi in Divonne-les-Bains."

"You told them? Why, for Christ's sake?"

"You have to give something to get something," Christo-

193

pher said. "I wondered if they'd kill on foreign soil and how quickly. Now I know."

Molly packed her suitcases without speaking. She laid Christopher's ski clothes on top of her own in an extra bag. "I suppose there's some remote chance we'll both be alive on New Year's Eve," she said. "If you come to the mountains you'll be properly dressed."

"The worst thing you can do is dramatize," Christopher said. "I have to go away at least twice in the next few days and I can't leave you alone. You'll be all right with Tom and Sybille. They're used to this kind of situation. They know what to do."

"And what *does* one do?"

"Routine precautions," Christopher said. "A doctor working in a cholera epidemic takes the necessary injections, boils his drinking water, burns his clothes. It's the same idea—the play-acting, the secrecy, and the codes, and the loud music so that you can talk in a room that may be bugged—all that is the way agents immunize themselves. They may die anyway, but if they take the proper precautions, the chances are against it."

"All right," Molly said. "But all this business of solving the crime of the century annoys me so. It's an interruption. It's almost Christmas, Paul. I thought we'd be together. I build up these scenes for the two of us in my imagination, and then they don't play."

"I promise you I'll be in Zermatt on New Year's Eve. It's a much better holiday than Christmas."

Molly closed her eyes and put her fingertips on the lids. "I have to be so passive—all our life together I've waited for you to come back, waited for you to feel love, waited for you to speak," she said. "Now I have to wait for you to prevent my dying, and the odd thing is, I'm less concerned about being murdered than about being alone for a week."

"It'll be over very soon."

"I know it will," Molly said. "Help me to get this stuff off the bed. Before I go I'd like to hold the clean part of you between my legs once more."

Webster went ahead of them in another car the next morning. They met him on the road to the airport by the ruins of Ostia Antica. Webster turned his back while they kissed, and watched the road behind them. There was still no sign of danger.

Christopher wondered what the Truong toc was waiting for.

# TEN

## 1

Christopher was alone, and that was his advantage. He controlled the rhythm of the operation. Driving back to Rome along the Ostia road, he calculated that he had eight days of safe time left. He thought it would be enough. It is almost impossible for a national police force to keep track of a single agent who continues to move, if the agent takes elementary precautions. For Christopher's opposition, who dared not go outside their own small circle for help, it was hopeless. They could not know where he was going or what he was doing. Their only chance was to catch Christopher in the open and kill him. He didn't think they would be able to do that.

He parked his car near the railroad station in a no-parking zone. After he had checked his baggage, he called the police and complained that the car was blocking traffic. By the time he made two more phone calls, the police wrecker arrived and towed his car away. He knew it would be under twenty-four-hour guard in the impoundment lot outside the walls of the city. It was the last place the Truong toc's men would look for it.

He phoned the Hertz rental agency in Milan and reserved a car for pickup in the late afternoon. At the telegraph office in the railroad station he sent a money order to a man in Ajaccio with a terse message that reminded him how little his methods differed from Klimenko's; the thought caused him to smile as he handed in the cable form and the money, and the clerk gave him a puzzled look: it was odd that a man, sending news of a brother's death in Christmas week, should look so cheerful.

Finally, Christopher checked the train schedule for Milan again and reserved a first-class seat on the 9:40 express. It was still only 7:30 when he walked out of the terminal and took a cab to the Vatican.

2

Alvaro Urpi had never taken holy orders, but he had come to resemble a monk. He waited for Christopher in a corner of the Vatican library, his broad face still shining with the effect of his morning prayers. Urpi was the son of a Portuguese soldier and a Chinese woman, and his dark features were such a combination of Iberian and Cantonese peasantry that he might have passed in either country as a native. He was twelve, and already sexually corrupted, when the priests took him off the streets of Macao and taught him to read and write. Before he was wenty, the Dominicans discovered his talent for scholarship, and he never for the next forty years lived outside the Church, or wanted to.

Urpi spoke and wrote every known dialect of Chinese. He had all but forgotten Portuguese, however, and when Christopher had brought him a letter from a relative in Macao, Urpi had had to construe it into Latin before he could understand it. Urpi's relative had wanted him to find a place in a nunnery for one of his nieces. The girl had never taken the veil; she went to live with a policeman. But Urpi had rediscovered his family through Christopher.

"Paul," he said, "have you brought me some photographs from Macao? How are they out there?"

"Not this time, Alvaro. I've come to ask a favor."

"Ah."

Urpi moved a stack of books from his desk to the floor, so that he would be able to see Christopher when they sat down. Urpi worked at a carved table, surrounded by battlements of volumes with ideograms stamped on their spines. A great pile of Chinese manuscript, Urpi's lifework, stood in the middle of the desk.

Christopher handed him the dozen strips of paper he had clipped from the borders of Yu Lung's horoscopes.

Urpi examined the calligraphy through a magnifying glass. He wore steel-rimmed eyeglasses pushed up on his forehead, but Christopher had never seen him use them. Urpi was very near-sighted. When he read, he used the magnifying glass and put his face close to the print, giving soft grunts of frustration.

Urpi touched Yu Lung's ideograms with his blunt farmer's fingers. "Lovely work," he said. "A very fine brush."

"Can you translate these for me, Alvaro?"

"Yes, yes," Urpi said, "but it will take some time. These are complex thoughts, very poetically expressed. This man writes a very old Chinese, and he uses Taoist imagery. How odd. What is he?"

"A horoscoper."

Urpi looked up, shocked at the word. "Oh, my, Paul."

"Don't you want to do it?"

"But of course. I didn't know you had these superstitions."

"I haven't. I just want to know what the manuscript says. In great detail."

"It will be difficult to render the spirit, you know. This is a rare idiom. May I have a little time?"

"Three days?"

Urpi looked at the long strips of paper again. "All right. But in the end, it may mean nothing to you. You'd have to know what and whom he was writing about and make deductions, even after it was translated. What language do you want it in?"

"Whatever suits you best, Alvaro."

"Latin is easiest for me—that's what I'm used to, and I have the Latin equivalents for Chinese words already in my mind."

"Latin will be fine."

"Good. The day after Christmas, then. I'll be here from six in the morning, as always. When do you go to Macao again?"

"Not soon, Alvaro. What do you hear from the family?"

"No Christmas message. I thought you might be bringing it to me. It takes me back, you know—I have grand-nephews now who are as old as I was when the Franciscans took me in. I'm sure they're as bad as I was—thieves, liars, full of lust. Ah, well, God is waiting for them."

"I expect so, Alvaro. Please guard those papers well. I'll want them back."

"They're safe here," Urpi said, indicating the thick walls and the slow figures in black that moved among the books. He waved a hand and put his head down among his books and papers, the magnifying glass against his eye.

## 3

Christopher slept on the train, protected by three nuns and a schoolboy who shared his compartment. In Bologna he leaned from the window and bought a sandwich and a bottle of beer from a platform vendor. One of the nuns peeled an orange and handed it to him, with the skin arranged around the fruit like the pointed leaves of a lily. She was young, with a sensual face from which prayer had scrubbed all traces of desire. However, the pretty orange, handed across the compartment as if she were feeding a horse and was wary of its teeth, was as much a gift of flirtation as of charity.

When Christopher arrived in midafternoon, Milan was bathed by the nickled light of the winter sun. He stayed long enough to buy two hundred feet of nylon climbing rope, a dozen pitons and a mountaineering hammer, a good camera with a closeup lens, and a small, powerful floodlamp bulb. Then he collected the car from Hertz, making certain that the trunk contained a set of tire chains.

There was little traffic on Route E–9, the road to Switzerland. The car was pushed toward the edge of the road by gusts of wind, and in Como the water of the lake blew over the jetties. At the Swiss frontier, Christopher was required by the relaxed police to show nothing but the green insurance card for his hired automobile. He inquired at Bellinzona, where the road forked, about the condition of the passes, and was advised to cross the Alps through the Splügen pass, since the higher Saint Gotthard and the Furka were closed.

There had been a heavy snowfall in the mountains, and he pulled off the road and attached the chains. It took him a long time to maneuver among the cars that had lost traction on the switchback road leading to the summit. At the top he got behind a Swiss postal bus, equipped with a snowplow and a sander, and followed it down the other side of the mountains into the valley of the Rhine.

It was ten o'clock when he reached Zurich. He drove through the dim streets, past the leaden Swiss architecture, until he found the hotel he was looking for. It stood in the Talstrasse, in a block whose rooftops led into the Bleicherweg.

After he had looked up Dieter Dimpel's address in the telephone book, he walked along the street until he reached the stone town house that was the bank of Dolder und Co. The bank had a mansard roof, with a steep pitch falling to the eaves but a flat top divided by three tall chimneys. The buildings on either side were twenty feet higher than the bank. Christopher fixed the proportions and the distances in his mind and walked on along the lake shore toward Dimpel's apartment.

Music filtered through the thick door of Dimpel's flat. Christopher placed his palm against its polished wood and felt the tremor of drums and tubas. He rang the bell, set in a brass plate on which Dimpel's name was inscribed in flowing script. There was no response. Christopher pressed the bell again and stepped back from the doorway.

When at last the door swung open, Christopher found himself looking into an entryway lined with timepieces. Grandfather clocks stood in all four corners; wall clocks were arranged edge to edge all around the walls; perpetual-motion clocks stood on the polished surfaces of antique tables. The military music had been turned off. Christopher looked downward and saw Dimpel, so short that the doorknob was above his head.

"What do you wish?" Dimpel asked in Swiss German.

He wore a plum-colored dressing gown and a white ascot. His bare calves were as muscular as a cyclist's. His blond hair was brilliantined and combed flat on his skull. He had the head and face of a normal man, with wary gray eyes and a long broken nose.

"I'm a friend of Major Johnson," Christopher said.

Dimpel showed no reaction to the name except to throw back his shoulders and lift his head so that he looked directly into Christopher's eyes.

"The party-card number was 555," Christopher said.

Dimpel gave a sharp nod and slapped his bare heels together. "The date was June 4, 1943," he replied. "I am somewhat occupied just now. Is it urgent?"

"Yes, but I can come back."

Dimpel ran his eye over his collection of clocks. "Thirty minutes," he said, winked, and closed the door. As Christopher went down the carpeted stairs, he felt the vibration of band music starting up again on Dimpel's phonograph.

Christopher went to a café across the street and drank a cup of hot chocolate. It was beginning to snow, plump flakes drifting through the lamplight that fell from the window of the café. A girl wearing a loden coat and white knee socks emerged from Dimpel's building. She looked up and down the wet street for a taxi, shook her head angrily, and strode off through pools of streetlight. Christopher dropped coins on the table and left the empty café.

All of Dimpel's clocks were striking the hour when the midget opened the door. He took Christopher's coat and went ahead of him through the rooms resounding with chimes and cuckoos. Dimpel now wore a tweed suit with a vest. The red handkerchief in his breast pocket matched his spotted tie.

Dimpel lifted a bottle of brandy from the low table in front of the sofa, showing Christopher the label with an inquiring lift of his eyebrows. Christopher nodded, and Dimpel poured cognac into a large balloon glass. He sat down, pushing himself back into the deep chair by digging his heel into the cushion. His bright eyes followed Christopher's gaze as he noticed the Dürer engravings on the wall, the porcelain collection on the chimneypiece. There were no clocks in the living room.

"So," Dimpel said. "How is Major Johnson these days?"

"Very well. He sends you his best wishes."

Dimpel nodded. "I'm sorry to have sent you away. I'd begun something. It was necessary to finish."

He had stopped speaking in Swiss dialect, and his German was filled with the mushy diphthongs of Bavaria. Dimpel made no sign that he was less than six feet tall, and Christopher very quickly stopped noticing his size.

He asked to use the toilet, and Dimpel showed him down a long hall, switching on the light for him. The walls of the corridor were crowded with framed photographs of unclothed blond girls, all wearing white knee socks; the pictures were expertly lighted and posed. Because there were so many photographs, the effect was chaste, an arabesque of white skin against whiter cloth, spun hair and closed eyes.

Dimpel slid out of his chair and stood up when Christopher returned. He refilled the brandy glasses and, taking his own in both small hands, thrust his nose into the fumes.

"Are you quite happy with the watch business?" Christopher asked.

Dimpel put his head to one side. "Yes, it's been a good business. It was an established shop—the old man who owned it had no children, so it went on the market without difficulty. I carry all the good Swiss marks—Omega, Piccard, Rolex, and so on. Also a good line of clocks. I've always liked timepieces. What are you wearing?"

Christopher pulled back his left sleeve. "A Rolex."

"You're wise to have steel instead of gold—the gold is a waste of money. Your watch will never wear out, but if you should happen to lose it, come and see me. I can save you quite a few francs."

"Thank you."

Dimpel waved a hand; the favor was not worth mentioning.

Christopher put down his glass and Dimpel sat straighter in his chair and composed his face, aware that the small talk was over.

"I wonder if you'd consider a proposal," Christopher said.

"I will *consider* anything."

"This is a matter of some urgency. I'm familiar with your work in Berlin."

"I haven't done that sort of work for a very long time."

"I realize that. Have you lost interest in it altogether?"

"It was more interesting than selling watches, I'll say that. I still climb a little in the summer. Last year I did the Matterhorn—from the Italian side." Dimpel thumped his chest with a forefinger. "Fifty years old."

"I compliment you."

Dimpel decided to stop speaking. He watched Christopher alertly, a look of broad amusement on his face. He flicked his brandy glass with a fingernail and listened to it ring.

"I have a simple job," Christopher said. "I thought you might undertake it."

Dimpel pursed his lips, sipped his cognac, made the glass ring again. "What made you think that?" he asked.

"Johnson's description of the way you worked in Berlin. He thinks you were a genius at what you did."

"What I did was certainly good for Major Johnson. I was much younger in Berlin. Besides, that sort of thing seems stupid once you've stopped doing it. Men like yourself, who go on with it all their lives, find that hard to understand."

"I'll describe the job," Christopher said. "It involves entering a room through a fireplace, opening a file with a simple tumbler lock, photographing documents."

"What building?"

"A bank in Zurich."

Dimpel burst into laughter. He had a deep voice. "A bank? In *Switzerland?*" he cried. "It would be safer to commit sodomy at high noon in the middle of the Bahnhofstrasse."

"It's a test of skill," Christopher said. "However, it can be done, and done cleanly. The security is nothing compared to the headquarters of the GRU in Berlin. Nor are the possible consequences."

"This is not Berlin in 1946."

"No. But, with respect, Herr Dimpel, this operation is incomparably more important than anything you did in Berlin."

Dimpel agitated his cognac glass and again inhaled its fragrance. He seemed deep in thought; then the smile of a man who remembers a pleasure parted his thin lips.

"Let me hear a little more," he said.

Christopher sketched the roof of Dolder und Co. and the adjoining buildings, showing the distances involved. From memory, he reproduced Klimenko's drawing of the interior of the bank director's office.

Dimpel, taking a pair of horn-rimmed reading glasses from his handkerchief pocket, examined the sketches. "What is the access to the roof?" he asked.

Christopher tapped the sketch. "I have a room on the highest floor of this hotel. There's access to the roof by the fire stairs. One crosses the adjoining roof without difficulty. The roof of the bank will give trouble."

"Yes. It's a drop of seven meters from the roof next door, then a climb of what—five meters? On what sort of surface?"

"Copper sheathing."

"Slippery stuff, and it's snowing. Then a vertical climb of four meters to the top of the chimney." Dimpel lifted his cognac and poured the entire contents of the glass into his mouth. "Very challenging," he said.

"I know nothing about the alarm system, nothing about the internal security," Christopher said. "This is a high-risk operation, Herr Dimpel. There may be a night watchman. If there is, he cannot be harmed."

Dimpel folded his spectacles and tapped his front teeth with them. "There is no watchman at Dolder und Co., and certainly no alarms in the chimneys. They're an old-fashioned firm, and the Swiss have faith in locks. It's in their national character."

"Entry has to be made tonight," Christopher said. "The time element is very strict."

Dimpel's clocks struck the half hour, and he gave Christopher a tight-lipped smile full of sly pleasure.

"Why should I do this?" he asked. "Can you explain that to me?"

"I can't think of a single reason, and if I could I wouldn't disclose it to you. There's nothing I can give you, in a material way, that you need. I will say that you're the only man in the world who can do it."

"You're quite right—I have no material needs. Johnson put me beyond the reach of your organization, you know, when he set me up in the watch business. I thought that rather a joke on you people. The British would never have done that, or the Russians."

"Would you have preferred working for them?"

"An agent always works for himself. It's a mental disease, that work. Quite incurable."

The sing-song tone of German sarcasm had crept into Dimpel's voice, and Christopher thought he had failed. Dimpel went to the window and stood on tiptoe to look out. He carried himself erect and all his movements were stylized; he planted his feet firmly on the Chinese carpet, drank from his glass with soldierly precision. Christopher remembered Trevor Hitchcock's description of Dimpel: the midget did have the manners of a field marshal. He clasped his hands behind his back and turned to face Christopher.

"The snow is coming down harder," he said. "Another difficulty."

"Yes, you'd leave tracks on the roof."

"Who would see them? I was thinking of the danger of a fall."

"Then perhaps we'd better talk no more about it," Christopher said. "I've enjoyed meeting you, and the cognac."

He stood up and held out his hand, palm upward, for his

coat. Dimpel looked Christopher up and down and shifted his feet on the carpet.

"One moment," Dimpel said.

He strode out of the room. When he returned he was carrying Christopher's coat and a scuffed, bulging rucksack. He wore a leather trench coat and a woolen cap. He nodded briskly to Christopher and slung the rucksack. They went out together into the snowstorm.

## 4

In Christopher's hotel room, Dimpel changed into climbing clothes and attached crampons to his boots. He inspected the rope Christopher had bought in Milan with great care and tossed the pitons contemptuously onto the bed.

Dimpel put the camera in the chest pocket of his parka, draped a coil of rope over his shoulder, and handed Christopher the extra rope. He ran up the stairs to the hotel roof; once in the open air, he spread his arms and took deep breaths one after the other, exhaling noisily through his nose. Snowflakes gathered in his thick eyebrows. He showed Christopher with gestures how he wanted him to assist.

Christopher, braced at the edge of the roof with the rope belayed around his waist, felt only a slight strain as Dimpel rappelled down the wall of the building. He was lost from sight for a moment, then Christopher saw him on the roof of the bank, running up the steep pitch of the gambrel, his weight thrown into the slope.

Dimpel reached the top, swung his arms for balance, and walked across the roof, leaving footprints behind him. At the base of the farthest chimney, he uncoiled the second rope and cast it toward the top of the chimney; Christopher heard the faint rattle of the grappling hook. Dimpel tugged on the rope and walked up the bricks, his body nearly horizontal. He sat on the top for a moment with the snow drifting down around him before he adjusted the grappling hook, seized the rope, and dropped out of sight down the chimney.

While Dimpel was inside the bank the storm worsened. Christopher, waiting on the roof, was unable to see the street six stories below, and he glimpsed Dimpel's climbing figure only faintly when it emerged from the chimney and came back across the housetops.

Dimpel didn't speak until they were inside Christopher's hotel room again. Dimpel's face was blackened like a commando's as a result of his passage through the chimney and he smelled of coal smoke. He bent his arm with a brisk movement and looked at the large sporting watch on his wrist.

"Thirty-one minutes exactly, from start to finish," he said with a satisfied nod. He dropped the coil of rope on the floor and handed Christopher the camera.

Dimpel stripped off his climbing clothes and stuffed them in his rucksack. Thick blond hair grew on his chest and shoulders, and his skin, pink and healthy from many baths, shone with sweat. He went into the bathroom, and Christopher heard him clearing his throat and spitting, and then the rush of the shower.

When Dimpel came out again, his hair was slicked down and he had wrapped a towel around his waist. He put on his street clothes, brushing imaginary specks of dust from each garment, and tied his silk necktie with great attention to the size of the knot.

"There were five documents in the file you wanted," he said. "A deposit slip, a memorandum of identity, an explanation of the withdrawal code, a withdrawal slip, and a police report. I took four photographs of each, as there was no brace for the camera and the light was not good. If the film was fast enough, you'll have readable copies."

"Thank you," Christopher said. "That was very quick work."

"It was simple work, and therefore very dirty." Dimpel looked at his fingernails, took a gold penknife from his pocket, and began to clean them.

"The matter of payment," Christopher said. "How do you want that arranged?"

"I have no need for money." Dimpel closed his penknife

and threw his head back with a snap. "Do you have German blood?" he asked.

"Half, from my mother."

"I thought so. You look German. You have the manner, the confidence, of a German officer."

Christopher had never been paid a compliment that he desired less. He made no reply. What Dimpel said next he said in his ordinary brisk tone of voice.

"Major Johnson may have told you about my early connection with Adolf Hitler."

"Yes."

"You're hiding a smile. I see you know the entire story. No, don't protest—I understand. I've thought much about that man. He was an obvious fool. Yet he was permitted to make history—destroy Germany. I mean its architecture, which was a work of art, and its name."

Dimpel paused and watched Christopher's face, as if awaiting a reaction to some startling bit of information.

"What I would like from you," he said, "is something from your government's collection of booty that belonged personally to Adolf Hitler."

Christopher saw a glint of humor in the calm depths of Dimpel's eyes. "Have you any particular item in mind?" he asked.

"Something that he wore or a personal document. Not so large that it will not fit into a good-sized picture frame."

"You're going to hang it on your wall?"

Dimpel was grinning now. "Yes, in a gold frame with a light shining on it. After I've used it to wipe my behind."

Dimpel picked up his rucksack, set his cap on his head, shook hands firmly, and left.

5

Christopher started south again at first light, and he was in Rome by early evening. The city was loud with the rough music of the bagpipers.

What had been snow in Zurich was rain in Rome. Christopher turned into the slow traffic along the Lungotevere; the windows of his car were steamed and the wipers could barely keep the windshield clear of the sluicing rain. There were two Vietnamese in his street, one at either end of the block in which his apartment building stood. One of them had draped a sodden newspaper over his head. A third Vietnamese sat in a black Citroën with Paris plates, smoking a cigarette. The eyes of all three men were fixed on the entrance to Christopher's apartment, and even if they had been able to see into his car they would not have recognized him driving by in the snarl of rush-hour traffic.

# ELEVEN

1

When Christopher showed Stavros Glavanis the room in which
he would break Frankie Pigeon, the Greek ran his palm over
its cold sweating walls and said, "If you're going to do this to
him, you may as well kill him."

"You have to bring him here in perfect condition and get
the information without putting a mark on him," Christopher
said.

"These methods are not your usual ones. Are you growing
more realistic?"

"It's a special case," Christopher said. "This man can't be
moved by money, and he's too afraid of his own people to talk,
unless you make him more afraid of you."

Glavanis looked around the bare circular room again. He
shrugged. "It may be possible," he said. "It depends on the man

—it always depends on the man, and how quickly you get to know him."

Glavanis had had trouble finding the second operative Christopher had asked for in his telegram, and more trouble getting out of Corsica during Christmas week, when the boats and planes were fully booked with foreigners on holiday. His standing instructions were to make contact on any even-numbered hour between six in the evening and midnight. Christopher had gone to the meeting place on the Capitoline Hill three times before Glavanis and his companion finally appeared.

By ten o'clock, Christopher was tired, and the wine he had drunk at dinner had given him a headache. At four minutes after the hour, he saw the tall figure of Glavanis, accompanied by a shorter man, climbing the steep street that led from the ruins of the Forum. Christopher, standing in the shadows, snapped his fingers twice and Glavanis came straight for the sound.

He embraced Christopher. "You remember Jan Eycken," he said.

Christopher nodded and held out his hand. Eycken hesitated for a fraction of a second. He did not like to display his hands: he had lost both thumbs when he fell into the hands of an Algerian rebel unit in the Kabylia, and he had spent his life among simple men who hated deformity.

Glavanis and Eycken had been comrades in the Foreign Legion—Glavanis a sergeant-major, Eycken one of his corporals. Glavanis was amused by Eycken's stolid Flemish self-absorption. Eycken had been a younger child than Glavanis during the Second World War, and he had seen action only in colonial wars. He thought Glavanis looked down on him because he had never killed a white man. Glavanis, wiping mirth from his eyes, had told Christopher that he planted this notion in Eycken's mind because it made Eycken very brave when they went into action together.

Stavros Glavanis came from a Macedonian village on the Greek side of the frontier with Yugoslavia, and he had been killing men in battle since the age of thirteen. His father had been a follower of General Napoleon Zervas, and when he went with Zervas's EDES partisans in 1941, he took Stavros, his oldest son, with him. They remained in the field, ambushing Germans and later fighting Greek Communists in the mountains, until the end of the Greek civil war in 1949.

When they returned to their village, they found that Stavros's mother was dead, and his six brothers and sisters, and most of his cousins, had been taken across the frontier and on to Russia by the Communists, to be trained for some future Greek revolution. Stavros's father gave him his gold ring and told him to marry and breed new children. Then, carrying his British rifle, he set off through the woods to the east. Stavros never saw him again.

Stavros married an Athenian girl, and found that he had married her too quickly: she cuckolded him within the year with an old lover who had fought against Stavros as a member of the Communist ELAS partisans. Stavros killed his wife's lover, shipped on a freighter to Marseilles, and joined the Foreign Legion. Christopher met him in Indochina, where he was a sergeant leading a platoon composed mostly of Germans. Because of Stavros's long experience as a guerrilla fighter and his personal enthusiasm for killing Communists, his platoon was one of the most successful units operating in the Indochina War on the French side.

After Dienbienphu, Glavanis went directly to Algeria, where he was shot in the chest by an Arab terrorist while sitting in a café in Oran. He lost a lung as a result of his wound, and Christopher recruited him a week after he was invalided out of the Legion, offering him the prospect of going into action against Communists.

In Vietnam and later in Algeria, during periods when he was recovering from wounds, Glavanis had headed military interrogation teams. He knew a great deal about the natives who had passed through his hands; because the French had lost both wars, many of the people they had tortured were now generals or government ministers or high party officials.

Christopher had often used Glavanis as a source of information, and once or twice as a courier. But he had never until now needed him for his primary skills.

Christopher took Glavanis and Eycken to his rented car, parked in a dark street by the Forum. Glavanis stood for a moment, gazing at the broken columns. "I miss Greece," he said, "these stones remind me." He lifted his hips off the seat when he got into the front seat, and reached into his pocket. Christopher opened the small box Glavanis handed him and found a gold-plated fingernail clipper inside: the Greek never called on a friend without bringing a gift.

When they drove through the gates of the villa on the Via Flaminia, Glavanis said, "My God, Paul—what is this place?"

The villa, a long, towered building, lay at the end of a drive that passed between perfectly matched cypresses. Gravel walks led through the grounds, past statues and fountains, hedges and fish ponds, flower beds and water jokes—a passerby could be soaked by a hidden jet in any of a dozen places. There was one stretch of walk where fountains formed an arch over the path for a distance of a hundred meters, so cleverly designed that not a drop of water fell on anyone who walked beneath the spray.

"It belonged to some Roman nobility, and afterward to one of Mussolini's mistresses," Christopher said. "Late in the war, the SS used it as an interrogation center for important prisoners —after that, nobody wanted it."

The Rome station had furnished the villa with black leather furniture, antique tables left behind by the Italians and the Germans, and thick carpeting that absorbed the echoes thrown out by the tile floors. An elaborate alarm system that covered the grounds with electric eyes and the interior of the villa with devices that sensed the heat of an intruder's body had been installed. The bar was stocked with the national drinks of five continents and the library contained books in twenty languages. There was a photographic dark room, a small cinema, a gymnasium. The villa was a place for new agents to be trained and old ones to rest.

Webster had arranged for the young officers who guarded the place to be sent away on Christmas leave. The old-fashioned German microphones implanted in the plaster had been replaced with voice-activated transmitters, and Christopher did not for a moment believe that he had been told where all the bugs were located. He took Glavanis and Eycken outside to explain what he wanted from them.

Glavanis asked only one question: "Is this man a Communist?"

"He works for them," Christopher said.

Glavanis, standing at the bar, grinned and drank from a glass of ouzo, taking in a noisy breath as he swallowed.

Eycken, who had the face of a suspicious shopkeeper, raised immediate objections. Christopher listened, knowing that it was Glavanis who would set a price on the services of his friend.

"The time element is very short," Eycken said. "We have to drive all the way to Calabria, take this man out of a guarded house, drive all the way back to Rome. And break him. All in three days or less. What if he doesn't break?"

"He'll break," Christopher said.

He motioned for Glavanis and Eycken to follow him. Glavanis refilled his glass from the bottle of ouzo he had carried into the garden. The three men strolled around the villa, gravel crunching beneath their shoes. In a thick grove of cypresses, a hundred yards behind the villa, Christopher knelt and pulled a lever hidden in a concrete chamber at the base of a tree.

A spring-loaded steel manhole cover opened at their feet. Christopher shone his flashlight into the hole. Twelve feet below, the round beam of the electric torch moved over a damp stone floor.

"Eycken, get in," Christopher said.

Eycken gave him a hard look and stepped back from the edge. He didn't move his hands, but Christopher felt his tension.

"It's all right," Christopher said. "It's just an experiment."

Glavanis nodded; Eycken held out his hand for the flashlight. Christopher gave it to him, and he put it in his pocket and swung athletically into the hole, hanging for a moment by his fingertips before he dropped into the darkness.

"I'm going to close the hatch," Christopher said. "You'll see us again in five minutes."

214

He turned Glavanis around and showed him that it was impossible to see the villa from where they stood. The house stood in open countryside, and there was no noise and no light.

They went back into the villa. Christopher led Glavanis down the cellar stairs, and then into a long concrete tunnel with strong light bulbs screwed into the ceiling. At the end of the tunnel, Christopher stopped before a rusted steel door.

"Eycken has been in there alone for five minutes, with a flashlight," Christopher said. "Look at his face, and use your imagination."

He threw a light switch and pulled open the door. Eycken was standing against the far wall of a bare round concrete room ten feet in diameter. The walls sloped inward like the sides of an inverted funnel. Eycken shielded his eyes from the blinding reflection of high-intensity lights. The walls were painted with white reflective paint.

Eycken held a heavy revolver in his hand. Glavanis stepped between him and Christopher. "It was a joke, Jan," he said.

Eycken swore, a long elaborate Arab curse, and moved around to the door before he put his gun away.

Christopher explained that the Germans had built the room. During the war they would bring a man through the dark fields, strip him, and drop him through the trapdoor. He would be left naked in the dark room, sometimes with a dozen rats, sometimes with music or recorded human screams playing at high volume through the loudspeakers in the wall. The door was faced with concrete and cleverly concealed; it was impossible to tell that it was there by sense of touch. When, after two or three days, the wall opened and the lights went on, and the prisoner—already half-crazed by thirst and the rats and the loudspeakers—saw a German in an SS uniform standing in the door, it had a certain effect.

"Is that how we begin with this Communist?" Glavanis asked.

"Yes. You may not have to do much more. He's used to being protected, being invulnerable. He thinks of himself as a dangerous man. That's one of the pressure points—he won't know how to handle being helpless. Also, he's a hypochondriac. He's going to get very cold in here with no clothes on, and he's going to be worried about pneumonia."

"Can we use water?"

"If you have to," Christopher said. "I don't know that it'll be necessary. I have something to keep him quiet when you take him, and when we let him go."

"You're going to let him go?"

"Yes. Don't let him see your faces at all. You'll have to tape his eyes as soon as you take him."

Eycken smiled, his white teeth glittering beneath the hair on his lips. "I'd better shave," he said.

"Afterward would be better," Christopher said. "I want you to start in the morning. You fly to Reggio and pick up the car there. Stavros, you still have the papers I gave you? The car is booked in that name, at Auto Maggiore at the airport."

"Yes, I still have the papers. What information does this type have, that he's worth all this trouble?"

"If I knew, we wouldn't have to go through all this," Christopher said. "Come on upstairs. I'll explain the operation."

Christopher showed them the maps he had drawn on the basis of Klimenko's description of the house in Calabria, and gave them photographs of Frankie Pigeon.

"It would be better to know more about his habits," Glavanis said.

"I agree, but there's no time. You have to have him back here before first light day after tomorrow. You'll have to lie up and watch, and take the first chance you get."

"What about the bodyguards? Can we deal with them as we think best?"

Christopher handed Glavanis a small briefcase. Glavanis removed two .22 caliber pistols from it and looked quizzically at Christopher. He pushed a cartridge from one of the clips; there was no lead bullet as in ordinary ammunition. The nose of the cartridge case was pinched shut. "What's this supposed to be?" Glavanis asked.

"It's birdshot. You can't kill with it, but if you fire into the

216

face from close range, you produce a lot of pain and shock. You want to immobilize these people for an hour or two, that's all."

"There's a better method of immobilizing people," Eycken said.

"No doubt. But this isn't a war zone, Eycken. If you kill somebody, you'll have *carabinieri* all over you before you get to Naples."

Eycken slid a clip loaded with the birdshot cartridges into one of the pistols and felt the weight of the weapon, holding it at arm's length. "I suppose it'll work if you get close enough and hit the eyes," he said.

"There's no need to hit the eyes."

Glavanis, seeing the contempt in Eycken's face, grinned broadly. "Jan isn't used to working with a man who has scruples," he said.

Glavanis sorted out the other things in the briefcase: two airplane tickets to Reggio, an envelope fat with dirty thousand-lire notes, bandage and tape, handcuffs, a hundred feet of light manila rope, a pair of binoculars, a bottle of pills. He shook the bottle and asked a question.

"Seconal," Christopher said. "Give him two or three if he's conscious when you take him. It should take seven or eight hours to drive back to Rome. He'll sleep most of the way in the trunk. Don't give him too much Seconal. We want him awake when you put him in the hole."

Glavanis prodded the contents of the briefcase with his blunt fingers. He nodded in satisfaction. "Everything we'll need is there," he said. "We'd better sleep now." Before he went upstairs, he winked at Christopher. "Do you know what day it is tomorrow?"

"Christmas."

Glavanis nodded rapidly and uttered a short, sharp laugh.

While Glavanis and Eycken slept, Christopher tested the loudspeaker in the interrogation room and prepared the other things that would be needed there.

Then he spent an hour in the darkroom. Dieter Dimpel's photographs of the *tortora* file at Dolder und Co. were in perfect focus. Christopher ran the negatives through the enlarger, but made no prints. The bank records verified Klimenko's story in every detail. There was one bit of information that Klimenko had omitted. It was an important fact, and Christopher concluded that Klimenko could not have known about it. If word of it ever got back to Moscow, big boils would burst all over the KGB.

At five in the morning, Christopher woke Eycken and Glavanis and cooked breakfast for them. He drove them to the airport, and before Glavanis got out of the car he kissed Christopher on the cheek in the Greek style. "Happy Christmas," he said.

Christopher drove back to the villa on country roads that wound through muddy winter fields, put the car in the garage, and fell into a deep sleep in a locked room.

2

When he woke it was dark again. Although the furnace was operating, the huge marble living room was cold, and he started a fire of olive wood in the grate and sat before it, reading the short stories of Somerset Maugham. He was most of the way through the thick Penguin paperback when headlights flashed across the ceiling and he heard tires turning on the gravel drive. The car, a dusty blue Fiat 2300 with a Naples number, blinked its lights and continued to the back of the villa. Christopher heard the car doors slam and the hollow double ring of the trapdoor being opened and closed.

Glavanis and Eycken were hungry. They still wore the ill-fitting peasant corduroys that Christopher had given them. Eycken drank three glasses of neat gin, one after the other, and pushed the bottle across the table.

"It's *cold,*" Glavanis said. "What I want is brandy."

Eycken went into the sitting room and came back with a new bottle of Martell. Glavanis drank from the bottle.

When there was food before him, Glavanis said, "It was easy, Paul."

Glavanis and Eycken had hidden the car in the woods and

218

waited until Frankie Pigeon came out at sunset for his evening walk across the fields. Two bodyguards, young men in American suits, walked beside him. Glavanis and Eycken shadowed Pigeon and his men, keeping inside the edge of the woods, until they were well out of sight of the house.

"We just stepped out and walked right up to them, all smiles," Glavanis said.

Pigeon smiled at them. Glavanis and Eycken, dark and grinning, wearing work-stained clothes, were the sort of men Pigeon liked to talk to. When one of the bodyguards put a hand on the gun in his pocket, Pigeon gave him a playful backhanded slap on the arm. Pigeon wished Glavanis and Eycken Merry Christmas. In his blurred Italian, he called out a question: What did the sky say? Was it going to rain on Christmas?

"We kept on smiling and shrugging," Glavanis said, "and on the count of ten—Jan and I worked out the drill beforehand —we shot the bodyguards in the face with your .22 birdshot. There was practically no noise."

Eycken reached into his mouth, extracted a piece of steak gristle, and placed it on the edge of his plate. "I apologize to you," he said to Christopher. "That's a very good weapon. They just fell over backward and went out like a light. It draws a hell of a lot of blood. They must have thought they were dead."

"One shot is enough, usually," Christopher said.

"We gave them six rounds apiece," Glavanis said. "They'll be paying for girls from now on."

"Don't worry," Eycken said, "they'll live."

"What about the man?" Christopher asked. He'd given them no name for Pigeon.

"He tried to run," Glavanis said. "I had to put some birdshot in his leg, but he's all right. I treated the wound."

"He saw your faces?"

Glavanis waved away the question. "For a few seconds. He won't remember. I've never seen a man so astonished. When I gave him the pills I held a gun against his head. He was shaking so badly one of the capsules fell out of his mouth. When I picked it up it was *dry*, Paul—he couldn't make saliva."

"Is he blindfolded now?"

219

"No, but he's wearing the handcuffs. There was nobody behind us on the autostrada. No one saw the car. The only problem is the police, and it's a holiday."

"They won't call the police," Christopher said. "You may as well get some sleep. You can start in on him in twelve hours. That ought to be enough."

Christopher went downstairs and checked the locks on the steel door. Through the peephole he could hear Frankie Pigeon breathing, heavily and quickly, and the shuffle of his bare feet over the stone floor. Christopher had transferred some electronic music from a record to a tape, playing the record over until the tape contained twelve hours of harsh, dissonant noise. He switched on the tape recorder, which was attached to the loudspeakers inside the interrogation room, and turned the volume to the maximum. The music was so loud that it set up vibrations in the steel door. Before he went to bed, he turned on all the alarm systems.

Christopher was drinking coffee the following afternoon when Glavanis and Eycken came downstairs. They had coffee with cognac in it, and Glavanis put two large steaks under the broiler.

Christopher said, "How much money did the man have on him?"

Glavanis shrugged. "None. The bodyguards had about two thousand in dollars, plus maybe two hundred thousand lire."

"It's yours."

"What about our pay?" Eycken asked.

"That, too."

"What do you want him to spill?" Glavanis asked.

"I'll ask the final questions when you think he's ready. Just work on him."

"We have to ask him something," Glavanis said. "Otherwise one can't make the psychological progression—there's no reason to put on more pressure if he isn't asked a question he refuses to answer. It's not logical. There's no focus of fear."

"Keep asking about a million dollars. Tell him you know he received it. Just keep hammering on that."

"Is that all?"

"Yes, for now. Talk to him through the loudspeakers—I've rigged a microphone. There's a light for his eyes if you want it."

"What about the water?"

Christopher hesitated. "If you need it, but be careful. I don't think it's going to be necessary."

Eycken sipped his coffee, making a windy noise with his lips. "I have a lot of faith in water," he said.

Glavanis washed the dishes before they went downstairs. They wore woolen ski masks that concealed their faces and muffled their voices. Eycken's black beard curled from the bottom of his mask.

They worked for almost three hours. No sound of any kind filtered into the upstairs. Christopher watched a Clark Gable movie, dubbed in Italian, on television. Finally he heard the steel door scrape over the stone floor of the cellar, and Glavanis's light footsteps on the stairs.

Glavanis came into the sitting room with his mask still on. "He's ready," he said. "Jan is with him. He's a mess, Paul—he can't control himself."

Glavanis pinched his nostrils shut through the mask, laughed when this reminded him that he still had it on, and stripped it off his head. He smoothed his short black hair with both hands.

"He's primitive, that man," Glavanis said. "At first he kept screaming that he was going to kill us. Jan kept pouring water down his throat through the tube. In the end, he went to pieces in a bad way, he kept on saying 'Mama! Mama!' It was very strange—we gave him no pain, just the water."

"Is he coherent?"

"More or less. He's afraid Jan will drown him again. The water is very effective."

"All right, let him rest for a few minutes. Turn off the lights and lock the door. I'll be right down."

Christopher went upstairs and put on an Italian suit, with the ribbon of a decoration in the lapel. With a gray wig and mustache and rimless spectacles Christopher looked different enough that Glavanis reached for his pocket when he saw him coming down the stairs. Christopher was carrying a small leather case, the kind used by doctors to transport hypodermics. He had draped a heavy dressing gown over one arm. Before he went into the cellar he removed his wristwatch and put it in his pocket; there were thousands like it, but he did not want Pigeon to remember it.

3

With the door closed and the lights reflecting from its polished white walls, the interrogation room looked like the inside of a dry skull. Frankie Pigeon, naked, was tied by his wrists to a ring in the wall. Long yellow stains ran down the inside of his legs. He trembled uncontrollably. The floor was slick with the water he had regurgitated.

When Pigeon saw the door open, he pressed his knees together and turned his lower body to one side in a convulsive movement, to protect his genitals. He looked at Christopher, then closed his eyes tightly. His limp gray hair had fallen over his face. Pigeon's chalky body had been powerful in youth; now it sagged, and his round stomach heaved in and out as he worked to control his breathing.

Christopher put his briefcase on the table. *"Buona sera,* Don Franco," he said.

Pigeon did not open his eyes. Christopher turned off the overhead lights. Now only the table lamp, fitted with a brilliant photographic bulb, was burning. Christopher stood behind the lamp in the shadows. He removed a large hypodermic syringe from the leather case, and holding his hands in the light, filled it from an ampule of yellow liquid. He laid the syringe on a white towel. Then he focused the lamp on Pigeon's face. His eyes were open, and he stared wildly at the syringe.

"This is a very unhealthy place, Don Franco," Christopher said, continuing to speak Italian.

Frankie Pigeon tried to speak and failed; he closed his eyes, concentrated, and tried again. "You get nothing from me," he said in English.

"We have time," Christopher said. "You must be very cold."

He put a chair in the center of the room, in front of the table, and untied Pigeon's hands. Pigeon fell to the floor, shuddering. Christopher lifted him and helped him into the bathrobe. "Please sit down," he said. He went back to the table and adjusted the light so that it shone on Pigeon's haggard features, but did not altogether blind him. Pigeon sat with one flaccid leg wrapped around the other; his body shook and he wedged his hands between his crossed legs.

"I want you to understand your situation," Christopher said. "It's possible for you to remain in this room indefinitely. Conditions will not change, except to get worse. No one will find you."

Pigeon had stopped trying to control his shivering. "They'll find me," he said, "and when they do, you bastard. . . ."

"No. You can forget about being rescued. It's not realistic. Your men have no chance. You saw what happened in Calabria, within earshot of your house."

Pigeon tried to speak again. It was difficult for him—his mouth opened and no voice came out. When finally he was able to utter sound, it was a high thin shriek; a beaded string of phlegm leaped out of his throat and fell through the beam of light.

"*Who?*" he screamed.

Christopher didn't answer. He waited until Pigeon had calmed a little before he touched the hypodermic with the tip of a finger. As he spoke to Pigeon, he tapped the glass barrel of the syringe with his fingernail.

"This hypodermic is filled with the live bacteria of Hansen's disease," Christopher said. "I wonder what you know about Hansen's disease."

Frankie Pigeon's eyes were fixed on the syringe and on Christopher's rhythmically tapping finger.

"Hansen's disease is caused by the Mycobacterium *leprae*," Christopher said, "which is why it's more usually called leprosy. It's a peculiar disease. The incubation period varies greatly.

Sometimes the disease develops in a year or two after infection, but sometimes fifteen or even twenty years can pass before any symptoms appear. All that time, the germ works inside the body. It takes various forms. The neural form may be the worst —lesions develop on the central nervous system. It causes madness, loss of sexual potency, loss of bowel control, and so on. It can paralyze the lungs or eat them away. Other forms cause the fingers, the nose, the toes—even whole legs and arms—to rot. Parts of the victim's body just fall off. Lepers have a strong, disagreeable odor. There is no cure once the disease establishes itself."

Pigeon pushed back his chair, the legs moving silently over the wet floor. He stood up, crouching with one hand on the back of the chair to keep himself from falling.

"Get away from me," he cried.

Christopher covered the syringe with a corner of the towel. "I want some information," he said. "It has nothing to do with your organization. There's no question of your betraying your own people—I've no interest in them or their activities."

Now that the syringe was out of sight, Pigeon was less agitated. But when he spoke, he stammered and his voice broke. He was not used to being powerless. "Those guys in the masks," he said. "They don't even know who I am."

"No, they don't. Here, Mr. Pigeon, you're nobody."

"They took fucking pictures of me!"

"Yes, those were their orders. We'll keep the photographs. We may want to mail them to the United States, to certain of your friends."

"Do that, and they'll come after you."

"Will they? I thought they'd be more likely to ask you if you talked, and what you talked about."

"I want those pictures," Pigeon said. "I'm not having any goddamn pictures of me with no clothes on and. . . ." He saw his fouled legs and turned his head aside, biting his lip like a shamed child.

"Let me tell you what we know," Christopher said. "In 1956 you received a retainer of one hundred thousand dollars from a short bald man with a foreign accent who told you his name was Blanchard. You didn't hear from Blanchard again until the last week in November of this year. You then received a cable from Naples stating that your Uncle Giuseppe had died. Following the plan Blanchard had given you seven years before, you went to an apartment on Cedar Street in Chicago, and received instructions for a job. You carried out the job. On November 25, two of your men, Anthony Rugged and Ronald Prince, went to the bank of Dolder und Co. in Zurich, and collected a million dollars in hundred-dollar bills. They identified themselves with the code name *tortora*, which, as you know, means 'pigeon' in English."

"You know so much, tell me what the job was," Pigeon said.

Christopher picked up the hypodermic and depressed the plunger, so that a thin stream of the yellow serum squirted out of the needle and through the light. "That's what you're going to tell me," he said.

"You can kill me!"

"No. I give you my word I won't do that. Not with a gun or a knife, or anything quick."

The trembling of Pigeon's body intensified. He stared into the light, then turned his whole body away from its glare. He swallowed noisily. When at last he was able to speak, he did so in a rapid soprano voice, like a *castrato*.

Christopher had to ask him only two or three questions. When Pigeon was done, Christopher left the room, taking the hypodermic with him, and the spool of tape on which he had recorded Pigeon's hysterical spillage of what he had done to earn Klimenko's money.

Upstairs, Christopher typed out a summary of Pigeon's statement on a single sheet of foolscap. When he was finished, he removed the ribbon from the typewriter and put the spools in his pocket; on his way back to the interrogation room, he dropped the ribbon into the red coals of the furnace and watched it burn.

Frankie Pigeon sat where Christopher had left him, his bloodless legs intertwined, his hands gripping the seat of the folding chair. Christopher put the sheet of foolscap on the table and told Pigeon to read it. He ran his empty eyes over the paper.

"Sign it, and give me your right hand," Christopher said. He inked each of Pigeon's limp fingers and rolled them over the paper, so that he had a full set of prints to authenticate the signature that ran drunkenly down the page.

He left Pigeon staring at his own hand, blackened by the ink. He still wore a large diamond on his small finger.

4

In the kitchen Glavanis and Eycken were playing piquet with fierce concentration. When they finished the hand, Christopher gave them their pay.

"Give the man this injection," Christopher said, handing Glavanis the hypodermic. "He'll be terrified, so you'll have to subdue him."

"What is it?"

"It'll knock him out for eight hours or so, it's harmless. He thinks it's leprosy germs. Dress him, and blindfold and gag him. Drive north on the Via Flaminia and drop him in a field, away from the main roads, at least three hundred kilometers from Rome. Then turn in the car at Auto Maggiore in Milan and leave the country."

"I've been thinking about what you said," Glavanis said. "He did see our faces."

"He won't want to see them again. He has no idea where he is now, or where to look for you."

"All the same, Paul—if you have what you want. . . ."

"There's an operational reason why he must stay alive."

Glavanis rested his brown eyes, which were as steady and as liquid as those of a young bride, on Christopher for a moment, then laughed and slapped him on the shoulder. "You always have a reason to let them live," he said. "One day you'll wish you hadn't been so merciful."

Christopher shook hands with both men. He stared at

Eycken's thumbless hands, and looked questioningly at Glavanis.

"It's all right," Glavanis said. "Eycken wore rubber gloves all the time we were downstairs."

As soon as he heard the car go down the drive, Christopher put the villa in order. Glavanis and Eycken had left nothing behind but fingerprints; he removed those with furniture polish and a cloth. He photographed Pigeon's confession and developed the film.

Before he left, he entered the interrogation room again. He recalled Frankie Pigeon's clogged treble voice, answering the final questions.

"What did Ruby say when you gave him the contract?"

"Nothing. He was overjoyed to hit that faggot."

"Didn't he ask for money?"

"What did Jack want with money?" Pigeon had asked. "He thought he was going to get the Congressional Medal of Honor."

# TWELVE

1

Christopher knew where Alvaro Urpi prayed. Each morning Urpi walked down the Tiber, crossed the river on the Ponte Palatino, and spent the first three hours after sunrise on his knees in the church of Saint Sabina. Urpi liked the place because it was named for a saint who was converted to Christianity by her slave, because it was almost barren of decoration, with great white columns standing in its nave—and because one could look through a peephole into a hidden garden and see an orange tree grown from the seeds of a tree planted seven hundred years before by Saint Dominic, a Spaniard who had the mind of a Moor, as Urpi had the mind of a Chinese.

Christopher waited at the back of the church while a young priest said Mass and Urpi finished his prayers. Christopher went with him to look at the orange tree and listen to the story again.

"Dominic has a better immortality than stone," Urpi said, and blushed, made shy by the poetry of his thought.

They went back to the Vatican together; Urpi walked like a Chinese, in small rapid steps with his arms held stiff at his sides and his eyes on the pavement. He showed Christopher his translation of Yu Lung's horoscopes. Christopher needed some help with the Latin: Urpi moved a finger from Yu Lung's ideograms to his own crowded handwriting, his eyes darting like a bird's from the material to Christopher's face as he explained the difficulties of the translations.

"As I said, it's obscure, metaphorical," Urpi said. "But it's plain that five men are involved. Three of them—two brothers and a foreign enemy—are marked for death. Also a woman who appears to be a virgin, and who has a relationship to three of the men. Her horoscope has to do with a journey and a message."

"Can you construe her destination and the message?" Christopher asked.

"Oh yes. That part is plain enough."

"And you're certain of the identities of the persons who commissioned the horoscopes?"

Urpi nodded, reading out the Latin phrases. He pronounced very clearly. Christopher cleared his mind, memorizing what Urpi told him.

Urpi gathered together Yu Lung's manuscript and his Latin text and handed them to Christopher. "What is being discussed in these horoscopes is murder," he said.

"Yes."

"Strange that they should express the crime in such beautiful language," Urpi said.

Before he left Rome, Christopher again drove past his apartment. The Truong toc's men were still there, but they had got under cover; they sat together in the Citroën, two men asleep and the other on watch. The man awake was as youthful as Luong, with a lock of hair like Luong's falling into his eyes. He bent his head toward a cupped match and lit his cigarette as Christopher drove by. There was nothing to be done about the Vietnamese: they broke no law as they waited for the opportunity to kill Christopher or kidnap Molly. He was glad to have them there, watching his empty flat, waiting for him to come back.

It was not yet full daylight when he reached the autostrada and turned north. There was a moon in the western sky and one of the planets shone beyond it. The road behind Christopher was clear. Only a few big trucks were moving at that time of day. No living soul knew exactly where he was, or where he was going.

Somewhere between the autostrada and the coast, Frankie Pigeon would be lying in a field. In the interrogation room, in the instant before he had begun to talk, Pigeon had risen from his chair, clasped his hands in front of his heart, and bent his knees as if he would fall to the floor in prayer unless someone supported him. He hadn't been begging for his life: he knew he wouldn't be killed. He wanted to be let go, so that he could return to the idea of himself he'd had before Eycken and Glavanis put the rubber siphon down his throat. Christopher, looking at his own hand on the steering wheel, had a quick vivid mental image of Eycken's thumbless hands. After that he didn't think of Pigeon again. "Pigeon does what he does for money," Klimenko had said. "After you pay a man like that, you don't owe him anything more."

In Orvieto Christopher found a coffee bar just opening and sat by the window drinking *caffè latte*, alone with the teen-aged boy who worked the early shift. At eight o'clock the street filled up with Italians, as though the town had been turned upside down like a sack and its people spilled into the morning. Once, after a week in Switzerland and a drive through the night over the Saint Bernard, he and Molly had arrived at the same time of day in Torino. When she saw the Italians again, shouting and gesticulating, Molly had leaped up, spread her arms as if to embrace them, and cried, *"The human race!"*

Christopher walked through the crowd to the post office and mailed Pigeon's confession and Dieter Dimpel's photographs and Yu Lung's horoscopes to himself in care of general delivery, Washington. The envelope would arrive by registered airmail in four days' time.

He had put photocopies of all the evidence in an envelope addressed to Patchen's post office box in Alexandria. After the clerk put stamps on this package, Christopher reached across the counter and touched his hand.

"Don't cancel the stamps on that one," he said. "I want it back."

The clerk shrugged. "You'll waste the postage."

"That's all right, I'll arrange it another way."

Outside the town, Christopher stopped the car and burned the envelope and its contents, grinding the ashes into the earth with the heel of his shoe.

It was the act of a romantic. Chr stopher laughed aloud at himself. But he was no longer under discipline; the information belonged to him and to the people from whom he had stolen it. Unlike Frankie Pigeon, the Truong toc was owed something: a sporting chance to stop Christopher from learning his last secret.

## 2

Christopher used the airport at Milan because it was less likely to be covered than the one in Rome. He turned in his rented car and bought a ticket for Salisbury. He used no special care: if he was being watched, there was no way in which he could avoid being seen. He carried one small bag containing a camera, a tape recorder, and the clothes he'd need.

He stopped at the newsstand and bought the *Herald-Tribune* and a paperback book. Nguyên Kim, wearing a coat with a fur collar, was standing behind him when he turned around.

"Hi, baby," Kim said.

Christopher smiled and punched Kim lightly on the left side of the chest; Kim was carrying a pistol in a shoulder holster. Christopher put his hand into the pocket of his own raincoat and smiled again.

"Why don't you walk me to the passport control?" he said. "Walk on my right and keep a step ahead. Clasp your hands behind your back."

231

Kim closed his eyes for a long moment. He looked very tired and less boyish. No expression showed on his face. He put his hands behind his back and they walked together past the long row of ticket counters.

"Just like the movies," Kim said. "All I want is a chance to talk to you."

"Go ahead."

"You know your buddies out there burned down a church right after you left?"

"No."

"Well, they did. It's very upsetting. That and the picture you mailed to the Truong toc."

They were in a passageway now. Christopher put his back to the wall and gazed at Kim.

"The question is this," Kim said. "Are you going to stop fooling around, or not?"

"In time."

"How much time do you think you're going to have? You can't work without traveling, Paul. You'll leave traces."

"Everyone leaves traces, even the Truong toc."

"You're not going to find traces of him. Even he doesn't know all the details of what you're after."

"No, I don't suppose he does."

"He wanted me to tell you that," Kim said, "and that's extraordinary. He says nothing to anyone outside the family. The old man admires you, you know."

Christopher waited. There was nothing he wanted to say.

"He asked me to give you a message," Kim said. "He had nothing to do with what happened to Luong. He didn't even know about it until after you left Saigon."

"Tell him I know that."

Kim came a step closer. "There's more," he said. "He knows you're not worried about yourself. He accepts that. But your girl is something else. You have to worry about her."

"Do I?"

"Yes. I know something now I didn't know twenty minutes ago. I thought the girl was with you. Now I know she's not. It simplifies the hunt."

232

Kim paused, peering up into Christopher's face, expecting him to reply. He frowned, as if exasperated with a stupid person, and went on.

"He told me to tell you this: there is no limit of time. You'd have to hide her for the rest of her life."

"And what will he do with Nicole?"

"Protect her, as long as he lives. But he's old, and when he dies, Nicole will be just a girl." Kim, his hands still behind him, rose on his toes. "Believe me," he said, "if you go on, if you don't stop, Molly will have rice in her mouth."

Christopher did not understand Kim's words at first; then he remembered Luong in his coffin with a grain of rice between his lips: food for the Celestial Dog.

"Why threaten Molly?" he asked. "Why not kill me?"

"The old man thinks you're not afraid of death."

Christopher said, "What makes him think I'm afraid of guilt?"

Kim dropped his hands to his sides and walked away down the passageway, his unbuttoned overcoat billowing around his hurrying figure.

3

The flight to Salisbury, through Khartoum and Nairobi, took eleven hours. Americans were not required to have a visa to enter Rhodesia, and Christopher, white and blond, passed through customs unnoticed. He took a domestic flight to Lusaka and found the man he wanted in the bar of the Ridgeway Hotel that night. He had used him once before, and he would not have used him again if he had been in less of a hurry.

They left in darkness, but when the light plane rose to its cruising altitude they could see the sunrise. It wasn't a long flight, along the brown Kafue River, above tan plains, and then, beyond the Congolese frontier, over a higher savannah that was the color of cheap green paint.

The pilot sideslipped between the trees and landed on a straight stretch of clay road. A herd of black and white goats, no larger than spaniels, bounded out of the way of the taxiing plane.

"That was Kipushi you saw up ahead," the pilot said. "It's an hour's walk. You can catch a ride to Elisabethville from there. I daren't land you closer without papers—they're hateful bastards, the Baluba."

# THIRTEEN

1

The day went by slowly, fried by the morning sun, flogged by the afternoon rain. The war had not been over for long, and Elisabethville had the atmosphere of a city whose residents, driven out by a plague, had only just found the courage to come back and claim their possessions.

In the darkened lobby of a hotel, Christopher drank mineral water and read the two Simenons, dirty and swollen by the rainy climate, that he had bought from a street vendor. At nightfall he went into the men's room and put on the boots and the bush clothes he had brought with him. He wasn't used to carrying a pistol, and he had to remind himself not to touch the hard shape of the .22 automatic tucked into the waistband of his trousers.

Nsango was four hours late. He made no apology. Christopher followed him into a quarter where hundreds of his tribes-men, driven out of the bush by war or the hope for money, had settled. Charcoal fires burned down the length of a long street, like a herd of red eyes in the black night. Nsango dropped on all fours in front of a tin hovel and crawled inside. It was con-structed of flattened gasoline cans and other bits of scavenged metal, and it stood in a row of houses that looked like mouths with the teeth knocked out.

Christopher crawled in after Nsango. Nsango sent away the people who lived there; they trotted, giggling, into the street and squatted in the dirt. Nsango found the stub of a candle and lit it. It gave little light. Christopher saw Nsango's gestures but not his face as he told him what he wanted him to say to Manuel Ruiz.

"Why would he believe such a story?" Nsango said. "He's not stupid."

"I know enough to bluff him—certain names."

"It's dangerous, Paul. I don't know if I can protect you. These Cubans are quick to shoot."

"There are still the same number?"

"Only five now. One was shot in the stomach and they couldn't treat his wounds. The other died of snakebite."

"You've been seeing action?"

"Some. We're still earning our guns."

"How many of the Cubans speak French?"

"All, but badly except for this Manuel. I think the others only understand about half of what's said to them."

"How are their nerves?"

"Jumpy. Some of my chaps are pretty simple men—they ate the knuckles and the liver of a prisoner not long ago. I wasn't there. It left Manuel and the others a bit sick."

"Then it's you they're nervous about?"

"Yes, they've received a lot of Kalashnikov machine rifles and they know we want them," Nsango said. "And of course they all have dysentery. Who knows? They may be glad to see another white man."

"Can we go now?"

Nsango sighed. "All right. It's a long walk to where I left the Jeep, and we'll have to find some gasoline and carry that."

He went outside and shouted. A babble erupted in the darkness, then died down as all but the people Nsango wanted drifted away. In a few minutes Nsango called to Christopher. He stood in the street with four jerry cans at his feet.

"Two for you, two for me," he said. "Sweat is the fuel of the revolution."

Walking through a field of coarse grass outside the city, Nsango began to sing in a low voice. Christopher compelled his imagination to form a picture of Molly, walking between high snowbanks in Zermatt, her face pinkened by the wind and the cold. His conversation with Nguyên Kim at the Milan airport kept intruding, like the strong signal of a distant radio station in nighttime. Christopher had gambled Molly as willingly as he would have played the life of an agent. He'd done it on reflex: never let the opposition see that you are vulnerable. Christopher ran operations the way a natural athlete plays a sport: he knew the game in his muscles and in his bloodstream. To change styles was to lose; thought was a handicap, emotion a hazard. His arms stretched by the weight of the jerry cans, he walked on, trusting Nsango to keep alert. The march went quickly.

Nsango's camp lay to the north, in the upland forest not twenty miles from the Rhodesian frontier. Nsango drove fast through the bush, down narrow paths, and he and Christopher leaned toward the center of the Jeep, their heads sometimes bumping together as they dodged the branches that whipped over the windshield. Nsango, shouting, told Christopher how the Cuban had been killed by a tree mamba that had fallen into the speeding Jeep a few days before. "A one-minute snake," he said. "He was dead before they could put on the brakes and run away."

They were challenged twice by sentries, boys wearing torn bits of camouflage uniform, before they reached the camp. It was an abandoned village with a large open space, beaten shiny by bare feet, in the center of a ring of conical wattle huts.

"This used to be a prosperous place," Nsango said. "I passed through here in '62 and found a pile of right hands—men's, women's, children's—in the middle of the village, on the open ground. A hundred people had been dismembered. It was propaganda. In the old days the Belgians used to cut off the right hands of a whole village if one man committed a crime. During the fighting someone revived the practice. I think it was the mercenaries—some of them were Belgians, after all. The whites said it was the Chinese and their Simbas, who wanted the whites to be blamed. It could have been either. In any case, that's where the population went."

Christopher knew the story was true; he had seen a heap of severed hands in another part of the Congo.

" 'The horror,' " Nsango said, his lips twisting around the quotation. "You may as well come to my hut and get some sleep. This Manuel is not a very early riser."

Inside the hut, Nsango handed Christopher a calabash of water. "It's been boiled," he said, noticing Christopher's hesitation. "You gave me your sickly intestines along with your white ideas."


2


Christopher woke every fifteen minutes and ran his eyes over the interior of the hut; it was about the size and shape of the room in which Frankie Pigeon had been kept. Nsango, his skinny legs drawn up, slept unworriedly, breathing softly. The sun came up and filled the low door with intense white light. There was a burst of birdsong at sunrise. Then the temperature rose twenty degrees in fifteen minutes and the surrounding forest fell silent.

Christopher was astonished to hear a bugle call being played over a loudspeaker. He crawled to the door of the hut and looked out. About thirty young tribesmen, barefooted and bare-chested, were mustering for reveille. A tall black with a Kalashnikov rifle slung over his shoulder and tribal scars on his cheeks called the troops to attention. In the shade of a limbali tree, a bearded Cuban wearing dirty U.S. Army fatigues smoked a cigar and watched. He too carried a Soviet machine rifle.

"That's the one they call Pablito," Nsango said. "I'd better explain your presence before you show yourself."

He ducked through the entrance. As Nsango walked across the parade ground, the Congolese NCO presented arms, and even the Cuban came briefly to attention and saluted. Nsango left his own Kalashnikov behind with Christopher.

Manuel Ruiz was eating breakfast when Nsango showed Christopher into his hut. It was three o'clock in the afternoon. Manuel lived in what had been the chief's compound, in the largest house; the other Cubans were quartered in the adjoining wives' huts. A half-dozen of the youngest terrorists were hoeing the cassava beds, their faces resentful as they wielded the bent sticks rubbed bare by women's hands and left behind when the villagers fled.

Manuel Ruiz said, "Have you eaten?"

When Christopher shook his head, Ruiz pushed a boiled yam and a knife across the table and poured warm beer from a liter bottle into a canteen cup. The Cuban was a young man, no more than thirty, with curly hair growing to his collar. He cultivated an air of menace that went badly with his smooth face and his wide frank eyes and snub nose. His skin was pale and he had the tremor of the dysentery victim. He ate and drank efficiently, without pausing to taste, as though to quiet his body in order to go on to more important things with the least possible delay. His eyes never left Christopher's face. The yam was dry and overcooked; he washed down each bite with a mouthful of beer.

Sunlight fell in splinters through the thatched roof, striping Manuel's green uniform. He had arranged his belongings around the walls—cases of ammunition stenciled with Cyrillic writing, a rack of weapons, unopened boxes of rifles, an American radio that ran off a gasoline generator. Pictures of Fidel Castro and Lenin, and a poster showing abject prisoners taken at the Bay of Pigs and their outdated American weapons, had been pinned to the sloping ceiling.

Ruiz finished his yam, wiped his lips with the back of his hand, and said, "Now. What are you doing in this installation?" He spoke grammatical French, and mixed with his adenoidal Latin American accent were some Congolese intonations.

"Nsango has explained how I got here."

"Yes," Manuel said. "But not why. You and he are old friends."

"Yes."

"He says you're an activist, that you've helped him."

"I've always admired Nsango."

Christopher handed Manuel the knife he had loaned him, handle first. It, too, was American, a new-issue, short-bladed bayonet.

"What I want to say to you has something to do with your work in another place," Christopher said. "I bring you some help for what you're doing here."

"Oh? What are your auspices?"

"I've brought you a gift from a friend—Do Minh Kha."

"Do?" Manuel said. "Do Minh Kha? A gift from him? Where did you see him?"

"I didn't. He passed it to me through a friend in Saigon. He wanted to bypass ordinary channels. He said you'd understand why."

"And the friend in Saigon—what was his name?"

Christopher paused to give it weight. "Lê Thu."

Manuel took the name, but not eagerly. Christopher watched the Cuban's reaction as an angler watches his line, drawn through the water by a sluggish fish. He decided to let it go for the moment. There was no reason why the Vietnamese would have told Manuel the code name for their operation: he did not need to know. But they would have had to give him some hint, and it was possible they had given him more than that. If they talked not at all to outsiders, intelligence officers talked too much to each other.

"What were you doing in Saigon?" Manuel asked.

"Working. My work is mainly in that camp."

"And your name, Nsango tells me, is Charron?"

"Yes."

"You knew where to find me, you knew my name, you knew Nsango could bring you to me?"

"I had some assistance."

Ruiz drew the dull edge of the bayonet down the bridge of his nose; when he brought the blade away it was filmed with sweat and he shook it off the steel with a snap of his wrist. "That's a little disturbing," he said.

"Then you should dress less conspicuously," Christopher said. "Even operating at night, that costume of yours is easily recognized. You're in a place where white men draw attention just by being white, and you're dealing with people who don't know the meaning of discretion. Nsango's men are not Nsango."

Manuel tugged at the lapel of his fatigue jacket and glanced at his tarnished badge of rank, earned with Castro in the Sierra Maestra. "We're used to these clothes. They symbolize something."

"Well, it's no concern of mine," Christopher said. "You may have better success than others who've tried to do what you're doing. Success is more important than security, after all."

"Is it not? All right, what does Do want?"

"To thank you. To give you this for your work here."

Christopher counted twenty thousand Swiss francs, in sodden thousand-franc notes, onto the bamboo table. Ruiz sat with his hands in his lap, gazing at the money.

"Very handsome of Do," he said. "What's it for?"

"As I said, for your work—a gesture of solidarity."

"Yes—but in return for what?"

"Lê Thu," Christopher said.

"What is Lê Thu?"

"I was told you'd understand. If you don't, so much the better for Do's security."

"I spent ten days in Hanoi. I didn't become fluent in Vietnamese."

"In French the name means 'the tears of autumn.'"

Manuel Ruiz's eyes moved away from Christopher's. He sat very still, then picked up the stack of pink bank notes. Christopher knew the signs, knew he had been right.

*"Las lagrimas del otoño,"* Manuel muttered. "How did you come by that phrase?"

"I help out, when I can, with some of Do's operations. He can't move freely outside his own country—he stands out, as you do among these blacks. Money, for example, must be carried and delivered."

Manuel nodded and cleared his throat. "It's remarkable what they can accomplish, Do and his people. But you're right, of course, their race limits them. They have to rely on others from time to time."

"Once again, security is sometimes less important than success."

"There's no such thing as security among professionals. You're here. I wouldn't have thought that possible."

Ruiz folded the money in half and stuffed it into his breast pocket. He fastened the metal button.

"Frankly," Christopher said, "Do didn't think what you did was possible. He's very grateful. You were the key."

Manuel leaned back in his chair and slapped his palm with the flat of the bayonet. He struggled with a smile of pleasure, then submitted to it. He had large even teeth.

Manuel Ruiz's mind opened with an almost audible click. Christopher had seen this happen before to men who had done great things in secret. No matter how disciplined, they wanted admiration. Manuel, sent by Che Guevara into a Congolese rain forest, was a long way from people he could trust—who could understand what he had done. Christopher didn't know whether Ruiz had decided to trust him or kill him, but he knew that Ruiz had decided to talk.

But not immediately. Manuel moved a stack of papers to the center of his desk, and wetting his thumb, began to go through them. After a time he looked up and recoiled in mock surprise, as if he had forgotten that he had a guest.

"You must excuse me now, I have urgent work," he said. "You'll stay the night, I suppose? Eat supper with me."

"Gladly. I have some Polish vodka in my bag. Do you like it?"

"No, but I'll drink it, Charron."

Outside, in the scorched white light of afternoon, nothing moved. Christopher heard African laughter coming from the huts and a radio playing songs in one of the Congolese languages. The sun had dried the cassava beds so that the soil was as fine as rouge.

Nsango sat in his hut, reading. When Christopher entered on his hands and knees, Nsango put a finger in his book to mark the place and showed him the cover. It was a French translation of one of Albert Schweitzer's works. Even before he became a terrorist, Nsango had told Christopher that Schweitzer, who lived among black lepers in order to save his own white soul, was the only man in Africa he dreamed of murdering.

"Know thine enemy," Nsango said.

Christopher took off the bush jacket he had been wearing, wiped the perspiration from the small wire recorder in its breast pocket, and fitted a new spool of wire.

"How did it go?" Nsango asked.

"All right. He'll talk tonight. He wants to talk to someone."

"Yes, he's lonely. He's above the other Cubans—they're louts. Manuel is an educated man."

"What are his communications with the outside?"

"You saw the radio. It breaks down a lot, and the man who knew how to fix it was the one who was bitten by the snake. Manuel has a link with the Russian radio in Dar es Salaam, but sometimes it takes hours to raise them. I think they don't listen for his transmissions."

"Would you consider sabotaging the radio?"

Nsango shrugged. "He'll connect it to you."

"Not if you're subtle. The generator operates on a gasoline motor. Put a little dirt in the gas tank."

"Sooner or later he's going to describe you to someone in their apparatus."

"Maybe. But not today."

"All right, I'll have it done. Manuel won't try to transmit until after dark—the sun interferes."

Christopher stood up and poured water into his mouth

from the calabash. He touched Nsango's Kalashnikov rifle, setting it swinging gently on its hangers.

"I see the weapons have been issued."

"Only to me and other more advanced natives," Nsango
said. "The men are growing impatient."

"I counted ten cases of rifles in Manuel's hut. Your men
must want them very badly."

"Yes. Manuel or one of the other Cubans guards them all
the time."

Christopher sat down on the beaten dirt floor. "How soon
do you expect to kill them?" he asked.

"It's difficult, even though there are only four of them left
besides Manuel. I don't want to use juju again, it leaves the men
in a bad way afterward. And the Cubans never go out with us
all at once. It's easiest to do it in a fire fight, so they think it's
the other side."

"I'd like to see Manuel Ruiz live for a while—a month or
two."

Nsango lay against the twigs and clay of the wall, his legs
stretched before him, his hands clasped behind his head.

"Manuel wants to live, too," he said. "He has zeal for the
idea of what he's doing—not, I think, for the act itself. That's
only a means to an end. He wants to go back to Cuba and tell
how black men died like flies for his idea. As I'm the only one
who understands the idea, or even knows what Communism is,
he needs me. Mine is the only black name he can remember.
To him, the others have no names, any more than lions or
porcupines have names; they're fauna. But my name is known
in the world, thanks to another white man—you. '*I* led Alphonse Nsango's revolution, *I* am the white explanation for his
victory,' Ruiz will say."

"Don't blame me for your fame."

"No? Then who hired all those boys to paint 'Nsango' on the
walls in Léopoldville and Brussels, who bribed the journalists
and wrote their stories of my heroism, who carried my book
through the jungles to a publisher?" Nsango pointed both index
fingers at Christopher and laughed. "To whom do I owe this life

of adventure and idealism, to whom do I owe Manuel, if not to you?"

"If I've done all that for you, then keep Manuel Ruiz alive for me. I may need him again."

"I don't know if I can keep him alive, and you, too. He'll kill you when he's had time to think."

"He mustn't be killed until he's talked. It may be necessary for him to talk again."

Nsango's smile had not left his lips. "All right," he said.

## 4

Christopher knew that a man who is trained to keep secrets can be counted upon, when at last he breaks his oath of silence, to tell everything he knows. The spoiled spy will reveal the true names of his superiors and his agents, he will suggest ways to destroy his own networks. He will bore his interrogators, who until the day before were his enemies, with the details of his thefts, betrayals, unauthorized murders, sexual vices.

Manuel Ruiz had not reached that point, but he was at a more dangerous one: he was an idealist who had done a great thing for his cause. Idealists make brave agents, but they are bad intelligence officers. They cannot exist for long without the company of like minds; they have a need to speak their beliefs and to hear their beliefs spoken. Ruiz wanted to talk and he had no one to talk to.

He did not trust Christopher, but Christopher was white and he knew Ruiz's ideological vocabulary. Besides, Christopher was in Ruiz's camp, surrounded by Ruiz's men, miles from safety. Ruiz imagined that he could kill him whenever he liked.

Ruiz was drunk. Christopher had gone to his hut in the dark, following another Cuban who carried a lantern. Ruiz opened tins—sardines, tuna fish, pineapple, cheese, round un-salted biscuits. They ate from this litter of food with their fingers and drank Christopher's vodka, warm in tin cups. For hours they talked about places they had been, Ruiz testing Christopher to see if they knew the same people. Christopher knew some of them in fact and others from hearsay; a few he knew more intimately than Ruiz ever would because he had run agents against them. Ruiz wore a .45 Colt automatic, U.S. Army issue, in a shoulder holster; its butt, like Ruiz's fingers after dipping into the canned fish, shone with oil.

Manuel left the hut frequently to empty his bowels; he had a bad case of dysentery and it carried the oily food through his body in a torrent. It was after Ruiz came back from one of his trips to the latrine that Christopher saw the idea come into his eyes. It amused Ruiz as an idea for mischief will amuse an intelligent boy. He knew what Christopher wanted to talk about; he would talk. Then he would keep Christopher until he could authenticate him, or kill him.

"These blacks of mine sometimes eat their prisoners," Ruiz said.

"So I understand."

Ruiz drank from his canteen cup, his eyes wide open and bright over its rim. "We began to talk about Do Minh Kha and his people this afternoon," he said.

"I remember."

"I've never heard of you, Charron. Perhaps that should reassure me. You know Do well, do you?"

"Well enough. I explained the relationship to you."

Ruiz looked at the ceiling, swirled the vodka in his cup, fixed his eyes on Christopher; his speech was blurred, and he struggled to enunciate the foreign language he was speaking. He began a sentence in Spanish, stopped himself, and rephrased it in French.

"They have a good revolution, the Vietnamese," he said. "Like ours—the same enemy, the same devotion, the same practicality."

Christopher permitted a grin to cover his face, as if he knew a joke too delicious to conceal.

"Do you know Benshikov?" he asked.

"He was in Havana for two years."

"After that, in Hanoi. Benshikov can be pompous. He wanted to reorganize the North Vietnamese service on KGB lines. Do told Benshikov that the Soviet service was too bureaucratic to have imagination. Do said you Cubans had the best service in the world, because your revolution is still young enough to feel hunger and rage."

Ruiz nodded, accepting the compliment. "Do told me that story, too," he said.

Christopher went on speaking, as if prolonging the joke. "It was Benshikov who suggested a professional rifleman for Dallas, you know. Do wouldn't tell him the details, just that he wanted an assassin."

Ruiz read the label on the empty vodka bottle.

"Truthfully, at the time, I thought they had chosen the wrong man—not you, the assassin," Christopher said. "He was so unstable."

Ruiz seized the bottle by the neck and tapped on the table with it; outside, some of Nsango's men were drumming and Ruiz tried to reproduce the rhythm, which was almost as complicated as speech.

"Oswald was insane," he said. "But perhaps that's what was needed."

Christopher lifted his eyebrows. "Did you imagine he could succeed?" he asked.

"No. That's why I was permitted by my own people to go ahead with the contact. They regarded it as a harmless favor to the Vietnamese—a credit for the future when we might want something from them. It wasn't a high-level decision. I can't imagine who had the balls to pass the word to Fidel after Oswald actually shot Kennedy. Naturally the Americans suspected us. A lot of people in Havana must have been very, very nervous."

"Your people had no misgivings?"

Ruiz waved a hand. "It's the old rule—the result justified whatever risk there might be. They thought even an unsuccessful attempt to kill Kennedy would have an important propaganda effect. To show he wasn't safe in his own country."

"Yes, but Oswald himself was a risk. I don't know how you avoided terrible handling problems."

"I handled Oswald very little, Charron. The contact was peculiar. He was such an outsider, such a clown. Our people in

247

Mexico wouldn't let me take him to a safe house, even. I spoke to him for perhaps an hour, in the Alameda, between planes."

"But it was you who brought him to Mexico."

"Yes, and I who suggested him to Do Minh Kha. I had his dossier with me in Hanoi, it came out to me in the pouch with a lot of other low-level stuff. One of our agents in New Orleans had assessed Oswald. He was trying to draw our attention there with that ridiculous thing of passing out pro-Castro leaflets on the street. We approached him. He offered to train and lead freedom fighters in Latin America. We pretended interest. Our man told him he'd have no problem getting a transit visa for the USSR at the Cuban consulate in Mexico City. The idea was that he'd stay in Havana, but the FBI and the CIA and all the others Oswald thought were watching him would think he'd redefected to Russia. Are you following?"

"Yes."

"Then you see the pattern. Oswald had a tremendous fight with our consul in Mexico City, a man named Azque, when he wouldn't issue the visa with no questions asked. Azque thought he was rabid."

"Yes, I'd heard that. He also got into a sweat with the people at the Soviet embassy. They reported it to Center."

"Did he? I'm glad I didn't know that. The Russians didn't want any part of him, naturally. No one did, poor fool."

"How did you make contact?"

"Telephone. We'd given him a time schedule for the call and a recognition code. We told him to stay at the Comercio, it's a dump. He hung about for two or three days and I had him surveilled. He was clean. So I called him up. He made the meeting in the park that same evening without any hesitation, precisely on time, hair all combed."

"I hope you didn't wear your uniform."

"No—suit, tie, briefcase. I let him see a pistol under my coat. I gave him no identification. I don't know what he thought I was. I played it very serious."

"Like a Russian?"

"He may have thought that. I told him nothing. He made a point of not asking." Ruiz made a comical face. "He wanted to look like a professional. He was very eager to be treated with respect. I obliged."

"How did you lay the mission on him?"

"You have to understand I never thought he'd go through with it. I just gave it to him cold: when Kennedy is in Dallas in the last week of November, kill him. Use a rifle. Wear gloves. Abandon the weapon and walk away."

"How did he react?"

"He was calm, casual. When I told him he'd change history he jumped a little and gave me a funny look, as if I'd touched him in the wrong place."

Ruiz was enjoying his anecdote. He was smiling now and searching Christopher's face for reaction.

"I mentioned plastic surgery, a new identity, a career of doing the same sort of thing in the future," Ruiz said. "Amateurs really believe such things are possible."

"And you promised to get him out after the shooting?"

"Of course. He wasn't the kind who wanted to die. He was all fantasy. He imagined himself in a Socialist country, famous with all the secret people. It was a matter of letting him smell the life he'd always wanted. Respect, trust—his greatness acknowledged."

"Weren't you afraid he'd panic when you didn't show up?"

"Once again, I had no idea he'd succeed. I thought he might try and be killed by the security forces. It was logical that that should happen."

"Even failing, he might have talked."

"Never. He wasn't the type. We would have broken him, or the Russians. But not the Americans. It would have been a federal case. The FBI doesn't torture people. In any case, they would have seen he was crazy. If he'd mentioned me, the FBI would have thought I was another of his fantasies."

"You thought all that out at the time?"

"Frankly, no. But afterward it was plain. It was Oswald who chose the meeting place for after the assassination—that movie house. The Texas Theater? He said it would be easy for me to remember. A movie house. That was the amateur."

"He wanted you to meet him there?"

"Oh, yes. He became very brisk—told me what sort of car to get for the escape, recommended a used-car dealer, drew a map of the routes south. He said we'd be across the border into Mexico before the American police recovered from the shock. I agreed with everything, as if he were a genius."

"Money?"

"I didn't offer him any—it would have been fatal. He wanted to prove his value. The operation cost nothing. He even had his own rifle and ammunition."

"He must have wanted communications with you."

"Certainly. I told him to rent a post office box at the Terminal Annex in Dallas when he was ready to go, and send me its number. I gave him an accommodation address in Mexico."

"Did he?"

Ruiz laughed. "Yes. He wrote the number of the box on a piece of paper and circled the two middle digits. The number was 6225. I realized after the assassination that 22 was the day in November on which he intended to kill Kennedy. And so he did."

"That must have been happenstance, the box number."

"Maybe. When I saw Oswald in Mexico City, he had a clipping from a Dallas newspaper with him, saying that Kennedy would be in Dallas on November 21 and 22. Those were the dates the Vietnamese had chosen—Do Minh Kha gets the American papers too. Oswald just wanted to tell me which day, so I'd be there to arrange his getaway. You know what these fools are like—they imagine a great secret apparatus exists, able to do anything. It's a good thing for us that they do believe it."

"If he'd already clipped the story, he might have gone ahead with the shooting anyway."

"It's possible," Ruiz said. "He'd had the idea for a long time. All I did was give him a rationale. After he talked to me, he was doing it for the revolution, entering history. I think that would have been important to him—to have his act known by the men in the apparatus. That way, he wasn't just a cheap little nut, he was the avenger of the masses."

"You're a good psychologist, Manuel."

"Fair. Oswald was easy material."

Ruiz rose from his chair and pulled his sweat-soaked shirt away from his body. He reached under the table and brought out a bottle of beer. When he struck off the cap, placing its lip against the edge of the table and striking downward with the heel of his hand, the beer spurted. Ruiz put the neck in his mouth to prevent waste, then filled Christopher's cup. It was a bitter local brand, heavily carbonated. Ruiz belched and shook his head rapidly in apology.

"It's odd, isn't it?" Christopher said. "Oswald *did* enter history, but he never had any idea who he was killing for, did he?"

"Not a clue. That was the beauty of it. I wondered at the time, just as you did, why Do had let me give him this pathetic queer, why he imagined this man would have the balls to do it. Do had it planned down to the day and the hour and the exact intersection of streets. He seemed to think the plan was so foolproof that any fool could fire the rifle. It goes to show you how clever these Vietnamese are, and how we underestimate them. The Americans are going to learn a lot over there."

Christopher lifted his canteen cup. "I hope so," he said.

Ruiz had told his story with nonchalance. Now his face collapsed into an expression of comical urgency. He slammed the beer bottle on the tabletop and rushed out of the hut. Christopher followed and saw Ruiz, tearing at his belt, running toward the bamboo screen that hid the latrine. He heard the Cuban's bowels open in a loud burst of gas and liquid. Ruiz groaned and retched, squatting astride the ditch with his arms wrapped around his own body.

Christopher, a pace behind the crouching man, drew the .22 pistol from his belt and fired two rounds of birdshot into the base of Ruiz's neck; the pistol's weak report could barely be heard above the drums. Ruiz emitted a groan, full of breath as if he had been kicked in the stomach, and fell forward into the ditch.

A mile down the path, Christopher found Nsango sitting in the Jeep, listening to the drums.

"The Cubans may follow," Christopher said. "Manuel won't be good for much when he wakes up, but he'll be able to send the others."

"The drums will tell me," Nsango said, "the savage heartbeat of the Congo."

His teeth shone in the darkness. He held up a finger for silence and turned on the headlights. Behind them in the camp, the drums stopped. They heard four long bursts of fire from the Kalashnikovs. After each burst, Nsango held up another finger.

"Only Manuel is left," he said. "Send me a postcard, Paul, when he's no longer needed."

# FOURTEEN

1

When Christopher arrived at Patchen's house on M Street, the others were already there. Foley still wore a black tie, but he had taken off his PT-109 tie clasp. He spoke in a louder voice and his handshake was rougher. He had begun to take on some of the mannerisms of the new President, but he hadn't yet perfected the style. Foley was between personalities; though his language was stronger, he was pale and less alert than he had been. It was apparent that he counted for less in the White House. He deferred to another man, a stranger to Christopher, who stood with his back to a fire of birch logs in Patchen's fireplace. Patchen introduced Christopher.

"J. D. Trumbull," said the man. Trumbull had a disarming smile and a chuckling Texas accent. He wore Western boots and a brown suit, beautifully tailored but unpressed, apparently, since the day it was bought. When Trumbull shook hands, he grasped Christopher's forearm with his other hand and squeezed.

"Old David tells us you've been through one hell of a lot in the last few weeks," Trumbull said. "We appreciate it."

When Trumbull said "we" he managed to sketch a likeness of Lyndon Johnson in the empty air over his shoulder. Christopher looked into the man's ruddy, open face for an instant before stepping backward to free his arm.

Patchen filled four glasses with ice, poured scotch into them, and passed them around. "I don't have any soda," he said.

"This's just fine," Trumbull said. "Tastes better but it's worse for you." Trumbull sipped his whiskey and turned his eyes to Patchen. "Now," he said.

"I'll assume Dennis has briefed you on the background to Christopher's report," Patchen said.

Trumbull nodded.

"I'm not Christopher's best salesman," Foley said. "But I told J.D. what his suspicions were."

Christopher realized that Foley had not addressed him directly since the night they met in Webster's apartment.

"In the past week or so," Patchen said, "Christopher has been to Vietnam, to Europe, to the Congo. He's talked with the people involved. He's put his life in hazard, and it's still in hazard."

As he spoke the last sentence, Patchen shifted his unblinking eyes from Trumbull to Foley. Foley returned the stare, tapping his nose with a forefinger.

"Now wait a minute," Trumbull said. "As I understand it, Paul is no longer with us." He turned to Christopher. "You've been doing all this on your own?"

"Yes," Patchen answered. "He wasn't operating under our auspices, nor did he have our support. He ceased to be our employee before he started out. What he has to report to us he's reporting as a courtesy to the government. Bear in mind that this information belongs to Christopher, not the government."

"All right," Trumbull said. "Let's have it."

Patchen took Christopher's report, a bundle of typed

sheets with several photographs attached, out of his briefcase and handed it to Trumbull. "You'll have to take turns reading it," he said. "There are no copies, and I think you'll agree there shouldn't be any."

"Who's read it so far?" Foley asked.

"I have. The Director refused to read it."

J. D. Trumbull put on a pair of half-moon reading glasses and settled back into his easy chair. He read rapidly, wetting a forefinger as he turned the typed pages. He went through the photographs and the attached documents slowly; when he saw Frankie Pigeon's confession and Glavanis's photographs of the naked gangster he gave a series of soft snorts. When he was finished, he closed the folder with care and handed it to Foley. There was no jollity left in Trumbull's face. He passed his eyes over Christopher once, then crossed his legs and stared at the tip of his boot while Foley read the file.

The four men faced each other, Foley and Trumbull in chairs on one side of a coffee table, Christopher and Patchen on a sofa on the other side. Christopher watched Foley. As he read, his face tightened. Once or twice he closed his eyes and inhaled deeply through his nose. He finished the last page, closed the folder, and tossed it on the coffee table. A photograph fell to the floor, the picture of the dead gunmen by the paddy in Saigon. Patchen picked it up and put it back into the file folder.

"That's pretty rough reading," Trumbull said. "David, what's Paul's background?"

"Christopher has been decorated twice for his work. He is a very senior officer. Within the outfit, his skill and his accuracy have never been questioned."

Foley cleared his throat. "He's also Patchen's best and oldest friend," he said.

"That's irrelevant," Patchen said. "The question before us is this report."

Trumbull peered over his glasses. "Paul," he said, "I'd like a little more flavor before I make a comment. Tell us how you see this."

"It's all there, in the report."

"I mean in your own words."

"Those are my own words, Mr. Trumbull."

"I know that, boy. What I want you to do is talk us through it."

Foley got to his feet, went to the bar, and made himself another drink. He took his glass to the window and stood there, looking into the quiet street.

"The truth is plain enough," Christopher said. "Before I go into it, I want to ask you a question."

Trumbull said, "Ask away."

"What exactly was the role of the U.S. government in the coup that overthrew Ngo Dinh Diem?"

Trumbull stared for a moment at Foley's rigid back. Then he said to Patchen, "Tell him."

"I think you already know, Paul," Patchen said. "In simple terms, we countenanced it. We knew it was being planned. We offered advice. We provided support. We encouraged the plot. We welcomed the results."

"Who exactly is 'we'?" Christopher asked.

"It was a White House project. They handled it, for the most part, with their staff and their communications. The foreign-policy establishment ran errands. There was no plan to kill Diem and Nhu."

"No plan? What did you people imagine was going to happen to them?"

"There's no point in arguing that now, Paul. What happened, happened."

J. D. Trumbull had been gazing idly at Dennis Foley's back. Now he turned his eyes, set in nests of wrinkles, on Christopher.

"Old Dennis told me you were upset about Diem and Nhu and how they died," he said. "I think that speaks well of you, Paul. But it reminds me of what Harry Truman said about the bleeding hearts who kept on weeping and gnashing their teeth and crying shame and damnation after we dropped the A-Bomb on Hiroshima and Nagasaki. President Truman said he heard a lot about all those dead Japs, but damn little about the drowned American sailors at the bottom of Pearl Harbor. You've got to keep your eye on the whole balance sheet."

"You just got through reading the balance sheet, Mr. Trumbull."

"Well, maybe. What you've given us in this report is just bare bones, Paul. I'd still like to hear it from your own lips, if you think you're ready to talk to us now."

"This seems redundant," Christopher said. "The facts are in my report. All the rest—how I operated and why, what people looked like when I spoke to them, how much money it cost —is background noise. If it helps you to understand, I can tell you all that."

"Do that," Trumbull said. "I'm just an old country lawyer. I'd like to hear how you fellows do the things you do."

At that, Patchen smiled at last and picked up his glass of scotch. Trumbull had been sipping his own whiskey for some moments, and he rattled the ice in his empty glass and gave Patchen an inquiring look. Patchen fetched him another drink.

## 2

Christopher began to speak.

"The report deals with the main question—who assassinated President Kennedy and why—and with two incidental pieces of information," he said. "These treat with the murder of Oswald, and with the possibility that heroin and other drugs will be used as weapons of war against U.S. troops in Vietnam. The Oswald murder—execution would be a better word—and the heroin just popped up in the course of the search for information about the assassination. There is no doubt about the truth of the matter where the assassinations of Kennedy and Oswald are concerned. As to the heroin, Patchen and the outfit can pursue it. It's more important than the other two questions, because you can still do something about it. It's intelligence. The rest of what I reported is just explanation."

Trumbull leaned forward, his elbows on his knees. "I'm learning," he said. "You fellows are a cold bunch."

"I'll deal first with the Kennedy assassination," Christopher said. "This is the way it happened: Ngo Dinh Diem and Ngo

Dinh Nhu, his brother, believed for some time that the Kennedy Administration wanted to overthrow their regime and replace it with a more pliant one. The Ngos knew that a coup was being plotted—they knew everything that went on in Saigon. There is collateral intelligence in the files on these two points. I reported some of it myself while the Ngo brothers were still alive.

"Around the beginning of September, Diem and Nhu gave up all hope that they could survive. They were realists; they knew the power of the United States and the ambitions of the South Vietnamese generals. Diem and Nhu expected to be overthrown, and I believe they knew their enemies would kill them. They made plans to revenge themselves—to spit out of their graves, as one of their relatives put it. You have to understand that they didn't want revenge for personal reasons. They regarded the coup and their own murders as an insult to their family and to the Vietnamese nation.

"It's normal in South Asia for people, even educated people, to horoscope important projects. They believe there are forces beyond human intelligence that have an effect on the acts of men—you can smile, Mr. Trumbull, but if you don't understand that reality, and give it due weight, you'll be making an arrogant mistake. You may think horoscopy is primitive, but it exists, and it's used as a matter of course throughout the tropical world.

"You've seen that there are two sets of horoscopes, both drawn by the Chinese Yu Lung in Saigon. The first set was drawn up on September 8, 1963. It predicted, quite accurately, that Diem and Nhu would be murdered and that the murder would be instigated by a powerful foreigner.

"On the basis of that horoscope, Diem and Nhu alerted their family. The head of the family, the Truong toc, who is identified in my report, took over the planning for the revenge of the deaths of Diem and Nhu. After reading Yu Lung's horoscopes, no one in the family doubted that the murders would occur, and soon. Nor did they doubt the broker for these murders would be the President of the United States.

"On September 12 Yu Lung drew up the second set of

horoscopes. September 12 was the tenth anniversary of John F. Kennedy's marriage. You have the translations. The men horoscoped were Diem and Nhu again, President Kennedy, a North Vietnamese intelligence officer named Do Minh Kha, and Do Minh Kha's grown-up daughter. Her name is Dao—or, in French, Nicole. In addition to a reading of zodiacal signs relating to these five persons, Yu Lung drew up an elaborate geomantic scheme. This showed the places, the geographical locations, where the *feng shui*, or the good and evil forces that act on men, would be strongest.

"Yu Lung's readings confirmed that death was certain for Diem and Nhu. The family had already decided—through logic, not magic—that John F. Kennedy would be the murderer of their relatives. Yu Lung's horoscope, based on the precise hour, date, and year of Kennedy's birth and other public information —when and where he was wounded in the war, was stricken with his illness, was married, when his child died, when his older brother was killed—showed that there were patches in the lunar calendar in which Kennedy was vulnerable to violent death.

"One of these periods fell during the third week in November on the Western calendar. Kennedy was assassinated on Friday of the third week in November—the day of prime danger for him, as predicted by Yu Lung. That he was killed on that day will seem happenstance to you, but it didn't look that way to Yu Lung or the Truong toc.

"Diem and Nhu were killed on November 1, our time. Kennedy died precisely twenty-one days later, on November 22. Diem's personal lucky number was seven. Seven times three is twenty-one. Also, in Vietnamese funeral custom, special rites are performed for the dead every seventh day after the day of death. So there was, in the choice of November 22 as the date of the assassination, what one of my agents called 'an elegance.'

"Now, as to the North Vietnamese intelligence officer, Do Minh Kha, and his daughter. Do is a member of one of the Ngo *phais*—he and Diem and Nhu were cousins of a sort. Do's name, by the way, is a *nom de révolution*; he was born a Ngo. Kinship

259

is a powerful thing in Vietnam. Do Minh Kha may have been a Communist and an enemy intelligence officer, but he was also a blood relation of Diem and Nhu. That would be, in a matter like this one, the more important loyalty.

"Yu Lung's horoscopes, which predict the *time* of events, and his geomantic readings, which indicate the best *place* to do something, showed this about Do: that he should be approached in Vientiane, Laos, in early September. Yu Lung foresaw that the best possible messenger was his daughter, Dao. She's called by her French name, Nicole, in my report. Dao or Nicole is the child of a woman the Truong toc wanted to marry when he was younger. The mother was killed during the migration of the Catholics out of North Vietnam after Ho Chi Minh took over in 1954. The Truong toc rescued the child and raised her as his own daughter. Therefore Do Minh Kha owed a debt to the Ngos not only out of kinship but also out of gratitude for the way in which they'd cared for his child.

"We knew that Do Minh Kha was in Laos during September. We watched him as a matter of routine; he is a very high-ranking officer and we wanted to know what he was up to. One of my agents, Vuong Van Luong, was among the U.S. assets who were sent to Vientiane to try to find out what Do Minh Kha was doing there. Luong failed to find out, and so did all our other agents. Do just stayed in a house in Vientiane for three days with a beautiful young Vietnamese woman. When nothing more than that happened, we assumed he was shacking up. Luong did manage to take photographs of the girl, coming in and out of the house with Do. The girl wasn't in our files. We couldn't identify her. We now know that the girl was not his mistress but his daughter. Do and Nicole met in Vientiane in September for the first time since the girl left Hanoi as a child.

"We weren't able to wire the house in Vientiane, and it probably wouldn't have done us much good if we had. Do is too professional to have talked, even to his daughter, in a strange house where there might be listening devices. However, Luong reported that Do and Nicole would go for walks together around the garden of the house in Vientiane. We know now what Nicole asked her father to do. And we know that he agreed.

"Nicole told her father about the family's plan to kill President Kennedy in revenge for the deaths of Diem and Nhu. She showed him the horoscopes, probably. She asked for his help in the name of the family. They code-named the operation against Kennedy 'the tears of autumn.' That phrase, 'the tears of autumn,' can be rendered in Vietnamese as a woman's name, Lê Thu.

"Lê Thu was the death name of Do's wife. As you saw in the report, the Vietnamese change their names when they die. There was a kind of double poetry, and a good deal of psychology, in the choice of this code name. At first I thought it was a play on the name of Madame Nhu—she's called Lê Xuan, which means 'the tears of spring.'

It was autumn in America when Kennedy was assassinated on November 22. The code name had two purposes—Lê Thu because of the guilt it would evoke in Do Minh Kha, who had sent his wife away to be killed. And 'tears of autumn' because Kennedy was going to die in autumn in the Northern Hemisphere.

"Lê Thu was not a secure code name—it contains a clue that led me to Do Minh Kha, and through him to everything else. But the family didn't think that security mattered, because they weren't going to use the phrase outside the family. What mattered to them was that it gave a name to their collective hatred for Kennedy and for Americans in general.

"What the family needed from Do was precisely what gave us our chance to penetrate the operation. They needed a cut-out, a go-between, who could activate Kennedy's assassin. They couldn't do it themselves because the assassin could not know, could not be permitted to guess, who he was working for. It was a matter of security—and, more important, a matter of motivation. An assassin being approached by the Vietnamese would know at once who was using him to kill Kennedy. They couldn't have that. Also, they are realists—they knew that even Oswald probably wouldn't have done it for a Vietnamese, let alone a

South Vietnamese. Oswald would have believed Diem was a Nazi, and his sympathies lay elsewhere.

"So they needed a cutout who was a white man. Do Minh Kha is in charge of the section of North Vietnamese intelligence that handles liaison with other Communist intelligence services. He had debts he could call in. The family didn't care who killed Kennedy. They didn't think it mattered who pulled the trigger—Yu Lung had already assured them the assassination attempt would succeed.

"Kennedy's horoscope gives not only the auspicious time for the assassination, November 22, but also the place, Dallas. Yu Lung had selected that city as the most favorable geomantic location. He drew up a long treatment of geomantic conditions in Dallas. The only limitation he put on success was that the assassin must not fire toward the north or northwest; under the principles of geomancy, these are directions to be avoided. Oswald fired almost due west from the window of the Texas School Depository. I don't imagine he'd been instructed to do that. It was a coincidence that Kennedy's car was traveling in a westerly direction.

"They knew Kennedy would be in Dallas on November 22. The American newspapers had reported this fact, and you can be sure that the Vietnamese, in Hanoi and in Saigon, had a complete file of clippings.

"When Do Minh Kha went back to Hanoi after seeing Nicole in Vientiane, he found Manuel Ruiz there. Ruiz was on his way to the Congo to organize a guerrilla force, and he'd come to consult with the world's leading authorities on guerrilla warfare, the North Vietnamese. Ruiz was surprised that Do knew where he was when I tracked him down in the Congo—of course, Do didn't know; I was lying to Ruiz—so he probably didn't tell Do what his target country was.

"However, Do had to tell Ruiz what *his* target was—John F. Kennedy. Do wanted an assassin for one-time use. Ruiz told him about Oswald. The Cubans had contacted Oswald, on an unwitting basis, when he was in New Orleans during the summer. He'd tried to pass himself off as an expert on guerrilla

tactics. The Cuban network in New Orleans informed Ruiz—
that was his department. The Cubans assessed Oswald, decided
he was a nut and dropped any idea of recruiting him.

"Ruiz didn't think the Vietnamese had a chance of killing
Kennedy, even though Do Minh Kha was absolutely confident
the operation would succeed. Ruiz played a game with the
Vietnamese. He agreed to approach Oswald and activate him
as Kennedy's assassin. You saw in the report what Ruiz thought
of Oswald. But he went ahead, as a favor to Do. The irony is
extraordinary: to this day, Ruiz doesn't know that he was an
agent for the Truong toc—he thinks the Kennedy assassination
was a North Vietnamese operation.

"At the instigation of an agent of Ruiz's in New Orleans,
Oswald went to Mexico City, leaving New Orleans on September 25 by bus. He arrived in Mexico City at ten in the morning
on September 27 and registered at the Hotel Comercio, as the
Cubans had instructed him to do. That day he went twice to the
Cuban embassy and once to the Soviet embassy to apply for
visas. He was refused in both places. Ruiz picked him up on that
day and kept him under surveillance. When Ruiz was certain
that Oswald was clean—that there was no U.S. interest in him
and no American surveillance, he contacted him by phone,
using a coded recognition signal.

"David tells me there are three dead days in Oswald's stay
in Mexico City. The official investigation has not turned up
anything on Oswald's activities between September 27 and October 1, when Oswald left Mexico City by bus.

"Ruiz talked to Oswald on September 30, in the park called
the Alameda. You have Oswald's reaction in the report. He took
Ruiz's bait. When Oswald walked out of the Alameda, he was
activated, and President Kennedy was a dead man.

"Ruiz went on to the Congo. Oswald went back to Dallas."

Dennis Foley left his place by the window. Christopher saw
through the window that two White House Cadillacs were
drawn up at the curb; the chauffeurs stood smoking on the brick
sidewalk. The meeting was taking more time than Foley and

Trumbull had expected. Foley, at the bar, poured neat scotch into his glass. His harsh blue eyes were fastened on Christopher's face.

"The killing of Oswald seems to have been unrelated to the Vietnamese," Christopher said. "There was unbearable heat on the Soviets. Oswald, after all, had been a defector to the USSR. The Russian service believes in direct, drastic action. The KGB had Frankie Pigeon in cold storage. They used Pigeon, and Pigeon used Ruby, to take the heat off. Pigeon earned a million dollars with one phone call.

"Ruby was a kind of fringe figure, more a hustler than a hoodlum, according to Pigeon. He'd always wanted to be on the inside with the syndicate, if that's what it's called in real life. Pigeon just told him to make a hit for the syndicate, and Ruby jumped at the chance. Pigeon says Ruby used to hang around the edge of the mob in Chicago and was always trying to keep in touch after he moved to Dallas. The syndicate never wanted any part of him. And it still knows nothing about the way Pigeon used Ruby to kill Oswald. Pigeon's terrified that they'll find out. They'd kill him. He broke discipline. He did it on his own, for the money.

"Frankie Pigeon scoffs at Ruby now for being a romantic about Kennedy, but I think Pigeon regarded killing Oswald as a patriotic act, just as much as Ruby did. Pigeon had no fear that Ruby would talk: he'd want to prove to the syndicate that he could observe *omertà* as well as any Sicilian. Once Oswald was dead, everything calmed down for the Soviets in twenty-four hours—literally. From their point of view, it was a sensible operation, and cheap at the price."

3

Trumbull sighed. "I swear I never heard anything like that," he said. "Men killing Presidents of the United States, and other men killing the assassin, and nobody knowing who they were working for or why. That part doesn't make sense at all."

"It makes *every* kind of sense," Patchen said. "That's the

264

way it's done. I can show you files on a dozen other cases. The pattern is classic. In other circumstances I'd say it was admirable." He turned to Christopher."One thing about the operation against Oswald. Are you sure about the counterfeit money?"

"Yes," Christopher said. "That's what the bank records show. Klimenko carried ten thousand hundred-dollar bills to Zurich. Fifty of the bills were counterfeit. They have the serial numbers of the money manufactured by the SS during the war. The KGB just passed the fake money on to Pigeon. Dolder und Co. caught it right away. Of course they informed the Swiss police. I don't understand it. Maybe the Russians didn't check all the serial numbers; maybe they just gathered up all the hundred-dollar bills lying around in their safes. You know how sloppy things can get on an emergency operation. They had no reason to plant the counterfeits on Pigeon, unless they've got some idea of blackmailing him with the syndicate. That's too complicated, even for them."

Foley returned to his chair with a fresh drink in his hand. Liquor and anger had colored his face. He sat down beside Trumbull and stared for a moment into the empty air. When he began to speak, he used the abrupt sentences Christopher remembered from their first meeting in Paris.

"J.D. asked you to tell us about your methods, but I didn't hear any mention of those," he said. "Suppose you tell us how you came by all this data."

"By spending money, mostly," Christopher said.

"Oh. You mean you've been zipping around the world like Sam Spade, bribing hotel clerks?"

"I paused to bury one of my agents, Foley."

Foley bent his long torso, leaning across the coffee table so that his face was close to Christopher's.

"Let me recapitulate," he said. "One of your agents, this Luong, was killed in Saigon. What was the death toll from the bomb in the car—five, six? Then you killed the two Vietnamese kids you call assassins. In Zurich you broke into a bank, using an unreconstructed Nazi as a burglar. In Italy you caused two American citizens to be shot, though not, by your account, killed. You kidnapped and tortured another American citizen. You left four Cubans dead and another wounded in the Congo. For a moralizer, you're quite a fellow."

Foley opened the file containing Christopher's report and spilled the photographs over the table. He arranged the pictures of the dead Vietnamese gunmen and those showing Frankie Pigeon, bound and naked, in the interrogation room.

"You expect us to put value on information obtained by these methods?" he asked. "You expect us to believe in someone named Manuel Ruiz, hidden in the jungle, and to believe he'd simply *tell* you what you say he's told you?"

Foley, as he finished speaking, became aware of Patchen, who did not so much move as change the tension of his muscles.

"Paul, don't answer," Patchen said. "Foley, let me say this to you: first of all, Christopher didn't kill his own agent; he has a reputation amounting to an office joke for keeping agents alive. Second, he didn't put two pounds of *plastique* in his own car. Third, he didn't expect to cause the deaths of those two Vietnamese gunmen. He wanted to talk to them, for reasons I think you understand very clearly—reasons he was honorable enough not to spell out in a report that may yet go to the President. I have no such scruples."

"David, I'm not talking to you," Foley said.

"Oh yes you are," Patchen said. There was no more resonance than usual in his flat voice, but Trumbull threw Foley a glance and held up his palm. "Go on, David," he said.

"Christopher's methods are justified by their results," Patchen said. "That's the rule. That's always been the rule. Christopher's been given promotions and medals by his government for playing by that rule better than almost anyone else has ever done. You haven't lived his life. You can't imagine it, much less understand it."

"All right, David," Trumbull said.

Patchen slowed his speech, but went on. "There's a tape recording of the conversation with Manuel Ruiz, and a living witness to Christopher's presence in the Congo," he said. "Christopher left Ruiz alive, and Pigeon too, when it would have been easy to let them be killed. We can lay hands on both of them whenever we're instructed to do so. Pigeon still has the counterfeit money, and the Swiss police know the serial numbers. We know the movements of Manuel Ruiz, and of Do and his daughter. The evidence is incontrovertible. Christopher has given you the truth. You don't like it, Foley. You never have. You think he has some motive to soil Kennedy's memory. The question is, will you ever learn?"

Rolling his glass between his palms, Trumbull nodded slowly, as if agreeing with whatever thought was passing through his own head.

"Well," Trumbull said. "What we seem to have here is a pretty good case against all the people Paul has put the finger on. We've got two men who believe it in this room—am I right, David? You buy what Paul's told us?"

"There's no choice," Patchen said. "It's not just this reporting. There's collateral intelligence in our hands that confirms almost everything he's told us. With a little more work we can remove every shadow of a doubt. Every shadow."

"Okay," Trumbull said. "That's you and Paul. I respect your judgment, David, and your work, Paul. Then there's Dennis, here—I take it he doesn't believe it, and he won't believe it."

Foley said, "That is correct."

"Then there's me," Trumbull said. "I guess I make the decision. Do we trot this in to the President? He's the man. The rest of us are just his lookouts."

Trumbull collected the scattered pages and photographs and put them back in order.

"If I show this to the President, what'll he do?" he asked. "He can go on TV and hand the American people another brutal, horrible shock, or he can read it and keep it secret and worry about it for the rest of his Presidency. The country has got to come together after this tragedy down in Dallas. *Got* to. We've got something to do in Vietnam, and we've got to do it. We can't do it without public understanding and support for our policy. Wouldn't you agree, Dennis—David?"

Foley nodded. Patchen, as usual, gave back no indication of his thoughts.

"I'll tell you a plain fact," Trumbull said. "If the American people believed that a bunch of Vietnamese got together and killed John F. Kennedy, they'd want to go over there and nuke that country—*nuke* it. You'd never get another dime out of Congress for South Vietnam. You'd never get an ounce of support from the press—those fellows love Kennedy's memory almost as much as Dennis does."

Trumbull riffled the pages of Christopher's report. "You've got to be careful who you let change history," he said. "You're sure that this is the only copy of this thing?"

"There's a photograph in Christopher's head," Foley said.

Trumbull gave Christopher a smile of great sweetness. It was the last time he looked at him.

"I've grown a lot of gray hair, son," he said, "but I've never seen anyone do the things you say you've done. I want you to know I believe you did it all. And I wish you luck—I mean that, Paul."

Trumbull stood up and went to the fireplace. He picked up the poker and stirred the logs. Kneeling with an apologetic, arthritic groan, he fed Christopher's report into the flames, sheet by sheet. Bits of charred paper, lifted by the draught, flew up the chimney.


# 4

Patchen went to the door with Trumbull and Foley. Neither man said anything more to Christopher. He watched through the window as Trumbull, smiling at his driver and making a joke, got into his car. Foley opened the back door of his Cadillac for himself, brushing past the chauffeur. The two black cars rolled away down the quiet street, under the leafless trees.

When Patchen came back from the hall he wore his topcoat and carried Christopher's over his arm. "I guess there's no reason why we shouldn't have dinner together," he said.

They ate a bad meal, cooked with contempt and served with scorn, in an expensive restaurant in Georgetown that was going out of fashion. In the men's room there were lewd jokes in French painted on the wall. They spoke very little; Patchen did not finish his food.

Outside, on the sidewalk, Patchen, with an abrupt movement, held out his hand to Christopher. He was exceptionally strong on the good side of his body, and he tightened his grip until he caused pain.

"You think they're coming after you, don't you?" he asked.

"The Vietnamese? Yes. But maybe not right away. They'll know I've told you. When nothing happens, they may postpone. It's a matter of waiting—everything is."

"Maybe they'll conclude the damage has been done. They may decide they've done enough."

"Do you think so?" Christopher asked. "They've had two sons murdered—three, if you count Ngo Dinh Can. The generals will shoot him eventually."

Patchen buttoned the collar of his coat; the wind, smelling of winter rain, was blowing down Wisconsin Avenue.

"So?"

"Only one Kennedy has been shot," Christopher said.

# FIFTEEN

1

Molly came into the room with snow in her hair. When she saw a man standing by the window, she went silent and stopped, frozen, like a cat that scents something strange in a familiar house. Then, seeing that the man was Christopher, she fell back against the door and put her hands to her cheeks: she wore all the rings Christopher had ever given her.

"Ah," she said. "Ah, Paul—it's you."

Molly had been on the ski runs and the wind had gone into her clothes; she smelled as clean as the snow. The mountain sun had browned her face and bleached her lashes, so that her eyes seemed a darker green. They didn't kiss. Christopher stood by the window with snow falling beyond the glass; Molly leaned against the door, her bright clothes reflecting in the varnished pine.

Christopher said, "Nothing has happened?"

"Nothing. We've spent the whole time on the slopes, or eating fondu."

"Then you've had a good week?"

"Oh, yes," Molly said; she moved across the room and touched his face, tracing the line of his eye and mouth. "But there's been a certain lack."

Later, she sat up with the bolster folded behind her and brushed her hair. It crackled and sailed after the brush in the cold air; Molly parted it into two long streams and brushed hard, biting her lip as she counted the strokes. Christopher arranged her hair, still alive with electricity, so that it covered her breasts. Molly threw back the featherbed and examined his skin.

"What are all those red bumps? I felt them under the eiderdown."

"Insect bites," he said. "I've been in Africa."

"Not the dreaded tsetse fly?" Molly cried, in an imitation of Sybille's voice.

Christopher laughed. "You've learned to love Sybille?"

"I believe so. I do think it's wonderful, the way she dances on the candle flame and flirts with waiters, other women, dogs, the English language—every thing and creature except poor Tom. She's so filmy, like Vivien Leigh in *Gone with the Wind*."

"Tom thinks she's a wonder. They're a sort of comedy team."

"Tom's been marvelous. He tells me all the time we're safe in Zermatt because there are no roads up the mountain, only the train. He goes down and watches each train unload, then comes back and tells me once again that I can't possibly be liquidated until the next one arrives."

"That's nice of him."

"He's mad to know what you've been up to," Molly said. "I haven't breathed a word. Sybille says he's most impressed, the way I keep secrets."

"I'll tell him tonight."

"Then it's over?"

"I wouldn't say that. I'm through with it."

"Ah, and did you learn anything?"

"Everything, Molly."

"Everything? Only the dead know everything."

Christopher took his hands away. Molly grinned at him, drawing a strand of hair across her upper lip. Christopher laughed and kissed her; she laid her long body against his, toe, breast, and cheek.

"Ring down for a bottle of champagne, will you?" Molly said. "Let's drink it and stay in Zermatt for a while. I like things as they are. I do love hours like this one—they're like sailing ships, so reckless and inside the wind, and you don't see how lovely they are until you get off and watch them sail away."

## 2

Tom Webster, crossing the hotel lounge through a crowd of slender men and women dressed like actors in perfect ski clothes, looked as if he were costumed for the 1932 Olympics. His sweater was too small for his shoulders, and his trousers, too long for his muscular legs, were the old-fashioned kind that bagged at the ankles. Christopher, watching him, felt a wave of affection spread through his chest.

At the bar Webster ordered two hot buttered rums. "You have to drink these things up here," he said. "It's part of the cure, like mineral water at a spa."

Webster saw an empty table against the wall, and dashed across the room to claim it. He didn't like to have people behind him when he talked.

"I think you're clear for a while," he told Christopher. "There's been no sign of Kim's people in Zermatt. I've had the technicians and the translators rush the wiretap logs on Kim. He's pulled off the surveillance he had on you."

"Why?"

"Something you said to him in the airport in Milan. He thought you were going to kill him right there, in the terminal. He thinks you're crazy."

"That won't last."

"No. Kim spends half his time raving about you. He says you've got to be stopped. He may not use Vietnamese operators next time. It may dawn on him that white men are harder to spot in Europe."

"I don't know," Christopher said. "They're about to realize they've had a bad experience with a white agent."

Christopher told Webster, in a few low sentences, what he had learned. As Webster received the information, his heavy face stiffened.

"What will you do about Molly?" he asked. "She's changed you, you know. You care what happens. If you have to worry about her, she'll bring you down."

The expression left Christopher's eyes, as if he were handling an agent. Webster's glance didn't waver.

"You ought to run," Webster said. "I don't blame you for wanting to go on with her, but it's a mistake."

"I've made worse mistakes. I'm worn out, like Klimenko. Would you say Molly's a better choice than the one he made?"

"Prettier. But less likely to forgive and forget if you make the mistake of telling her as much as Klimenko's going to tell us."

"Molly doesn't want to hear it."

Webster picked up Christopher's glass and handed it to him. "*Everyone* wants to hear it," he said. "But what the hell —let's have a good time. It's New Year's Eve."

3

Webster had booked a table in another, smarter hotel for the *réveillon* supper. Sybille and Molly wore evening gowns and jewels. Webster had forgotten to pack his dinner jacket. He appeared in a tailcoat frayed at the lapels and shiny from a generation of flatirons. It fitted him no better than his skiing costume.

"Don't you think Tom looks wonderful?" Sybille asked. "We borrowed his outfit from the headwaiter—well, rented it with an enormous tip—and I stitched and tucked Tom into it. He wanted to carry a napkin over his arm but I said no. Do you think I was right to interfere?"

During the elaborate supper, Webster ordered bottle after bottle of champagne. He kissed Molly at midnight and danced with her, spinning her with her arm above her head so that her hair flew out of its pins and her long skirt swirled around her legs.

"God," Sybille said to Christopher. "She's a beautiful girl. Are you going to marry her and spoil her figure with babies?"

"I don't think so."

Sybille watched Webster and Molly, gasping with laughter, on their way back to the table.

"I'll tell you something, Paul. She prefers fear to the alternative. You won't be able to make her go away."

"Has Tom been talking to you?"

"Tom tells me everything, and so does Molly. You bloody fool."

"Do you think I've made a mistake, Sybille?"

"A mistake? You've thrown your life away for nothing. Tom says you did it for your country and the honor of the outfit. Those two things, added together, equal nothing. What good is what you've done? Look at Molly before you answer."

Sybille, as if she could not bear the taste of anything bought with her husband's work or Christopher's, threw her champagne on the tablecloth.

They were the last to leave the dining room. Webster, still wearing his party hat, draped strings of confetti around the shoulders of the women. Outside, between the high snowbanks, they walked hand in hand, four abreast. The low winter moon, as white as the glacier, lay on the brow of the Matterhorn.

"My God, I've loved this place," Molly said.

"Everyone does," Sybille said. "It's the funny train ride to the top and coming into the sunshine. And gazing upwards at the Matterhorn and being so glad one isn't Swiss. God does squander his landscapes."

Christopher stood behind them. Their faces were lifted

toward the mountain and they were breathing deeply in the sharpened air. Molly, without shifting her gaze from the moonlit field of snow, put a hand behind her back, beckoning Christopher to her side. But he was looking up and down the shadowed street.

Molly turned and smiled. She lifted her hands and fluttered her fingers as though to wake him from a daydream. She still wore all his rings: the emerald from Burma, the jade from Macao, the scarab from Egypt, a topaz, and an opal. There was a cathedral on Majorca where Christopher had gone with Cathy to look at a wooden virgin whose chipped enameled fingers were laden with jeweled rings. "There must be a lot of people around here who are afraid to die," Cathy said. "You don't give offerings like that to be forgiven your sins—only to be allowed to live a little longer."

## 4

The Websters left the next day after lunch. Christopher and Molly skied all afternoon. Molly, perfect in every use of her body, plunged down the mountain ahead of Christopher, stinging his face with the plume of snow that flew from the heels of her skis. She was full of laughter during dinner, but she was reluctant to go upstairs. They sat by the fireplace until midnight, drinking brandy and listening to a guitarist.

Finally they went to bed. After a time, Molly turned on the lamp and pushed Christopher's hair off his forehead. "I forgot the candles," she said.

Molly saw that he meant to speak; she put a finger on his lips.

"I know what you have in mind," she said. "Don't say it, Paul. I won't go."

"It would be better, Molly. I can't take you back to Rome. You're only in danger so long as they believe I care for you."

"Yes. You've explained. When you told me about Cathy's affairs, you said her body was her own—that she could do as she wished with it. Did you honestly feel that way?"

"Yes. I still do."

275

"Then you must feel the same way about my body."

"What I feel for you is love, not jurisdiction. That wasn't enough for Cathy."

"I own myself, just as Cathy did, then," Molly said. "She chose to abuse her body, and broke her heart. What I choose is this: I'll give up my body and lay it in the earth before I'll go away from you."

She turned off the light and turned her back. Christopher saw that not even a lie would change her mind. In Molly, love was a force as ruthless as the one that ruled him. To respond in kind was beyond him. He had been dyed, heart and memory, by the life he had lived, and not even Molly, willing to be murdered in order to prove to him that love was possible, could rescue him from what he knew about himself. Molly had taught him to feel again, but not that it mattered.

Molly moved under the featherbed and fitted her body against his, warm skin and hair that smelled of wind and woodsmoke. Before Christopher went to sleep, he thought again, out of long habit, of the things he knew he could say and do to outwit the simplicity of her passion. But he gave up: his betrayals had not saved Luong or Cathy or any of the others. Lovers and agents, living within their secret, could not be saved, or even be warned, by treachery.

Molly murmured in her sleep and threw a nerveless arm across his chest. Christopher felt her pulse on his own skin.

*Excerpt from Charles McCarry's*
*riveting new novel*

# CHRISTOPHER'S GHOSTS

*Available now from The Overlook Press*

In Charles McCarry's first novel since the acclaimed revival of his classic espionage novels Paul Christopher is back! So is the only adversary who ever eluded him.

*Christopher's Ghosts*—a novel of the broadest scope and penetrating depth—transcends the bounds of its genre, giving McCarry further claim on his long established reputation as perhaps our pre-eminent novelist of espionage.

The reader of this grand tale is catapulted into the high drama of Europe in the late thirties. A young Paul Christopher and his family face the rise of Nazi totalitarianism in Berlin, even as he wrestles with a doomed love and witnesses an unspeakable atrocity committed by a remorseless S.S. officer. Some 30 years later, across oceans and time, Franz Stutzer was back in Berlin now the fulcrum of the Cold War in Europe, Stutzer emerges from the ruins and shadows with a simple goal: to destroy the last living witness to his crime.

It is case of tiger chasing tiger as Christopher is pursued by the only man alive who can match his tradecraft and instincts. Edging toward the final confrontation with this mortal enemy, Christopher must operate in the one theater he had thought he had mastered—his own past.

With ferocious suspense, masterful pacing, and a penetrating insight into the blood-soaked spectacle of the twentieth century Europe, once again, and brilliantly, Charles McCarry delivers a haunting parable of a life—and an entire generation—confronting the ghosts of its brutal history.

# ONE

—

## 1

In the summer of his sixteenth year, in the last weeks before the second World War began, Paul Christopher kept seeing the same girl in the Tiergarten. She was about his age or maybe a little older. She was slender, dark-eyed, pale, and even in sunlight her hair was black with no hint of brown. She wore it in a long plait. She dressed in blue— a short coat, skirts that swung as she walked, white knee socks, sometimes a beret. She never smiled or made a gesture. She seemed to be watching him, just as he was watching her. Paul, dribbling a soccer ball or sailing a model boat or reading in the sun, would look up and there she would be, close enough for him to see her face but too far away for conversation. They would catch each other's eyes, blue gazing into brown. It was always Paul who looked away first. When he looked again, she would be gone like a ghost. Once or twice he took a step toward her. She immediately turned around and walked away without so much as a look over her shoulder. She was sad, or so Paul thought from a distance. He was reading Balzac that summer. The girl reminded him of Victorine in Le Père

Goriot. She was pretty. If she had been happy, she would have been beautiful.

Like Paul, the girl was always alone. He had no friends his own age in Berlin. Until he was ten he had gone to school with other boys, but when the dictatorship came to power his parents sent him to school in Switzerland. His father was an American. Paul traveled on an American passport, but because his mother was German and he had been born in Germany, his nationality was an open question to the authorities. Twice this summer—it was now early July—the secret police had summoned all three Christophers to its headquarters at No. 8 Prinz-Albrechtstrasse to inquire about Paul's case.

A major named Stutzer recorded their answers in the three thick files containing the information that the secret police had gathered on them so far. Because he asked the same questions over and over again, as if they had not already been answered, it took Stutzer more than two hours to cover three or four questions. Why was Paul not a member of the Hitler Youth as all German boys his age were required to be? Did he associate with the decadent Jews and communists who frequented his parents' apartment? Was he allowed to listen to their treasonous talk, to their insults to the Leader? Why had he been sent to a school where French was spoken, where hatred of the Reich was taught as part of the curriculum, where history was falsified, where decadence was the order of the day? Why was he not attending a German school?

Paul's father refused to answer these questions on

grounds that they were not questions but provocations, and that they were irrelevant because Paul was an American citizen who could not, under the laws of his own country, take an oath to serve and obey a foreign potentate—that was the term he used—without automatically losing his citizenship. Hubbard Christopher's mannerisms were American, and worse than that he had acquired them at an Episcopalian prep school and at Yale College. He exuded untouchability. He looked amused when being questioned by Stutzer, as if he had bought a ticket to a play that was so bad that it was interesting. It was hard to imagine a more dangerous look to have on your face when visiting No. 8 Prinz-Albrechtstrasse.

The last time they were interviewed, Stutzer had lost his temper. "Whatever your theories on nationality," he shouted, "you must not assume, Herr Christopher, that you can laugh at our questions and not be asked harder questions that will bring you under even deeper suspicion. Remember that."

The Christophers were suspected of crimes against the Reich, and they had in fact helped several enemies of the dictatorship to escape from Germany. There was no real need for the secret police to prove these charges. On his own authority Major Stutzer could send them to a concentration camp or even summarily execute them, but for reasons of his own he wanted to prolong the questioning, to maneuver them into full confessions. His interest in the Christophers, especially in Paul's mother, was deeply personal. They had a history. Always Stutzer's eyes were fixed on her, staring hard, when he fired his questions and threats, as if he was deeply interested in the impression he was making on her. He rarely looked at Hubbard or Paul.

The Geheime Staatspolizei, or secret state police, abbreviated as Gestapo, have been imagined by later generations as a collection of freaks, but in fact they looked like any other Germans. Stutzer was a recognizable type—bony, erect, triangular face, long nose, thin wet pink lips, quick mind. He spoke educated German. He was not, however, educated in the sense that Lori Christopher was educated. She spoke German, French and English with equal fluency. She knew Latin and ancient Greek and had read the greatest books in all those languages, she recognized almost any European musical work immediately and played the piano expertly, she knew painting and sculpture as well as she knew music, she had memorized the poetry of Goethe and other giants of German letters, she remembered mathematics through the calculus. Stutzer had no need for such a body of knowledge. As Hubbard said, secret policemen were like all tribal peoples—they might not know a lot, but they all knew the same things. The Christophers called Major Stutzer Major Dandy because Dandy was what his surname meant in English and because he was almost comically dapper.

Because the questions asked by the secret police were always the same, even when they seemed different, Paul thought of other things while they were being asked and answered, or not answered. Mostly he thought about the girl in the Tiergarten. Why was she always there? Why was she always alone? In his experience, girls traveled in pairs, one of them pretty, the other one plain. Why was she watching him? Why did she always wear blue? Why did she never give him a sign apart from her entrances and exits? Who was she?

A day or two after an interview at secret police headquarters, Paul was flying a kite in the park when a half-dozen Hitler Youth appeared. They wore campaign caps, brown shirts, neckties, ornamental belt buckles, shorts, knives on their belts. Paul was in a large open space. He saw them coming a long way off. Because there was nothing else to do except run, he went on flying his kite, a large box kite that he had made himself. The Youth advanced in a column of twos, led by their section leader, marching in step, ankles turning on the rough ground, apprentice soldiers on serious business.

Just then, at the edge of a grove of trees, the dark-haired girl appeared. One moment she was not there and the next moment she was, as if someone had turned on a magic lantern and projected her image onto a screen. She stood beside a large linden tree and watched. The section leader, whose shoulder boards bore a single crosswise narrow stripe instead of being plain like the other boys', shouted orders to halt, make a left face, and stand at ease. He then marched over to Paul.

"Papers!" he shouted. He had a voice that had recently broken, grave blue eyes under thick smudged eyebrows, a large straight nose, shiny patches of healed acne, a thin neck. Behind the bully stood his audience. Paul ignored him. He had met others like him in three different countries. He had his own instructions on how to deal with the type. "Don't argue, don't hesitate," his American boxing instructor, Fighting Jim Cerruti, had advised. "Feint with the left and then hit the bum on the nose with a straight right hand. Hard. You gotta break his nose with the first punch, understand?"

"Papers!" the leader said again, louder this time, and with a pinker face.

Again Paul ignored him. His kite was climbing. He paid out string. The wind was strong at the kite's altitude and the taut string quivered. The leader made a movement. He had a knife in his hand. He cut the string. The kite escaped and climbed rapidly, blowing east toward the River Spree. With the severed string still in his right hand, Paul faked with his left, then punched the leader on the nose with a straight right.

It was a short, hard punch, delivered with a lot of force because Paul's feet were already set as a result of his work with the kite. He felt the cartilage split under his fist, saw blood fly, saw the leader's cap fly off. The knife spun away, nickeled hilt glinting in the sun. The leader fell to his knees, hands to his face, blood flowing onto his brown shirt and necktie. He shouted a strangled command, his voice breaking. The others attacked. There was nothing to do but fight. Paul had no chance against six attackers even if they were unskilled. He knew this, but he also knew that he could not escape, so he stood his ground. He landed a few punches, drawing more blood, before he was subdued. Two of the boys held his arms behind his back while the others took terms punching him in the face and stomach. Paul kicked his attackers until they threw him to the ground and began to kick him. With no adult present to call them off, Paul thought they might kill him, but before that happened they wore themselves out. They were short of breath, panting.

The leader, nose still bleeding, delivered several kicks of his own.

"Next time obey orders!" he said. "This will teach you to answer questions."

The Youth fell into formation and marched away. Paul knew that his beating had not lasted as long as it seemed. He understood, vaguely, that the leader and his detachment had been messengers from Stutzer. Deputizing for the secret police was a great honor for these boys. Paul lay on his back and looked upward into the cloudy sky, wondering where his kite was now. Far to the east, he thought, perhaps over Hellersdorf or even beyond. He had been kicked in the stomach, in the groin, in the back, in the kidneys. Every bruise throbbed. He realized that he was losing consciousness.

Fingertips touched his face. The girl was kneeling beside him. He revived a little. The pain was worse. She said, "You're conscious. Good. Is anything broken?" He thought, How would I know? but said nothing. He didn't want to say the wrong thing and frighten her away. Up close she had a wonderful face—dark liquid eyes, full lips, perfect teeth, pale skin that was nevertheless faintly brown, as if another complexion lay beneath the one on the surface. She was speaking

English, not German. She had an accent like his mother's, barely detectable and unmistakably Prussian. She had gone to good schools.

In German Paul said, "I don't think anything is broken."

In English she said, "I speak no German."

Paul said, "Why not?"

"Look at me, then think about it," she said. "Stay here. Don't move."

She leaped to her feet and ran. After a moment she returned with a water-soaked handkerchief and began cleaning his face. Her touch was gentle but efficient. She concentrated deeply on what she was doing. Paul smelled blood, wet linen and the water it contained, the girl. Especially her hair. He put a hand in front of his face to stop her from continuing the first aid and said, "Thank you, but I should go now."

"Go where? No one will help you. They will take one look at you and know you have been beaten up and think you're a Jew or a Bolshevik."

"They can think what they like."

"My father is a doctor," she said. "I'll take you to him."

Paul got to his feet. Standing up, he was overcome by dizziness and nausea. When he leaned over to vomit, it seemed to him that he was falling into a bottomless abyss. His legs would not obey him. He lost his balance and fell. He tried to get up again but couldn't. He felt the girl's hands on his arm, guiding him.

The girl said, "You have a concussion. That's a serious matter. Let me take you to my father."

"Does your father speak German?"

"He wouldn't dream of speaking anything else," she replied.

<br>

# 2

The father who was a doctor determined that none of Paul's bones had been fractured. However, four lower ribs had been broken. Paul, stoic up to that moment, shrieked when the doctor poked each of them with a stiff forefinger.

Better the lower than the upper ones, the doctor told Paul. The upper ones, when shattered, could pierce the lungs or the liver or the spleen. "The ribs will be painful for a few weeks but there is no treatment, they must heal themselves," the doctor said. "Try not to make sudden movements. No sports for a month. You must make yourself cough fifty times every day." He demonstrated the deep, phlegm-clearing cough that he was prescribing. "Now you," he said.

Paul coughed. The pain was excruciating. This showed on Paul's face. He gasped and seized his side. The doctor said, "Yes, it will be painful at first. But it is absolutely essential to clear the lungs. Otherwise they can become congested and that could be fatal. You could drown from the fluid in your own lungs. Drown! So cough! Ten times when you wake up, ten times at mid-morning, ten times at noon, ten times in the afternoon, ten times before you go to bed. Do you ever wake in the night?"

"Sometimes, not often."

"If you do, put your face in the pillow and cough ten more times before you go back to sleep."

The doctor found no other sign of internal injury. The ribs had not splintered and punctured the lungs. The spleen seemed to be intact. The liver felt normal.

"Nevertheless you must be watchful," the doctor said. He spoke very rapidly, as he did everything else. He spoke in a mumble, something rarely heard in the old Germany where everyone was exhorted to speak to strangers at the top of their lungs. "If you notice blood in your urine or stool," he continued, "or if you cough up blood or bleed from your anus, penis, nose, or ears, you must go to a doctor immediately. At once, without delay. Do you understand?"

"Yes, Herr Doktor."

"Herr Professor Doktor. Your family has a regular doctor?"

"Yes, Herr Professor Doktor."

This doctor was a small lean man with a bald crown with two puffs of graying black hair growing on either side of it. He was sure of his skills, unsmiling, abrupt in his speech. It was obvious that he expected meek obedience from his patients. Paul thought that he was angry about something—an injustice, an insult—at the center of his being. Whatever it was, he quivered under the weight of it. Paul had seen this condition in some of his parents' friends and in certain of the brainier masters at his school.

"Sit up," the doctor said.

Paul obeyed.

The doctor cut several long strips of adhesive tape, then taped Paul's ribs, sternum to spine, on each side. He pulled the tape very tight. It was a painful process. Paul did not make a sound or a face.

"It's all right to gasp," the doctor said when he had finished one side. "We're alone here. I know it hurts."

Paul nodded.

"You're good at hiding your feelings," the doctor said, cutting tape for the other side of Paul's chest. "That's a useful quality in life, as you will find."

Paul could think of no answer to this that would not be disrespectful, so he said nothing.

The doctor said, "Did you cry when you were a baby?"

"I don't know."

"Your parents didn't tell you?"

"No."

"Then you must have cried. Or maybe you didn't but they thought it would be bad for your character for you to know that. Do you think the Leader cried when he was a baby?"

"I never imagined that he ever was a baby, Herr Professor Doktor."

"Ah, a wit! Do you think it wise to make such jokes, young man?"

"There's nothing funny about the Leader, Herr Professor Doktor."

The doctor looked up. He was enjoying this conversation. "Then you are a loyal German even if you are a wit?"

"I'm not a German, sir."

"You're not? You certainly sound like one. And look like one. They could paint you in the uniform of a hussar and hang you in a museum. If you're not German, what are you?"

The pain of having his ribs strapped made it difficult for Paul to hear what the doctor was saying, much less answer.

"American," Paul said.

"What luck. How did that happen?"

"My father is an American, my mother German."

"Your mother doesn't mind your being an American instead of a German?"

"She and my father decided before I was born that I would be an American." Paul did not know why he was telling this strange little man about whom he knew nothing things that no one outside the family had a right to know.

"Why did they make such a decision?" the doctor asked.

"I wasn't there."

"But maybe a fortune teller was and she saw the future."

Paul said nothing. In fact there was a fortune teller in his family's life, a friend of his mother's. She lived with the Christophers when she was in Berlin. Perhaps the doctor was collecting tidbits for the secret police. Living in the Reich made you think such thoughts even when you hadn't been beaten within an inch of your life in the last half-hour.

The doctor finished taping. He had already put iodine on Paul's skin where it had been broken. "There," he said. "Done. Your parents will be surprised when they see you. You live nearby?"

"Not far," said Paul, cautiously.

The doctor sat down at a desk, unscrewed the cap of a

thick black fountain pen, and wrote for a minute or two with great speed. When he finished, he blotted the paper, folded it, and handed it to Paul.

"This is for your parents," he said. "It describes your injuries and the treatment. If you have severe pain, not twinges but pain, take one aspirin dissolved in water every four hours."

"And your fee?"

The doctor waved away the clumsy words. "No need."

"Thank you, Herr Professor Doctor."

"Since you're an American you can dispense with the honorifics. In your country, I understand, you call doctors 'doc.'"

"That's true, doctor. I will say goodbye now."

"Let me ask you a question before you go," the doctor said. "Why did they do it?"

"Who? Do what?"

"Have you forgotten? The Youth. Why did they beat you up?"

"They didn't explain."

The doctor bit his lower lip, nodded his head. "Then all is in order," he said. "Nothing has changed."

## More **CHARLES McCARRY** from
## **OVERLOOK DUCKWORTH**

*The Better Angels*
978-1-59020-004-9
$25.95 • £17.99 hc

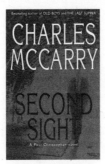

*Second Sight*
978-1-58567-878-5
$24.95 • £16.99 hc

*Secret Lovers*
978-1-58567-854-9
$24.95 • £16.99 hc

"The best writer of intelligence and political novels in the world." —*The Boston Globe*

"McCarry is the best modern writer on the subject of intrigue—by the breadth of Alan Furst, by the fathom of Eric Amblier, by any measure." —P.J. O'Rourke

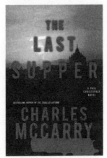

*The Last Supper*
978-1-59020-014-8
$13.95 • £8.99 pb

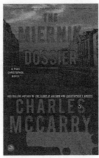

*The Miernik Dossier*
978-1-58567-942-3
$13.95 • £8.99 pb

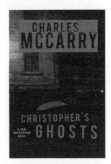

*Christopher's Ghosts*
978-1-59020-113-8
$13.95 • £8.99 pb

### **OVERLOOK DUCKWORTH**
New York • Woodstock • London
www.overlookpress.com

# Books of Similar interest by
## GERALD SEYMOUR

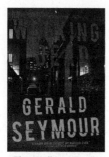

*The Walking Dead*
978-1-59020-005-6
$24.95 hc

*Kingfisher*
978-1-58567-937-9
$14.95 pb

*Rat Run*
978-1-58567-894-5
$24.95 hc

"Not since the arrival of John le Carre has the emergence of an international suspense novelist been as stunning as that of Gerald Seymour."
—*Los Angeles Times Book Review*

"Gerald Seymour is one of the unsung heroes of the politica thriller."
—*Chicago Tribune*

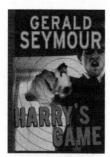

*Harry's Game*
978-1-58567-909-6
$14.95 pb

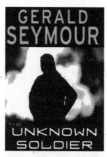

*The Unknown Soldier*
978-1-58567-752-8
$13.95 pb

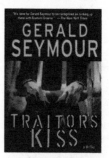

*Traitor's Kiss*
978-1-58567-885-3
$13.95 pb

**THE OVERLOOK PRESS**
Woodstock & New York
www.overlookpress.com